Will's Wake

Will's Wake

TIMOTHY DRESZER

 Umgapa Sky Productions - Santa Cruz, California

Published in the United States by Umgapa Sky.
Santa Cruz, California.

Cover Design by Zianora Dreszer
and Umgapa Sky © 2025
Photography by Timothy Dreszer

https://www.youtube.com/@umgapasky/
https://www.instagram.com/umgapa/
https://soundcloud.com/umgapa-sky/

Library of Congress Control Number: 2025916131

ISBN: 979-8-218-81700-8 (paperback)
979-8-218-89732-1 (e-book)

ASIN: B0FTSBGNP9 (paperback)
B0FTSGJN6L (e-book)

To my middle brother,
who convinced me to be nothing like him.

To my worried mother,
who was never a monster, despite what I said.

And to several others,
you know who you are,
who drive me crazy, keeping me sane.

Molecules

Prologue: Ripples

A warm drop of water rolled slowly down her hand, then grew on the end of her pinky. Shree stared into the tiny orb until she recognized the world around her reflected on its surface. But as still as the afternoon was, the reflected world kept stretching and contorting until the microcosm of water freed itself and launched towards the deep. Shree's focus involuntarily darted after her satellite just in time to see the perfect image of herself implode as her water drop merged with the collective whole. Shree watched the ripples spread out to the sides of the basin as her little ship bobbed in their wake.

As these waves perturbed his peace, Mr. Trains rose from his seat at the tiller and prepared for battle. Leaping to first one side, then the other, he rocked the aluminum hull, churning waves into a pitching storm. "At last we'll see the character of this craft. Can she stand up to a squall? Will she take on water? Be breached by the storm's fury?"

"Don't you dare, Mr. Trains! We'll sink for sure."

"But are you certain, my dear?" Mr. Trains was in his element. "We will never know until we find out. One does not arrive in Timbuktu without ever setting sail!"

"Isn't Timbuktu in a desert?"

"Life lived in fear is not a lived life!" No sooner had he said this than Mr. Trains lost his balance. Their ship, it seemed, had started spinning. They took a moment to comprehend the meaning of this new development. Then suddenly, "Whirlpool! Whirlpool! Everyone for themselves." And with this, Mr. Trains started climbing the mast.

Shree could only watch as their little craft was pulled against its will into a deepening vortex. Somehow, the water in the basin was draining away. Already, the sides of the pond had risen around them, obscuring their surroundings. All that was left was the spinning sky above, the accelerating water below, and the boat teetering like a pendulum, under the weight of Mr. Trains. Shree looked desperately for a means of rescue. Yet no rope to safety offered itself. She grabbed hold of the bottom of the mast, knowing full well that Mr. Trains was not to be followed in a crisis. The sides of the aluminum boat began to warp, and water poured in. There was no avoiding the inevitable now, Shree thought, as she struggled to catch a breath against the tide. The boat fell fully on its side under the influence of Mr. Trains atop the mast. Shree felt the grip of the current. With the strength of a python, the water pulled her down towards the gaping hole at the bottom of the basin. Out of the corner of her eye, she caught Mr. Trains sweeping past, and she grabbed his flailing hand. But his descent would not be stopped as he slipped through her fingers, into the drain, and out of sight. Shree cried out in horror that he was lost, and in a moment, she would be too.

The wreckage of her crumpled boat arrived at the opening and lodged itself firmly against the torrent. Shree's left leg found its way into the hungry mouth, but the rest of her clung to the wreckage and the rim of the hole. Willing her savage strength against the immense current proved utterly useless. Now she felt certain she would lose her grip or the twisted aluminum would sever her leg, and in pieces she would follow her friend into darkness. Her mind gave in to the chaos of panic.

Yet the rush of water slowed, as the basin emptied and the last dregs calmly drained away. Quiet answered her chaos. All that was left from the storm was the pile of crushed aluminum, a soggy sail, and Shree. She carefully extricated herself and found her way out of the basin to dry in the light of day.

As she understood that the danger was over and she had

survived, Shree also understood that she had lost her friend. Her just-dried face was soon dripping with tears. How could it be that he was so quickly gone? "Oh Mr. Trains, how could I have let you go? I'm so sorry I didn't hold you tighter. Mr. Trains, I can't…"

"What's that you say?" Shree looked up to see Mr. Trains's head emerging from the spout above the sink. In a moment, the rest of his body joined him inside a giant drop of water, then splat, he was down in the sink, admiring the wreckage of the aluminum boat that Shree had made.

"Mr. Trains, don't ever scare me like that again!" she said with an ironic smile to her imaginary friend.

Book I

1. Hollow

August 18th, 1981

Sunlight exaggerated the accumulated dirt and bug parts on her windshield, so Rebecca dutifully spritzed and swept her field of view with the wipers. Now, great smeared arcs were made luminous by the same insistent sun. With a paper napkin from the glove box, she rolled down her window and reached out to clear a small portal from which she could see the road beyond. It was already 5:26 pm by the time she left the office. Rebecca knew an impatient daughter had been waiting at the pool for half an hour, and worries about her ex-husband burned in her thoughts.

Yet just as she pulled onto the freeway, another concern superseded her daughter's fate. A mysterious buzzing that Rebecca originally thought might be evidence of engine trouble, suddenly revealed itself to be a large yellow and brown wasp, angrily bouncing between her cleared portal and the dusty black dashboard. It was only a matter of moments before the wasp, now flying in figure eights between front and rear windshields, would decide that Rebecca was to blame for its confounding entrapment. So, feigning calm, she steered for a freeway exit, trying not to draw attention to herself. When the wasp abruptly stopped buzzing, she discovered it evaluating her from between her two hands, which tightly clenched the steering wheel. Mesmerizing sienna eyes dared her to flinch, pulling her deep into their alien depths. Suddenly brake lights approached. When she glanced down again, the wasp had vanished, though its sinister silhouette still darkened her retina.

At last, the car arrived at a safe place to stop. Her angry companion could be heard taking its frustrations out under the front passenger seat. With all windows down and her door wide open, Rebecca waited outside. Not certain that the tormented demon had found its freedom, Rebecca eventually decided that Shree had waited long enough. She drove with the windows down, imagining she could still hear buzzing beneath the rushing wind.

The final swim meet of the summer had been over for almost an hour by the time Rebecca arrived at the Rec Center. There was no sign of her daughter. Shree would have gotten tired of waiting and walked home, Rebecca rationalized at first.

It wasn't until she pulled into their driveway that Rebecca felt certain that something wasn't right. She charged into the empty house, half expecting to find Anthony there. She advanced from room to room, calling out, much as her ex-husband had done only a few nights before. Within moments, she found herself opening her own closet door, irrationally thinking her daughter would be cowering inside, just like she had. Its emptiness halted her at a cliff's edge. Yet in another moment, her brain was tumbling into the depths. *Breathe, Rebecca, breathe.*

Could it really be happening? Where else could she be? 'Don't leave the pool!' I'm sure I said it. Did I? Yes, at breakfast. Told her to stay put! Be there as soon as I can. Must have heard me. Could I have missed her? Swimming?

Rebecca hurried back to the car, and as soon as she sat down, a bolt of pain struck the back of her right leg, just below the knee. The triumphant wasp extracted itself from her leg and zipped out of the still-open door to freedom.

Yet Rebecca's attention remained on her daughter. She quickly drove back to the pool and went through the gate this time. No sign of Shree anywhere. She even made a kid check the boys' changing room. She interrupted a coach who was running drills with the high school team. Her air of desperation must have made an impression. The coach took her to the office and got Shree's coach on the phone. He had not seen Shree at that day's meet. He was sure. Shree had not been to the meet and had missed all her scheduled races.

Rebecca called Jimmy. While waiting for her brother to come to the phone, her leg still throbbing from the wasp, Rebecca thought about the last moments she had seen Anthony. *He was shocked! Had looked at me in fear, stumbled back. Fled!* The burnt smell, still fresh in her memory. Rebecca had wondered if it was the last time she would see him. The police had come that night and had concluded that the blood on the light switch had been from his breaking the window. She had been relieved then. Now, a thought flashed through her brain that if things had turned out differently, Shree would be with her right now. This triggered a new spiral into darkness. *What will he do to her? Has his fear morphed to anger? Is Shree worried? She doesn't even understand the danger she's in. Will she find a way to call? Will she even want to call?*

Finally, Jimmy picked up the phone and extinguished the one flicker of hope remaining. He had left Shree at the pool. Watched her walk through the gate. But Jimmy had offered one new possibility. Shree was with her friend, Wendy. Rebecca drove to Wendy's home and nervously knocked on the door. A stern woman answered and called to her daughter. No, she hadn't seen Shree. Not today, not in many days. "Was she in trouble?" Wendy had asked. Rebecca said no. The word had just come out, 'no'.

Rebecca returned home in a daze. Now she felt herself moving, but it was as if she were only going through the motions. Her body walked into the house, but she was not quite there. Pain from the wasp sting hung in the background, a tiny kite string. Her body sat down on her daughter's bed, yet she was a million miles away. She didn't think. Didn't feel. It was as if it were someone else's life.

Jimmy showed up. *Why's he here? Oh yeah, something terrible.* With effort, she swam back to the surface. Shree. *Tony took Shree.* Must call the police. Jimmy called them and put her on the phone. Yes, it is a kidnapping. Yes, it's her father. Yes, he's dangerous. Yes, she had fired a gun at him.

Shortly after dark, a police car arrived. It was Officer Lovell and Officer Donnilon, the same two who had come on Friday night. No, they couldn't do anything until Shree was gone for twenty-four hours. "Your husband will probably call in a couple of hours. In all likelihood, he'll bring her home shortly. These things have a way of resolving themselves." With that, they left.

Jimmy stayed. He tried to say encouraging things. That Tony loves his daughter and would never hurt her. That Shree was a smart kid and would call soon. By 11 pm, not much was being said. It was clear there would be no call that night. Anthony was not bringing his daughter home for bedtime. Rebecca sent her brother home. She told him that she was okay. But the words were hollow. What does it mean, 'okay'? She was what she was, peering into someone else's life from far, far away. She lay down in her daughter's bed and looked at the car lights as they drove across the walls and ceiling. *This is what Shree sees every night,* she thought.

2. Dark Ages

May 20th, 1981

It hadn't been easy to get off early. As a computer operator, Rebecca was often the only one left to run the mainframe, and afternoons were especially busy with other departments bringing in huge jobs to be loaded at the end of the day. Rebecca, tall, wavy auburn hair landing on her thin shoulders, bangs raising curtains on dark eyes, high cheekbones, and a prominent nose, assured her boss that she would return in the evening. But she had to take her daughter to a dentist appointment at three forty-five.

"It's not very professional to run out on us with little notice. Next time, get permission a week in advance so we can adjust the schedule," Mr. Spruill, short, thin, and balding, his mustache a mere sparrow's feather, scolded his newest employee. He had been against hiring a woman for this job, and just as he predicted, the motherhood thing was interfering with her work.

As the car's air conditioner struggled to overpower a muggy afternoon, Rebecca tried to assemble a speech for Shree while she drove down the freeway. With growing anxiety, she realized Shree needed to be warned. If Anthony tried to see her when Rebecca wasn't around…. What words would convey seriousness, but not frighten her daughter? Again and again, Rebecca's own fear and anger invaded her composition. In high school, she had dreamed of becoming a writer. Such naiveté. Words are easy if nothing is on the line. In frustration, Rebecca decided she would wing it. Shree is a smart kid; she will understand how important this is.

~ ~ ~

"Annabelle thinks she's such a princess! And Jeanie n' Sharron B. follow her 'round everywhere. It's embarrassing! I'm not gonna go to her stupid party, even if she does have a pool."

"Wendy, don't you think you're being too harsh? Anna's nice, she's always kind to me. Of course, Jeanie and Sharron B. are stuck up. But Anna can't help it if she's the prettiest girl in fifth grade. I think she's a little sad. Why don't you like her?"

Wendy went unexpectedly quiet for a moment, her face flushing red. Finally, she came out with, "She's two-faced." Then quickly she charged ahead. "If I have to go to her dumb party, I'm not bringin' no gift. She's rich, so she's got everything already," Wendy rationalized. Shree suspected Wendy actually did want to go to the party.

Rebecca caught sight of Shree a block from school, walking with another girl. "Shree! Shree, get in!" she called out of the half-opened window as she rolled to a stop next to them.

Shree's stomach leapt into her throat as she saw her mom. Last night had gone surprisingly well, but something told her that a lecture was coming. "Do I have to come now, Mom? Wendy and I are heading to her house," she lied. Wendy was about to say that she couldn't have guests over, but then she caught the glance her new best friend sent her way, and Wendy kept quiet.

"Remember we're going to the dentist," her mom said factually. The presence of Wendy was, nevertheless, a welcome refuge for Rebecca too. "Well Shree, why don't you introduce me to your friend?"

"Mom, this is Wendy, she's in my class. Wendy, this is my Mom, she lives in my house." While this little joke was the inverse of one her mom had told before, Shree meant it more than her mom ever had.

"Hello, Mrs. Kreigle." Wendy was proud she'd remembered Shree's last name.

"Hi Wendy, do you live nearby,' Ms. Kreisler replied. "Can we give you a lift? We have a little time."

"That's okay, Mrs. Kreigle, I can walk."

"Come on Wendy, my mom'll drive us to your house," insisted Shree. Wendy resisted, embarrassed about where she lived. But her friend was giving her a pleading look, so Wendy climbed into the back seat with Shree.

"Well I'm sorry girls, but you will have to put off your playdate for another time, maybe tomorrow. Shree knew she had this dentist appointment."

"Okay Mom! I forgot," Shree confessed in resentment. Rebecca noticed the attitude.

"Wendy, where did you say you live?" Rebecca may not know how to talk to her daughter, but she knew she was in the driver's seat.

"Turn right on El Camino. I live in, um, La Hacienda Park," answered Wendy in quiet resignation that her shame was now exposed.

"Oh yes, La Hacienda, Shree and I almost moved there. They have some lovely homes." Rebecca tried to hide behind this compliment. Her true feelings were pity for this poor child growing up in a trailer park. These concerns were entirely foreign to Shree. While she had no idea what La Hacienda Park was, she had thought many times that living in a mobile home would be cool. She imagined the homes being driven all over the country and people seeing the world from their kitchen window.

Soon, they pulled into the entrance, where Wendy asked to be let out at the front gate. But Shree pleaded to see her actual mobile home. It turned out to be nothing special. It was barely distinguishable from most homes in the park. Not nearly as nice as the manager's deluxe unit with a second-story deck and flower boxes, painted bright red with white trim. But it was much nicer than where Wendy pointed out "Creepy Mr. Carsten" lived. The garbage bags and weeds almost hid his rusted-out pickup with a camper on the back, coincidentally also red and white. No, Wendy lived in an ordinary three-bedroom double-wide with a view of the lovely yellow lace curtains in the next trailer, three feet away.

Just before she jumped out, Wendy gave Shree a conspiratorial look. "I'll go to Annabelle's if you'll do!" Reluctant goodbyes were said, then Shree and her mom were alone.

Despite her intention to go directly into warning Shree about her father, Rebecca was still too unnerved about what words to use. So she spent the drive to the dentist quizzing Shree about school, and about her new friend.

~ ~ ~

Inside the dentist's office, in a rush of chilled antiseptic air, Dr. Heshing struck up a conversation with Shree's mother. Quickly it advanced beyond normal chitchat when they discovered they both had attended UMass in Amherst, though Shree's mom had dropped out to work and raise her. Soon Rebecca and Gretchen were laughing about a humanities professor who was, evidently, very full of himself. But then it was time for the dental work, and her mom left for the waiting room, while the affable dentist applied large, powerful hands to Shree's helpless little mouth.

After what seemed an endless enemy incursion of prodding and poking, the now tight-lipped dentist announced that she would be drilling into a cavity. Then the incursion gave way to full warfare, replete with bone-jarring, tooth-shattering, hand-to-mouth combat, and a stabbing pain that Shree couldn't withstand. She finally managed to pull away from the gruesome scene long enough to vocalize her pain, only to have the dentist insist it was trivial and then redouble her efforts to conquer the offending tooth. Shree couldn't believe this was happening. She had been to dentists multiple times before, but it had been nothing like this. She knew something was wrong, but this stern woman overpowered her, and no one was there to help. Years later, when Shree first learned the word 'sadistic', she would think of Dr. Heshing. But at this moment, she only thought about wanting her mommy to come rescue her.

"Just a little bit longer if you will keep still. You don't want me telling your mother that you wouldn't cooperate." Shree squirmed under the drill because she couldn't help it. The pain in her tooth was blindingly bright. Through eyes clenched shut, she could see the searing pain, like staring into a lightbulb, then dimming to a red glow before searing back up to blinding white agony again. Every muscle in Shree's little body tensed against the awful man-sized arms, forcing the pain upon her. Finally, a young assistant entered the room, and the dentist pulled her arms back. "There is no reason to cry, young lady. I swear she seems frightened of the drill." When the dentist turned her back, the younger woman put her hand comfortingly on Shree's knee and looked sympathetically into her eyes. Yet she kept silent. The drilling was done, but the horrible hands were in Shree's mouth for another fifteen minutes before all combat finally ceased.

Rebecca appeared again but didn't notice her daughter's tears. Dr. Heshing cheerfully described the dental procedure as routine. "It was a small cavity that didn't even require Novocaine, which saved you some money, by the way. Unfortunately, your daughter was a little frightened and uncooperative, so it took longer than needed. She will never make it through Professor Keating's Modern and Post-Modern Expression if her thoughts remain firmly in the dark ages," Gretchen said, ending in an upper-class English accent.

"Oh that sounds just like him!" Rebecca welcomed the jest.

Out in the car, with Shree still in shock and pain, Rebecca praised Dr. Heshing again and again. There were no words that Shree could formulate to tell her mom what had just occurred. Shree sank further into herself. Gradually, she left behind the notion that her mommy would have rescued her if she had only known. And tentatively, Shree approached the idea that since her mom had arranged for the torture session with her friend, that maybe she actually, probably needed to be saved *from* her mom. It was during this drive home, with Shree in shock, that Rebecca turned to the subject of Shree's father.

"I need to have a talk with you," her mother began as they entered the freeway. "I realize that your dad showing up here was a surprise to you, and perhaps you were hoping to meet with him. However, I need to explain why that isn't a good idea."

Shree kept silent, not at all ready to talk. She wanted to blurt out that she knew her mom was lying.

"We discussed before how your father is different. His brain doesn't work as ours does. Because of his illness. We've also discussed how we both really want him to get better. Unfortunately honey, your father is still a long way from getting better. The good news is that he has been given some time out of the hospital in what is called outpatient care." Rebecca didn't mention that her ex-husband had been out of McLean for over two years. It occurred to her that it was easier to talk to Shree about this while they were in the car, and especially with Shree in the back seat as she was now. Instead of looking directly at each other, Rebecca had to watch the road, and Shree seemed to be staring at her knees. "His doctors want to see if he can live with his mother and continue treatments…"

"But why can't he live with us?" Shree's words escaped before she could stop them.

"Well honey, he's too sick. He needs special care, and he can't take the stress of living with us." To this, Shree returned to her previous stifled silence. Rebecca had to slow down suddenly as a beat-up pickup truck pulled into her lane unexpectedly. "Besides, we're now in Texas, and he needs his mom in Boston. I know you would like him in our lives, but it would be bad for him. He can get confused, forget where he is, forget who he is." Rebecca knew this was a poor description of Anthony's condition, but she was trying to paint the simplest picture for her daughter. Freeway traffic slowed to 20mph, and Rebecca began to feel that the same forces were conspiring to bog her talk down to a crawl. "Unfortunately, your father needs a great deal more care from the doctors… in Boston." Rebecca felt determined to get her words out, even as all forward momentum had ceased in their lane. "He is an outpatient, but the doctors have warned that he may need to return to the hospital if things prove too stressful." Okay, so far, so good, Rebecca thought, as she switched into another lane, but now comes the tricky part. Shree sat motionless, now staring out the window. Cars crept by, one by one, in the lane they had just abandoned.

"The reason I wanted to talk to you, though, is that it's troubling that your Dad came to our house Tuesday night. His doctors are worried about him and need him to return home. They're worried that he's confused and may accidentally get hurt. I could see he was confused… when he was at our door. He'll get help soon, but until he does, we need to stay away from him." Cars on either side of them eased forward, while Rebecca and Shree sat perfectly still under an unforgiving sun.

"So I need you to be very brave and good. He may show up at our house again, and if he does, I need you to stay away from him. If you see him, call me immediately. If you can't reach me, call

Uncle Jimmy. Don't let him in the house, don't talk to him, and don't go anywhere with him. This is very important." Imprisoned in their car, at a dead stop, surrounded by a dozen other glass and metal cells. Families, couples, those going solitary. Whole other worlds existed, so close and yet unknowably distant. Shree saw a young woman singing to the radio. Rebecca envied an elderly couple laughing about something. The traffic inched ahead, and Rebecca soldiered on.

"Your father is really very sick, and his brain isn't working right. I know he doesn't want to hurt you, or me, or himself. But he might accidentally hurt someone! Sweetie, it is very important that you keep away from him. You need to promise me that you will stay away from him!" Shree sat in silence. "Shree honey, he probably won't come by. But if he does, promise that you'll stay away from him! For his sake. Shree, promise me you will."

Shree felt certain that everything her mom was telling her was a lie. She had heard her dad, and he wasn't confused. *Dad isn't brain sick. The only one who's brain sick is Mom.* But she knew that her mother was never going to stop this horrible talk until Shree promised. *Well if mom can lie….*

"Shree, honey, I know this is hard for you to understand, but you have to promise me that if Anthony, if your dad tries to talk to you, tries to come into the house, or tries to get you in his car…, you must promise me that you'll keep away from him. For his own good, so that his treatment can work and he can get better. Promise me."

"Okay, I'll stay away," Shree quietly acquiesced, staring down at her knees pushing up against the front seat. In the end, Shree felt lucky they were in the car. Her mom often knew when she tried to deceive. But the noise of the air conditioner, her quiet response, and the fact that Shree was seated directly behind and out of sight of her mom, all helped to disguise this lie.

These four words were all that Rebecca wanted. They were both freed from further torture. Rebecca's frightening thoughts could be pushed to the back of her mind again. Even the glacial traffic melted, and they flowed past the elderly couple. Now all Rebecca wanted was light-hearted distraction. Though Shree was reluctant to talk, her mother asked her to read aloud the birthday party invitation. That's when they both learned that the girls were invited to sleep over. Yes, Rebecca thought, Shree would have a normal childhood.

3. Tha James

May 19th, 1981

Despite suspecting that her eleven-year-old daughter had faked illness to skip school that day, Rebecca had no evidence, nor energy to confront her. Consequently, domestic life adhered to the same routine in the Kreisler household. Shree read in her room while Rebecca prepared macaroni and cheese with broccoli. She tried to engage her daughter while they ate, but Shree was quieter than usual. So Rebecca switched on the radio and they listened to "The Fourth Tower of Inverness". After Shree's bath and before sending her off to bed, Rebecca mentioned a dentist appointment, scheduled for the next day. No mention was made about her ex-husband, though he lingered like an apparition in each of their minds the whole evening. All was quiet in the house for an hour and a half, so Rebecca made sure Shree's door was closed and dialed the number to the phone outside Jimmy's dorm room. "Hello, is Jimmy Kreisler, room 17, available?"

"Tha JAMES! Phone call for Tha JAMES!" came blaring out of the receiver.

Rebecca waited on the line for a couple of minutes while a door was pounded on and loud, inaudible voices were heard. Then, in her brother's cheerful voice, "Hello?"

"So you're 'Tha James's now?"

"That's just Nathan, or as he likes to call himself, 'Tha Scalpel'. There are a surprising number of frat boys here, especially considering this is grad school. I think a lot of these guys are at the medical school. Nathan, I know, plans to be a heart surgeon."

"So the stereotype is true?"

"What stereotype is that?"

"That surgeons are all jocks, frat boys."

"Well it's true about Nathan, anyway. How's Shree? Is she feeling better?" After dropping everything to pick Shree up for his sister, James was hinting for a thank you.

"Yeah, she's fine. She says she felt better after she got home. But I meant what I told you this morning. Tony *is* dangerous."

Jim couldn't imagine his brother-in-law ever being dangerous. "So you say, but you don't actually think he would hurt his own daughter, do you?"

"Yes I do, Jimmy. You have no idea what he can get like. And I don't appreciate your thinking you know him better than I do." Rebecca needn't have added the last line; her tone of voice said it all clearly.

"Okay, okay! I'm on your side. But can we talk about it a little? Just trying to understand."

"Okay Jimmy, what's to understand?" Rebecca responded, the tension in her voice ebbing. "Tony had to be institutionalized. Several times. And before that, we were living with him. You were away at school and missed all the fireworks."

"But he was in the hospital and was treated", Jim reasoned. "Stress and grief can do a number on you. Didn't his sister overdose around that time?"

It wasn't that, Jimmy. Of course Tina's death hit him hard. But she died over a year before Anthony's first breakdown. His doctor said it was a classic case of schizophrenia. It runs in his family."

"Maybe so," Jim acknowledged without conviction. "But he's had years to recover. I've talked to him. You wouldn't believe how clear-headed he was. It wasn't just a normal conversation, Becca.

He's very aware of the pain he caused, and he wants to repair the damage he's done. He…"

"Shree was five years old," Rebecca said flatly. "Her daddy was babbling about mind control and voicing bizarre conspiracies involving dead people. It makes me physically ill to remember…." Three students passing down the hall were talking loudly about how hard it was to understand one of their professors. Jim guessed it was Dr. Theissen, even though he was trying to catch every word his sister said.

"…from the window. Shree remembers some of it but doesn't understand what was happening. I helped make sure she didn't understand, Jimmy. To her, Daddy was just being funny, just playing games. He would say the scariest things to her, and she would laugh and laugh." A door down the hall opened, and Pink Floyd's 'Interstellar Overdrive' poured out with its chaotic rhythms flooding the bare hallway.

"…had to take her away. We would get in the car at 3 am…" Nathan yelled for Greg to turn down the horrible music. Jim felt solidarity with Greg, even though he was trying to follow what his sister was saying.

"…would wake me up asking, not about why we were sleeping in the car, in a strange parking lot, but where her daddy was. I had to call the police on him. And then I was terrified that he would be so wild they would shoot…" Some girl with deep blue hair, that Jim had never noticed before, was asking when the phone would be free and asked him to knock on 23 when he was done.

"…told her there was a cat stuck in a tree, and Daddy helped the police get her down. Well she isn't five years old anymore, and she won't be fooled by my stories! So no, Jimmy, Tony is not coming back into our lives."

"Wow, Becca, I didn't realize how hard it was." Jim tried to sympathize, though he restrained himself from pointing out that all took place years ago.

"I could fill in some even uglier details, but I'd rather not reenter that labyrinth. There is one more reason why I won't let him in her life, at least while she's growing up. And this one I would think you ought to appreciate. Schizophrenia is hereditary. Shree's his daughter. If she has even a drop of schizophrenia in her, then I want her to have the very best chance of overcoming it. And everything I've read tells me that having a stable, healthy childhood with lots of love is the best hope for her. What is the term I read… 'premorbid adjustment'. I want to make sure Shree has the best premorbid adjustment that I can give her. And Tony will destroy any hope of that, no matter how okay he may seem now."

"Jeez, sis. You've put a lot of thought into this. Maybe you're right, but…"

"Maybe?" Rebecca's irritation began surging back. "This is the only way it can be. You know, his mom told me to leave Boston. Lydia is great and has helped me in so many ways, dealing with Tony. She helped me get the divorce and full custody. And she loves Shree, her only granddaughter. But she told me that it was her job to take care of her son, and I have to take care of my daughter."

"Wow, that's really sad. Okay, I guess I see where you're coming from, sure, but…," Jim tried to catch himself. "But… and I don't have any better idea how to raise a kid, obviously, but I just think it's so sad. Sad for Tony. Sad for Shree. Sad for you."

"Yes, it's sad for Tony. Of course it's sad for Tony. Everything about his condition is sad for him. I loved him enough to marry the guy, so I have ached over the cruel hand that life has played on him. It broke my heart over and over. But at some point, I have to cut him out and put Shree first. And it will be a whole lot sadder for Shree if Tony is in her life. Sadder if she grows up with his chaos."

"But…," Jim tried to continue.

"Look, I'm not saying she should never know her dad. Maybe when she's in college she can get to know him. But she's only eleven! Let her be happy without worrying about her dad. And especially let her not have to wonder if she'll wind up being like him. I don't ever want her thinking some emotional outburst, a strange thought, or her childhood imaginary friend is a sign that something is wrong with her. You know how inventive she can be. Thoughts that maybe there's something wrong with her can be self-fulfilling."

"Oh yeah, that would be tragic," Jim agreed. "She doesn't deserve any of that self-doubt. But she *is* like her dad, in ways. No matter how she's raised, some things will come through. She looks like him, you know."

"She does. Her hair, her eyes especially. The way she laughs…."

"And she's going to be like him in other ways. You can't prevent that. If she's destined to be schizophrenic, there is nothing you can do about it, Rebecca."

"Not the determinism bullshit again, Jimmy. I know you believe there's nothing we can do about our fate, so why try."

"That's not what I believe…"

"Whatever. I know that how she grows up will have a big effect. And if you want me to play your determinism game, well I can't help but do what I have to do. So I will keep Tony out of Shree's life and don't try to interfere."

Something inside Jimmy finally erupted. "Rebecca, he's her father! You can't do that. You can't do it to him, and you can't do it to Shree." Though he felt like he was strongly standing up for fathers everywhere, his voice echoed his childhood whimpers when Rebecca had teased him.

His sister replied as an adult, with icy determination. "Yes, I can, Jimmy, yes I can. I have legal custody, and I'm her mother. If there is one thing I'm sure of, it's that I have a responsibility to protect my child. And I will protect her from him."

He felt certain that, as Shree's father, Tony should have a role. But Jimmy didn't have the energy to battle his big sister. "Okay Rebecca, okay. I can't stop you. I do think Tony's fine now, but I know how you feel, and I know you're doing what you think is best for Shree. What is that line in Candide? 'You have to cultivate your garden?' You have to raise Shree as you think. I can't tell you how to do it." Maybe someday he could say more, he thought, but not now. "But I do want to help, uh, help you and Shree when I can. I love being her Uncle Jim."

"Okay Uncle Jimmy, I'm glad we had this talk, though I was dreading it. I know how you look up to Tony. Now tell me, did you give him our address?"

"I did," he meekly confessed. "I'm sorry, but we had such a great talk, and he seems so healthy and self-aware. I just thought you'd be happy to see him."

"I wish we'd talked about him sooner, but I wasn't expecting he would show up in Houston. Did he say anything about where he's staying or how long he'll be in town? Did he leave you any way to contact him?"

"He didn't say. He mentioned that he'd been programming for some company in Boston. Sounded like he still works there, so maybe he's only in town for a few days. He did say he'd come by again, though."

"Just tell him that he can't be in Shree's life. I have full custody, and I *will* call the police."

Jim was again startled by his sister's threat. "Okay… okay, I'll let him know how you feel." What a miserable task he'd just agreed to. As he thought about this and fatherhood, he realized he had been staring at a doodle of a duck that someone had left on the wall by the phone. It said, "I may be a Quack, but at least I'm not a Coot."

"Well I'm glad we had this talk, Jimmy. And congratulations on your seminar."

"Thanks, it went pretty well," he responded without enthusiasm.

"Nitey nite 'Tha James'!"

"Goodnight Becs! And I'm sorry I gave him your address without asking." With that, she hung up, and he followed. Exhausted by the conversation, he still couldn't square his sister's view of Tony with the guy he saw the day before. He lingered by the phone with a defeated look on his face before he noticed that the girl of deep blue hair was sitting on the floor outside room 23, observing him. He nodded to her.

"I'm sorry for eavesdropping, but I really needed to get out of that room. You sounded pretty intense on the phone," she commented with a sympathetic look. "You alright?"

"It's fine. It was my sister," he said, returning a smile.

"You're James, aren't you? I'm Sirrus."

4. Curdling

May 19th

"Raise your hand if you know the first step of 'Fraction Subtraction'. Remember, kids, we're on the fraction subtraction express, and as long as we keep chugging along on the tracks, we're all going to arrive at the station." Ms. Warner and her cheery enthusiasm for teaching were not helping Shree's state of mind. It also didn't help that she had learned fractions the previous year at her old school. And now it seemed Ms. Warner's saccharine voice was going to magnify Shree's growing headache.

She had woken up to the memory of her dad's visit and soon was daydreaming how he would move in and their family would be whole and happy again. She was remembering his funny voices and the silly games they used to invent.

But mom had rushed her through breakfast and into the car, scolding her for putting on yesterday's shirt. Shree remembered her mother's cold voice late at night. Then, in the car, her mom asked her directly if she had heard anything last night. Shree had frozen, not ready to admit that she had been listening to the whole conversation. What her mom said next twisted inside her. Her mom said her father had stopped by but couldn't stay.

Ms. Warner's cheery voice cloyed for attention, but Shree was too much in turmoil to follow. Now she recalled Mom threatening to call the police. *What on earth could possibly make her be so mean? Dad just wanted to talk, but Mom wouldn't listen to him.* Shree felt a dread rising, strangling hope and crowding out her confusion. Just when she learned her dad wanted to come back, she discovered that her mom was the obstacle.

If only she had said something in the car. If only she had told Mom that she heard every word and she knew! *Dad loves us. Why didn't you listen to him? We can be a family again. But Mom! Why were you being so mean?!* Shree's stomach kept churning.

"It's really quite simple, class, this 'fraction subtraction extraction contraption'. First, you find a denominator…." The stew of emotions brewed further. If Mom wouldn't listen to Dad, then *maybe it was up to me to get Mom to listen. I'll have to tell her she's wrong.* But she knew she never could. An unbridgeable void. *Though if I say nothing, if I pretend nothing is wrong, we could lose Dad again.* It all seemed hopeless, under the pounding in her head.

"What denominator, you ask? Why, you need to find a 'common' denominator? And will any common denominator do? Why yes it will, but why make it hard? The higher the harder, but the *lower* the less work for you." Ms. Warner was on a roll. Her high school production of 'Music Man' was reborn in fifth-grade math. Any moment now she might burst into a song about the Denominator with a capital D. Unfortunately for her, most of the class was thoroughly on top of fractions, and the couple of kids still struggling were getting even more confused by all the catchy jingles.

"Remember, the LCD makes it easy for me."

Desperately trying to find a way out of her twisting thoughts and that stultifying room, Shree stared out the window. Suddenly something caught her eye. The dusty pane scattered the sunlight, and Shree felt a buzzing. Bzzz. Did she just see that? "Bzzzreee, bzzzz Zzzhree, Shrrreee come quickly. Shree, you have to save him! Shree, you have to get home and save him." Shree's exhausted mind had strayed, and her imagination had found a crack in that lovely window out of that ugly room. "Shree, come quickly." It was Chaser. To anyone else, he was just a housefly. But to Shree, Chaser was a friend.

"Chaser, what are you doing here?"

"Well you know me, always buzzing about. Bzzz, I have come to get you out of herrre."

"But why, Chaser? And what do you mean 'save him'?"

"You know where I was this morning? Buzzing about in my favorite bathroom window. It was great, sun streaming in, breeze through the screen. I was minding my own business, rattling between the glass and the screen. Making all kinds of rrracket. The acoustics in that bathroom window are just perrrfectt."

"Chaser, get to the point."

"Well I eventually paused the buzzing to listen for other flies. And that's when I hearrrdddim, hearrrrd him, Mr. Trains, of course. Who else? That guy is always making noise. Knocking things over, jangling keys, complaining about food. Chewing."

"Chaser!"

"Well, this time he is pinging on a bottle. Just ping ping pinging on a botttttle. So I flew to investigate as one does, and you will never guess where I fffound him. Never guess… g-g-guess. Guess!"

"Uh, next to a bottle?"

"Insiddday botttle! Insiddde! Now how did he get in therre? The bottle is clothed, closeddd, you see."

"That Trains does get into things he shouldn't." Shree was enjoying this little distraction of hers.

"I'll say he shouldn't! It was one of your mother's liquorrr bottles. You know he shouldn't be be in ththerre. He told me he'd been trrrapped in there since last nine night. Seems he slipped in when your mmmom had a drrrink last night. But then she closed it before heek c-could essscapppe. He'sss been trying to keepppp hiss head above the liquorrr ever sin siss since!"

Shree suppressed a laugh, which she disguised with a cough. A couple of kids looked at her, but she quickly regained her bored expression.

"Well I laughed too, Shreeree, but it's accctually very serrrious. I think Mr. Trains may ddrr may dddrown! So you need to get home rrright away to get him out of th-that bottttle."

With this, Shree decided to do something she had never done before. She raised her hand. Ms. Warner seemed delighted that someone had a question about fractions. "Yes, Shree?"

"Ms. Warner, I th-think I'm sick."

~ ~ ~

Her car door closed with a satisfying solidity, and Shree felt secure, having escaped from school for the day. Uncle Jim was soon in the driver's seat, and his easy "Let's get out of here" imbued a lightness to the mood. Shree was so relieved that her uncle showed up to take her home. While waiting in the nurse's office, she began to realize that a ride home with Mom was exactly the opposite of an escape. But Mom had called her long-haired little brother Jimmy, and Uncle Jim came to Shree's rescue.

"So are you feeling okay, Shree? Do I need to take you to a doctor or anything?"

"It's okay, I'm starting to feel better already."

"Just needed a break from school? That's okay, we all do sometimes."

"I was feeling bad earlier, but I guess it isn't so bad now. I probably could have stayed in class, but I'm out now. You won't tell Mom, will you?"

"Don't worry about it, Shree," her Uncle said with an implied alliance. "Glad you're feeling better. Are you doing okay in your classes?"

"It's only the one class, and half the stuff they're teaching I learned last year. This year is so boring. And easy."

"Boring? Easy? Then you'll be fine if you miss a day. Besides, skipping school is in your DNA. Don't tell her I told you, but your mom would skip school and go to the beach. One time, she and her friends got caught when their car broke down on the way back. So you, Shree-Ra, are just doing what comes naturally. Besides, you did exactly what you were supposed to do. Really couldn't have done anything else." As he said this, he suddenly realized that he had missed his turn and now needed to circle around.

"Well if Mom finds out I'm not really sick, she will tell me exactly why I should've done something different. I'd be in big trouble. Half the time, I'm actually sick, Mom wants me to get up and go to school anyway. She always thinks I'm faking it."

"Don't worry about it Shree, really. Things will work out perfectly. Your body told you to leave school, and you had to follow. It's cause and effect. You know we are biological machines following the laws of chemistry, of physics. Millions, no, trillions of interactions of molecules build up waves of pressures pushing you to take a breath, crave ice cream, or hum a catchy tune. All this stuff is going on before you're even conscious of it." Shree stopped following what her uncle was saying. Uncle Jim was known to talk about weird things. Her mom would tease him about it, rolling her eyes at Shree with a smile. "Next thing you know, you're flying down the road with your Uncle, feeling that warm Houston air racing by. You didn't skip school. School spat you out, and now the day is yours. What are you going to do with it?"

"I don't know. Maybe read?"

"If I were you and had a free day, I'd be cranking up the tunes. Unfortunately, I have to get to an immunology seminar I'm leading later today. No rest for the wicked. What music do you listen to?"

"I don't know, whatever is on the radio. Mom listens to KILT."

"What! Don't listen to that crap. At least switch to K101. I expected you to be listening to the B-52s or Talking Heads." At this point, Uncle Jim pushed a tape into the deck, and some very dramatic guitar and drums filled the car. It was so loud that the rest of the conversation was shouted. "This is my favorite band, 'Yes'! This is called 'Sound Chaser', and this guitar is amazing."

Shree didn't know what she thought about his music; it was so loud. But with it blaring and Uncle Jim shouting, she had plenty of room to slip back into her thoughts. She liked her uncle a lot, especially the way he didn't talk down to her. But he also never seemed to realize when no one understood what he was talking about. Mom called him 'Brother Oblivious' sometimes. *Hmm. Was Mom being mean to her brother too? Maybe that's why she always calls him Jimmy, even though he told us he prefers Jim.* Shree felt closer to her uncle at that moment, even though she kind of felt like he was from a different planet. With guitar rockets blasting, his spaceship turned onto her street.

The car rolled up to their house, and Shree opened the door. Uncle Jim held his hand up, waiting for the right place to turn down the music. "Do you want me to come in, fix you some food, or something? I can stay a little while, but I do have to prepare for the seminar."

"No, I'll be okay. I can feed myself. I'll just read until Mom comes home. Thanks Uncle Jim!"

"No worries, Shree Ra of the Free Day! Remember that everything you do today is perfect. It is exactly what you're supposed to do." With this, Uncle Jim smiled a friendly, knowing smile, cranked his music back up, and drove off. Shree turned on her heel, bounced up the step, and unlocked her door to a free day.

Home alone without a care. What will she do?

~ ~ ~

"Mr. Trrrains! Don't forget Mr. Trains." Chaser buzzed by Shree's head and flew in a contorted helix towards the kitchen. Shree climbed onto the counter and opened the cabinet above the fridge where her mom kept the liquor bottles. There were two, one was a half-empty bottle of red wine, the other was something called 'Baileys'. She opened it and Mr. Train's poured out of the top, spilling onto the floor.

"Well it took-ed you long and all. Long hall. Took, took you a long time!" Mr. Trains looked like he'd been at sea for six months and had forgotten how to walk on dry land. He was swaying, and as soon as Shree offered to help him, all his muscles stopped participating. With more than a little difficulty, she dragged him from the kitchen to her room and put him on the bed. His eyes were closed, but he kept trying to say something. "Tha tide was raisening, was going bigger. Like bread dough that swallowed its pizza. Is there pizza? Oh no, I'ma be sick. I, uh, no false alarms, false teeth. Do I have real, real, uh. What took you so? You cared about my… my shoes are soggy." Shree shushed him, and soon his semi-random words reduced to an odd syllable here and there. "Gurl!" Then, after a long pause, "wrap", and all of a sudden, "Fractions!" and he was out.

Shree looked at Chaser, who just arrived from the kitchen. "You know th-th-that stuff is st-st-strrrrong!" Oh Chaser, not you too, Shree thought. She watched as Chaser nose-dived, literally into Mr. Train's nose. Then he too was out.

Returning to the kitchen to find something sweet, Shree realized the bottle was still on the counter. Well, a little taste can't hurt, she thought. Wow, that is surprisingly yummy! Most of the strong burn of alcohol was hidden by the sweet, creamy deliciousness. But after the sip went down, the sting was left to linger. Shree took three more sips before deciding the aftertaste was too much. Besides, she didn't want her mom to see that some of the liquor was gone.

She considered adding water to hide what she drank. But water wouldn't be right, since this liquor was a creamy light brown. Milk? Should she try adding milk? After tossing it over in her head, she convinced herself it was the right thing. Not only did she spill the milk, but she put too much into the liquor bottle. And the milk didn't mix with Baileys. She closed the bottle and shook it up. Now it looked like it was curdling! She poured out the excess into a glass, where it looked like an oozing, slimy mess. Since she couldn't quite remember how much was in the bottle, she worried there was still too much. Or maybe too little. Changing her mind again and again, she poured back and forth between the bottle and the glass half a dozen times. Finally, she resolved to drink what was in the glass and put the bottle away.

When she left the kitchen, feeling more than a bit woozy, she left a sticky counter, the towel stained and smelling of alcohol, the glass only partially rinsed, and the sticky bottle of Irish milk, with a wet peeling label, pushed to the back of the cabinet. Shree hoped that her mom wouldn't see the bottle and would forget about it. At that moment, she was pretty sure she had gotten away with everything that day. What would she do now?

5. The Reservoir

May 19th

The sky was ominous with dark clouds hanging low. In the distance, gray sheets of rain were hiding the usual outline of the First Baptist Church. But at the reservoir, Shree was blessed with a patch of blue sky as she arrived on her bike. So much of where she lived was regimented with suburban block after perfectly scripted block. The exact same houses in slightly different muted earth tones, repeating every fourth home or so. But the reservoir, or so it was called, was a break amongst the mowed lawns, boxy hedges, and flower-trimmed rock gardens. Large heaps of dirt, broken concrete, and dry grass pushed haphazardly into an embankment surrounded a deep chasm of tangled riotous growth at the edge of a brown pond, with black and smelly orange mud laid out as an unwelcome mat. Shree had climbed down to the water for stone skipping and tadpole hunting in the green slime several times already. She had slit open her bare foot on broken glass two months before, and now looked warily and longingly at the blood-stained wildness below. Further on were bike trails where she had seen kids racing down and over jumps. Admiring, she wasn't quite brave enough to try it herself.

Instead, she found her spot just below a higher ridge, shielded from street view. There Shree disappeared into the scenery. An ordinary girl of ordinary size. Shree's straight, almost black hair, pale complexion, and pointy nose were accented by regal eyebrows and gray-blue eyes behind dark rimmed glasses. Most adults recognized that she was smart and assumed she was well-behaved. And many kids avoided her for the same reasons. Since moving to Texas, she mostly kept to herself. Now, at the reservoir, she felt alone in the world. The effect of the Baileys having evaporated, the previous night's scene was returning to her thoughts. Yet someone had recognized her and was heading her way.

May 18th

Bedtime came for Shree before she was ready. Her mom never negotiated on a school night, but the routine didn't mean that sleep was near. Instead, Shree cracked the window and listened to the sounds of the neighborhood, imagining she could hear the trees talking. While the movement inside her house had ceased, outside irregular gusts of wind were roughing up supple leaves with misplaced insult. A branch in mourning scraped against the house next door.

A car drove by, and a window-shaped light drove across her wall and stretched onto her ceiling. In the far distance, a dog was barking while a woman yelled for Angus to quiet down. Shree heard a couple of people walking along the sidewalk discussing whether Lonnie was aware of what was going on. The gossip pulled her in, but the voices faded before Shree herself could learn what Lonnie hadn't. A car drove in the other direction, and another window shape illuminated the bookshelf and then, like a prison spotlight, searched across the wall where three stuffed animals sat frozen in their escape. Shree yawned and realized that slumber would find her soon. She closed her eyes and let the wind and the barks of Angus drift further from her mind. As always, she saved her last few thoughts for her daddy. She knew he was far away but imagined he was thinking of her. The trees were talking about ants, and a partial moon was tiptoeing silently between their branches, but Shree was lost to it all.

"You can't be here." Shree started at the sudden stern words from her mother. It took a moment before she realized that her mom wasn't ordering her to retreat. Her voice was directed to someone standing on the front step mere feet from her window. Shree couldn't see anything, but their voices were as clear as the moonlight.

"I just want to talk to you, Rebecca." Those words brought Shree to her full attention.

May 19th

"Shree, I knew you was faking! Mind if I join you?" Wendy was dragging her bike over the hill and dumped it next to Shree's.

"If you want, Wendy, but I was enjoying the quiet." Shree knew Wendy, of course, but had never seen her outside of school. In fact, Shree had purposefully avoided Wendy after their first conversation. Wendy was bigger than most of the kids in fifth grade, with reddish brown hair, a too-friendly smile, and freckles. She seemed so talkative and gossipy. Shree felt like she was in a crowded room when there were only the two of them. So she braced herself to wait out this new obstruction to her peace.

"So why the big ex-scape from school today? I know Mrs. Warner was drivin' the fraction subtraction train off the rails, but was that the ax'chul reason ya ditched?"

"It wasn't that, I just had something on my mind and needed to get away."

"Don't worry, I won't say nuthin' and I'm sure Mrs. Warner don't 'spect neither. She was prob'ly too busy dreamin 'bout Mrs.

Halloway to notice."

This piqued Shree's curiosity despite herself. "What are you saying?"

"Well, have y'ever heard of less-beents? You know, ladies who only like ladies?"

"I think the word you mean is 'lesbian'."

"Yeah, yeah, less-beands, well I saw Mrs. Warner 'n Mrs. Halloway huggin! Last week, after school. I had to stay late, n'when Mrs. Warner da-smissed me, she went to Mrs. Halloway's room and they was huggin and I saw it when I passed by the door."

"Well that doesn't mean they're lesbians. My mom has hugged plenty of women, and she's not a lesbian. Come to think of it, last year in Boston, we lived next to a lesbian couple, and I don't think I ever saw them hug."

"You lived next door to lesbeans! Wow! Weren't they arrested?"

"Wendy, you seriously don't know what you're talking about! This is 1981, no one is arresting people for that."

"Well I'm perdy sure it's 'gainst th'law. I heard my momma and daddy talkin' and it sounded like the courts were s'posed ta lockum up."

Shree remembered her mom telling her that some people had very strange beliefs, especially in Texas, and that she should not worry about it and just let them be. But Wendy seemed badly off the mark. "Wendy, there are all kinds of people in the world. People who love opera, and people who love spiders, people who believe in Martians, and people who eat snails, and people who make movies. I kind of think it makes the world more interesting. I don't think we have the right to tell someone else who they should be. I also don't think Ms. Warner is a lesbian just because you saw her hugging Ms. Halloway."

Wendy thought about this for a while. Shree was kind of

surprised that her words had made Wendy quiet. She was also surprised that her mom's words, spoken more than a year earlier, had come out so naturally just now. This realization was even more vexing, since Shree didn't know what she felt about her mom at that moment. Mom certainly didn't accept Dad as he was.

"Maybe yer right. Who're they hurting anyways?" decided Wendy with a look of seriousness.

"Anyway, I left school today because my mom was so mean last night!"

"What, why? I mean, I know what it's like, but what'd she do?"

Shree was startled that she was sharing with Wendy, yet it all poured out. "Well my parents are divorced, and I almost never get to see my dad. Last summer, my mom moved us here from Boston, and I thought I would never see Dad again. Then last night, after I was in bed, I heard him at our door. He was here! Asking to see me!" By now, tears were streaming down Shree's cheeks. "But my mom said no and told him to go away!" A torrent of feeling took over. Shree finally understood that she was angry. "She sent him away when he came across the whole country to see me. What kind of a mom does that?! She's such a bitch!" The word had never crossed her lips before. "She says that she loves me, but then she does that! She wants to keep me all to herself. Like her servant. And Dad, I could hear the sadness in his voice! He wants to see me, and she threatened to call the police! She just closed the door on him! How could she be so horrible? How could she?!"

"Oh Shree, it's gonna be okay."

"Then my mom lied this morning! She lied about it as if everything was fine. That Dad couldn't stay and had to leave town again. She was lying to my face!"

"Shree, it's okay. It'll be okay." Wendy found herself hugging her friend without thinking about it. She felt strangely strong, while she also felt helpless. She didn't know what to say to Shree. But she felt like hugging her was the only thing in the world she should be doing at that moment. She couldn't remember when she had last been hugged herself. Her family never gave hugs or said 'I love yous' or anything. But now she felt like this moment was overpowering her. She realized she was crying too.

And then the moment subsided. Shree pulled back, wiped her tears away, and Wendy turned her face in embarrassment. "Thank you for that," Shree said quietly. "I'm sorry for crying, but it just came out."

Wendy turned back to her with tears still filling her eyes, "I ain't sorry at all, Shree! I think I needed it too." They exchanged a smile of recognition through watery eyes, then Wendy continued, "I don't know what's up with yer parents, or why yer mom is bein' mean. But I know what it's like to not matter to 'em. My older brother can be cruel. I mean he hurts me! But my parents don't see it, don't even care. He nearly drownd'ed me last summer, 'n mom yelled at me for mak'n a racket 'n disturbing her nap."

Wendy wondered if her complaint was trivial and self-centered after Shree's painful revelation. But Shree didn't seem to notice or didn't mind. She pulled Wendy into a quick side hug and said, "We'll just have to stick together then, you and I. Our mothers be damned!"

"And brothers!"

6. Turtle

May 23rd

The house was huge. Wendy thought that her house could fit in Annabelle's living room. One whole side of it was solid windows, from floor to ceiling and wall to wall. The windows looked out onto a shaded patio, which itself looked onto a swimming pool sparkling in the hot Texas sun. Back inside, the opposite living room wall was a gigantic stone fireplace, topped with a wooden mantle the size and appearance of a stage. A backdrop for this stage was a painting of thousands of grayish green people in rags, swarming at the foot of an immense cross towering towards yellow sunbeams breaking through gray-blue clouds. Wendy noticed the cross was tilting backwards from the weight of the pile-up of people. It looked like it was painted mid-fall. For stage curtains, there were two identical massive bookshelves filled with photos of cars, horses, and churches, arrayed symmetrically. Finally, the stage contained actors costumed as expensive-looking crystals, a clock with chimes, and two tennis trophies.

A huge couch in about twenty sections seemed to circle most of the room. On this couch were half the kids from their class. Annabelle was on the floor with most of the girls facing her. She jumped up to greet Wendy, who was surprised by the attention, since they rarely talked to each other in school.

"I'm so glad you could make it to my party, Wendy. I wasn't

sure you would come."

"Well y'invited tha whole class, so I thought I better show up. Thanks for having this thing. Here's your gift." Wendy felt so awkward at this moment, like they both were only saying what they had to. But while Annabelle seemed so natural in her welcome, Wendy could tell that her own words sounded insincere, which made her feel even more embarrassed. She also really hoped Annabelle wouldn't open the gift now. Her dad had taken her to the mall and grudgingly gave her ten dollars to spend. Wendy hadn't a clue what to buy a rich kid and finally just got something she wished she had herself, a small coin purse that looked like a turtle. As soon as they left the store, Wendy knew it was a stupid gift and that Annabelle and her crew would laugh at how cheap and stupid it was. She almost refused to go to the party, but her dad had already paid for the gift, so he would be furious if that was wasted. Besides, deep down, she wanted to go to the party. She wanted to swim and see Annabelle's house. And she knew her new best friend, Shree, would be there.

"Thanks, you can just put the gift on the table," Anna said with a friendly smile, motioning towards a giant table in the adjacent dining room, which was piled with gifts already. "Did you bring your bathing suit? You're going to spend the night, aren't you?"

Wendy had blocked out that it was to be a slumber party for the girls. She had never been to a sleepover before. But she also thought that Annabelle had actually only wanted her followers to stay over, so she hadn't even asked her parents. "I ain't sure I kin stay tha night."

"What'd you mean? Please stay over. We're gonna have so much fun. After the boys leave, we can have an all-girls party. I'll be disappointed if you don't stay." Anna looked so sincere that Wendy remembered why the other girls followed her. The resentment and embarrassment from a year ago evaporated. She wanted to stay and have fun with Annabelle again. Perhaps she could call her parents. But then she remembered her stupid gift and the coming ridicule, so she decided not to call.

Just then, Johnny came in, and Anna, like a good hostess, turned all her attention to greeting him. Wendy noticed that Johnny seemed even more awkward than Wendy had been. Returning from dropping her gift at the table, Wendy saw that Shree was just arriving. So Wendy took a seat on the giant wrap-around couch, saving a place for Shree, and watched to see if Shree handled the greetings any better than she and Johnny had. Shree was doing okay, but when she noticed Wendy making a face, she burst into a smile, hugged Anna, and wished her a happy and fun birthday. So that is how it's done, Wendy thought.

As the party started, Annabelle's mom, wearing a fancy bright yellow dress and holding a tall pinkish drink, in a voice that sounded like it fell from a very great height, suggested that the games begin. So Anna and her followers announced that everyone should break into two teams for charades. Shree and Wendy used this time to look around the amazing house again. It was Shree who pointed out the chandelier over the table of presents. It looked like it was made of thousands of diamonds. Suddenly, Shree called out 'Planet of the Apes', which surprised Wendy, since she didn't think Shree was paying attention to the game, and also, who ever heard of a movie called 'Planet of Apes'?

Later, Annabelle's mom appeared, now wearing a light blue poofy dress, and suggested in her most disinterested voice that everyone go outside to the pool. There, four of the boys, led by Doug and Johnny, dominated the water and repeatedly splashed everyone. Wendy and Shree sheltered on the patio, where Sharon G. did a pretty funny impression of the fancy way that Anna's mom talked. Like there was a bad odor coming from the kids.

When the rambunctious boys finally got out of the pool, several girls slipped in. Shree swam straight to the bottom of the deep end and stayed for so long that Wendy wondered if she was okay. When she came up, she gasped, "Did you see them?"

"See what?" asked Sharon G., before Wendy could.

"Bubble rings!" exclaimed Shree. This led to a friendly competition and tutorial on how to blow bubble rings, which Wendy felt confident Shree had won, until Lloyd put everyone to shame. Say what you might about slow Lloyd with his deep Texas drawl and cowboy shirts, but he could sure blow some perfect bubble rings.

Drying in the sun on their towels, Shree and Wendy overheard some of the girls talking about how Anna was the only one wearing a two-piece swimsuit. The talk bothered Wendy. She thought maybe she could never wear a two-piece because kids would laugh and taunt her. She didn't have a slim body like many of the girls. She could hear her brother teasing her that she looked like a chubby boy. He and his friends had called her 'hippo'. Now, hearing the talk of two-piece suits made her want to hide under her towel and sneak away. Then Shree looked at her and rolled her eyes in the direction of the other girls, saying, "I thought swimsuits were for swimming." Those words draped over Wendy's shoulders, protecting her from self-doubt. She knew how to swim just fine.

Around five o'clock, so many boxes of pizza were delivered that everyone should have had plenty. Raymond declared he could eat ten slices, and Leon actually did eat eleven. Finally, after eating, everyone came inside and presents were opened. Wendy braced for humiliation, but only Annabelle and her devotees paid any attention to the presents. Laura was accusing Mickey of cheating off her on a spelling test, which caused most of the kids to take sides. Then Albert, for some reason, declared that he doesn't believe that there is a heaven, and all sorts of chaotic opinions about reincarnation, nothingness, devils, motorbikes, and hell spilled from the kids. Eventually, Elizabeth pointed to the cross painting above the mantle and sentenced Albert to everlasting damnation. But Albert just smiled and said he had wanted to see who would say 'damn' first. Elizabeth looked very upset, but the conversation moved on.

Unfortunately, thoughts of last year popped into Wendy's head as she waited for the same trio to humiliate her. A summer day forever scorched into her memory. Standing in the lot next to the vacant school, soaking wet. Sharron B. was threatening to tell Wendy's parents, while Jeanie called her an ugly criminal. The only one who could save her from these two jackals was Annabelle. Yes, she had stolen, but Anna had done it first. And she begged Wendy to do it too. Only in front of these two tattle tales, Annabelle changed her story. She hadn't stolen a thing. Why would she? She had money. "Just like your brother," Sharron B. had said, Wendy was "just a worthless criminal." Almost a year later, the shame and guilt were still fresh. Wendy resented and feared Jeanie and Sharron B. for what they knew. But Annabelle was an enigma. Either she lied to the jackals or she lied to Wendy. Either way, Wendy was too ashamed to speak of it.

"Where did you find the turtle? It's the cutest thing." Annabelle had left her crew to thank Wendy. Peering into her sweet smile, Wendy was too stunned to answer. "It was you who gave me this little guy, wasn't it? He's so cute!" Wendy smiled awkwardly and asked if she could use the phone. Shree noticed this exchange and wondered what it was all about.

7. Alignment

May 23rd

Their conversation six days ago had been easy and inspiring, so Tony was looking forward to seeing Jimmy again. Yet when the door swung open, his brother-in-law looked anxious and embarrassed. The reason soon materialized in the form of a body squirming in his bed.

"Hi Tony, ah, this is Sirrus. She's… in Hendrick's cancer lab." Tangled in orange blankets was a girl in her early twenties, with a mess of strikingly blue hair hiding most of her face. She nodded hello, and Tony realized that she had been crying. So he quickly offered to come back another time. But Sirrus jumped up, revealing that she was fully clothed in black and even had large red lace-up high-tops on.

"I truly have to leave now, so you should stay," she said to Tony. "Thanks so much for listening to it all, James. I'll let you know how it goes when I confront him."

"You know where to find me if you want a shoulder. And remember that it will all work out for the best, no matter what." With that, Jim squeezed her hand goodbye and closed the door. "Sorry, Tony. She's having a rough time with her boyfriend. How have you been?"

Boyfriend?! That girl's obviously interested in Jimmy, thought the new arrival. The way she looked *into* him.

Tony was a whole inch shorter than the six feet of Jim, yet unless they were side by side, anyone would have assumed Tony was taller. He was thin, but it was more his posture. He had a bearing of someone used to ducking to get through doorways, a sort of permanent lean forward and dip of his head. His dark, almost black hair was slightly long, wavy over his ears, and pushed out of his bright gray-blue eyes. Though his face was pale, his nose was sunburned. In comparison, Jim, though he was younger, looked more solid. His brown eyes were more eager, like he was still discovering the world. Straight brown hair framed his high cheekbones, draped over his chest, and down his back. He was clean, though his stretched-out concert t-shirt needed a wash. Tony, on the other hand, was unshaven and wearing his usual long-sleeve overshirt, hiding signs of dampness from the hot, muggy May afternoon.

Initial greetings over, Tony noticed that Jim was still tense. "So you're going by James now? Your friend called you James. Suits you." Jim failed to suppress his smile. Tony continued, "I went to see Becs and Shree after we talked. It didn't quite play out as I'd hoped."

"Yeah, she told me."

"You know for me, seeing her again, it's as if nothing's changed in all of these years. Her eyes are the same beguiling mysteries that I was drawn to twelve years ago."

"She's my sister, man," interjected Jim.

"And even while she was telling me to leave, I felt drawn to her. Like the universe knows we belong together, but she just hasn't noticed yet."

"Tony. Tony, I have to stop you right there." Jim didn't know how he was going to convey his sister's rejection. Tony was so innocent in this moment, and Jim, five years his junior, feared wounding his idol. When his older sister first brought Tony home, Jimmy, at twelve, had worshiped his music tastes, political views, and his knowledge of history, science, art, just about everything. Now though, Jim knew something his hero didn't. And he understood it would hurt Tony deeply. "Don't go there. Rebecca told me that you have to leave her and Shree alone."

Tony leaned back on his heels and listened to Jimmy, marveling at his discomfort. What could Jimmy know of his sister's true feelings, standing so far outside their relationship? *Obviously Jimmy's just a messenger.* Tony reflexively ran two of his fingers over a small hole that had appeared in his corduroys some months ago. *It's painful to us both as he tries to avoid Becca's words and yet express them as he was told.* In their last conversation, Tony was struck by how much Jimmy had grown up while away at school. Now, Jimmy seemed as young and naive as ever. A green poster of the Pyramids adorned the wall, and Tony found himself drawn into it, losing focus.

"But Rebecca is adamant. You cannot be together. She says that you're not good for Shree."

What?! Not good for Shree?! I'm her father! Rebecca is being cruel. Why is Jimmy going along with her? He looks like he's about to cry. No no, Rebecca has played this game before - I know she can't mean it. Not good for Shree! What isn't good for Shree is that I am not in her life. His index finger pressed through the small hole in his pants and felt his warm thigh. For a moment, he had difficulty extracting it again. At this point, Tony grabbed the thread of conversation and let Jimmy know that Rebecca didn't actually mean this nonsense. "She's just scared," he managed to say. Still Jimmy persisted. *This kid's getting irritating. Need to remember, not his fault. The bottom edge of the poster, intentionally at a slant, angles up as if pointing at the lower right corner of the window. But the angle's slightly off. She said I can't see Shree till she goes to college?!* His middle finger pushed its way into the growing hole. "She's eleven! I'm not going to be kept from my own daughter till she's eighteen. These years we've lost have already been bad for her." *That angle is very distracting. Why didn't he mount that thing so it lines up?* "And bad for me," *torture. Pyramids, after all - angles matter.* "How can Rebecca suggest such a thing?" *If raised by only a centimeter, it would align perfectly with the window corner and the corner of the building across the street. 'Obviously these years have been painful to her too.' Did I say it or just think it?*

Jimmy felt powerless to alter the course of the ship of Tony. Instead, he felt himself dragged in his wake. Who was he to say to a father that he isn't needed? Especially that Tony's own father had disappeared when he was young. Oh why had he agreed to be his sister's messenger? "Tony, this is how Rebecca explained it to me. Your condition is the problem…."

My condition?! My condition is fine. That poster, on the other hand, is a travesty. Here it all is again. A few years ago, maybe. Not as if I haven't done the work. All of it. The textbook on the desk at least doesn't pretend to rhyme with the decor. Ganz sees it. Better not keep poking the hole or it'll rip. Jimmy knows I'm fine. Besides, it's slightly Freudian, isn't it? Molecular Biology of the Cell. Rebecca will see it too. Just worried. Scared. Now, I see it! The title points towards the door hinge in one direction while aligning with the desk lamp above it. Bet she's talking to mother. Why can't my mom let me live my life?! Like the hands of a clock, the rhythm of angles. Jimmy is absolutely tearing himself apart, talking about 'my condition'. Beard stubble feels even better than the hole. Poor lost soul is afraid to offend me, but his sister has sent him in with her live grenade. She hasn't recognized that I've gotten beyond it. And Mom will never let me be healthy. Yet here I am. Wonder what it says about microtubules?

Jim concluded his speech to silence. Tony had, graciously,

remained quiet through the whole uncomfortable thing, and now Jim awaited the harsh verdict. Finally, Tony reached out and touched his shoulder. "It's okay. It is going to be okay, Jimmy, er, James. Obviously I don't agree... that I'm bad for Shree. Rebecca wants her to have a normal, loving environment to grow up in. So do I. And I know I'm an essential part of that environment. I've been missing, but I won't be much longer. Rebecca doesn't recognize it yet, but she still loves me. I know Rebecca put you in an uncomfortable position, telling me this. Well you can let her know that I got the message. But just between you and me, James, I know that she'll come around and we will be a family again."

After briefly extemporizing on the value of humans seeking patterns in their environment, Tony casually moved a single tack in the lower left corner of Jim's Pink Floyd poster. One side now bulged from the wall. "You'll thank me later," he said, then slipped out the door. After a couple of hours, Jim decided that the small change made the poster foreground appear slightly 3D. He left it as a memorial to the enigmatic genius that was his brother-in-law. Until his backpack caught on it a week later, and the poster ripped.

Just like with Rebecca, trying to talk with Tony about their family left Jim exhausted and defeated. He knew that Rebecca and Tony saw two extremely different futures. All the causes and effects, unavoidably led to this sad mess. His trite words to Sirrus echoed in his mind. No, little Jimmy, no matter how it worked out, it would NOT be for the best.

8. The Goodie Bag

May 24th

Shree's mom's car rolled to a stop, the back door swung open, and Wendy stepped out in front of her house. Goodbyes were said, and the car pulled away. She was sad that the break from her life was now over. Wendy clutched her goodie bag containing plastic jewelry and candy lipstick. Of little actual interest to her, she held it as if it were treasure, entitling her to a better life. But Max noticed her arrival and descended to remind her otherwise.

"Where were yew last night? Wetting tha bed at someone else's house fer a change?" called Max from behind her.

"I was at a sleepover, something you ain't never been invited to." Wendy didn't even turn around. She felt her muscles tighten for what she knew was coming if she didn't make it through the front door in time. But as her hand was reaching for the door handle, Max grabbed her shoulder, swung her around, and before she could twist away, he had pinned her to the ground, a knee on either shoulder.

"Look at me when I'm talking at yew, ya little bitch!" Max spat the last word with all the hatred a brother could muster. "Mom-n-Dad and I were talkin when yew was gone las' night. Ther as sick-a-yew as I am. Mom called th'doption agency. Ther gonna take yew back." Wendy had heard this one too many times already. She had believed it might be true when she was six. But Max wasn't going to drive her to tears so easily now. Max continued his venom,

"Before she called, Mom said if they don't come, we gotta take matters into our own hands. Yew know what that means, don't ya Wizzy? Don't yew?"

"Get off me, Max, get OFF!" Wendy tried to twist and throw her brother off of her, but Max was too heavy.

"Mom said th'only reason she ain't cut ya ta pieces awready is cuz it would be too big-a-mess. She was laughin', saying she'd do it this time, mess-er-not! We wuz all laughin' at the image of it. Of yer cut-up-eyeballs all over the floor."

Wendy started crying despite her determination not to. Of course she knew that their mom wasn't planning to cut her up. But the image flooded into her brain nevertheless. This wasn't the first time he had used 'cut-up eyeballs all over the floor', but repetition never dulled its power. If anything, that phrase grew in potency, triggered a convulsion of tears, each time more powerful than the last. She saw her mother in a rocking chair, knitting, with that wicked smile of hers. And cut-up eyeballs, Wendy's eyeballs, looking up at the bottom of her mom's shoe, rising and falling above.

"Get the fu— GET OFF ME!" Wendy struggled through spasms of tears.

"Not til yew gimme yer candy!" Max said, grabbing Wendy's goodie bag. When he realized there was nothing worth having, he laughed. "They only gave ya girly crap. Your friends just sent ya home with their garbage. That's what they think-a-yew. Garbage!" Then, tiring of his game, Max had one last insult. He hocked up a snot-filled 'loogie' and let it drip slowly from his lips till it was dangling just above Wendy's left eye. Wendy wrenched her head to the side, and it landed in her ear and hair.

Max jumped off of her and strutted down the lane. Wendy looked around the seemingly deserted trailer park. A half-dozen mobile homes up the lane, a man was working on his car and listening to the radio. No saviors live around here, she once again realized. She pulled herself up, swore to herself that she would kill Max one day, picked up the torn goodie bag, and went inside to the bathroom. God, she hated her brother.

9. What Makes A Lake Glow

May 23rd

After the boys had all been picked up, after the organized games were done, and the s'mores mess was cleaned off the tables, floor, chairs, and hair, Annabelle's mom appeared again. Now in pink, with another tall drink in her hand, also pink, she ushered everyone upstairs to the den. The thirteen girls remaining, two now dressed in Annabelle's clothes, noisily made their way to this new floor. Like the living room immediately below, one whole wall was glass. But here, royal blue curtains blocked out all trace of the trees, stars, and neighboring houses beyond. Sharron B., wanting to emphasize that she had been in Anna's den before, lamented that it was too dark to see Clear Lake.

But it wasn't the view that the girls were assembled for. Annabelle directed everyone's attention to the large television at one end of the room. It was the largest, bulkiest television Wendy had ever seen. Shree looked at her watch, wondering what TV shows started at 9:18 pm. But Mrs Riddley stood in the door with three VHS tapes. Anna asked the girls whether they would like to see 'Grease', 'Carrie', or 'Gidget'. Shree and Wendy looked at each other. Neither had ever seen a video player at someone's home. Annabelle's mother, looking beyond the kids, dragging her words out in her flat tone, said it would be okay if they watched all three, as long as it was not too loud. When she was gone, Anna said that her mom's bedroom was at the opposite end of the house, so they could stay up as late as they wanted. The couches and chairs were pushed back against the wall, bedclothes were changed into, blankets and pillows were tossed into the salad of fifth-grade girls as 'Grease' started playing.

Shree found the movie a bit irritating. While the stylized clothes and intentionally stereotypical characters may be charming to adult viewers, Shree was put off by how fake it all was. Wendy also lost interest, but mostly because she didn't like the singing. Does anyone even like musicals, she wondered? Before long, they were huddled in the back behind the curtain, looking out the window at a moonlit lake marred slightly by a telephone pole in the foreground. They started revisiting the characters of the day. Francie getting marshmallow stuck in her hair, Doug trying to push everyone into the pool, Lloyd blowing the perfect bubble rings, Eddie naming the jets flying overhead, Mary finding a big brown walking stick bug, and not letting anyone hurt it. They laughed, quietly, all over again when remembering Sharon G. imitating Anna's mom, then later imitating their teacher.

"Who knew Elizabeth was so religious?" Shree said cautiously. God was never talked about in her family, but she had been warned that other families were very religious and that she shouldn't talk about things that might upset people. But now she was curious about her new friend. Did Wendy believe in God? Did she believe people go to heaven or hell? She hadn't thought about it much herself.

"Yeah, she kinda took the whole thing too seriously, didn't she?" Wendy, too, felt the need to walk cautiously in this conversation. Her mom thought Shree was Jewish, whatever that was. "Do you believe in God?" The question came out of Wendy's mouth, but who had put it there?

There it was, thought Shree. A question she was never asked before and had never answered even to herself. "I, uh, think I don't." With this, she took a side. Was it the right side, she asked herself. Or would she burn in Christian hell with Albert? With each passing moment, she felt sure that this was right. She did not believe in God.

Wendy on the other hand, had always believed what her parents believed, had gone to church for years, had prayed to God for protection from her brother. She had prayed that morning that no one would laugh at the stupid turtle purse. But now she sat before her best friend, in sight of God's moonlight, making the lake glow. And she wondered how that God of moonlight could send her to hell? She was just a kid, but if she died that moment, would God really cast her into the fire? In this one moment, her whole life seemed to shift. Does she choose God, an invisible being that, for unknown reasons, hadn't performed any new miracles in two thousand years? Or does she choose her flesh and blood friend right in front of her, also glowing in moonlight? What should she believe? The years of sermons and vacation bible school and saying grace before eating, all of that seemed like a boring script, as fake as the movie playing on the other side of the curtain. Actually, more fake than that, because 'Grease' was a lot more fun than church. So Wendy began to suspect that maybe she, too, *didn't* believe. But saying it seemed too much for the moment.

"I'm not sure if I believe in God. But I *am* sure that I don't believe in prayin', or none a that church stuff. I think the bible can't possibly be true. God may've created the world, but people made up that church stuff, and it's so stupid." Wendy was shocked with herself, but God didn't smite her. That morning, she never would have said such things. But now that she said them, she wondered if maybe she felt them all along.

The two of them talked for a long time about religion and their experiences. Wendy had a lot more experience with church than Shree had, but Shree appreciated hearing all about it. They both were empowered by how comfortable it was to talk to each other about unspeakable things. Shree respected Wendy for holding onto her belief in God, for seeing the magic in the moonlight. And Wendy felt at ease with Shree letting go of God and seeing physics in reflected light. Much like their shared tears at the reservoir, this evening bound them closer together. Each, in their own way, felt like the conversation was a secret hug between them.

Just then, a commotion occurred by the TV. Shree and Wendy raised the curtain to see that there was a man, no doubt Anna's father, standing in the doorway. He hadn't been seen the whole day. "Annabelle, won't you introduce me to your friends?" he said in a booming voice. Wendy suddenly realized who Annabelle's father was. It was Reverend Sebastian Riddley. He was on TV, Sunday mornings, on a show called 'Praise Unto the Lord'. Wendy's mom loved to watch it. Her dad called him a snake oil salesman because Mom had sent him money. Now the guy was standing in shorts and bare feet in front of them.

Annabelle stood in front of her dad, his arms hugging her as he rocked back and forth. "This is Jeanie, you know Sharron, that's Francie, Laura…"

"Why aren't y'all just the cutest little girls in all God's creation! I hope you'll be comfortable tonight. You don't mind if I borrow my Annabelle for a little while, now do you?"

"Dad, please, we're about to go to sleep. Don't make me stay up longer," Anna pleaded with a surprisingly whiny sound to her voice. The reverend said something low into her ear, then disappeared with a frown. Anna's eyes leaked tears, though she tried to wipe them away before anyone noticed. Jeanie went to her, but Annabelle turned her back and left the room. After that, no one talked until it was clear that most girls were falling asleep. Shree and Wendy soon followed down that same path. Wendy listened for

Annabelle's return but fell asleep to muted sounds of an old beach movie.

10. Roly Poly

May 25th

Clearly, he had made a mistake. Parked across the street from the school and slumped down in the front seat, he hoped not to be noticed. He had run the air conditioning during the drive from the motel, so the windows were rolled up when he parked in full sun. For the first fifteen minutes, he hadn't given it a thought. But when he grabbed the steering wheel to pull himself up a bit, he cursed and yanked his hand away with a seared palm. Now he realized he was being cooked and desperately needed to get out of the car. Just then he realized that someone three houses down from his oven was watering their lawn. How soothing it would be to hang his head down into that stream of cool water. But the problem was that the woman holding the hose was eyeing his car. Did she find it suspicious that he was slumped low in a car across from the school? Was she thinking he was a creep stalking kids? Could he explain to her that he was a father, while drenching himself with her garden hose? His head was burning by this point, a fever inside of a broiler. If he drove off, then came back to park under the shady tree near the corner, her suspicions would grow. If he got out and introduced himself, then hid as soon as school was released, her suspicions would multiply. But he couldn't wait openly and risk being seen by Rebecca.

Her demands were still ringing in his ears. He had visited Rebecca again, two nights earlier, hoping to make peace. Standing outside her house in the moonlight, he was captivated once again. She looked so naturally perfect, the home from which he'd lost his way. But she was aloof, not ready to receive him. They both loved Shree; he hoped they could start there and rebuild. But she was a wall. Shree wasn't home, and Rebecca insisted he leave town without seeing his daughter. Desperate for peace, he relented. Promised. Lied. He knew he could never leave town without seeing her. And now he waited, his soul burning in this hell car.

Besides, he wasn't even sure this was Shree's school. It was the first elementary he had found near their house. Just then, the school bell rang and kids began leaking into the neighborhood. He realized he may have made another mistake. The kids were being picked up by parents on the far side of the school. If Rebecca picked up Shree and they drove off in a different direction, then he would have learned nothing. Should he drive to the other side of the school? Was he already too late? Would the vigilant gardener take down his license plate and watch him drive away? It dawned on him that his car had Massachusetts plates, making him even more suspicious. His head was pounding in the heat, yet he was paralyzed as to what to do. Then he saw her. Shree was walking with another girl, towards the street he was on. The one thing he had done right was park on the side of the school closest to his daughter's house. Shree was walking home, which was just perfect.

She looked so tall, not the roly poly little girl that he had so much fun playing with. It was always so natural, goofing around with her. She would laugh at every stupid joke he made. It wasn't easy to get Rebecca to laugh in the later years, but Roly Poly just loved to laugh at his funny voices and silly walks. Bedtime was the best. He would read books to her in silly voices, and she would add her own cute voices until Mama would call out "Quiet Time," and they would muffle themselves while almost bursting with giggles. And then he would read her one more story, but this one slow and dry. She would quiet down into the nook of his arm, lean her head against his shoulder, and slowly nod off before he had gotten halfway through. And now look at her. When was the last time someone read her to sleep? At eleven, she is certainly doing all the reading herself. Tony watched as his daughter turned the corner with her friend and walked on in the direction of her house.

He decided to see if she would separate from her friend before he tried to speak to her. Now he scooted himself up, started the car, rolled down the windows to some relief, started the air conditioner, which only blasted more hot air, gingerly tapped the steering wheel, and turned the car in the opposite direction from Shree. If the garden spy was taking notes, then there would be nothing to attach him to Shree. He drove around the block and a few blocks down, closer to Shree's house. Here he found a shady spot to park, left all the windows open, and waited for his beautiful girl to walk right by him.

What should he say? She took longer than he expected, and he began to wonder if she took another path or perhaps had another destination in mind. Then he saw her slowly making her way down the block, alone. His nervousness grew. Would she be happy to see him? Or did Rebecca tell her terrible stories? Was he a monster to her? What was he doing here? What if she screamed and ran? What if cops were called? As if on cue, a patrol car turned onto the street. Maybe the gardener had called. Maybe someone on this block had spied him from a window. The police car rolled up to his car and then passed on without a stop. He looked right at the officer as he passed. But the officer had not even noticed the out-of-state car with all its windows rolled down, complete with a suspicious character waiting for an unsuspecting little girl.

Now she was on the same block. Now she was fifty feet away. What would he say? What would she do? Ten feet, he froze. He couldn't look, he couldn't speak. He sat frozen to the spot and heard her footsteps walk right up to the car and then right by. He couldn't believe he didn't move. He was petrified by what she would say to him and petrified that he had just let her walk by. He couldn't let her go. He yanked on the door handle and leapt out of the car.

"Roly Poly! Shree Riley Roly Poly!"

~ ~ ~

Shree was feeling the heat on the way home. After Wendy split off towards La Hacienda, Shree daydreamed she was trekking across a desert, leading her camel by the strap of her backpack. It was wishful thinking that she could drench herself in the coolness of that scene. The camel was too tired from a journey of a thousand days and couldn't be bothered to converse. Meanwhile, a car swerved in on a corner and caused Shree to jump right back into the dull Houston suburbs. The sidewalk cement was hot enough to be felt through her shoes, and the tar pooling up in the asphalt road was glistening like black licorice. Fortunately there were tire marks and even footprints to provide archeological evidence that hot tar was worse for shoes than cement. Shree recalled her mom's voice when she'd discovered tar footprints on the carpet.

Sidestepping cracks along the sidewalk, she noticed that the one shade tree she counted on along this block was unexpectedly occupied by a stranger in a car with all the windows rolled down. Rather than stop for a breather in the shade, she kept up the pace, determined to stoically reach the next good shade tree, which was a block and a half away. Without warning, though, the car door opened, and she heard a man leap out. She turned to look back while still marching intently forward, caught her toe on a crack in the cement, no doubt pushed up by the roots of her stolen tree, and felt herself pitch suddenly forward as she heard a familiar voice calling her name.

Dad? Dad!, she thought as she hit the pavement hard. In an instant she was filled with joy, embarrassment, then pain, then joy again, each feeling vying to overwhelm all others. She wanted to answer her dad in words, but only managed tears. He ran to help her just as she rolled over to greet him, accidentally hitting him in the face with her flailing hand.

He jumped back, fearing that she was fending him off, imagining that his daughter didn't recognize him, believed him an attacker, or maybe even thought of him as a monster: her crazy father escaped from an asylum.

While all of this happened, the actual owner of the shade tree was peering out of an olive-green curtained window, wondering if she was witnessing an abduction. The shade tree had served as bait for years, allowing the elderly woman to learn all sorts of things about her neighbors without having to be friendly. However, the scene playing out now might prove to be the most scandalous yet.

"Shree, it's me!"

"Dad! Dad, I know! I'm so happy…," Shree managed through her tears. "I'm so happy you came for me!" Behind the neighborly curtains, Deloris was both relieved and disappointed.

"Oh Shree honey, I've missed you so so much!" Tony had by this time picked up his daughter and was hugging her and kissing her hair, and she was squeezing into his neck. This embrace went on for a few long moments, and then Tony thought to check her wounds from the fall. "Let's see how you look. Are you okay? Your hands are bleeding." Together, they inspected the damage. She had one bloody scrape on her right palm, with a few pebbles still pressed into the wounds. Also her knees were scraped, but not too badly. Tony wiped away her tears, and they just smiled at each other for a while. Then Tony turned to business.

"Is your mom expecting you? Is she at home?"

"No, she doesn't get home till about five-thirty."

"Well does she call when you get home, at least?"

"Yeah, I'm supposed to call her."

"Okay Shree, we should drive you home to get these wounds cleaned up, and you should call your mom. But Shree, is it okay that we don't tell your mom that you saw me?" This was the business at the back of his mind. He knew Rebecca would be furious if she found out. But he didn't want Shree to do anything she wasn't comfortable with.

"That's exactly what I was going to ask you! Mom is being so mean, and I don't want her to know about us. I heard her the other night. She said she would call the police on you! She's being so mean to you, Daddy. And she's mean to me, too."

"Oh Shree, darling, your mom just wants to protect you."

"From you?! From my own Dad?!"

"She's just worried, that's all. But she should know that I could never hurt you. Well, uh, I mean…," her dad looked down at her bleeding palm and stroked it, "…I will never intentionally let you get hurt, sweetie."

"Oh I know you'd never hurt me, Daddy! And I think Mom is crazy. I think she is blinded by meanness towards you. She is always…".

"Shree, really, it's okay. Your mom loves you, and I love you, and I love your mom. And someday we will be a family again. But please let's not talk about your mom now. Other than to say that I think it's best that, for now, we don't say anything to your mom about our meeting. Okay?"

"Okay, Daddy," Shree agreed and hugged him one more long squeeze before they got in the car.

They drove the three blocks to her house. Tony was planning on staying outside, till he realized that he should help Shree clean her wounds and put bandaids on. Inside, their bathroom looked ordinary. That is, nothing caught Tony's eye as particularly familiar. But when they emerged from the minor surgery, his eyes caught glimpses of many things that reminded him of the years they had been together.

While Shree called her mother, Tony dove into memories triggered by the clutter of Rebecca's life. The framed Salvador Dali postcard they got at the Museum of Modern Art in New York, the lamp they bought in a garage sale, photos: of Shree just born, Shree bundled in the snow in front of their first house, Rebecca's parents, Saul and Ruth on a sailboat. He recognized his old stereo and found some of his favorite albums mixed in with hers. She had never liked Coltrane, but there he was, next to her worn copy of Carole King's Tapestry. A lot of new books he didn't recognize, but some old ones too. Steppenwolf, The Sirens of Titan, Childhood's End, The Brothers Karamazov. He remembered giving her Dostoevsky the summer after freshman year. He thought it might be too much for her, but she read it through. She had given him Gravity's Rainbow, but he never finished it. And there was the painting he made of her and Shree, his Madonna and Child, he used to say. All in reds and blues, the two of them swirled together into a galaxy. At least that is what he tried to do, but now it looked like a pretentious mess. And yet she kept it framed, on the bookshelf next to a framed finger-painting by three-year-old Shree. Rebecca had made such a big deal of Shree's use of yellows and oranges. Then he noticed some of the newer books. Living with Schizophrenia, The A-B-Cs of Divorce, Parenting Solo.

"Mom doesn't suspect a thing. Want to see my room?" Shree broke the spell, just as her father was slipping into sadness.

"Well, Shree, I don't think I should be in your house. How about we go to a park?"

~ ~ ~

The air-conditioned car was more comfortable than the park Shree guided them to. So they kept driving. In no time, they were revisiting funny voices from the bedtime stories he used to read her. And the lake where he had taught her to swim. Sheltered from the heat outside, Shree recalled the snowman they decorated in Mom's dress and named Abigail. Shree also admired how her dad had climbed onto the roof in his underwear to rescue their cat, then slid off into the bushes below. Tony recalled believing the cat was an alien and the detergent in his jeans was poisoning him. But he didn't share that with his laughing daughter. Eventually, they pulled into a shady park on the shore of a lake.

"So this is Armand Bayou?! They mentioned it at the motel. Let's take a quick look." The two hopped out into the warmth and, despite the sun, Tony led them out onto a wooden pier. There was a tangle of fishing line and some dried blood, evidence of a fishing trip which had been either successful or disastrous. As they reached the end of the old wooden structure, Tony sat down and began. "Shree, unfortunately I can't stay in Houston."

"But why not? You just got here!"

"I promise that I'll come back, but I have to return to work. I've been looking for a job here, but I haven't found anything yet."

"Take me with you, Daddy! I would love to go back to Boston with you."

"Roly Poly, I would truly love it if you lived with me in Boston, but we can't do that yet."

"Please, Daddy! It would be perfect. Mom is such a Bi…, she is so mean. Please take me with you! I want to live with you."

"Seriously, Shree, I can't take you away from your mother. She loves you very much."

"Don't you love me?"

"Of course I do, I love you most in the universe. I love you with every molecule in my body."

"And I love you, Daddy! But I don't think Mom loves me very much. I certainly don't love her like I do you."

"Shree, don't ever say that. I know your mother has her faults, but she loves you more than life. Anyone can see that. You know that, Shree."

"I'm not so sure…."

"Shree, I can't take you away from your mother. But I promise you I'll be back and things will be better. We'll be a happy family again. I truly believe that. We are meant to be a family."

"But if you're gonna come back, why don't you take me with you and then we'll come back to Mom together?"

"I'm sorry, Shree. But I have to leave you with your mom. She needs you. I will come back as soon as I can, though. Hopefully I can arrange things by the end of summer." Shree felt depressed. Her dad had come to her, and they finally have a moment alone, and already, she was missing him.

"I don't understand why you have to go. I've missed you for forever. Why d'you have to go away already?"

The two sat still at the end of the pier. A soft breeze made the sun bearable. Birds were chirping in the trees behind them, and a crane was hunting in the shallow water near shore. Tony wasn't sure how to answer her. He calmly took his shoes off, and she followed suit. They dipped their toes in the soothing water. "I don't have a good reason for you, Shree. I have to go because of money. I have to return to my job. But more importantly, I have to be steady. I have to do things properly and show your mom that I've changed. We are going to be a family again, and the door to making that happen is in your mom's heart. However, I'm not going to get to open that door until I convince her that I'm reliable. That's why I'm returning to Boston. Sometimes you have to take a step back in order to move ahead." Just then Shree gasped. Between her dangling toes, a huge prehistoric fish swam calmly but menacingly.

"Whoa, that thing is huge!" Tony said, grabbing his daughter's shoulders.

"You're telling me!" Shree had yanked her legs out of the water and was clutching them to her chest.

"That must be an alligator gar. I can't believe one just swam between your feet! That was amazing!"

"That was gi-normous. And it was so freaky looking! So fricken scary! I think my heart jumped out of my chest. Did you see the mouth on that thing!" Shree was jumpy, but enthusiastic. "That was twice as big as me," Shree exaggerated.

"At least. That was incredible!" Tony backed her up, pulling his much longer legs out of the water, dripping. "I'm not waiting for that monster's friends." They both laughed. "This… THIS is what nature does." Tony said with an air of satisfaction. "It creates the most amazing things and then springs them on us to scare the bejesus out of us." They picked up their shoes and socks, and walked barefoot back to the car.

On the way home, Tony told her that he would send her messages from Boston. "I can't write to you because your mom doesn't want me to. But I will write to your mom. If you watch for my letters, know that anything I write on the envelope will be for you. Know that I am thinking of you always. We are destined to be together. You may feel impatient, but I've found that the universe knows what it wants. It opens the door in its own time, and we just need to be ready to walk through. I'll be back before you know it, and we will be a family again!" They had one last embrace, which was hard to let go of. Shree's tears started falling, and Tony felt like his would too if he stayed a minute longer. But Rebecca would be home soon, so he needed to go. Shree watched for a long time as he drove off. Only after she went inside did she realize that she had left her shoes in Dad's car.

11. A Plan

May 27th

School finally broke for summer, and liberty was no longer just a word in the daily pledge. Most kids had imagined the final bell would trigger a mad rush for the doors as the imprisoned throngs raced away from school without looking back. In reality, though, freedom meant they could be as lazy as they wanted, lingering on school grounds, laughing with their friends about all the fun things they would do that summer, comparing plans and boasting of adventures too grand to be real. Raymond was going to Alaska, Albert was going to Israel, Mary was going to sing in a production of Annie Get Your Gun. As if jealous, Mickey announced he would be acting on television. Then the races began. Eddie was going to fly a plane, Lloyd was going to race boats, and Doug was going to race motorcycles. Wendy and Shree glanced at each other, not believing most of the boasts, but not bursting any of the exuberant bubbles rising on the breeze. Laura heard a bit too much, though. "Doug, I know you never rode no motorcycle in your life. And Lloyd, you're gonna be on the swim team all summer." But the afternoon was too perfect to respond to the naysayers.

Eventually, the majority of kids were picked up by parents or wandered off in threes and fours. Sharon G. was one of the last. She confided in Shree and Wendy that she would be moving to New York over summer break. She didn't want to make a fuss, but she was going to miss them. Maybe she could write? It seemed so grown-up, Wendy thought, to know someone who lived in another state. Shree and Wendy wrote their addresses in Sharon's notebook. Soon, Mrs. Gibson arrived to take her daughter away, and they all hugged and promised to stay in touch. Each of the three girls quietly suspected that would be the last contact they would ever have.

As the two of them started walking home, to break the silence, Wendy suddenly suggested to Shree that they meet at the reservoir in thirty minutes. She hoped this would be their first plan of the summer.

"I can't. My mom is making me work this whole week." Shree was too embarrassed to say anything earlier, but now it was just the two of them.

"What? It's the start of summer?!"

"Yeah, but she's mad I lost my shoes?" Wendy looked down and saw new tennis shoes on Shree's feet, then looked back up in confusion. "I left my shoes in Dad's car two days ago. Mom came home and threw a fit."

"You were in your dad's car?"

"I told you! We saw the alligator gar." Shree looked at her friend in exasperation.

"I remember THAT! So your mom is mad cause you saw your dad then?"

"No, I didn't tell her about Dad! I told her I lost my shoes at the reservoir. Then she got mad that I went to the reservoir. She made me take her there, and we looked for my shoes till it was getting dark. She was so mad. She yelled at me that I was making her poor." Shree distorted her mom's words. "Said shoes cost a fortune, and I would only eat ramen for the next month. Then she took me to Kmart and got me the ugliest shoes she could find."

"I think they're cool. And all the time your old shoes were in yer dad's car? Why didn't you call'm?"

"Well obviously Mom would have heard. Besides, I don't know his phone number. He's staying at a hotel." They stopped at the corner where they would usually part, Wendy heading north and Shree continuing west.

"So she grounded you?" Wendy stepped into the street, decidedly heading west along Shree's route.

Shree welcomed Wendy's decision without acknowledging it. "Mom laid it out in the car ride home. I have to do yard work and clean the house for the first week of summer. I swear it's what she wanted all along." Shree didn't tell Wendy about the additional things her mom calmly mentioned on that drive home. Including the evidence that Shree had snuck the Bailey's. "Even though she's at work, she'll be checking my progress every day when she gets home. If she isn't satisfied, then she'll make me work another week. She's so unfair. She acts like I lost my shoes on purpose. She just wants me to work for her. Dad said she needs me. She only needs me to be her slave! I should run away. That would show her."

They walked on in silence for a while, then Shree announced, "That's my plan for the summer! I'm going to run away and go live with Dad! I'm not sure how yet, but I'm gonna do it." Some part of her wondered if the plan was as ridiculous as the stories the boys had been making up. Yet she also felt determined to actually do it.

Wendy imagined that Shree was just joking, so she leaned into it. "Kin I come too? I never been outside a Texas." And with that, they gave voice to their wild imaginations, which included riding bikes around Washington D. C., taking a hot air balloon to the top of the World Trade Center, and a racing submarine to France.

When they arrived at Shree's house, Wendy announced, "Well I kin help with the yard work. Maybe we kin get the work done quicker n'your mom'll let ya off b'fore the week's up?" Wendy didn't like the idea of working in the hot sun when the summer break was finally here. But hanging out with Shree seemed a lot better than being alone.

"Wendy, you don't have to help. Besides, if Mom caught us, I might be in more trouble."

"Oh don't worry 'bout me. I ain't gonna do none-a-tha hard stuff. And if yer mom comes, I'll say it's all *your* fault!" Wendy smiled deviously, hoping Shree was on board with her own first plan of the summer.

"I'll tell Mom that *you* stole my shoes!" Shree didn't know how this plan would play out, but she was happy to at least have Wendy's company for the time being.

The yard work that afternoon was slow but not so terrible. Shree's anger towards her mother kept reappearing, though. Wendy listened while Shree repeated her threat to run away. Mostly, it was just angry words, Wendy thought. But Shree started making lists of what she would need. The next day, Wendy showed up shortly after Shree's mom left. They worked off and on till noon, pulling weeds, using an edger. After a long rest inside, playing a few games of crazy eights, and discussing how much a plane ticket or a bus ticket to Boston would cost, they returned to weeding around the paving stones.

On the second full day, when Shree's mom showed up at noon, Wendy just managed to sneak around the back without being seen. Rebecca saw the nervous look on her sweaty daughter's face and felt guilty. She looked at the messy job that Shree had done. There were plenty of weeds among the flowers, and the sidewalk edging was more like a zigzag going into the lawn. But it was clear that much effort had been made. Piles of unraked weeds and trimmings were enough evidence that Shree had felt 'consequences'. Rebecca sent Shree in to wash up. Meanwhile, she tried to rake and sweep some order into the yard, surveyed the remainder, and resolved to mow the rest of the lawn herself on the weekend.

In the evening, Shree called Wendy to tell her the good news. "The slave driver let me off for now. Do you want to go to the pool tomorrow?"

"It's a plan!"

12. Envelopes

June 10th

There is a quiet perfection to solitude at dawn. Suburban streets that are so ordinary in the everyday afternoon, awake somehow gleaming with magic promise before most people even stir. Birds flit from branch to branch, chirping joyously, at the light's return. The smell of dew-covered grass hangs low, like mist upon a Scottish moor. Golden light creeps across rooftops as guilty shadows retreat. A cat peers enviously from inside a bay window, as a lone bicycle glides down the middle of a deserted street, unchallenged by any other soul. This became Shree's daily meditation by the second week of swimming.

The shock of sudden immersion in cold water is what woke her up that first morning, though. Her alarm rudely summoned her at 5:45 am. The warm narcotic of slumber cradled her under the blanket, but her mom called out from the other room. Swim team meant out of the house by six-o-five and in the pool by six-thirty. Instead of getting a summer pool pass like all the other kids, Shree's mom had signed her up for the swim team. After initial disappointment, the idea of being on a team sparked her interest. She was pretty good in the water. The first shock of cold that morning however, extinguished any flame. Willingness was drowned by lap after lap after lap after unending lap. Her coach blew his whistle if she tried to climb out, yelled insults if her pace slowed. All she could think about was how this was all her mom's doing. By eight-thirty she felt too exhausted to ride home. Just as well, she had no desire to get home before her mom left for work. No doubt Mom would make her do the dishes or clean the bathroom. It wasn't till the third morning of swimming that she began to recognize the magic of her early morning ride. And it wasn't till the third week that she began to skip practices and ride her bike for miles unbroken.

But back to that first morning. In an exhausted fog, she went straight back to bed. Unexpected sounds inhabited her empty house. A refrigerator hum, the unanticipated rush of chilled air from an unnoticed vent. Sprawled across her unmade bed, Shree beckoned for sleep, which dangled just beyond the next thought. She saw herself on Dad's doorstep after running away. *He's lonely. He needs me to stay.* She pulled the blanket overhead to block the sun. *Dad will be laughing in our old yard. I'll tell him how mean she is. I'll never come back. Do people take buses all the way to Boston? Is twenty-five dollars birthday money enough?*

"You could get off your lazy posterior end and get a job!" Mr. Trains was hanging upside down from the light fixture. "Or you could rob-a-bank!"

"I can't get a job, I'm a kid!"

"But you could rob-a-bank! What? Kids aren't allowed?" Mr. Trains had swung down and balanced ever so precariously on the bedpost. "We can get Chaser to be lookout. And your lizard friend can drive the getaway car." Shree smiled, eyes still closed, picturing slow Zak in a getaway car, darting and stopping every twenty feet, his head turning back and forth at lizard speed, before every cross street. Mr. Trains looked offended at her mirth. "Obviously, I'll have to crack the safe. That leaves me wondering, how you'll earn your cut? What exactly is your job in this heist?"

"See! Told you I couldn't get a job!" Shree felt pleased with the turn of conversation, but this thought evaporated with a rap on her window. A figure in shadow, silhouetted by sunshine beyond, Wendy was peeking in. Embarrassed about her imaginary friend, Shree ran to the front door. On the way, she knocked Mr. Trains to the floor and kicked him under the dresser.

June 18th

The first letter arrived three weeks into the summer. Shree had been checking the mailbox every day and had already slipped into fears that her dad had forgotten about her. Now she had a bulky blue envelope that said otherwise. On it was a swirl of drawing that reminded her of something she had seen before, but couldn't quite remember where. It took her a while to realize the swirls were actually made out of words in very fine print. She read 'loved you and always', folding over the edge of the envelope so she had to flip it to follow the sentence. She spent some time looking for the beginning, only to realize that the message cycled on, repeating itself. "You must never doubt that I have always loved you and always always will as time whistles through our lives like wind through the trees, the years come and go, yet the trees keep growing, so listen and you can hear the wind say, 'You must never doubt that…,'" and so on, repeating word for word. And word by word, the image of a tree with swirling branches grew across the envelope, until the whole thing wiggled back to the beginning. Shree wanted to hide the letter away so that it would be only ever hers, tangible proof of her dad's love.

Yet she accepted she must leave the envelope in the mailbox for her mother to find. Just as she knew the outside was hers, she knew the inside was meant for her mom. Hopefully Mom's heart would be melted by the secrets inside. How could she not realize how they all belonged together?

Yet her mom threw the letter out! During weekly chores, Shree had found it in the waste basket while vacuuming her mom's room. *Not only do I have to wake up and go to practice because Mom hates me, but on top of that, she makes me clean her messes!* Dad's letter had been ripped into pieces. Shree tried to put the pages together but couldn't understand what they said. "Remember the time of coffee marlin and diffendence…," or "fransigly the ranernams". Her father wrote quickly in cursive, and Shree found most of it impenetrable. She wondered if her mom could figure it out. Maybe her mom couldn't read it either and had torn it up in frustration? Shree wanted to hold onto the torn envelope, but worried her mom would notice, so she left the magic tree, shredded by her mother's chainsaw hands, in the trash.

The next letter showed up two days later. The envelope was white and bulky again, and this time there were no words at all. Instead, a fish that looked like the gar they had seen, swam across the back of the envelope, leaving swirling eddies on the paper that just happened to form two big hearts and one smaller one. The front of the envelope had a cartoon moon, with big goofy craters making ears, eyes, and a smiling mouth. Her mom disposed of it without a trace. A third letter appeared the very next day. This one had a large monkey face smiling, saying "Love is all we need" like the Beatles song. Behind, a parade of unicycle and goat riding monkeys played tubas and juggled what looked like even smaller unicycle monkeys. This one, she showed to Wendy, before her mom could destroy it. Sure enough, the next day, there was no sign of it, not even in the outside garbage.

"My dad really loves her, but he has no idea. When I get to Boston and tell him what she's doing with his letters, he'll see what a monster she is. He won't send me back then! And Mom will know what it's like. Dad and I will be happy without her, and *her* letters will be the ones torn to bits."

July 10th

A few pages of a letter were reclining on top of the small bookshelf, otherwise draped with a drying towel, several reprints of science papers, a flyer for a grad student mixer hosted by the astronomy department, and a dated copy of National Lampoon magazine. Left alone while James checked his laundry in the basement, Sirrus didn't restrain her curiosity. Not bothering to find the first page, she jumped right in.

```
softly curving repetition of wavelets along a
river surface, catching sunlight like a
chattering texture. The bottom, streaks of aqua
silt alternating with cavitating stones bathed
in limpet stutter. Singular grass stalks on the
bank, still heavy with seed, tossed by wind in
a great chorus of harmonizing individuals,
visual music in their multitude, waves
answering and repeating in melody. As countless
grains of sand underfoot, sculpted into ripples
imprinted upon warm-golden dunes, relieved by
creeping shadows, dragged beneath arriving
nimbus daydreams, stretching and tuning with
vivid gloaming hues, counterpunctual voices
with the polyphony of visual music below. In
all of this, I am lost and found!

Why do these complex and yet simple and
harmonizing patterns induce pleasure in this
brain? Hard and soft-wired detectors of
patterns, neurons fire in time, synchronizing
with more dendrites firing multi-time, while
more and more sets of purring cells join into
this drum circle, creating new polyrhythms on
top of syncopation till the very tops of the
moire waves tickle pleasure circuits reserved
for special occasions? Why? Why are those
circuits in our brains?! Entranced by
```

reflections, instead of hunting fish. Dazzled by fire is of a kind, tho that hypnotism is also a mystery. Not just warmth and work that humans have come to expect. Don't see an obvious selection path to the invention of brain circuits for the purpose of transcendence! Akin to the regenerative powers of sleep? But clearly much less fundamental to survival, considering how rarely we achieve universal oneness. Also a pathway to fixation, given our elevation of music. And some search for nirvana through noticeably unhealthy methods. Did Neanderthals falter from hypnotic revelry?

Yet, not all products of evolution are due to survival selection! Stochastic luck and linkage. There is no reason to expect a reason for everything under the skull. It's just possible that the serenity we feel from whatever inspires us is a lucky accident, due to secondary stimulation of brain circuitry intended for entirely different purposes (well-fed, warm, safe, sleeping offspring). On the one hand, this theory of innate joy as an unexpected side-effect of evolution is depressing… enlightenment is an aberration! On the other hand, the universe has rung its own bell and wrung another paradoxical beauty out of itself.

James had appeared in time to witness Sirrus completely focused on her crime. When she realized she was discovered, her embarrassed laughter was her only defense before Judge James. Yet he was more interested in what she thought of the letter.

"Who wrote this? Part of me wants to think it's brilliant, but mostly it seems written to prevent anyone from understanding it."

"Well I think it's brilliant. My brother-in-law, Tony wrote it. It's a continuation of a conversation we had when he was here. We were talking about art then, but he has extended it to beauty and transcendence. He's saying that maybe our appreciation of beauty is an accident of evolution," James said with confidence.

"I think I understood that, but he comes across as so arrogant. Like he has discovered some great secret of the universe, but will only reveal it if you can decipher his blather."

James was visibly shaken by Sirrus's judgment. "No, you don't understand. It's like poetry. He's trying to say so much in a few words. He wrote it to me after all, and he knows I'll catch on."

"Have you? Then what's he talking about that the universe 'rung its own bell'?"

Now James was even more flustered. "Um, I think he's saying that the universe, uh, sees itself, its own beauty, through us. And that moment of recognition is like ringing a bell." Sirrus remained Sphinx-like, leading James to try again. "Or maybe that it's a paradox that spiritual transcendence only exists because of a mistake or something, and that mistake is like ringing a bell that doesn't exist. Or only exists because it was accidentally rung."

"Okay James, whatever he was trying to say, I do appreciate the beauty in watching you struggle to explain it."

"My sister thinks he's schizophrenic. But I think mostly he, uh, just experiences things at like a different level or something." Sirrus, the Sphinx, just blinked. "Though he's, maybe, a little obtuse," James concluded with an awkward smile, hoping Sirrus would move on.

With cat-like eyes, she asked, "You going to this astronomy thing?"

July 21st

Gliding on her bike one morning, Shree suddenly skidded to a stop. On an unknown lane, amongst the long shadows of skinny trees, diagonals drawn across still-wet lawns and sleeping cars, Shree had noticed one yellow license plate. Maine, *Vacationland*. It was the perfect solution, discovered on a perfect morning. Standing on her bike, it all played out in her head. It was beautiful! Shree couldn't wait to tell her dad. And now she knew she would. Later that day, Shree and Wendy called Sharon G.

13. Talisman

June 23rd

"Come on, Tristan, you promised us you could bring the goods!" Max didn't believe for a second that Tristan would pull it off. But he wasn't sure if Luis would score some weed, and he didn't want to spend the day fishing if they weren't gonna get buzzed. When they met outside the Rec Center though, Luis had a grin that could only mean one thing. Blob showed up as well, looking as if he was already stoned. They all got into Luis's worn-out Corona, and Luis had to show Blob how to hold the door closed with a coat hanger. Max accepted the back seat to avoid door duty. And as they pulled out of the parking lot, exhaust poured into the back, causing Max to regret his choice. "I'm dying back here, Luis!"

"Shoulda called dibs on the front, Maxwell," Luis replied with his victory grin. His stocky build and muscled arms dwarfing the steering wheel.

"We hav'ta pick up Tristan," Max announced. "He says he's gonna swipe a bottle a vodka from his mom."

"That pussy'll never make it," Luis ruled like a judge. "Bet his mom caught him and he's grounded."

"If his mom catches him, he'll be grounded for the summer!" was Blob's ante. Blob's long black hair, which usually covered half his face, was now blowing wildly in the wind.

"Maybe till he graduates," Max raised, having met Tristan's

mom. Max was shorter than Luis and Blob, but from the tight back seat, he towered over them both. No doubt, he was trying to supplement his oxygen with the fresh air blowing in through their open windows.

"Well, that would never work 'cause Tristan'll pro'bly outlive his momma!" With that, Luis took the prize, but left both Max and the Blob confused. "Because he'll never graduate… but he can't stay grounded forever." The other two laughed, and Blob congratulated Luis.

Despite all doubts, Tristan had a bottle of vodka in his backpack. And the rest of the car ride, and part of the path to their fishing hole, Tristan recounted the intricacies of the caper. Unfortunately, the whole story was that his mom was out of the house, and he just took the bottle from the TV cabinet where she keeps it. So even though he was a hero for getting vodka, he was ignored again within moments of joining them.

The trail along the bayou was overgrown, and Max, in the lead as usual, took them through a couple of uncharted loops and once led them straight into a mush of orange brown mud and cattails. Now Luis took the lead, backing them out of the muck, while Max noisily sucked his shoes out of the brown goo. Suddenly Luis shrieked and jumped back. Then Blob exploded with laughter even louder than the scream.

"That was a water moccasin! That's no laughing matter." Luis tried to reclaim his dignity, while his heart still raced. "One bite from a water moccasin and you'll be dead in 15 minutes."

"But you jumped like a little girl. And that scream. You were hil-AIR-ri-ous!"

"Shut the fuck up!" Luis pushed Blob good-naturedly. "Can't a girl scream if she wants to?" Only Luis could pull that one off. By abandoning his dignity, it was fully restored. Tristan, in particular, admired Luis's grace. But when he tried the same move himself, later that day, Max just called him a faggot.

By now Max had kicked and stamped all the mud from his shoes and reclaimed the lead. Luis had no intention of going first. When they got to the snake spot, there was no sign of anything. Without anyone acknowledging it, though, all four of them jumped past the spot and quickly put twenty or so paces between them and any hint of snake.

As soon as they got to their fishing spot, they got down to business. They hadn't bothered to bring fishing gear, but they each had a lighter. Luis proceeded to roll up a joint, using two leaves, pulled like Kleenex from a pack of Zig-Zags with the image of either Jesus Christ or Tommy Chong on the cover. Tristan pulled out the vodka, but Max motioned to wait. The ritual of passing the joint would take precedence. And without them realizing it, they did treat it as a ritual. Luis, the bringer of the goods, was the priest who lit the incense. Blob, who somehow floated above the world, the guru of being stoned, was presented with the joint next. His face lit with a kind of peace, his one good eye peeking through the gap in his long hair, looking timeless as he toked. No doubt his ancient indigenous ancestry imbued him with the aura of wisdom in the others' minds. Next was Max, of course. Max would take giant tokes. They joked that he could smoke down to a roach in one breath. Tristan half-worried he would. And finally, it was Tristan's turn. He swore to himself that he wouldn't cough this time. But Luis just stared at him with his happy grin until Tristan lost it. They all laughed, then Luis took up the joint again.

They were dazed by the time the roach was too small to hold. Luis and Max started talking about a boat that used to be there. Blob, head hanging from slouching shoulders, gazed at a spider web that caught the sunlight in a most inspired way. He was thinking that the many boxes, spaces between the silk of the web, were like individual panes of glass. He realized the spider was an architect, and the web was the most amazing building he had ever seen. Meanwhile, Tristen was staring at his shoelaces. They were twisted, and he didn't think they ought to be. He began to untie his shoe with plans to straighten each twist, so that the laces weaved the shoe closed with perfect repeating folds. But before he got to his plans, he forgot about them entirely, having realized that Max was pulling on his backpack.

Max pulled out the vodka, took a swig, then handed it to Blob. Tristan thought he should be the one handing out the vodka. As if hearing his thoughts, Blob looked right at Tristan and thanked him loudly. Luis and Max did the same, in much quieter tones. "And thank yo' momma too!" Blob concluded.

The rest of the afternoon was lost in drunken nonsense. Luis and Max did find an old dinghy hidden in the weeds. They tried to paddle out to the island, but instead abandoned it a few feet from shore, when it was taking in water with all four of them in it. The boat sank in three feet of water, and they lay on the muddy banks until they dried out. Tristan said what they all were thinking, wet clothes were like having personal air conditioning.

The rest of Luis's pot was dry, thanks to the ziplock baggie, but his papers were pulp. Max and Luis spent more than enough time saying rude things about girls they all knew. Tristan wished they would stop, especially when they were talking about his sisters or Ginny, whom he thought was sweet. Blob ignored them and took his pocket knife to an aluminum can. "I bet this'll work as a pipe!" he offered. Immediately the group gathered around the new talisman.

It didn't matter that the Mountain Dew can had, moments ago, been garbage, left in the mud for who knows how long. No one cared about the bit of dried mud that stretched up to the mouthpiece. Nobody noticed the tiny snail still inside. The guru of being stoned had created a magic pipe out of nothing, and his three disciples thanked their lucky stars to have been present at the performing of this extraordinary miracle. The moment would become essential lore of their tribe. Three years later, two people who had never met 'The Blob', would describe the miracle to a young novice, who utterly failed to comprehend its importance. "So they smoked dope out of a coke can?"

Somehow, the small congregation managed to get home without snake bites, drownings, or crashing the car. But they were not treated like crusaders returned from the holy land. Tristan did get punished for two weeks, with a threat of military school. Luis's car overheated on the way home, then broke down within the week, never to run again. Blob's grades arrived in the mail that day, and rather than repeating, he learned that he had already attended his last day of school ever. No one who knew him was surprised or terribly concerned. As for Max, well his parents smelled his crimes and locked him out that night. He finally fell asleep in the backseat of their car. He knew how to get past the door lock, and dreamed of what he would do if he learned how to hotwire it. "Perhaps my education is important after all," he whispered to the empty night.

14. Cookies

July 23rd

Sharon's house was further away than either Wendy or Shree had biked before. They left their own subdivision, crossed under a freeway, passed a festering old mattress, abandoned tires, and broken bottles. Her secret plan was aching to be shared, but Shree held it close the whole way. Wendy, getting tired, wondered why they couldn't just say goodbye to Sharon G. over the phone. They rode past empty fields with grasses so tall that they imagined wild animals stalking them, continued through streets of half-built homes, roofers smoking cigarettes, a churning cement truck, and someone yelling for Julio. Finally, they arrived in the next inhabited subdivision, which looked remarkably like the one they had left. Sharon G. was waiting for them on her front step.

They had to go inside so that Sharon's mom could meet them. She apologized for not offering them iced tea. The movers were due in a week, and there was so much yet to pack. The living room was filled with cardboard boxes. Some full and labeled, many more leaning, flattened, against a wall. Sharon interrupted the apologies and explanations to assure her mom that she and her friends had somewhere else to go. Sharon was determined to leave the house as soon as she could. Almost out the door, her little brother turned up, whining to go with them. But the older sister was having none of it. When the bickering turned to insults, their mom laid down the law… Sharon could spend time alone with her friends. Kevin had to start packing his room.

Sharon led her two visitors on foot, back the way they had come. After two blocks, the cars, lawns, and even driveways vanished. Three empty houses, almost fully built, stood deserted on their own block, castles on an island of dirt surrounded by a concrete moat. Sharon led them through to the backyard of the second house and promptly pulled herself in through an open window to a back bedroom. First Wendy, then Shree awkwardly struggled up to the window frame, pivoted over, then dropped onto a cement floor scattered with sawdust and stray nails. They looked around in admiration and burst out laughing for the sheer joy of this life-sized doll house.

"Sharon G., you have your own home?!" Wendy managed to say approvingly.

"It isn't much, but once I get the decorators in, it will do," she replied in the same voice she had used to imitate Annabelle's mother. She took them on a tour, which included walking through some walls that were yet to be plastered; a tiled bathroom with mirrors, sink and tub, but no faucets; a grand kitchen with cabinets and countertops but no refrigerator or stove; and a rough staircase without a railing, that opened onto a second story living room with a view of trees in the distance. Here, Sharon unveiled her preparations. Before her friends had arrived, she had already gathered several lawn chairs and had made a low table out of a piece of plywood and two crates. She also had a large bottle of Fanta strawberry soda, paper cups, and some cookies in her backpack. She had obviously given some thought to how to entertain her visitors.

At first, the soiree was filled with questions about why she was moving (her dad's job), where she was moving to (Long Island, NY), and when she was going (in two days to stay with her grandparents while the actual moving was done). Next, their classmates were dissected, their teacher flayed, and several events of the past year were recalled in greatly exaggerated detail. But eventually, Sharon steered the conversation to something more intimate as befitting a celebration of their first and final visit.

"What is the one secret that you've never revealed to anyone?" Sharon asked mischievously. "What's up with you and Anna, Wendy? I know you've been keeping that a secret!" A flush of red matching her soda-stained lips, swept across Wendy's face before she could say a word. *Again, she was in that store. Again, the broken sunglasses. The accusing stare.*

"Not ready yet? Okay, I'll start," Sharon G. offered. "I mean, I'm moving away, so you can't use my words against me for too much longer.

"I've never shared this with anyone. I thought I would go to my grave with it. When I was six, we were at the grand opening of King's Shopping Village. It was a real big celebration, you remember Wendy?" Wendy looked on blankly. She was caught up in the web of her own shameful secret. Sharon continued, "There were free balloons, and a clown, and goats to pet. I remember my mom let us have hot dogs, popcorn, and cokes. I think they were free, 'cause I got two cokes!"

Annabelle had been trying to get the attention of some boy, Wendy recalled. Todd was older, in junior high. The boys were having water balloon fights, and Todd asked the girl hanging around if she had any balloons he could use. That's how it all started. When Wendy ran into her, Anna confided that she'd just swiped some balloons from the U-Tote-Em to give to Todd. Wendy was amazed. She never knew anyone her age stealing from a store. And Anna! She always thought Annabelle was a real goody-goody. And here she was, showing off her stolen treasure!

Sharon rolled on at an excited pace. "Anyway, we were there for a long time visiting stores, petting the goats, watching performers. Then my little brother needed to pee, and my mom wanted me to go too. But I insisted I didn't have to. You see, I really didn't want to miss the magician. So Mom and Kevin left, and I got to stay all by myself in the front row of the show."

Right away Wendy could see that Annabelle had stolen the wrong thing! Her balloons were long and skinny, like the kind used for balloon animals. They don't work well as water balloons. Todd rejected them as Wendy knew he would. That's when Annabelle turned her bright blue eyes on Wendy. "Please help me get the right ones," she had pleaded. And Wendy couldn't resist her. She had always wanted to be Annabelle's friend, ever since they met in kindergarten. Even her name was hypnotizing. But Annabelle constantly had girls around her, and somehow Wendy was perpetually pushed off to the side. Yet right then, it was just her and Annabelle, and Annabelle was looking into her eyes like they were the only two people in the world. Wendy would do whatever Annabelle asked.

"Only as soon as they left me, I realized that I actually did need to pee," Sharon laughed. "The guy on stage started doing his show, and the tricks were amazing. He made scarves come out of a chicken's butt, and everyone was laughing. But I kept looking for my mom, and she wasn't coming back. And I really needed to pee! It was like an emergency. I couldn't wait."

Inside the store, it was suddenly real. Could she really do it? Steal? Would she get caught? Only one person seemed to be working in the store, a woman standing at the cash register. A man in greasy overalls was buying Marlboros. Wendy quickly went behind the two rows of shelves and found the balloons where Anna said they'd be. Maybe there will only be the thin ones? Or maybe they would all be sold out? Wendy grasped at hope. But there they were, a whole box of little plastic bags filled with assorted colored balloons, each saying 'Happy Birthday!' in white script. Wendy heard the one and only customer leave, so she was all alone with the cashier. She listened and heard nothing. She reached for the balloons, and as she touched them, she turned to look down the aisle and jumped. The cashier was standing at the end of the aisle, looking straight at her.

"Don't do it!" The cashier said this simply, but firmly. She was about her mother's age, but thicker and with a tattoo up her arm. She looked mean, like she kicked dogs or something. Wendy acted like she didn't know what the cashier was talking about.

"Do you have any," Wendy wished she could have said anything but… "balloons?"

By now Sharon's voice had risen as the tension of her predicament grew. "Only the guy on stage saw me squirming around. So then he came down and pulled me up on the stage with him. At first, I thought he was gonna take me to the bathroom, so I followed him. Before I knew it, I was on stage and all these kids and parents were staring at me. Yet I'm still dying to pee!"

"Eighty-nine cents a bag. Pay for them up front," the cashier said with little trust that Wendy would pay for them. Just then, the bell on the door jingled as another customer entered. The cashier pointed her finger at Wendy, gave a severe look, and turned to guard the register. Wendy waited to see that she was occupied with the customer, then grabbed as big a handful of bagged balloons as she could, and stuffed them in her pocket till it was bulging. She couldn't pull her hand out; it was so stuffed. Then, once she did get her hand out, several packets of balloons came out with it. She stuffed them back in, but one dropped to the floor. She started to reach for it and heard someone coming around the corner of her aisle. Wendy stepped on the bag, but she could see red and yellow balloons peeking out from the side of her dirty white tennis shoe. Casually, she reached up for a set of plastic birthday candle holders, then examined them carefully, trying to act like a real shopper. Should I get the blue ones or the pink ones? When she glanced over at the other person now on her aisle, she was relieved to see it was an older man selecting gum. He turned and winked at her. She smiled but felt like she

was about to throw up.

"The magician guy was trying to get me to hold his hat while he tapped with his wand. And I'm twisting in place, my knees clamped tight, trying to hold it in, while he's saying something to the audience."

Eventually the old man left the aisle with his gum, but he didn't seem to be going to the cash register. Wendy planned to wait till someone was checking out, so she could slip out the door without being noticed. But the store was quiet. She discreetly picked up the balloons on the floor and put them back into the box. She was just deciding to pull out the balloons in her pocket, when she saw the cashier in the next aisle staring at her through the shelves, bottles of insect repellent and lighter fluid framing her gargoyle face. Wendy froze as the cashier again said, "Don't do it!" Just then, the man with gum called out to say he was ready to check out.

As soon as the cashier left to take care of him, Wendy turned to escape, but was surprised that another customer, this time a mother with a sleeping baby, had joined her in her aisle. Wendy walked the other way, towards the front, then doubled back on the next aisle to the back of the store. From this point on, the cashier would see her if she looked up from the register.

Sharon was squirming in her seat, acting out her scene. "Then he started pouring a whole pitcher of water into the hat I'm holding. I finally saw Mom and Kevin arrive, so I tried to get off the stage. But the magician pulled me back and kept pouring the water into his hat! And I just couldn't hold it anymore. It just started happening, my legs got warm, and the warmth just spread. My bladder felt so relieved, but the rest of me was horrified."

Wendy circled around the store quickly in order to exit from the far side. The door in sight, she turned her head to see if the cashier was watching, and walked right into a display of sunglasses, knocking herself and multiple pairs to the floor. By the time she got up, the cashier had finished with Mr. Gum and started heading towards her. Wendy tried to get the glasses back in the display, then took a determined step towards the door, just three feet away. Only as she stepped, an unseen pair of sunglasses crunched beneath her foot. Now there was nothing to do but get out that door as fast as possible.

"First one kid, then another, started pointing," Sharon continued. "The magician stopped whatever he was saying and looked real concerned. By now everyone was laughing and pointing at me! And I started bawling while my shoes were filling with pee and my socks were sopping wet. And I just kept peeing," Sharon said with an air of resignation. "The puddle grew so big it was dripping off the stage. I felt like my whole life was over!"

Just as Wendy reached for the door, a girl grabbed for the handle from the outside and started pushing in, while Wendy was barreling out. What was Sharron B. doing there at that precise moment?! She could hear the cashier almost catching up, yelling that she had to pay. Wendy was certain all was lost as the cashier's hand reached for her shoulder. Yet grace intervened to help her shoplift. She instinctively twisted around the door, pulling it forward so that Sharron B. stumbled inside while she dashed out.

Wendy ran as fast as she could, sprinting into the busy road, sure she had dodged between two cars. Suddenly brakes screeched across the pavement like chalk on a blackboard, and a car abruptly stopped, inches away. The man behind the wheel flushed white, but Wendy only saw an angry judge condemning her for life. She turned and ran, not daring to look back, finally disappearing between houses, running through unfenced backyards until she had to jump a fence to avoid going back towards her crime. Her shirt got caught on the way over, and she fell at the feet of a woman watering her tomato plants. "What do you think you're doing?!" demanded this new judge. Wendy couldn't get words out and just nodded as she stumbled to her feet and ran for the gate. She just kept running and running till she got to where Annabelle was waiting for her.

"It was the most embarrassing thing that ever happened to me!" As Sharon concluded, she was grinning. "Life goes on," she said, "and now I know never to drink two cokes at a time. Nor trust a magician. Mom said it looked like the water magically disappeared into the hat, then reappeared in my pants." Shree erupted with giggles and guessed that maybe Sharon had told her story before.

"Now your turn," Sharon said, turning to Wendy. "What actually happened with you and Anna?" Wendy flushed deep red again.

Until she reached Annabelle, Wendy's only thoughts were how sickeningly awful the whole thing was. She didn't want to steal, she didn't want to lie, and pretend to shop when she had no money. She hated that the cashier now knew she was a thief. And the fear of almost getting caught twisted her stomach to the verge of vomit. She promised herself, as she gasped for air, unable to talk from running, that she would never ever steal again.

But Annabelle was so pleased and kept praising her and thanking her. Slowly, Wendy started enjoying Annabelle's gratitude. After all, she truly had escaped! She even felt a little proud, telling her story, minus her fear. She faced real danger yet came through it victorious. She and Annabelle offered the balloons to Todd, and Anna praised her to Todd, and Wendy praised Annabelle back. Before long, they were in the middle of a water balloon fight, though Todd switched sides to throw his balloons at the two helpless little girls.

Wendy and Annabelle were both smiling and soaked when Jeanie and Sharron B. found them. And in the hail of shame and name-calling that pelted Wendy, Anna's camaraderie vanished. The two of them were not together. Anna hadn't stolen. She had bought her balloons. Wendy alone was the criminal. "Just like her brother."

"Other Sharron said you accused Anna of stealing, but they

said you were the thief. Well not Anna. She told me later that you were innocent, but she wouldn't tell me more. So it's been like a year. What's the real story?" Sharon looked at Wendy expectantly. "Well, Wendy? Tell us! What happened between you and Anna? Everyone believes Sharron B., but what's the real truth?" Sharon G. was no longer smiling in her insistence. Instead, she had a sympathetic look, like she only wanted to help.

"She and I just had a misunderstanding. I thought she wanted me to steal something for her."

"Did you do it? Did you steal something?"

"Well, I, uh, don't wanna talk about it," Wendy said quietly.

"She doesn't have to say anything if she doesn't want to," Shree broke in, feeling protective of her friend. "Let's change the subject." After all, a certain secret was aching to come out of Shree.

"Sure, we can change the subject," Sharon agreed. "Only I just want to say, in case you didn't know, I have never liked the other Sharron. She's a fake. She is the worst B word I know. And if there is a choice between you and her, I'd pick you any day!" Wendy's shame was replaced by embarrassment. She'd spent the last few years thinking Sharon G. didn't really like her.

"Well now it's my turn to tell a deepest secret, only mine hasn't happened yet!" With this, Shree started on her story of her divorced parents, and her cruel mom, and her shining knight of a dad. "So I'm going to run away to Boston! I'm just trying to figure out how I can get there." Shree had yet to voice her secret plan aloud. Not even Wendy knew it. Now the moment had finally come....

Suddenly there was a loud pop, and the glass in the large window beyond their table cracked. Shree and Wendy were both in shock, staring at the window, but Sharon turned immediately in the direction of the stairs and yelled, "KEVIN! I'M TELLING!"

Kevin had a slingshot and a defiant look on his face. "You can't tell Mom, cuz I'll just tell her about y'all playing house in here. Where did you get those cookies?"

"How long have you been here?" Sharon and her brother looked at each other with daggers in their eyes.

"Long enough to hear *her* say she's runnin' away," replied Kevin, pointing his slingshot hand at Shree.

"Listen, Kevin is it? Please don't say anything." Shree imagined Ms. Gibson calling her mom after Kevin told on them. "I was only talking. I'm not going to run away," Shree lied. "And your sister isn't doing anything wrong."

"Yeah she is! She's not s'posed to go in these houses. Mom-n-Dad said so. So she ain't gonna tell on me for bust'n tha window."

"I mean it, Kevin. You breaking things can get us all in a bunch of trouble. Not just with Mom-n-Dad but with the police. We better leave right now. And you better apologize to my friends if you know what's good for you." With this, she got up and started packing her backpack.

"Yer friend'll get in so much trouble when I tell Mom!"

"Hey, no one's gonna get in trouble! No one needs to be a nark!" Wendy felt like it was up to her to talk everyone down, as she was the only one without a gun to their head. "Look, we wuz jus tellin' secrets. Well, my secret's that I broke some guy's winder once. Ya see, MY big brother'n his frien's were throwin' rocks over a fence into a swimmin' poowl." While Wendy was telling the story, she took the bag of cookies from Sharon. "I saw th' splashes 'n I thought it wuz cool. So nex' day, me'n another kid tried ta make some splashes, ar'selves. Only th' firs' rocks we throw'd, they didn't hardly makit ta th' poowl. So I threw one as hard as I could." Wendy casually offered a cookie to Kevin. "An' it broke a winder! I was so ser-prised! D'I even do that? Then suddenly some guy comes runnin' outta his house yellin'. Says he's gonna whup our you-know-whats n' hand what's lef' over ta th' poe-leece!"

"Wow! Did he catch ya?" Kevin asked, with his mouth full of cookie.

"Ah weren't gonna wait 'round ta give'm th' chance! I ran faster'n I ever did'n malife. But th' other kid weren't so lucky." She gave Kevin another cookie. "After half n' hour or so, I casually walked by th' house. And saw a police car! That kid got caught, and he went to juvie! I couldn't get ta sleep that night, thinkin' 'bout what a stupid thing I'done. I never saw th' kid again, neither. I still feel awful 'bout it, years later. So STOOPIT, 'n so lucky I didn't get *ca-ught*. Tha' poor kid, tho, went to juvie 'cause a me!" Kevin was silent, while Shree marveled at the mysterious hypnotic power of Wendy's Texas accent.

"So let's get outta here before the workers or the poe-leece come," Shree concluded.

The rest of the afternoon, Kevin stuck close, thwarting his sister's plans, as well as Shree's. Still, Shree had paid attention, and she picked up what she needed to know for her plan to work. When it was time to ride home, the second set of awkward forever goodbyes was a bit more heartfelt than on the last day of school. Sharon G. was certain she would write to her friends with her new address. Yet for some reason, she never did.

On the long bike ride home, Shree finally got to reveal her secret plan to get to Boston, and most of the way home, the two chirped joyously about how they would both ride on sofas, watching TV, all the way to New York. This plan was sure to work!

But as they approached their own neighborhood, a pensive mood rose in Wendy. "It was Max who broke that window, not me," she announced. "And one of *his* friends got caught. Though he didn't actually go to juvie for it," she clarified. Then she took a deep breath and confessed, "But I did steal from U-Tote-Em. That's the secret I ain't never gonna talk about."

15. Shards

July 30th

"You are not to have anyone here while we're gone. Do you understand me? Maxwell? Gwendolyn?"

"Of course, Dad, we know the rules. No one is coming over." Max sounded so mature that Wendy actually believed him.

"The name and number of the hotel are on the pad by the phone. Your Aunt Sally might come by to check on you. There is plenty of food in the fridge. Don't make a mess and do the dishes after you eat." They could see their mother in the car, reaching for the horn. "Well I better go," Dad concluded with a sharp 'beep' for punctuation. "Be good. Be safe."

"Bye Dad! Good luck at your tournament. Hope you and Mom win!" As soon as the car door closed, Max went into the kitchen. Wendy stayed to see their mom wave as the car pulled away.

Her parents lived to play bridge, it seemed. It was the most boring game Wendy had ever seen. They usually took her with them on these bridge trips. Sometimes the hotel had a pool. But she had also been stuck hanging out at a tournament with absolutely nothing to do. A giant room with a hundred tables and all these old people with serious or angry faces for two straight days. She would walk up to the table her mom and dad were playing at, and invariably get a mean look and a "No kibitzing!" from the other players. Once or twice, another kid her age would be there. So they would be stuck together for the whole weekend with nothing in common but a shared dislike of bridge. Finally, she was old enough to be left at home.

"I'm having my friends over, so leave." Max didn't even look at Wendy, just kept eating a whole package of lunch meat straight out of the refrigerator.

"No one's allowed to be here. And that lunch meat is for our lunches." Even as she said this, she knew it was pointless. Something told her that she shouldn't leave the house to Max and his friends. So she went into their parents' room, picked up the phone, and called Shree. Max was always nicer when Shree was around. Well mostly he just ignored them, which was a lot better than when she was alone with him. Shree agreed to come over, but her mom wouldn't agree to her spending the night unless Wendy's parents called to invite her. Obviously that wasn't going to happen.

By afternoon, Shree joined Wendy in her room, playing Monopoly and discussing Shree's plan to get to Boston. Though her door was shut, pounding bass and drums invaded through the common wall to the living room. Still, between putting up houses on the yellows and going 'directly to jail', dreams of an adventure were voiced. "Like stowing away in a moving hotel room!" "We'll fill the fridge with root beer, and keep ice cream sandwiches in the freezer." Wendy almost believed that she too, would go. Shree promised that her dad would let Wendy stay. Though Wendy imagined her parents being forced to come get her. The vacation from Max would be worth any punishment.

Yet after the first vision of adventure settled, and the music had been cranked up a few more notches, Wendy began to see cracks. There would be no electricity, so the TV wouldn't work. Probably no light for reading, even during the day. No ice cream sandwiches, no 'collecting two hundred dollars'.

The heavy metal that Max and his friends were blaring in the living room kept increasing in decibels with each new song. They had to raise their voices louder and louder just to be heard. "Where are we gonna poop?" Wendy shouted, just as a brief diminuendo cleared the air. They both burst out laughing, which was swallowed up by power chords. Rent at 'Marvin Gardens' proved too steep for Wendy.

Suddenly a crashing sound overcame the pounding bass. Breaking glass was clearly part of it. Jumping up, Wendy ran to the living room with Shree cautiously following. There were Max and Luis, fighting on the floor with the glass table shattered beneath them. Yet it wasn't the time to think about what her parents were going to say, or even wonder if someone was hurt. The two were not finished twisting and wrenching at each other. Max was on top of Luis, but Luis had Max's head locked under his arm. They were both vividly turning shades of red and purple, sweat flying and mixing with the mess as their bodies would suddenly jerk and reorient, trying for leverage. Neither was capable of speech, so despite the music, the fight was strangely soundless.

Blob finally started shouting at them, "Stop both of you. Just stop!" And though it didn't stop, both fighters seemed to slacken a bit from exhaustion. The two of them calmed to a stillness. Neither of them budged for another couple of minutes. The music came to an end, but no one paid attention.

Max eventually spoke. "Are you bleeding? Let's at least get off this glass." So they unwound themselves and the redness in their faces drained away. Luis was bleeding, and when he took his shirt off, it looked like a flap of skin was sliced from his shoulder blade. A lot of blood was coming out. Almost everyone was too shocked to think of what to do, until Tristan jumped up to him, took the shirt and pressed it hard, closing the wound and hiding it from disturbed stares.

"We got to get you to the hospital, man!" With that, the boys pushed out of the wrecked living room. Max stayed behind for a moment, looked straight at Wendy, who was still too shaken up to comprehend.

"Clean up this mess!" Then he followed his friends out the door. Wendy didn't even react till minutes after everyone had left.

"Do you think he's gonna die?" Wendy was overwhelmed by the thought that a shard of glass had just stabbed into Luis. And her brother had been the cause. Was he trying to kill him? This didn't really happen, did it? Wendy's traumatized thoughts went places before she could stop them.

"No, I'm sure it'll just be some stitches," Shree said with some confidence. While the whole scene had been super disturbing to Shree, somehow the wound and all the blood didn't bother her that much. Luis, or whatever his name was, was obviously hurt, but he had been pretty quiet about it. He had pulled off the shirt with both arms, so the wound probably didn't go deep, she thought.

Wendy, the cloud of worry about Luis and even her brother lifting, was finally confronted by the wreckage before them. Like an ominous clicking of a giant insect, the needle kept popping at the end of the abandoned album. Wendy crossed the battle scene and turned off the stereo. Shree started moving the chairs away from the glass. Wendy was going to stop her. The nerve of her brother making this disaster and telling her to clean it up. Bottles, broken glass and even cigarette butts on the floor. Wendy knew that if she didn't clean it up, their parents would blame them both, and she would be punished. So she joined in with Shree, clearing things out of the way so that they could first deal with the broken table.

Shree was amazingly helpful and supportive. They discussed what she would tell her parents about the table and blood stains in the carpet. Shree insisted she would tell Wendy's parents what happened. But Wendy didn't want to reveal that Shree was even at the house. No, she hoped that Max would agree to a story that he had been standing on the couch and slipped, breaking the table. Neither of them would tell about guests, and maybe their parents would be easy on them.

Eventually, Shree had to go home, leaving Wendy there to face her brother alone. But he wasn't home yet. She fed herself a peanut butter and jelly sandwich, put her plate and glass in the dishwasher with all the others, started it up, then went into her room to wait and worry.

At about nine, she heard her brother and went outside to face him and plan their story for Mom and Dad. But Max wasn't alone. While Luis wasn't there, everyone else who had been there that day returned to the scene. Wendy couldn't take it.

"Max, you can't do this! Shree and I just cleaned up your mess. You can't have all these people trash it up again!" She said this loudly so that everyone heard her. Max just smiled. "This is NOT fair! You broke the table, trashed the house, and I had to clean your damn mess! You can't have people here!" The guys looked embarrassed and even sympathetic, but Max didn't bend.

"Listen to little Gwendy cussing! What would Mommy and Daddy say?" His sing-songy voice, especially in front of his friends, was meant to provoke, and it enraged her.

"You broke the table and cut your friend. You coulda killed him! You're almost a murderer! They should lock you up in prison for the rest of your life! They will lock you up, I bet."

"Scaredy little Gwendolyn wants to run to Daddy! Scaredy lil' girl is afraid of a drop of blood!" Max felt like a puppeteer, pulling Wendy's strings for his friends' entertainment. "Maybe there's gonna be blood from yer… *Cut-Up-Eyeballs!*"

"It shoulda been your blood today. I wish it was your blood! I wish a shard of glass stuck in you! Went into your face!" Wendy was so mad she couldn't contain herself. If a shard of glass had been in front of her at that moment, she would have lunged at her brother and stabbed him in the face. "I'm gonna kill you someday!"

"Wendy sounds so scary! Ooh I'm so sca-wed! Wendy is gointa kill me." By this time, Max's friends couldn't stay silent. They all had siblings, and they all had ugly fights, but this seemed like it was heading nowhere good. Blob, who had an older sister and two younger half-brothers, was the first to say something.

"Dude, leave her alone." His voice was not loud, like it had been when he'd tried to stop the fight with Luis. He looked at Wendy with sympathy and repeated, "Leave her alone, man."

"She's my sister, and I can treat her how I want!" Max snapped back. But when he turned to look at his friends, he knew that they weren't enjoying his show. He had thought they were laughing with him, but they were either looking away uncomfortably, or like Blob, sympathetic to his sister. The fun was over, so he turned back to his pathetic sister. "Just stay in your room, okay?"

Wendy stood at the entrance to the hallway, shaking with anger. But Tristan, who had three older sisters, looked sweetly at her. "Thanks for cleaning everything up, man. We'll try to keep it clean tonight. D'you wanna beer?" Wendy mouthed thank you, but didn't take a beer.

Blob offered, "We'll clean up before your parents come home." He meant it at the time, but later that night, after some reflection, he admitted that he just couldn't picture them actually cleaning. But for the rest of the night, he did make a point to put bottles in the trash and smoked his cigarettes outside.

Wendy returned to her room and slept poorly under a blanket of loud music. Grand Funk Railroad and ZZ Top on endless repeat, while voices barked and laughed till late into the night. Why didn't the neighbors complain? Eventually, she realized it was quiet, or at least quieter.

When she awoke the next day, she thought the house was

deserted. As she opened the bathroom door, a strange man in his twenties or older was just coming out with vomit dripping from his overgrown mustache. Wendy pressed back against the wall to let him pass. "Have you seen Rankin?" he asked. Wendy had never heard of Rankin and just shook her head in reply. He staggered towards the front door, squinted his eyes as soon as it opened, then stumbled out without closing it.

Wendy surveyed the house and realized it was as bad as yesterday. Worse when you include the vomit on the bathroom floor. She cried. She didn't even want to *think* about cleaning again. Or how Max wouldn't lift a finger. Or her mom yelling at her, punishing her. "Go get my hard shoe." No doubt she would be cleaning the house for months on end now. The rest of summer was already lost.

She poured cornflakes into her bowl, then realized there was no milk left. So she made it with water and sugar like she used to. She took her bowl outside to sit in the carport and look at the trees. She was hoping for a few moments outside her own life before the marching began. Then it struck her. Mom's car was gone.

16. Bodysurfing

August 2nd

The drive to Galveston, about an hour, was filled mostly by listening to music and Shree's Uncle Jim. Everyone else in the car was dying to talk. Words were building up pressure, ready to escape like steam from five separate kettles. Instead, they were bottled up tightly. This tea was only to be poured into their proper cups. Shree had begged her mom to let Wendy come, and Wendy was shocked her mom let her go. Rebecca in turn, had begged her little brother to join them for a day at the beach. He, in turn, asked if Sirrus could come along. These invitations were, of course, about enjoying the company of those invited. But they were also strategic moves in each case, designed to block the paths of foes. Shree and Rebecca both worried what might happen if they spent the day alone together. Jim was hoping Sirrus would forget about her boyfriend for a day. He didn't recognize that Sirrus, too, was being strategic. She was using James's kindness to get away from her verbally dismissive and neglectful boyfriend. The fact that spending time with James was prompting Conner's suspicion wasn't lost on her. The fact that Conner's old girlfriend was in town was entirely unrelated, however.

So, while others were lost in thought, the car stereo played Stevie Nicks, and Jim was filling in the empty wordscape. "We're trying to piece together how immune cells can create so many different antibodies. Antibodies can be made to recognize nearly unlimited shapes. But they are made of protein, and there is nowhere near enough DNA to code all those possible shapes!" Poor Jimmy was oblivious to the fact that most of his audience had no idea what he was talking about. Shree knew what DNA was, but thought protein was just something like vitamins in food. Wendy had never heard of DNA. Rebecca could sort of follow, but wasn't interested enough to make the effort. Lucky for James, Sirrus understood what he was saying. But he had already told her about his research when he'd given her a tour of the lab. So during the car ride, she wasn't very attentive.

Eventually, Rebecca pushed him towards talking about determinism, mostly because she knew he was going to keep talking no matter what. She found his thoughts naive and laughable. In her mind, she was offering him enough leash to trip on in front of Sirrus. She smiled to herself as he took off running. "It's simple physics, really. Cause and Effect. Atoms and molecules are like billiard balls. They smash into each other and bounce off, but always follow the laws of physics. If you know the speed and angle at which one billiard ball hits another, you can know precisely where the other ball will go. What direction, how far, precisely. Cause and effect! The same with atoms and stars. They behave exactly as they should, as the laws of physics say they will. So theoretically, if you could know every particle in the universe, its mass, velocity, and so on, at a specific moment, then you could know exactly what will happen in the universe one second later. Cause and effect! And if you can know one second later, you can know ten billion years later. And since that is true, then there certainly is no free will. We don't make decisions. Our decisions are determined for us by chemical reactions, which are determined by physical laws. We are all riding on waves of cause and effect."

While Rebecca was feeling smug about her silly brother, Sirrus was listening closely. She strongly disagreed, but wasn't ready to lay out her case. For their part, Shree and Wendy were both taken in by these ideas. Wendy, for the first time, thought about free will, a term she had heard before. She was suddenly desperate to believe she had it. Shree felt like there was a trick being played. Like maybe Uncle Jim was making a joke and would eventually prove that black was white or something.

On a roll with a captive audience, Jim got to what he most wanted to say about determinism. "I think most people believe determinism, lack of free will, is like a horrible straitjacket. Like we're imprisoned by causes beyond our control. But I think it is exactly the opposite! If everything that happens is determined, then everything that happens is exactly perfectly right. Like every pool ball goes exactly into the pocket it's supposed to. And every decision we make is exactly right, even when it's the 'wrong' decision," he said using air quotes. "We can only do right! And even in pain and suffering, even death, it is freeing to realize that it is exactly what the universe needs. No more and no less. I find that comforting."

Rebecca had had enough. "Well I believe we have a responsibility to try to make good decisions. And if we don't, suffering does happen." Rebecca, the older sister, couldn't leave little 'Brother Oblivious' somewhat dangerous ideas hanging without saying something. "If you hide behind determinism to try and avoid responsibility for hurting someone, then that is worse than the hurting alone. Someone could use determinism to justify abhorrent things. Or at a minimum, avoid learning to be a better person." A mother must protect her daughter from bad ideas too, she thought.

"That isn't what I mean, Rebecca. Of course Hitler was evil, and of course we have a responsibility to be kind to others. What I am saying is that the struggle to do right is necessary; it is part of the cause and effect chain. But we shouldn't suffer for things that have already happened, only for things that are yet to happen."

"But regret is part of how we learn, Jimmy. We do struggle with the past, and it makes us better people. At least I hope so." With that, Rebecca turned onto the sandy parking lot. The beach lay just beyond the low dunes. They unloaded the car of themselves, a blanket, towels, cooler, sunscreen, and a dozen other things to drag across the hot sand. Within steps, both Shree and Sirrus were hopping with the pain of sticker burrs. But the relief of arrival at the promised destination erased the struggles just passed. In this, James's philosophy won out.

~ ~ ~

Within moments of setting their things down on the sand, Shree ran with Wendy into the water. It was shallow for a long way out, and warm as a bath. Shree wanted to hear what happened with Wendy and her parents. And Max. So they pushed out to the second sandbar, jumping up into the passing waves, splashing the water with their arms and faces, occasionally falling back, occasionally bouncing on hard shells or something gooey hidden by the almost opaque brown water. But through the fun, Wendy filled in the holes of her horrible Saturday.

"He wrecked Mom's car!"

"What! That's crazy. Was anyone hurt?" Shree was expecting to hear about Wendy's parents discovering the broken table, but she was literally knocked off her feet by the unexpected wave. "Start from the beginning, tell me everything!" she said, spitting out a mouthful of saltwater.

Wendy recounted the second party, the emptied house, the vomit dripping from the mustache, the missing car, the wreck of bottles, spilled beer, cigarette butts, and of course, vomit. The disaster of a house that Shree herself had helped clean. "The whole place needed to be cleaned all over again."

"Why didn't you call me?" Shree spat out more seawater.

"No, Shree, I wouldn't ask you again. You already did so much. Besides, the only one who shoulda been cleaning was Max. I decided I wasn't gonna do anything. I was gonna let Max deal with it. Let my mom 'n dad come home and see his mess. I knew I would get punished anyways. Why clean up his mess?" At this point Wendy went underwater, leaving Shree to imagine her stand.

"Then somewheres around noon, Max showed up on a bike and went straight to his room. I asked him 'Where's Mom's car?', but he didn't answer. I insisted that he clean up. Told him I wasn't gonna do any of it. He didn't say a single word. In a couple minutes, he came outta his room with his backpack bulging. Then he went into the kitchen, grabbed peanut butter 'n bread, crammed 'em in his backpack. He didn't even look at me. I followed him down the front steps. He got on the bike, which wasn't even his by the way, and took off without ever even say'n a word."

~ ~ ~

Back on the beach, Rebecca was unburdening herself to Jimmy. "Does Shree seem different to you? She's barely talking lately."

Jim pointed at the two girls splashing in the waves. "Yeah, she seems fine with her friend."

Rebecca acknowledged. "Maybe it's nothing. Maybe she's just been sullen and lonely. Doesn't want to talk to me, though," Rebecca admitted more quietly. "It's definitely a change. Most of the past year, she's been perfectly happy in her own little world. Before she even had a friend here."

"Well maybe she's just growing up," Sirrus chimed in. Her blue hair framed her child-like face that seemed so unspoiled and naive. Rebecca, who was prepared to find Sirrus irritating, nevertheless welcomed her offering.

"Yeah, that's what I was thinking. And I know there are a lot of things she'll be going through soon enough. But I'm just wondering what specifically is bothering her now. And how can I help?"

"I don't know if parents can help," Sirrus offered cautiously. "I remember when I was eleven, I would have been mortified to talk to my parents about my feelings. Don't get me wrong, my parents are very loving. But at eleven, I wasn't ready to accept myself. I'm not sure I could comprehend them accepting me." Rebecca thought this was both a new way of thinking about Shree's sullenness and a bit too over the top on Sirrus's part.

"I think Sirrus has a point," chimed in Jim. "I know when I was hitting puberty, the last thing I wanted was to talk with Mom." Rebecca laughed out loud at the thought.

"I know some bad years are coming. I just think it's still too early for that. But I guess all I can do is try to let her know that she can talk to me if she wants. And if she doesn't feel like it, that's okay too." What Rebecca was actually imagining was the glare and silence from Shree during any attempt at mother-daughter bonding.

"I'm sure that's what she needs to hear. You're such a good mom." Sirrus obviously wanted to make a good impression. Rebecca gave her points for trying.

"Well I'm sure glad she's found a friend in Wendy," concluded the worried mom. "At least I know she's talking with someone."

~ ~ ~

In the waves, Wendy was hopping on one foot, thinking she had been cut by something hard under the water. But she was okay. "After he left, I realized I had to at least try to clean up. So I put all the bottles and crud in Max's room. Before I finished, Aunt Sally showed up. So I told her everything." Wendy neglected to mention that she had burst into tears at the first sight of Aunt Sally, then took several minutes to calm down enough to tell her about Max and the car and everything, through sobs and sniffles. "Aunt Sally called my parents and told them. At least I didn't have to tell them and deal with their anger. Then she helped me clean and stayed with me the rest of the day, till my parents arrived."

"Wow, it's lucky your aunt came." So were your parents furious when they got home?"

"No they weren't. That was the biggest surprise. They were clearly upset and wanted me to tell them everything. But Mom asked me if I was okay, and my dad even thanked me for answering their questions and for cleaning up. Still, they were real upset, and I went to my room as soon as they let me. Later, I heard my dad talking on the phone and telling Mom it was the police."

"Why the police? Did they call your dad?"

"I'm not sure if I heard the phone ring. Probably he called them. Anyway, it wasn't till this morning that my dad told me they found Mom's car. It was wrecked. It was upside down in a field. There was no sign of Max. Dad asked me again about the last time I saw Max. I think it must have been after the accident. Dad asked if Max was injured, bleeding, or something. But honestly, I don't remember anything like that. His clothes were muddy. Maybe he went deaf, 'cause he didn't respond when I talked to him. But Dad said that wouldn't have happened in a car accident. He asked me about the blood stain on the carpet, but that was Luis."

"So Max didn't get hurt?"

"I don't think so. But we still haven't heard from him."

"What about anyone else? Was there any blood in the car?" After Shree said this, she wondered if she had gone too far. To Shree, it was like a detective story, but Wendy must be worried.

"I asked about that too, but I'm not sure Dad knows. The car was what they call 'totaled', which means there is no fixing it. It'll be hauled to a junkyard."

"How's your mom?"

"She hasn't said much, but she's been crying a lot. I think she just misses her car. She really loved that car."

"I'm sure she misses Max too," Shree suggested, thinking maybe Wendy needed to hear it.

"I'm not so sure!" Wendy said with acidity. "He was such an asshole! Look how he treated us all. If you ask me, I hope he never comes home." Even as she said this, she was uncomfortably aware that she was scared for Max.

"Where do you think he is?" Shree asked, quietly ignoring Wendy's bravado.

"I bet he's staying with one of his friends. Maybe that 'Blob' guy or Tristan. They were both kinda nice. I wouldn't be surprised if Max is leeching off them." In verbalizing this, she remembered that she hadn't mentioned either one of them to her parents, even though they had questioned her about Max's friends.

"You know what your Uncle Jim was talking about in the car?" Wendy wobbled towards voicing her dilemma.

"What, the immune system? DNA?"

"No, about deciding things, *freewell?* Is he saying we can't actually decide anything?

"Yeah, sorta. I don't think he really believes it, though. It's free will."

"Well I have a decision to make. I never told my parents about Blob and Tristan, cause I didn't want to get them in trouble. But what if Max is staying with one of them? Should I tell? Should I get them in trouble, but maybe find Max? I don't want Max coming home, but I'm sure it'll be better for him if he does. He's only fourteen, he can't live on his own?" Wendy was indeed struggling with the decision, but she was also proud of herself for bringing it back to 'free well'.

"I think you probably have to tell."

"So you don't believe in *free well?*" Wendy said with a laugh.

"*Will.* No I didn't say that!" not realizing Wendy had made a joke.

"I know, Shree. You're probably right, though. I better tell." Wendy thought she was through talking, but as she dove under another wave, she thought about one more decision. "One thing these past two days proved to me is that I don't wanna be anything like my brother. I'm gonna be *nothing* like him! That is *my* free will!" she declared, finally saying it right. "I was thinking about that when your uncle was talking. I am gonna *choose* to be nothing like my brother." Wendy felt stronger than the waves, just then. She let one hit her full in the face, but came through on the other side triumphant.

Shree had never been more impressed with Wendy. To be honest, Shree had been impressed with her friend many times. Mostly because Wendy frequently knew what Shree was thinking without her even saying anything. But now Wendy was way out front, and Shree was proud of her. After all this ugliness her friend had gone through, she seemed completely confident in herself. Wendy was deciding who she was. Shree thought she should be making decisions about who she is. Maybe going to live with her dad was just such a decision.

As if on cue, Wendy added, "Also, I don't think I can go to Boston with you!" Shree wasn't surprised. "I think with what Max has done, I need…"

Without warning, Uncle Jim appeared in the waves. "Hey, you kids ever try bodysurfing?" And with that, he introduced them to a new way to play in the waves. Soon they were taking to it like dolphins.

~ ~ ~

"So, do you like my little brother?" Rebecca had been wondering what was up with Sirrus and Jimmy for weeks now. Jimmy mentioned her multiple times, and she could tell he had a crush on this girl.

"James is great! Of course I like him. He's so sweet and helpful," Sirrus replied innocently.

Rebecca thought she had asked directly, but Sirrus was being evasive. "He thinks the world of you. You must know that"

"Yeah, he's really been nice to me. He's such a great listener. He has helped me more than I deserve."

What kind of game was Sirrus playing? More than she deserved? "Sirrus, I hope you aren't going to break Jimmy's heart."

"No no, we're not like that! We're just friends. Really good friends, but just friends. I have a boyfriend." Sirrus gave one of those sweet looks like she would never hurt anyone, and Rebecca could understand how Jimmy was smitten.

"Don't be so sure he only wants to be a friend. I know my brother, and I think he might like you a lot more than just as a friend."

"But James knows I have a boyfriend. He's been so helpful with him. I probably would have broken up with Conner some time ago if James hadn't helped me to understand him."

"Jimmy might be too nice for his own good! But trust me on this, he wishes you were something more than just friends." Rebecca hoped she hadn't misread her brother. "Now it's fine if you don't ever see him that way, but don't hurt him." Rebecca felt a certain satisfaction that she had forced the question. Of course she didn't want to interfere in Jimmy's love life. But from what Sirrus was saying, Jimmy was heading for some pain. So on balance, Rebecca felt very good about playing his protector.

Sirrus, on the other hand, didn't appreciate this conversation at all. She was perfectly happy letting things evolve. She wasn't sure if she could like James that way. He was sweet and smart and all. But was he really her type? He was kinda young and immature. Also, she was committed to Conner, even though he drove her up a wall. She knew she would break it off with him someday, but the thought of actually doing so seemed exhausting. If only he would break up with her. That would be so much easier. She did daydream that she might possibly get together with James, if only Conner were out of the picture. That image was a sweet one. But to make it happen herself?! That was an emotional Mount Everest to climb. Breaking up would not be one conversation. It would be a week of anger and pain and recriminations. Conner knew every button to push, every knife to twist. No, it would be so much better if he would just dump her. James was her rock, her island, to malappropriate from Paul Simon. James was the shelter she had come to rely on in an emotional storm. And Rebecca was going to force her to send him away. No, Sirrus did not like this conversation one bit.

"Seriously, please be gentle with my little brother. If you don't like him that way, make it clear. But don't pretend you don't know, because I am telling you right now. Pay attention to it or you're going to hurt him a lot."

"Okay, Rebecca, I'll pay attention. I wouldn't intentionally hurt him for the world. He truly is a, uh, very special friend to me. But I will be aware that he may feel things differently from me. I'll be clear with him where I stand." Sirrus said it, but she wasn't sure she could be clear with herself.

Rebecca looked her up and down and smiled in what she thought was a kind and forgiving way. But Sirrus felt it was more judgmental than forgiving. "Thanks, Sirrus. I'm just trying to look out for my little brother. I hope you understand."

"I know. We both want him to be happy."

And now, the three wet youths returned from the sea with laughing talk of that one that Wendy caught all the way to shore. They broke out the food and bottles of pop, or 'cokes' as Wendy and Sirrus called them, and had lunch. Their conversation returned to aimless banter, but at least there was less tension than there had been in the car. After eating, Sirrus took a walk on the beach. Jim wanted to join her, but she made it clear that she wanted to be by herself for a while. After Sirrus walked northeast a ways, Rebecca asked Jimmy to walk with her to the southwest. Shree and Wendy dug in the wet sand by the beach, finding butterfly shells with plenty of the unopened ones burrowing back down into the soupy sand.

"Jimmy, I don't think she thinks of you that way."

"I know. We're just friends."

"But you like her, don't you?"

"She has a boyfriend. Yeah, I like her as a friend. She's great. But we're just friends."

"Okay, Jimmy. She does seem nice. She's super cute." Rebecca couldn't help but want to stir things up. She didn't believe his denials for a second. But now to business. "By the way, have you heard from Anthony?"

"Yeah, he's written me a couple of letters. He says you don't respond to any of his letters or calls."

"Well he's sent me a letter about every other day! He has got to stop. I throw all the letters away, unopened."

"You don't even read them?!"

"I read the first one, and it was just drivel. How he wants me to forget everything that happened, and how we should get back together and be a family. I already told him that's never gonna happen. But after the barrage kept coming, I thought I'd better read one of the more recent ones, to see if he's losing it again."

"And…"

"I think he is! He's threatening me and, at the same time, talking about our cosmic responsibility and how the universe is speaking to him. Telling him we must be together."

"But that's just hyperbole. He's just being poetic." Jim reached down and pulled a tangle of seaweed up from the wet sand. Three tiny shrimp hopped out.

"Does he write those things to you too?" Rebecca watched the shrimp fling themselves back into the water, then disappear.

"He's written about how you're the center of his universe and things like that. I know you don't want him in your life, but I think it does sound sweet. He just really cares for you."

"No, Jimmy, these are the sorts of things he would say when he was losing it. He would talk about the universe controlling him. Everything was so dramatic and beyond his control. The longer he went, the more complicated the logic became. I'm pretty sure he's off his meds. It just goes downhill from here. Thank god he's back in Boston, and thank god Shree isn't seeing any of these letters. I sneak them out of the mailbox and throw them away at work. If she saw one, she would be drawn to it immediately and start asking questions. He draws all over the envelopes. He's talented with his drawings. Even though I throw them away, I can't help but admire his doodles."

"He hasn't drawn on the letters he's written to me," Jim said with more than a little jealousy. With a quick sidestep, Jim avoided a patch of black tar in the sand. At first, he thought it was some sea life.

"So have you written him back?" Rebecca asked, admiring the patterns that the receding waves had made. Little tributaries carved into the sand, branches braiding into harmonized ripples in brown and tan.

"Yeah, I wrote him. I told him that you and Shree are happy

and he shouldn't worry about you." He had hidden from Rebecca that he was corresponding with Tony. It was a relief to come clean. His feet, on the other hand, were now splotched with black from the tar he hadn't noticed.

"Okay, however next time you write him, I want you to tell him that he should never write to me again. If I ever want to talk to him, I can contact him. But no more letters. I won't have it. The more he does it, the longer it will be till he hears from me."

"So it's okay with you that I write him?" He couldn't help admiring Tony's style of writing. And besides, unlike Rebecca, Tony was interested in the research he was doing.

"Sure, if you want to, Jimmy," Rebecca said with some compassion. Then, on second thought, "Remember what I told you before? How he gets? You should pay attention to his mental health. Notice it's deteriorating. Stop trying to make sense of what he's saying when it gets weird. I plan to call his mom. Maybe she can get him on his meds again. Maybe you should urge him not to play with fire. But I warn you, it can be mentally and emotionally exhausting to try to reason with him."

Then unexpectedly, a puffer fish appeared at their feet, washed up from the waves.

17. Certificate

August 10th

"**M**om, what are you doing here?" Rebecca was truly surprised to see her mom standing on the doorstep with her rolling suitcase at her side, while a taxi departed in the background. She hadn't seen her mom since Thanksgiving, hadn't talked to her since Mother's Day. That conversation had been strained, with both of them holding back all the things they had wanted to say, in the interest of being pleasant. The only real pleasantness had been that their conversation ended in under four minutes. Now her mom was at her door, obviously expecting to stay for a while. What was even more surprising was how much her mom had aged. Her hair, once dyed red, was fully gray. Her frame, once imposing enough to intimidate Rebecca, seemed stooped and shrunken.

"Is that how you greet your own mother after a year?"

"Come in Mom, I'm just surprised to see you. Shree, your *Bubbie* is here!" Rebecca yelled into the house a little too loudly.

"Gramma!" Shree came running from her room and threw her arms around her grandmother. Shree had been staying in her room since her mom got home from work. They had yet to talk about the morning outburst, and with Grandma here, they never would. So Shree practically flaunted her affection for her grandmother as refuge from and victory over her mother.

"I just got on a plane this morning because it had simply been too long since I had seen my beautiful *eynikl.* You have grown so much. Just look at you, Riley." Her grandma never liked the name Shree and refused to use it. Shree never thought about why, but her gramma was the only one who ever called her Riley. In her mind, it was simply affection.

Shree and her grandmother continued catching up, while Rebecca was happy to fade into the background. She called Jimmy, who promised to come over later. She started making dinner, pasta and red sauce, with a salad. Eventually, they arrived at the dinner table, and Ruth turned some of her attention on her daughter. "Don't you have any dressing for the salad? This is just a bowl of lettuce," followed by, "I assume you have a bed for me."

"I can give you my bed. I'll bunk with Shree. How long are you here for?"

"Don't worry, it will just be the one night. I booked a room at the Regency downtown, but they made a mistake on the dates."

"You don't have to pay for a hotel. We can put you up. I just wanted to know how long we'll have the pleasure of your company. I know Shree has missed her *Bubbie*. I've missed you too," she added awkwardly. "You know, Shree had a great year in school. She won an award for a story she wrote. Shree, go get the story to show your grandmother." Shree ran off to look for it.

"I hear that Anthony has been writing you. I thought you were done with him." Grandma said this quietly so that Shree couldn't hear. But she said it in such a condemning tone that Rebecca could hear the message loud and clear.

"We can talk later, mother." Rebecca preferred that they never talk about Anthony again. She knew all her mother's thoughts on her ex-husband already.

Shree returned with her story. It was about a boat caught in a storm. The boat capsized in a horrible tragedy, but when the story ended, the boat turned out to be made of paper, and the tragedy was all in the imagination of a little girl. Shree had been given a certificate at the end-of-year school assembly. Her grandma layered on the praise and took a photo of her with the certificate and the story.

Soon Jimmy arrived, and Rebecca could fall further into the background, which was just what she wanted. Jimmy didn't leave till an hour past Shree's bedtime. And by then their mother was so exhausted from jet lag that Rebecca was confident she was off the hook.

"So has he been writing to you again? Are you letting him back into your life? I knew he was trouble from the first time I saw him." Clearly, Ruth felt energized by this most recent chance to tell her daughter exactly how she was ruining her life. Sleep would wait.

"No Mom, I am not letting him back in my life. I have legal custody of Shree, and we left Boston because he lives there."

"He was trouble back when you were in high school, and he's trouble still. His hippy anarchist ways. The drugs. I told your father he was going to impregnate you, and sure enough. Before you even graduated high school, you had a baby on the way. It just killed your father to see you like that. I thank God that you finally threw him out. I don't know why it took you so long to see it. Can you imagine the damage he would do if he were raising Riley?"

"Well he isn't, so you don't have to worry about that." Rebecca felt trapped under the same old conversation. Her mother was wrong in so many ways, but she was right in enough of them that Rebecca had no grounds to say anything. Besides, if she did say anything, this conversation, no this pummeling, would last another two hours. So she tried to say as little as possible. She just did her best to oil the path for her mother to speak her mind. Because Mother was gonna speak it. And Rebecca couldn't help noticing a new addition to the routine. Now she was blamed for Dad's passing. That was rich. Dad drove drunk into that lake while she was at college, and Shree was a toddler. It wasn't Rebecca getting pregnant that drove Dad to drink. We all know why he drank.

"Do you really think Houston is the right place to raise Riley? I hear the schools are atrocious." Rebecca was relieved that her mother had left her high school failures behind.

"This is Clear Lake City, Mom. We're right next to NASA. You can't throw a rock without hitting an engineer or a rocket scientist. The schools are some of the best in the state."

"The state of Texas, exactly."

"Mom, you're being prejudiced. There are a lot of smart people around here. It is a great place for kids to grow up."

"I heard a story on NPR about the teen suicide rate here."

"Yes, mother, all the kids are jumping out of the one-story buildings around here. It's practically raining depressed teenagers."

"Don't be sarcastic, Rebecca. I'm just wondering if you thought things through when you moved here."

"I did consider that Jimmy was here. I thought it would be nice for Shree to have family nearby." Rebecca instantly regretted saying that, as she suspected her mom was thinking about moving here too. "But I'm certainly not tied to this place. We will see in a few years."

"Your daughter needs a stable home. Speaking of that, is there anyone new in your life?"

Rebecca cringed. Her mom thought that she needed to remarry, that raising Shree by herself was a bad idea. "No Mother, there is no one like that. I'm not interested in anything like that at this time." Rebecca wasn't just saying that to escape her mother. Perhaps it was exhaustion after her marriage to Tony, but she couldn't imagine adding anyone else to their lives. Rebecca and Shree. In her mind, that was all that they needed.

"Well you're not getting any younger."

At that, Rebecca pointedly got up. "I have to get up early for work tomorrow. Do you need anything to make yourself comfortable? There are towels in the closet next to the bathroom." Rebecca showed her mom to her own bedroom, got a spare blanket, said good night, and went into Shree's room to sleep.

18. Tides of Chaos

August 12th, 13th

Just the storm I needed, Rebecca had thought when she looked at the wilting flowers on a late summer's eve. She knew Anthony was back in town as soon as she saw them. They were jasmine. She had told him in high school that she loved jasmine tea, and he had brought her jasmine flowers on special occasions ever since. In two days it would be their wedding anniversary, she realized, as she bent down to pick up the plastic cup of flowers. For a brief instant, she felt wistful. But the sentiment was soon overwhelmed by dread.

First Mother shows up out of the blue. Then Anthony returns with his chaos to prove Mom right. Hopefully I can keep her in the dark about this latest appearance. The more immediate concern is Shree. Had she seen him leave the flowers? Anthony had promised to stay away from Shree. *Has he broken his word? Did he descend upon Shree like a ghost?* Rebecca wasn't sure she would be able to keep their little ship of normalcy afloat.

Shree reported that she knew nothing about the flowers, and offered no hint that she'd seen her father. When chocolates and a letter showed up the next day, Shree again professed having seen no one. Rebecca made up a story that someone she met at work was her admirer, and took the letter into her room to read. Inside the plain white envelope, in his almost unreadable scrawl, Anthony was both pleading to see her and threatening that forces beyond their control were driving them together. He wrote of a grand test that was playing out now, and she needed to be open to the possibilities, both grand and dark. Rebecca wanted to call the police. She wanted to take Shree and leave that moment. Something bad was brewing in that man, and Rebecca and Shree were right in his path.

An invitation from her mother offered an unexpected lifeline. That evening, she offered to take her granddaughter into the city on Friday. They would do some shopping in a fancy department store, and attend the symphony that night. Shree would spend the night in the Regency downtown, then go to the Museum of Fine Art on Saturday morning. Rebecca and Jimmy would meet them for lunch before Ruth caught her flight back to Boston. With Shree out of the house, Rebecca would have a chance to plan their escape. Perhaps they could leave town. She had a week of vacation time accrued. Maybe Jimmy could talk to Anthony and convince him to return to Boston. If not... Rebecca didn't want to think about that yet.

~ ~ ~

Ruth had hoped her daughter would take the day off from work and join them. The plans to educate her granddaughter about art were meant to be a lesson for her daughter as well... in the importance of properly educating a child. She also hoped for more time with her daughter before she returned home. Unaware of Rebecca's real concern, Ruth assumed that Rebecca just wanted to skip spending time with her. Unfortunately, instead of being the teacher, Ruth now contemplated being the one taught a lesson. How was she supposed to entertain an eleven-year-old girl for a day and a half? If only it were ballet season. If only she had gotten tickets to a play. Instead, they would be hearing Mahler. Even she found Mahler boring. And what was she supposed to feed an eleven-year-old? Hot dogs?

August 14th

Mr. Spruill, a nervous man, was hesitant to let her take vacation on such short notice. So Rebecca told him about her ex-husband, about his mental illness, his sudden appearance, his frightening letter, and how she feared what he might do. Mr. Spruill became more sympathetic. Still, the soonest he could offer was Wednesday for starting her leave.

During lunch, she went to the police station. Across an impersonal desk in a busy room, she told Officer Beauregard about her ex-husband: the mental health problems, the restraining order, her move from Boston, his sudden arrival, and the fact that he had just left a threatening letter at her door. She pulled out the letter, but when she tried to point out the threatening words, she realized that the officer did not read them in the same light. He looked imposing as he told her that there was very little that the police department could do. The restraining order was issued in Boston and had already expired. She could seek a new one in Texas, but from his perspective, no crime had been committed, nor even clearly threatened. He suggested that she might stay with a relative for a few days if she felt frightened of her ex-husband. He also suggested that the best way to persuade her ex-husband to move on would be if she had a new man in her life. Rebecca left the precinct office feeling powerless and offended.

As she was leaving work, Mr. Spruill, with an uncharacteristically calm air, again called her into his office and closed the door. The thought leapt into her head that he was about to fire her. Instead, he handed her a gun. Rebecca was horrified, but she tried hard to not visibly react. He insisted she take it. "You will sleep better at night knowing you have this to protect you and your little girl." Mr. Spruill had always seemed a gentle, religious man, but clearly Rebecca had no idea what went on in his head. Not wanting to question him, she took the gun. She had never held a gun in her life. He showed her the safety, told her how to use it, and stressed that just showing it would solve most problems. "You have a right to use it to defend yourself in your own home," he said with an air of certainty. She carefully put it into the inside pocket of her bag. She had no intention of touching it again. She left the office more worried than ever.

She felt like the whole week, she had been sliding inescapably towards disaster. With each little step, from her daughter calling her the 'B' word, her mother's digs, Tony's threats, right up to her boss handing her a gun, Rebecca felt less and less in control of her life. She feared that it was beyond her abilities to reclaim the peaceful world that she and her daughter deserved. Unavoidably, chaos was taking her down.

19. Crazy Little Thing

August 11th

Shree's sobs took a long time to subside. She had actually confronted her mom! There was no undoing the fight. Couldn't unsay *that*. But her mom had been horrible. To her dad, to herself, and now even to Wendy. As if in sympathy, a summer rain tapped on the window until it drowned out the sound of her crying. Eventually though, she drifted deep into the morning and fell asleep. Almost two hours passed before she felt herself emerging at the far end of the recent storm. The sun by now had intruded past her curtains and pried its way through her eyelids. She sat up and wondered what she would do now. She was not allowed to leave the house and had been told to clean. Typical. She was just her mom's servant, her prisoner slave, she thought. She wanted to get on her bike and ride away forever. He said he'd come back for her. When? There were only three weeks of summer left. Why hadn't she left when she had the chance? She had only needed to open the latch!

She poured a fresh bowl of puffed wheat and sat on the couch in the living room to watch TV. Mom never let her eat in the living room. She was happy to disobey. Nevertheless, she was determined not to spill a drop. Puffs of wheat were escaping over the brim. She popped them into her mouth by ones and twos. She heard a car pull into the driveway, and she quickly turned off the TV and moved to the kitchen table, not to get caught. But instead of her mom's entrance, she heard a knock at the door. She kept quiet, hoping that whoever was there would soon go away. But the knock became a playful tapping. She knew it wasn't Wendy. Wendy would come around to the back door. Could it be…?

"Roly Poly? Roly Poly, are you homey? Can Shree come out and play-ay?"

Shree ran to the door, flung it open, and buried herself in her dad's arms. "Daddy you came for me! Oh Dad! I'm so glad you're here!" The two of them rocked in their embrace until they almost fell over.

"I've missed you so much, sweetie. My how you've grown!" Tony said this while holding her off the ground.

"Oh Dad, I haven't grown," Shree responded, laughing. "Maybe you've grown!"

"I have grown, Shree! I have. Are you ready to be a family again?"

"Yes! Yes! Daddy, take me to Boston and we'll be a family."

"Well that depends on your mom, where we live. I like Boston, but your mom is making a life here."

"She can have her life! She doesn't want our family. We should leave without her."

These words were not entirely unwelcome to Anthony. He worried that Rebecca was not ready to accept him into her life. But he had returned to Houston to resolve their future one way or another. Still, he hoped for the best of all outcomes. "Shree, your mother must be given a chance. We'll have to see what she wants. But I'm here for you, and things are going to be so much better from now on. I'm not going away again. If we leave, we'll leave together."

Even though these were words that Shree had been dreaming of all summer, she was startled to actually hear them. "Oh Dad, don't joke. Are you really staying? Can we really live together?"

"Yes it's true, sunshine of my life. One way or the other, we're going to be together."

"Are you going to live here in this house?" Shree wanted to believe what her dad was saying. But she remembered her mom threatening to call the police. "Will they let you?"

Anthony noted the 'they', but didn't know if it was significant. Yet he understood that Shree felt her mom was the obstacle. "Shree, I'm here in Houston. I am not leaving Houston without you. I know your mom may not be ready for me to live with you two, however. But we are going to work it out somehow."

"Mom is such a monster. You know she's grounded me! Just because I defended my best friend, who she insulted. We should leave Mom. She only wants me here as her prisoner! Her slave! I'm supposed to clean the whole house while she's at work." Anthony let Shree continue to complain about her mom without interruption. "She's been tearing your letters up. Your beautiful letters! And she tears them up and throws them in the garbage. We need to leave her behind and go! She's never gonna be nice to us. She is horrible. Please let's just leave."

"Now take a breath, Shree. I'm not sure what your mom is thinking, but we will give her a chance. We have to hope that she'll choose our family, Shree. The best things sometimes take patience, but we'll let her decide. It's important. We can't be happy if we leave her behind without trying. She deserves it. We deserve it. I see you're upset with her right now. I'm a little upset too. But… but if we're going to be a family, we must do this right. Can you understand that, Shree?"

Shree didn't understand it. Her mom had *had* all sorts of chances. But she looked into her dad's eyes as he sat on the front step beside her. He looked so kind and so loving and so expectant that she would understand. "Yes, Daddy, we can do it the right way."

And now Anthony felt comfortable that his plan might actually work. "Okay Shree, this is what we're going to do. We're giving your mom a week. You need to be on your best behavior. You need to keep our plans a secret. Don't let her know I was ever here. Okay?" Shree nodded. "Okay. You be on your best behavior, and I'll try to talk some sense into your mother. One week. If by Monday… if she can't accept us as a family, then we can leave without her." There, he had said it. The plan was out there. It was the grand test that the universe would give Rebecca. Either Rebecca would recognize the family and let him into their lives. Or Shree would come with him, and Rebecca would know what it's like. Would understand what he felt. It was a test for him, as well. The universe was asking what he was willing to do to bring them together again. It was even a test for Shree. Could she keep the secret? Would she be ready to go in a week? The plan was in motion, and the universe would have its way with them. One way or another. "What do you think about that plan, Shree?"

Shree was again startled that her dreams were becoming real, tangible things. Here was a plan. Though she wanted to leave immediately, Shree knew that was crazy. What would they do, just drive away? "Okay Dad. One week."

"Promise me that you won't tell her a thing!"

"I wouldn't dream of it."

"And promise me that you'll be good, do the cleaning or whatever. Just be the good kid that you are."

"Okay, I'll try." Shree felt relieved. She would vacuum the house. She was probably going to anyway. And when her mom came home and yelled at her, she would be able to wait it out. One week.

"And I may not see you much before then, because I need to do what your mom wants. She doesn't want me seeing you yet, so I can't risk her catching us."

"If you come by my swim practice, she's never there," Shree said helpfully. "It's at the rec center and ends at 8:30, Monday through Friday. Except today. There's a swim meet at 4 pm every Tuesday."

"You're swimming! That sounds like fun."

"All we ever do is laps. I hate it."

"And the meet? Is it a big thing? Will your mom be there to watch you?"

"She always has work."

"I may see you there, but if not, definitely by next Monday. I promise we'll be back together soon." Tony leaned over, hugged his daughter tightly, and told her he loved her more than anything in the world. He stood up, shared with her a look of happy conspiracy, walked to his car, smiled one last time, then drove off.

Shree floated back inside the house, got out the vacuum cleaner, and pranced in its roar. A radio song was stuck in her head, and she found herself treating the vacuum as her air guitar/ microphone. "This thing, called love. I just can't handle it."

20. Garbage Disposal

August 6th

It was six twenty-seven when Shree rolled onto Sharon's street, shaking just a little. The moving van stood imposing in its silence on the empty street. Even the birds were hushed as Shree climbed off her bike and leaned it against a neighbor's hedge. The overstuffed mass of her lopsided backpack swung her off balance as she slowly stepped up to the back of the truck.

All of the day before, she had been excited, picturing the moving van that had triggered her dream, while packing and repacking for the journey ahead. Peanut butter and jam, bread, water, flashlight, garbage bags, toilet paper. She remembered the van with the 'Vacationland' plate, beckoning, with its couch, refrigerator, boxes with blankets, and a reading lamp. There had even been a ramp that she could have wheeled her bike up. She would have what she needed. But when it was time to sleep that night, darker questions peeled a bit of her dream away.

Rushing through breakfast, she was out the door before her mother had woken. The ride over, milk and cereal arguing with her insides, took less time than she remembered. And now, confronted with the closed back end of Sharon G's moving van, milk leapt up her throat. A desperate bid to escape. Studying the door, she guessed how the latch worked. Reaching up to the handle, she understood she would have to climb up.

A flash of strange moving men invaded her thoughts. She

almost physically shoved them back, along with the curdling milk and shredded wheat. Instead, she tried picturing Daddy's surprised smile when she appeared at his door. Going for donuts and hot chocolate while they made plans for the rest of summer. But the thought of donuts caused the milk to surge again. Sleeping in her old room with the stars on the ceiling. Locked in a van in the dark, in the heat. Talking in silly voices with Dad for a whole day. She would take him to her old school, and he would sign her up for sixth grade.

Suddenly a noise. The movers?! Only a neighbor putting out his garbage can. He didn't even notice her. But panic had already taken hold. It chased her back to her bike. She flew to her own neighborhood. Familiar streets. Late, she arrived at the swimming pool, where she was supposed to be.

~ ~ ~

Wendy hadn't yet told her parents the names of Max's friends, when Max was arrested. He had been sleeping in Luis's grandmother's car, who called the police. He was arraigned on auto and bike theft, as well as possession of a controlled substance, driving without a license, and reckless endangerment. Wendy's parents hired a lawyer and got the auto theft charge dropped.

August 10th and 11th

The story appeared in the local news, and even though Max's name wasn't mentioned, somehow Shree's mom guessed that it was Wendy's family. This news, once confirmed by Shree, led to an anxious night for Rebecca. Wendy seemed like a good kid, but her brother was dangerous. Rebecca wondered what kind of parents they had and what kind of lifestyle Shree was being exposed to.

"I don't want you going over to Wendy's house anymore." Rebecca announced this in the morning with a confident tone, even though she wasn't at all sure she should say anything.

"What? But why? Wendy's my best friend," Shree responded, practically spilling her cereal. Immediately she knew her mother was being the same evil beast that was keeping her father away.

Her mother continued, "Well, it's probably not a good time. They have family tensions and need some time to themselves." While this was a reason Shree should stay away, Rebecca knew in her heart that she didn't want her eleven-year-old girl anywhere near Wendy's older brother. She also darkly imagined the parents as poor trailer trash, people who dropped out of school, couldn't hold jobs, maybe even shot up heroin. While she knew her fears weren't rational, her sleep-deprived brain kept throwing the worst sort of thoughts in front of her. No, Wendy was nice, her parents were probably nice, she told herself. But just to be safe, Shree must stay away.

"That's so unfair. Wendy and I play games in her room. They're nice to me." Shree lied. She wasn't even sure Wendy's parents knew who she was. They rarely spent time at Wendy's house. But Shree was deeply offended that her mom would try to restrict her. "Why don't you like Wendy?!" Shree's anger boiled. What was the monster doing? Insulting her best friend?! Like she insulted Dad?!

"Shree calm down. No one is saying anything against Wendy."

"You don't want me seeing her anymore. You want to keep me from my only friend!"

"Young lady, that's enough! I am doing no such thing. Wendy's fine. It's her family that I'm...," Rebecca stopped herself. "It's her family that probably needs some time to themselves."

"Why are you so mean to me! You are such a bitch!" Shree knocked her chair over as she fled the kitchen table and flew into her room in tears, slamming the door behind her.

Rebecca wanted to strangle her daughter at that moment, but also felt embarrassed that she hadn't handled the conversation any better. She found herself yelling, "You're grounded! Do not leave except for swimming. And I expect the whole house vacuumed when I get home." She was startled that those words came out of her mouth. Almost the exact same words had been yelled at her by her own mother. She picked up Shree's chair, poured her cereal down the garbage disposal, and then steadied herself on the counter. She felt dizzy. She had only been worried, and somehow she wound up grounding her child and giving her chores. Maybe her own mother had just been worried too.

Unfortunately, she was going to be late for work. There was no time to turn this mess around and have a hallmark moment with her daughter. She tried to think of what she could say to Shree right then, but her daughter had called her the 'B' word, and she couldn't *not* punish her. Rebecca resolved to just leave for work and try to make peace when she got home. She thought that time was probably what they both needed. As she left, she walked by her daughter's room and heard crying. It was both painful to hear and somehow comforting. Shree was still the little girl, and Rebecca was only trying to protect her.

21. Who Do You Think You Are?

August 14th

"You're such an idiot!" Sirrus beamed with the confidence her insult would be taken as affection.

"Me? What did I do now?" Jim got out of the way as Sirrus pushed past and plopped onto his bed. He tried to suppress his smile, given she had just called him an idiot, but his delight was hard to hide.

"You and your determinism BS. You can't possibly believe it," she said with a vicious smile in her eyes that he would remember for a long time.

"Why can't I? Of course I believe in determinism. I am a scientist," he replied as if that connection was self-evident.

"You had me stumped for a while. Obviously determinism is too simplistic, but I couldn't figure out how to explain why you're wrong. At first, I thought of Dostoevsky's Notes from the Underground. We prove our 'will' by the lengths we go to humiliate ourselves, we swear two plus two does not equal four, anything to maintain our sense of dignity, our free will." Sirrus was not being very clear about where she was heading. "But then I realized that *you* are proving Dostoevsky's point. And I will have to show you two plus two does indeed equal four. Your lack of free will is a sick joke you are telling yourself, and it has dangerous consequences. You need the three-step treatment. Are you ready to be cured?" Sirrus had settled in and knew exactly where she was going. It seems she had plotted out her intervention.

"Do I have a choice?" Jim asked with a sly smile.

"In this case, no," Sirrus replied with her own smile to reward his choice of words. "Step one. There may be determinism, but there's no *pre*-determinism. Your billiard ball universe is far too simple. The whole universe is staggeringly complex. The amount of math needed to model a single hydrogen atom is huge. But you suggest that if we knew where every particle is at a given moment in time and where it is heading, then we could calculate the universe at any point in the future. That would take the most powerful computer imaginable. That would take a computer bigger than the size of the universe. And that computer would take way longer to come up with an answer for the changes between time A and time B than the actual time between them.

"Think of the complexity of just one brain. Billions of neurons, each made up of trillions upon trillions of atoms in all sorts of combinations and interactions. How are you going to calculate, with certainty, what that brain will do next? Now think of trillions of living beings on this one planet among uncountable planets in uncountable galaxies. And that isn't even bringing in quantum mechanics, which says your billiard balls are predictable in aggregate but not individually. Statistically predicting is not the same as knowing. And it isn't as if you can isolate one brain or even one galaxy. No, James, we cannot possibly know exactly what is going to happen until it does. Each moment, tied to the past, is created in its present. We cannot be predetermined."

"Hmmm. I'm not sure I agree absolutely. But I will grant that there is no realistic way for us humans to ever know exactly what will happen until it does. But we can certainly estimate. We manage to play catch, after all." Jim was enjoying the show, with Sirrus overflowing to explain her ideas. But he did fear that he would be tricked into giving up his own.

"Okay, James, very good. That leads directly to step two!" She took a deep breath before charging on. "Perception is imperfect. We must make guesses… or theories. We look at a tree, recognize its species, notice if it is young or old, dry or sick, or thriving. But there is so much more to that tree than we see. We cannot put the whole tree inside our brains to truly know it. It's history, it's chemistry, the pH, or electric potential, or the number of chloroplasts in each of its cells. Does it sense the sun? Does it feel the saw? Communicate with its neighbors? There are so many things we don't know but could, and so many more that we could never possibly know. And we don't have time to know that one tree, because there is a bush over there, and some ants and a cloud and a snake and, well… we have to make shortcuts. We package up the perceptions as a tree. Think about the perceptions themselves! We see light reflected from the tree. Our eyes take in a few million photons, which strafe across our cones as we walk past, and in an instant, that blur of color and shape is processed into our perception of a tree. It isn't a tree; it is a quick guess we make, sculpting the flash of data into something that resembles our previously assembled model of what a tree is. All done mysteriously in the neuronal tangles of our brain. We have somewhere to go, so that quick assessment, 'tree', will do. Our brain has not come in contact with the tree, but we will have a theory about what its trunk feels like. All we got is some photons, but we may guess that apples will ripen in summer. We have never seen that tree burning, or made into cabinets, or paper, yet we can easily theorize that those things could happen. And yet, it is possible we only saw an image of a tree plastered on the side of a bus. Or only glanced at a realistic painting. Perhaps we didn't see a tree at all, but someone suggested a tree was on the left, and we didn't actually look. The tree in our brain forms of nothing more than faces appearing in the clouds."

"I'm not sure where you're going."

"Where I'm going is that our minds, which you believe are 'determined' by all the atoms in the universe, are in fact somewhat removed from the rest of the universe. And we can never actually perceive anything in full detail. So our brains are theory makers. We build models of things from imperfect and incomplete information. Our whole understanding of our world is just all the models our brain has made of the world. We think we know. We believe our models to be the true world. And we act on these models. We jump when our fear tells us a snake is striking, though we only glimpsed a rubber toy. We decide to make cabinets based upon a model of what we can do with wood, and theorize we can get wood by cutting down the tree. We started with the perception of photons across our retina, and that 'cause' led to the 'effect'… cabinets?! It may be a billiard ball universe, but our models lead to some really wild bank shots!" Sirrus was particularly pleased with that line, but Jim didn't even notice.

"Okay, the path to making cabinets out of a tree is clearly complicated," Jim responded. "But it isn't just a few photons of perception. It is a lifetime of photons sculpting the brain. We learned about carpentry by reading books, talking with carpenters, seeing cabinets being made. We acquire tools and need someplace to store them. The cabinets were made from a huge number of perceptions over the course of our lives," Jim asserted, feeling sure he had chipped away at her point.

"Indeed, my dear James, I think you're getting it!" Sirrus looked terribly pleased with herself, but Jim only felt like he was falling into her trap. "Are you ready for the third step?" He wanted to say no, but he just nodded for her to continue. "Step three. Theory of Self. What are our causes, and who do you think you are?" Jim knew it was a rhetorical question, but he almost jumped in to answer. Sirrus held up her finger.

"Because we cannot know, we make theories. And unlike everything else in your billiard ball universe, this collection of billiard balls that is us, has an interest in staying together. Non-living things have no interest in their future form. But we have a fundamental interest in staying alive. We value some outcomes over others. We want food and companionship and warmth and love. And above all, we want to *not* die. But fundamentally, we are operating on incomplete *and* inconsistent information. You read Godel, Escher, Bach. So what do we do? We build multiple models! We imagine an apple tree as a food source, firewood, or cabinets. A snake means a poisoned death, a campfire stew, a doctoral dissertation, or a pair of boots. The future is very important to us, and our multiple theories give us choices.

"But while we are theorizing about trees and snakes, we are spending a lifetime theorizing about ourselves. And we strongly believe we can do things. We know we can ride a bike, write an essay, find beauty in a flower. So every time we're confronted with a decision, we don't just think of the options, we think about what's best for *us*. The snake stew would feed us for a day, but might we feel guilty if we kill it? I want to know more about snakes, but how much time do I want to spend studying them? Would my children prefer a treehouse or cabinets? All these decisions and someone has to make them. Of course I will make the decisions, but I am just an elaborate theory. Our causes are not just simple billiard ball reactions but self-invented motivations. Unlike billiard balls, we value where we are going and bend forces to help us get there. Causes from the future. Causes coming *after* effects. I believe I can become an artist like Van Gogh, and so bend my life to painting, spend years in art school. Of course, I have no actual talent, and to everyone else, my paintings are worthless."

"I'm sure you're not that bad."

"Shush! I never painted in my life," Sirrus snapped, not

wanting to get distracted. "What I'm saying…"

"Yes, what are you saying?" Jim was pretty sure he understood, but wanted to encourage her to finish.

"What I am saying is that the universe is being born in each moment, that no one can know before it happens, we are insulated from reality, due to our inability to actually know anything beyond our flawed perceptions. We make a bundle of theories about all of it, and we ourselves are an elaborate self-built theory. And in the moment, the causes of our actions, our decisions, are very real inside ourselves, but somewhat removed from reality. We act! We decide! No one can know what we will do. We don't know what we will do ourselves most of the time. But if I want to kiss you, I have decided that. It isn't pre-determined. It isn't destiny. It's me, in the moment."

This last example of a decision threw Jim for a loop. Did she really say she wanted to kiss him? He had been ready with a response, but now he was tongue-tied and turning red. "Well, I, uh…"

"What's the matter? Predestination got your tongue?" Sirrus was anxious to rush past the awkward moment. She was surprised herself at the kissing example. It came out of nowhere. But now that it was out, she recognized its source. He was so earnestly listening to her, his sweet eyes in rapt attention, his lips so soft. She pulled herself together. "So do you get it?"

"First, I want to point out that your theory of free will seems to depend on our own self-delusion. A theory of ourselves that is inherently inaccurate." Jim thought this description would take the air out of Sirrus's argument.

"Yes, exactly! You may think this implies our free will itself is a delusion, but not necessarily. Instead, the more delusional someone is, the more obvious it is that our choices are not born in reality, but in our minds." Not quite satisfied, Sirrus added, "That said, our theory of self doesn't have to be bonkers. We still have free will, simply by virtue of acting on our own motivations, making choices that we think are best for us."

"Okay, I agree with most of what you say. Completely agree. But that doesn't at all negate that everything is a chain of cause and effect. Your model of you is determined by all of your experiences, which were determined by the billiard ball universe. All your decisions are still determined by all the causes that went into them."

Sirrus paused for a moment, not sure where to go next. Then rushed on. "Okay, perhaps we need a fourth step. Are you saying that all our decisions could occur without our consciousness?"

"Essentially," Jim sensed that he tripped.

"But the determinants, the causes, are based upon our models, our conscious understanding of the world. Our models. What reason would there be to have consciousness if it isn't needed?"

"Models can be unconscious. There is no reason we are conscious; we just are."

"So we are just along for the ride? We could sleepwalk through life and be just as successful, because the biochemistry would still work?" Sirrus was playing with James like a cat plays with a naive mouse.

"How do we know anyone is actually conscious? We can't know." Jim knew he was falling, but he clung to his familiar ideas.

"Well you know you're conscious. I know I am conscious. That is enough to prove to me that consciousness exists. And my consciousness is very elaborate. All my memories. How chocolate chip ice cream tasted the summer I turned six. How the rain felt on my eighth-grade camping trip. What my kindergarten teacher said about the Easter Bunny. I bet consciousness is a big expense for evolution. If it is just smoke, why did it evolve? Why did it evolve so elaborately? Do you really want to stick with your answer that consciousness is just along for the ride?"

Sirrus had spoken his language, evolution. "Okay sure, consciousness is the product of evolution. And it must require a lot of energy, use a lot of the body's resources, so it is probably useful," Jim affirmed. "It is more than just a funny nose on a monkey." They both smiled at his weird comparison.

"Okay. Well a very important part of my consciousness is my belief that I can make decisions. I can be obsessed with sorting through my various models in the struggle to make decisions. Why would consciousness evolve with this elaborate sense of the importance of making the right decision, if the decision is determined without me? Perhaps it is because there is a *right* decision to make. There is a value to deciding well, and that value is my own survival. I have evolved as if free will, my ability to decide, is important." She then held up her finger as if to announce she was making her most important point. "You may not believe in free will, but *evolution sure seems to*." With that, Sirrus felt like the canary that caged the cat.

Jim was flustered. He wasn't sure if he was ready to abandon allegiance to his determinism philosophy. But he couldn't think of what arguments he had at hand to defend it against evolution. "Well done, Sirrus, truly well done. I'm gonna have to think about this for a while." He really did feel like an idiot. She had given him some things to think over. At the top of the list was her viciously smiling eyes and that kiss comment.

"Okay, James, you know where to find me when you're ready to submit to my free will. She took his hand, and for a moment he thought she would kiss it. She caressed it between her thumb and fingers, closed her eyes slowly like a cat, then pranced out of his room without another word. He fell back on his bed, intoxicated with thoughts of her. Unfortunately, within a minute, his sister was at his door.

22. Her Problem

August 14th

"Did you enjoy the concert, Riley?" Ruth was struggling to find anything in her memory of the concert they had just left that she could talk about with her granddaughter. The music had wafted over Ruth, and while she did enjoy it, she had been in a reflective state during the entirety of Mahler's Fifth Symphony. By the end of it, she needed to will herself awake, stifling yawn after yawn.

The frantic waves of brass near the beginning found her thinking about her children. *Their lives are entirely without me now. Jim is so excited about his studies. Such a long way from the little boy I taught how to sew. Remember how proud he was when I taught him to play the Ode to Joy melody on piano.* She recalled family games of Monopoly, how he hated it when he lost. *Nathan, always the banker, slipped him extra money so that he could buy Tennessee Avenue.* The music now irritated her, demanding attention with its quick changes, when she was absorbed in her own thoughts. She had always hoped Jimmy would become a writer. *He wrote the cleverest stories. His third-grade teacher said he had a real flair. But he's been pulled in another direction. Why hadn't he come to the symphony tonight? We used to go to all the performances together when he was younger.* Ruth didn't understand his interests now. When he got into the whole biology thing, she thought he'd become a doctor, like his cousin, Albert. *Albert just got engaged to someone from his office. Wish*

Jim could meet a nice girl, but he spends all his time in that lab of his. Never going to meet a nice girl in a lab. Ruth tried to bar from her thoughts an unwelcome intruder. Maybe her son didn't like girls. *Can't be. But he's never had a girlfriend as far as I know. He's always had crushes, though. A mother knows. He had been smitten with that girl in the tenth grade. Julia? Thought at the time that Julia wasn't good enough for my brilliant little boy. Whatever happened to her, I wonder.* A French horn, then an oboe, pulled her deeply into herself. Her eyes were closed, and she imagined her lovely five-year-old boy playing in the yard during the Scherzo. She felt her head sagging, and sleep would feel so good at that moment. But a rapid crescendo and sudden end of the movement jarred her back to this world of uncomfortable chairs and too much perfume.

A deep sadness at the beginning of the next movement filled her with thoughts of her daughter. Rebecca would never reach her potential. *She was always daddy's girl when she was young.* Ruth had felt excluded from their games and jokes. *But somebody had to raise her; it couldn't be all play. Who potty-trained her? Who got her to clean her room, taught her to do her own laundry? How to cook? Make a budget? Nathan was too busy for things like that. And later she would talk back, say the ugliest things to us. And Nathan would just laugh it off as if it were a joke. She needed to show us respect. It was the seventh grade when she got in with those bad kids in school. I had wanted to transfer her to a religious school, but Nathan wouldn't hear of it. Said it was too expensive and that her friends weren't so bad. Nathan didn't have anything to say, though, when I found marijuana in Rebecca's room. I was at wits' end trying to deal with that child. Sneaking out. Getting a call at two in the morning from the police. And then the pregnancy!*

Why hadn't the damn child gotten rid of it? Ruth shifted uncomfortably, realizing that her granddaughter was sitting right next to her. *If that poor child could read minds,* Ruth flushed in embarrassment. *A child raising a child.* Rebecca had done what she could under difficult circumstances, Ruth admitted to herself. *She should have left Riley with us.* But that stubborn girl married her Anthony and got family housing near campus. Off they went, Riley in tow. It was surprising that Rebecca even got into college after her disastrous high school years, Ruth recalled. She was well-read, always liked her books. And she almost pulled it off. But then she dropped out. *Well we all lost ground when Nathan passed.* But she should have stuck with college. Riley was so adorable at *his* graduation. And things were coming together. He had a good job, their cute little house. *Then suddenly he's hearing voices or something. Must've been drugs.* Rebecca claims they stopped doing drugs when Riley came along, *but I know her husband must have been doing a lot of spitballs or loopers or whatever it's called.* He just went certifiable. *Lucky he didn't hurt the child.* Ruth had told Rebecca to leave him so many times. Eventually she had no choice. *She should have moved back in then.* But she insisted on the single mom thing. *At least she finally divorced that horrid man.* And got away from him, all the way to Houston. *It's good they're close to Jimmy,* but Ruth rarely got to see them.

And though Ruth hated the idea of leaving Boston, she thought she'd probably put in an offer on that second condo she saw. Her kids didn't seem to need her, but she would find ways to be helpful to them anyway. It was all she had left, really. And again, Mahler's strings were helping to take the floor out from under her. She would move another day; now she felt peace, as her chin found her chest.

She pulled herself back to the surface, certain that no one had noticed. She clenched her teeth as a yawn tried to break free. Finally, the music rose to the farewell crescendo, alerting the somnolent that it was time to clap. Scattered people were standing and loudly clapping, but Ruth wasn't certain that she could make it to her feet. As more people stood, she realized that Riley was standing too, clapping exuberantly.

~ ~ ~

Shree had been in a lousy mood for much of the day. She didn't much want anything during the shopping trip. Her grandmother had bought her two dresses that she didn't know when she would ever wear. Okay, one of them she would wear that night to the symphony. She was not looking forward to the symphony because her mom had warned her it might last four hours and that she had to sit still and be on her best behavior the whole time. No, she wasn't looking forward to the symphony.

At dinner, she had talked with her grandmother about school. Gramma asked her about boys, which was totally uncomfortable. She also asked a lot of questions about her mom and whether she had any man friends. At first Shree said no. But then she made up a fake boyfriend for her mom. He was a real tall Texan named Tex who rode a white horse. He taught them lassoing and cow shoeing. And took them in his helicopter every weekend to his half-acre cattle ranch in the Adirondacks. Gramma finally caught on, but it wasn't the helicopter or the shoeing that clued her in to the ruse. It was the Adirondacks for some reason.

At the symphony, Shree thought the first piece was pleasant, and was going to ask why no one clapped. Gramma just put her finger to her lips. They played a couple more pieces and then everyone clapped. Gramma leaned over to explain that the three pieces were one, called 'Mozart Concerto'. Next was some weird noise that didn't sound like music at all. Shree thought it was funny how all the people were listening calmly to the orchestra trying to offend them with what sounded like a broken bicycle being thrown into a garbage truck, which then crushed it till you could hear the tires pop. At the end, everyone clapped like that racket was the best music they ever heard. She was sure it was composed as a joke and somehow only she had figured it out.

Then the main symphony started with just a single instrument. Shree was pulled in and almost resented the rest of the orchestra when they joined in. The music drew her into her own thoughts. She was still in a bad mood, but this was the first time she thought about why. She realized it was her fight with Wendy that morning. After her mom left for work and before Gramma showed up, Wendy had come over. She had been so excited to tell Wendy that Dad showed up.

"I hope you have a good life back in Boston," Wendy had said with very little sincerity.

"Well you sure sound happy for me! What's your problem?" Shree was offended. "You know I've been waiting for my dad to come back, and now it's happening."

"Sure Shree, you're getting your dream come true. We're all happy for you."

"Well you sound like you're mad at me. I thought you wanted me to get to live with my dad. Didn't you?"

Wendy had to look away. "Sure, I'm happy for you, it's just that…" Wendy had paused as if she didn't know what to say.

"Okay, I get it," Shree had said. "You're so caught up in your life, and you don't care about what's happening in mine. All those times I was telling you how my mom is a monster, you were just waiting till you could brag about your miserable brother. I get it. Poor Wendy and her mean brother."

"Shree, you're such a stupid jerk sometimes.' Wendy said it with anger, though tears were filling her eyes.

"Well you're being the stupid jerk right now. I'm not sure I'm even going to miss you."

"Fine Shree, just go. Go to your Boston, or wherever. I don't need you telling me your lame problems anymore. Now you can have your perfect stupid life, and I will be back here with my fighting parents and my brother in jail."

"Yeah, poor Wendy, with ignorant parents and an idiot brother! What's your problem?" When she said this, she had been so angry. Now, when she repeated her own words in her head, she felt embarrassed. And bathed in dramatic music, making turns as quickly and chaotically as she, Shree realized she had been more surprised and hurt than angry. Wendy had always been a good friend. A great friend! What was her problem now? Of course she's had problems with her brother. He was a real, in her thoughts Shree lowered her voice when she said it, 'asshole'. But that's what he was, Shree had seen it herself. And now he was going to jail for it. But why would Wendy be mad at her, even if her home life was horrible? She still didn't understand Wendy. 'What was her problem?' she thought sympathetically. She wished they could have the conversation over again. But Wendy had ridden off on her bike, and Shree couldn't chase after her because her grandmother was coming.

The music had grown sad, and with it, Shree missed her best friend. For the first time, she considered her secret as possibly a bad thing. If her dad took her away, she wouldn't see Wendy anymore. Of course she would go anywhere with her dad, but now she hoped they would stay in Houston. Maybe her mom would let him live with them. She couldn't imagine it, but maybe that was the best thing that could happen, as Dad had said. Shree thought about this long and hard, while the music went from hopeful to sorrowful to playful to…, she didn't quite know what. But she did know that Mom was not going to let Dad live with them. And so it was likely that she would be saying goodbye to her best friend. She felt sick thinking about it. Like something was being pulled out of her stomach. Maybe now she understood what Wendy's problem was. It was her problem too. As the music moved on, a brighter spot impelled her to think of solutions. She must go with Dad, if he takes her. She can't choose Mom. But how could she hold onto Wendy? She felt like they were meant to be best friends for life. If she left, maybe she wouldn't return until they were adults. Maybe they could go to college together. But how would she even know where Wendy was going to college? They could write letters! With that thought, Shree perked up. Of course it wouldn't be the same as living close by, but she had heard of people having lifelong pen pals. Shree and Wendy would write letters to each other all their lives! It would be like having a diary, but much, much better. She couldn't wait to tell Wendy.

As she sat quietly in her seat, she noticed that she was enjoying the music, even if it was very long. It had gone along with her thoughts and helped lead her to a solution. She liked how the tense parts and the sad parts really sounded like what she was feeling. The music had been racing with abandon one moment, then it spilled into a quiet, languorous mood the next. This wasn't one of the simple radio songs she was used to. In one of these quiet moments, she heard her grandmother beside her start to snore. Shree smiled, remembering her mom's lecture on how she should behave. She couldn't wait to write Wendy about it!

"Did you enjoy the concert, Riley?"

"I really did, Gramma!"

23. Weight of Leaves

August 14th

After leaving work, Rebecca got some take-out food and went to a park to try to calm her thoughts. She increasingly felt she had no choice but to move again. She knew the police wouldn't protect her, and she was now a bit leery of her boss. The only person in her life who mattered was Shree, and Shree would be coming with her. But she couldn't afford to move. Who knows how long it would take to get another job? She was not calming down. And like hyenas descending on an injured zebra, the mosquitoes now found her and attacked. Rebecca fled the park in the gathering dusk, forgot where she had parked, then found a ticket beneath her wiper blade. Two large men across the street turned with a jump when they heard her frustrated expletives. She slid behind the steering wheel and let herself cry for just a moment before turning the ignition.

~ ~ ~

Looking for an ally, she found her way to Jimmy's dorm. "I saw Sirrus in the hallway. She told me that I should go easy on you because you had a hard day. What was that about?" Sirrus had been laughing, but Rebecca was so tense she only heard trouble.

Jim laughed. "Oh did she? No, everything's fine. She just proved that I'm an idiot, is all."

"Well we all knew that," Rebecca replied, proving that the

instinct to tease her brother was momentarily stronger than the cloud of worries thundering over her. She looked at Jimmy's tiny room from the doorway, the messy bed, hard wooden chair, and small desk teetering with books, then she proposed that they go for a walk.

"I can't handle them anymore. Either one of them!" She found herself shaking in the warm, humid air. "Mom shows up on my doorstep and practically blames me for Dad's death! The very next day, Anthony turns up with flowers and threatens dark consequences if I don't let him move back in. I just want a normal life for Shree. Is that too much to ask?!" Rebecca was so choked up that she couldn't keep talking.

Jim found his sister's weakness jarring. She was always the grown-up. Always the rock of responsibility, his older sister. Now, seeing her overwhelmed, nearing tears, he realized that he needed to be the grown-up. "Don't worry about Mom, she just says stuff without thinking. I'm sure she doesn't blame you for Dad. We both know he drank because of her." Jim had meant that as a joke, but his sister didn't acknowledge it as such. "I know when she's particularly annoying, and she has been these past couple days, I have to remind myself that she just wants the best for us. Of course she has no idea what that is. She grew up in a different time. So when she tells me I need a wife to look after me, I just try to keep my sense of humor. Maybe she needs a wife!"

Rebecca found Jimmy's words and bad jokes calmed her down. Though he had always been Mom's favorite, even he found her annoying. It was nice to be reminded that she and Jimmy were on the same side when it came to Mom. She would miss her brother if she had to move. Unfortunately, as the problem of Mom receded, the much more ominous problem of Anthony returned to the foreground.

"We'll be leaving town on Wednesday. I can't get off work any sooner. He's going to be a problem. I'm sure he's off his meds and spiraling." Jim looked appropriately concerned. "I'm hoping you'll take Shree Monday and Tuesday. I'm worried what he might do, and I want to keep Shree as far from it as possible." Rebecca was no longer overwhelmed. All she needed was to be reminded that at least one person would try to help. Now she was back to being the older sister. She was a mom.

Jim was relieved at the obvious return of his sister. "I do have work to do in the lab, but I can have her hang out. She might be bored while I'm working, so she should bring a book."

"Thanks Jimmy! Also, when you do see him, you need to convince him to return to Boston. If he doesn't, we're going to have to move again." Saying it aloud felt heavy. They had stopped near a large tree with massive branches. How could the tree carry that much weight, she thought? "We can't live constantly worrying about what Anthony will do. We'll have to leave Houston. I'll call Lydia, his mom, and I'll give you her number too. She may be able to help convince him to return home."

Jim felt the weight of Rebecca's words. Yet there was no time to turn them over in his mind. "Okay, Becca, I'll do all I can. Don't worry. I'm sure he'll return to Boston. No need to worry about uprooting your life again." Jim said these words and meant them. Before, he had been afraid of telling Tony to stay away from his own daughter. Now he felt protective of his sister and niece. Rebecca knew that sending Jimmy to deflect Anthony was like sending a paper tiger to stop a tiger shark. But she was doing all she could. Her defenses were being laid. She returned home feeling, if not the master of her fate, at least determined to weather the storm.

But someone was waiting on her front step.

24. Eating in the Rain

August 15th

Rain was coming in waves. James had circled round the Regency in downtown, expecting his mother and Shree to be waiting in the doorway. With no sight of them, he had to find parking. "Just f'ing great," he hissed as he stepped deep into a gutter stream getting out of the car. He was drenched before he managed to press coins into the meter. Fifteen minutes ought to be enough to walk the three blocks, find his mother, and then walk back. He gripped his flimsy windbreaker and faced the squall, leaping over puddles and balancing above a storm drain, which was at full torrent. When he entered the calm, carpeted lobby, he expected to be yelled at: his shoes emitting puddles, his clothes heavy and clinging, his hair and nose dripping in time. It was Shree who called out. He walked towards them, shivering in the cold, conditioned air.

"You're late! Where's Rebecca?" Ruth Kreisler felt it was disrespectful to keep someone waiting. Her affection for her son was easily forgotten whenever he arrived late.

"She isn't coming. There was a break-in at her house, and she went to the police this morning."

"A break-in? Is she all right?" Ruth stepped to her son, clearly worried. Shree was all ears too, but showed no emotion.

"Oh, yeah, she wasn't there. She was at work. Nothing was taken, but evidently there's a mess she needs to clean up. Looks like some teen vandals." Jim knew the true story, but presented the one his sister had suggested. "Hope you have an alibi, Shree." Jim said this with a big smile on his face to lighten the mood. Shree smiled, but her grandmother was not amused.

"There is no call for joking about such things, young man. So Rebecca isn't hurt? Does she need any help? I can delay my flight." Rebecca had been adamant. Do not let Mom delay her flight.

"No really, Becca is fine. Just a broken window. She doesn't need help." Jim wanted to finish with the white lies as soon as possible. "She told me that she's terribly disappointed that she doesn't get to see you off today." And with these words, Ruth suspected that the whole thing was just Rebecca's ruse to avoid spending time with her mother.

"Well I'll go call her. You two wait right here." Ruth made her way to the front desk before Jim had a chance to stop her. He was worried now that he'd probably get a parking ticket. Shree asked again about the break-in. While Uncle Jim repeated Rebecca's story, he had a fleeting thought that Shree knew more about what happened than he did.

After the call, Ruth was in an even worse mood. She insisted Jim repark his car in the hotel garage, though she also insisted on paying. She had arranged for them to dine in the revolving restaurant at the top of the hotel as a surprise treat. And even though they had missed their reservation and there were only three of them now, they were seated. Thick rain clouds blocked the view. Raindrops could be seen clinging to the windows, with monotonous gray beyond. Ruth had imagined the happy family together at this moment when she would announce that she was selling the house and moving to Houston. Instead, the conversation was awkward, with each one of them thinking, but not talking about the fourth, who wasn't there, and exactly why that was. Further around, as the floor turned, rivulets streaked across the windows, and wind could be heard, which worried Ruth. They were, after all, thirty floors up.

By the time ice cream was served and Ruth's coffee was poured, the sun broke through the clouds. The view of the light reflecting off glass buildings captured their attention. Now calm, the water's surface glinted magic, while distant greenery looked pristine. They spoke in whispers, pointing out the rosy tinge to the clouds, wisps zipping through buildings, and distant billowing cumulus atop dark shelves of nimbus. Jim named some of the buildings, pointed out the elevated freeway they had driven on, and asked the waiter if it was Buffalo Bayou that was reflecting the sky. Shree thought of the moonlight on Clear Lake and wondered what Wendy was doing. Without anyone being aware, the ghost of Rebecca had departed the table, and the three of them were smiling and enjoying their family moment.

Then time was up for Ruth's visit. Jim and Shree said their goodbyes to their mother and grandmother, respectively. They watched her board a van with other travelers heading to the airport. Jim was struck by how old his mother had become. She was just another old lady with gray hair, needing help up the stairs of the bus.

~ ~ ~

"So I didn't want to say anything in front of your grandmother, but after the break-in, your mom doesn't want you spending time alone at your house for a while." Uncle Jim was driving Shree home in the slow lane of the freeway. He found it much easier to lie to his mother than to his niece. What he didn't realize was that Shree knew right away what it was about. Her mom suspected what she and Daddy were planning. And this new rule was meant to prevent him from meeting up with her. Shree kept her thoughts to herself. The silence worried Jim.

"It's just for a few days. I'm sure there is nothing to worry about. She said you two were planning a vacation in a few days anyway." This was news to Shree. "But Monday and Tuesday, I thought you and I could hang out together. Do you think you could stand me for a couple of days?" Jim was nervous about her answer. He knew that he would have to work for much of the time, so Shree should be wary. Shree remained quiet.

"Are you okay? You can tell me if something is bothering you, Shree."

No she couldn't. Shree had a big secret burning a hole in her stomach. How was she supposed to take off with Dad if she was hanging out with Uncle Jim? And what was she to say now? Ordinarily, she would have been happy to spend a couple of days with him. He may talk a lot about boring stuff, but he was also funny and always ready to goof off. "It's just that…". *Think Shree, think.* "Well I had planned to do something with Wendy," she lied. She had no plans with Wendy. What excuse could she give?

"Oh, that sucks. But maybe you can reschedule your plans for another time?" He thought about inviting Wendy too, but that would be too weird. What would Wendy's parents say about their daughter sitting in a college dorm with an unknown grad student? Too weird indeed.

"And I have a swim meet." Shree latched on to the swim meet. It was her one hope. She had hated the swim team for eight weeks. Especially early morning practice. Maybe practice will pay off in the end, she thought, suppressing a smile.

Uncle Jim agreed to discuss with her mother about dropping Shree off at the swim meet. And he suggested they could swing by Wendy's to reschedule their plan. This made Shree a little nervous, given the lie she had just told, but more because she was worried Wendy would still be mad at her. Of course, the sooner she could apologize to her best friend, the better.

Unfortunately, no one was at Wendy's house. Uncle Jim suggested she could leave a note, which reminded Shree of her letter-writing plan. The first thing Shree wrote was Wendy's address, which she carefully folded into her pocket.

Dear Wendy,

I'm so so so so so very Sorry! I am such a stupid jerk, but you are the best friend I could ever have! I think we will always be best friends, and I hope you think so too. A certain parent may be taking me on vacation soon, and I will miss you so much. But I will write to you. There is so much to say. Like my grandmother was snoring at the symphony. And we ate lunch inside a rain cloud. I will write more soon.

Your Best Friend, Shree.

Shree tightly folded the note, wrote Wendy's name on the outside, and put it in the rusty white mailbox. 'A certain parent,' she thought. *Which one?*

25. The Test

August 14th

The sweltering heat of the afternoon had given way, but the air felt so thick that the warmth had yet to dissipate. Tony sat in the dark on the front step of the little house Rebecca and Shree were renting. He hoped for a cooling breeze sweeping through, but the plants nearby stubbornly refused to move. When he met her after swim practice, Shree had told him about her night in a hotel with her grandmother. This sounded like the stars were aligning for Tony. Everything was depending on this night. Over the course of the summer, as Rebecca had ignored his letters and refused to take his calls, his helplessness had grown. Yet somehow, he convinced himself there was hope. He remembered how she had ignored him for months when they first met. She later told him that his persistence had impressed her. So he persisted now, believing that she was secretly hoping that he would. Tonight was their anniversary. There would be just the two of them again. Back to the spark that started it all. She would surely reveal herself to him tonight. He had been in the weeds long enough. It was time for her to invite her husband back inside.

Her car pulled into the driveway, and he heard her getting out. Everything was on the line. He held his breath and waited for their big moment. After years in exile, months in purgatory, he watched his angel approach.

"What the fff….! What the hell are you doing here in the

dark!" Rebecca leapt back, almost losing her balance at the flash of a man in the darkness by her door. In an instant, her fear became rage as she realized it was Anthony.

"Happy anniversary, my angel!" Tony smiled hopefully and held out a fistful of jasmine.

"Oh no you don't! You don't get to scare me on my own doorstep and offer flowers. Get those things out of my face. And this is not our anniversary. We are no longer married!"

"But Becs, it has been long enough. It's time you let me back into your heart. You know it's time. Our…".

"Our nothing! There is no 'our' anymore. You don't listen. I told you back in May, and I'm telling you again. Get over this! You are not part of our lives. All of that ended!" Rebecca's anger had simmered over the summer. But over the last few days, as her life felt beyond her control, when going to the police proved useless, when she had to contemplate uprooting their lives once again, now the fury began to erupt.

"Rebbie, this is our moment! We have been tested enough. Now is the time for our family to reemerge as strong and loving as ever."

"You're not listening to me! LISTEN to me! LISTEN! Anthony, it is time to go home! GO HOME!" Rebecca knew her neighbors could hear her yells. That thought would usually shame her into a whisper. Now, she wanted the world to know her business. That business was to send Anthony away.

"But Rebbie!"

"But nothing, Anthony. Go back to Boston. Your time is up! Go home NOW!"

Tony was overwhelmed by the force of her. He couldn't remember all he had planned to say. He couldn't remember the tests that had been placed before him. He stammered, but she just pointed for him to leave. He wanted to say something, but she just spoke over him, shouting, screaming for him to go home. Sheltering his emotions from her painful bombardment, he retreated to his car and drove away.

His brain was a choking tangle of discordant thoughts and feelings. He tried to calm himself and figure out what had just happened. Why was she so insistent? What didn't he understand? He pulled into the first parking lot he saw. There he sat for hours running everything through his head. What did this mean?

~ ~ ~

After his car left her street, Rebecca went inside, locked the door, and slid down to the floor, shaking. This was too much. Her tears rolled down her cheeks. She wanted to believe that she had chased him away for good, but she wasn't that naive. She worried that she had missed her best chance at convincing him to leave them alone. But her anger had gushed out of her before she could control it. She knew she must have sounded crazy to the neighbors. Yes, crazy. That is what she had been. Her certified schizophrenic ex-husband shows up at her door, acting like flowers could erase the past, and the neighbors are going to conclude she is the crazy one. This thought was the levity that she needed to get off the floor. She wiped her eyes, poured herself a glass of wine. Wanting to turn away from her life, she turned on the TV to whatever nonsense was showing. She didn't follow it. Before she knew it, the late show was over, and she had virtually no recollection of it. She was exhausted. Too exhausted to think about the day, which was fine by her. Tomorrow would be easier, she smiled. It was only her mother she would have to deal with.

~ ~ ~

The crowds had left the bowling alley parking lot, and only

one car remained. Tony had sunk low in his seat. He had slept in his car on the long drives to and from Houston. Now he vanished into his thoughts and almost entirely out of view of passersby. At some point, a police car entered the all but empty parking lot. However, neither the Massachusetts plates nor the top of Tony's head triggered their interest.

The week was slipping away. It had all been leading up to this very night, and he had to understand what it meant. He couldn't accept that it was all over. A dozen years of their lives thrown away? No chance of being a family again? Never to fall into each other's eyes? Harmonic bliss, he once called it. No, no, it couldn't possibly be gone for good. They had been called to each other. What was he missing?

She told me to listen to her. Tony kept returning to this. *This is a test, and I am failing it. She wants me to listen to her. I am ready to listen! I want to understand her every word. She was trying to tell me something, but I don't get it. Am I to go home? But she IS my home! I have no other home but her and Shree. She knows that! Still, she is telling me to go home. She's telling me that I must go to her? This test isn't for her, it's a test for me! She is telling me that I must go home to her! Not ask her to be let in, but to let myself in. Yes, that must be it. If I am to go home, I shouldn't wait on the doorstep; I must go right in. Yes, that must be it! And she said it was no longer our anniversary, that we're no longer married? But of course we will always be married. The universe had brought our two lives together and bound them, bound us with Shree! Obviously, we're still married. Maybe that's it. We can't be married if I'm asking to be let in. We can't be married if I am doubting my place in our family. That has to be it! She needs me; she is waiting for me to show that I understand.*

Tony felt elated. This whole thing was a trial, a test of him to prove his love. He assumed she knew he loved her, but that wasn't enough. He must prove how much he loves her by being her husband again. The marriage will never be whole until he makes it whole. And she couldn't believe he knew it was whole, after these messy years, until he showed her. He would show her. He would walk into their house as her husband and Shree's father!

Still, he worried. Did he have it wrong? He had twisted things in the past to believe what he most wanted. Now he couldn't possibly believe that she didn't love him. *Yet she was so angry. From the moment she saw me, she was angry. Where was the love we'd shared? I can't believe it has left her. No way. We had burned for each other. We had known true deep connection, which only happens with soul mates. That can never go away. So why was she so angry? Could it be...? Of course! Of course, it's so obvious. She is angry because she's been waiting for me to figure it out. That anger is just her love suppressed. That is the impatience of her love. The power of her anger is directly proportional to the power of her love. And so I must overcome this test with the power of my understanding. The universe will unlock her love only through my love.* He was exultant. He twisted the key in the ignition and ended his silent night.

As the car rolled to a stop outside her house, Anthony took a long pause. Is this really what he's supposed to do? Is it really what she wants? What the universe prescribes? He knew this was the moment. This was his test. Either he goes inside or he doesn't. If he doesn't, he would be giving up on their love once and for all. Retreating from his family, out of fear. If he does go in, they will overcome this horrible separation and reignite their love. But what if he was wrong? If he misunderstood it all?

~ ~ ~

Rebecca woke to the sound of breaking glass by the front door. She jumped to her bedroom window to climb out. But the latch was stuck. She heard the front door shake and then open.

Quickly she hid in her closet. She heard Anthony's muffled voice. He entered her bedroom, calling out that he was home. She held her breath in fear. He turned on the light, calling for her to show herself. Whatever he was thinking, she was too terrified to imagine.

"Rebbie, where are you? I'm home, my love. You don't have to be angry anymore. Rebecca, where are you?" She felt him pace around the bed. He returned to the hallway. He was in Shree's room. In the living room, the kitchen. Without thinking, she found her bag in the darkness, found Mr. Spruill's gun with her fingers. She could hear his movements, though he had stopped calling out. She heard the sliding glass door and knew he'd stepped out to the backyard. Then there was silence. The thought of dashing out the front door flashed across her mind, but she was paralyzed. *Please go away, please, please go away*, she pleaded in the quiet of her head. She heard him in the house again. In her room again. He had stopped moving. His breathing was as soundless as her own. She heard his hand on the closet door. Her head bent down, she closed her eyes, and willed the light to stay away. "Why there you are, my Angel!"

"Tony, please!" Rebecca slowly lifted her head to see his silhouette against the lighted room. "Tony, you have to go away," quivered her voice. "Tony. I have a gun."

"Rebecca, my love, there is no reason to be angry anymore. I understand. I am here now." He didn't hear or didn't comprehend 'gun'.

She stood up now. She showed him the gun. He still didn't understand. That was nonsense. *Rebecca would never have a gun. She would never fire anything like that.* "Anthony, I mean it!" Rebecca was terrified he wouldn't stop. "Tony STOP IT!" He stepped into the closet and reached for her. The gun popped louder than she expected.

Tony fell back. It was all a whirr of sound. He couldn't tell what happened. But Rebecca stood over him, a gun in her hand. There was smoke and an unexpected smell like fireworks. *She shot a gun. At me!* He started kicking his legs and somehow, tangled in a bedsheet, knocking something over, he made it to his feet and ran. The look on her face, contorted with emotion, he couldn't understand what. He ran from that image of a crazed Rebecca holding a gun.

Rebecca was stunned. It took a moment to comprehend he was gone. She heard his car speed away, and still she wasn't sure what had just happened. The gun. She had fired the gun. *Did I hit him?* He was alive. She looked for blood. She didn't see anything. *Wait, it's there.* There was blood on her light switch. There were drops of blood on the carpet. *I did hit him?!* What was she supposed to do? Call a hospital? *Call the police?* She still had the gun in her hand. She shook it off her fingers, onto the bureau, next to the closet, where she still stood. She was an adult, she thought. She called the police.

26. Tears

August 18th

"What happened this time?" Sirrus stood in Jim's doorway with tear tracks through her thick black eyeliner and running half down her puffy red cheeks. Her obvious distress caused Jim to pull back unconsciously. It was one thing to be dazzled by her cleverness, quite another to be tending to her sobs over someone else.

"He said I'm a tease and that I'm the reason he is failing microbiology." She didn't mention that her boyfriend had accused her of teasing James. With this, she pushed past him and dropped onto his bed. In the moment, Jim felt conflicted. He wanted so much to drop onto the bed next to her and hold her. But he knew what would happen if he did. While she was crying for another hour, he would smell her hair and look at her delicate lashes. While she was telling him how much she needed Conner, he would be dreaming about kissing the nape of her neck. And when she would ask him for advice on how to return to Conner's good graces, he would be struggling to suppress words of poison towards his rival. So instead of joining her on the narrow bed, he sat on top of his desk and managed to poison his own feelings. It was surprisingly easy to do. Her swollen, blotchy red face and mucus-filled nose caused him to stare out the window while she regurgitated the latest fight. Her voice actually had a kind of grating whine he hadn't ever noticed before.

Sirrus noticed he was distant. "I'm not bothering you, am I James?" She sat up on the bed and looked up at him. The only light in the room was from the window, and the evening sunlight was filling the room with a soft glow. To Sirrus, James's serious face looked angry, yet still sweet. He was a man, yet still a boy.

"I don't understand why you don't just leave him." Jim had never before directly suggested that Sirrus break with Conner, afraid that it wasn't his place. He was also unconsciously mortified that Sirrus would end their friendship over the suggestion. But at that moment, with her irritating voice and sniveling tears over Conner, Jim didn't really care.

Sirrus was shocked. But it wasn't James who surprised her. Well, it was. James had always been so supportive and caring. But what shocked her was that she felt a twinge of joy when he said it. Where had that come from? Okay, she knew very well where it came from. But she was in the middle of aching over her feelings for Conner. With a few words, James had broken the spell. Now she wanted, needed to make James care for her again. But she had no idea how.

Jim was puzzled by the long pause after he told her to break up. The words had stopped, the crying too. Was she angry? He was afraid to look at her. He told himself that he would wait. Let her tell him he was cruel. Let her get up and leave. But he couldn't help himself; he had to look. She was staring up at him with still watery eyes, and he couldn't help but think she was radiant. The warm sunlight made her face glow in that moment. But he couldn't tell what she was feeling. He was about to say something, to take back his suggestion, when there was a knock on the door.

Conner was there, broad-shouldered, mature-faced, perfect hair, looking every bit like he hated Jim. But when he spoke, Jim realized that Conner wasn't the slightest bit concerned with him. "Dude, some chick is on the phone for you." And with that, he turned and slowly strode down the hall. Jim looked back at Sirrus. She remained on his dorm bed, now clutching his blanket. He left the door open, walked the few steps, and took up the phone receiver.

"Is Shree with you?!" Jim had known that 'some chick' was going to be his sister, but the barked question threw him.

He stammered. "Um, Shree? No no, Shree isn't here. I dropped her at the pool like we agreed."

"She's not here. They said they never saw her today."

"What?! I dropped her at the gate. I saw her walk inside." Jim was catching up now. He knew what his sister was thinking. *No, Tony didn't take her. Tony couldn't have taken her.* "She probably went over to that friend of hers. Wendy."

"You know what happened." Her words were flat. As if she were stating an ordinary fact. The chair is wooden. The carpet is blue. You know what happened. Jim knew this was not good.

"I'm on my way."

27. Rational Thinking

August 14th

He had fled in panic. Fear possessed him like a hurricane overpowers a coastal town. He didn't think about getting out of the house, didn't notice starting the car, wasn't aware of stop signs or directions. Yet somehow the storm passed. The howling winds calmed. The waves receded. Leaving collapsed homes, and the once sentimental, as garbage, to sift through, then clear away. The first thoughts that materialized, as he drove past a strip mall, were ones of shame. He had entered her house! Believed that it was somehow what she wanted. How horribly pathetic he was! Why didn't he believe her? He had convinced himself that she spoke in code. Because he needed her to want him. *She was safe in her home, door locked.* But he entered anyway! *What kind of person does that, terrorizing her? She warned me. She told me she needed to protect herself! From me!*

The steering wheel was sticky with blood. Should he go to the hospital? Would he be arrested? He had to figure this out. Had to get away. He drove to his motel. A river of white and red lights could be seen, the nearby freeway. But the parking lot was dark as he switched off his headlights. A summer storm of strobing clouds was noticeable in the distance. He darted into his room, pulled the curtains tight, then turned on the light. He was bleeding, but not badly. He examined his torso, legs, arms. Only his right hand. He remembered the broken window. Why did he break the window?

Why did he believe she was testing him? He thought he had everything under control. Thought he was healthy. Was in tune with the universe. Then he just broke into Rebecca's house. He had to get a hold of himself. *Think rationally. Stop fantasizing.* Otherwise he would be locked up. *Never want to go back to that.*

Is he safe now? *She said she would call the police. The neighbors must have heard. How soon before they find this motel? Where to go now? Had to give my driver's license at check-in. This is bad news. Over with Rebecca now. She tried to tell me. To stop me. But Shree? Think. The police will be called. It's over, can't be fixed. Must leave Houston! Abandon my whole plan? How would they find me? License plate. Must accept it's all over. My little Roly Poly girl?* Abandoning her was too painful to think about.

He drove more than halfway to Dallas, following the river of lights, before pulling off to sleep. He parked the car under some trees, knowing that the hot Texas sun would be rising all too soon. Sleep took its time finding him, as his mind raced through images of his shame. Practicing rationality.

The sun found him anyway. By nine, his head was pounding from the heat. Hadn't even rolled down the windows. *Again.* Parked in a town by a lake. Noticed a highway patrol car, parked only a couple hundred feet away. *Are they looking for me? Have to disappear, but too exhausted to drive.* Dark clouds were already covering half the sky. The first drop of rain knocked loudly on the roof, followed by a staggered procession.

He had cash; he should use it, he thought. Emptied the bank account back in Boston. Four thousand six hundred dollars were hidden under the seat. *Find a cheap motel, hide the car somehow?* In the next town, he checked into an old motel with a fly strip hanging from the antlers of a deer trophy, mounted next to a teenager reading 'A Separate Peace'. The kid didn't ask for ID or care about a license plate. Tony pulled the car to the back and collapsed on a musty bed. When he awoke, the rain had passed, and night was already returning. Groggily, he walked to a grocery store and bought food for his long drive back to Boston. But he couldn't bring himself to leave. Sadness descended on him with an old familiar weight. By the time he trudged back to his room, all he wanted to do was crawl back in bed and block out everything. How can he give up Shree?

Slowly, over the next two days, his thoughts picked through him and began to put him back together. It was true that he had made a horrible mistake, going into the house. He accepted this. But she had fired a gun! She could have killed him! *All the time she's telling me that I'm crazy, but wasn't THAT crazy? I've never almost killed someone! She's the crazy one! Sure I've had episodes. Anyone can go into the wilderness in this insane world. She proved the point. She almost murdered me, and I only blame myself?!? Maybe the reason we haven't gotten back together is that she's irrational! She couldn't see that we were meant to be together. Stop it, Tony! No, it's done.*

But Shree! He felt like his insides were ripping out. He told himself again and again not to think about it, that something would be worked out later. Yet every time he had managed to distract himself, a cloud of depressing pain would crowd around the periphery of his thoughts until he had to return to the glaring problem. He couldn't give up Shree. And no matter how he tried to barricade himself with rational thinking, a new sinister rationale began to seep in under the door. Rebecca was dangerous, and Shree needed to be protected from her. Shree had said it herself: her mom was a monster. His daughter, living in a house with a gun? Rebecca was irrational, disturbed, violent. He must do something. *The rational thing to do is to rescue Shree.*

Book II

28. Secret Agents

Shree felt defeated before the swim meet began. Lingering by the gate, she didn't want to accept the obvious. Monday had passed, and her father hadn't reappeared. Something had happened at the house between Mom and Dad. That something had resulted in a broken window and a broken promise. She entered the locker room to pull on her swimsuit, still wet and smelling of chlorine. She felt trapped. The meet, like her mom, could not be avoided, so she re-emerged into the Houston heat to find out what races she would swim.

"Shree, it's time!" Dad's voice took her by surprise, and she spun around to greet him. Yet he was nowhere to be seen. Had she imagined it?

Shree had dreamed of their escape for so long. Daddy would show up in their doorway, and she would run to him. Then they would climb into his car, and her mom would be furious. She'd yell 'Stop!', but they wouldn't stop. 'I'm living with Daddy now, and you can't do anything about it!' Multiple times, Shree had mouthed the words she would say. Then they would go to the airport and fly to Boston, where they would live in their old house near the park.

Their actual escape proved to be so much more exciting. "It's time!" called his voice from the hedges just outside the fence. The voice told her to walk quietly around to the next block, where he had parked. It was like they were secret agents, she thought, as she quickly changed back into her clothes. When she got to his car,

Dad was wearing a hat and sunglasses, but his smile was unmistakable.

"I'm ready to take you to live with me, now. Are you sure that's what you want?"

"More than anything, Daddy," she beamed, climbing in. They hugged, then off he drove down random streets, until eventually they got to the freeway. They even talked quietly, as if someone could hear them inside the car. But after a few miles on the freeway, Dad removed the hat.

"We have to be very careful for the next few days, Shree. Your mom will be pretty mad at me, and she may try to get the police to stop us. I have every right to have you live with me. I'm your father, after all. But if the police are involved, and the courts, well, it could take months or even years before they let us be. So, though everything is fine, we still want to avoid the police. Is that okay with you? Do you still want to do this?" The weight of what he was doing could be heard in his serious voice. He needed Shree to reassure him this would be okay.

Without missing a beat, her joyful mood carried him along. "Of course, Dad! I'm just happy you finally came for me." Shree couldn't stop smiling. They were really doing this! "And it's fun too, how you had me sneak out of the pool." She put on his discarded hat and beamed. "We're on the run!"

"Well I don't want you to be afraid or anything. The police are the good guys, after all," he laughed. "We'll just try to avoid taking up any of their time." Tony then told her the plans. "It's important to get out of Texas as soon as we can, but we're going to drive west. No one will expect that." He gave her a sly glance. "We'll be driving all night, so you'll have to sleep in the car tonight. Okay?" She nodded. "Also, if any police cars come by, I want you to lie down on the seat, so that they don't see you." All she could think of was how much fun it was.

She asked if they would fly to Boston once they left Texas, but he told her they weren't going to Boston. "We're going to live in a completely new place, but I'm not sure where yet." At first she was disappointed they wouldn't live in Boston or remain in Houston. But then it just made everything even more exciting. Who knows where they would end up! "Maybe Oregon, maybe Alaska," Dad suggested. These seemed like mythical lands to Shree.

They talked till late in the night, eating burgers and shakes in the car. They talked about what kind of place they wanted to live in. Dad wanted to live in the forest. Shree wanted to be near a beach. Dad talked about all the creatures that live in the forest, deer, skunks, raccoons. Shree suggested they could have a pet raccoon. Then Dad told a story of how he once met someone who had a pet raccoon. How it ran up his leg and kept climbing till it sat on his head. It was the cutest little baby raccoon named Ricky, but it was afraid of everyone except its owner. Then Dad said raccoons need their freedom as wild animals, but they might have a cat. Shree loved that idea.

Eventually the yawns caught up to Shree, and the talking trailed off. So Tony pulled over and made a nest in the back seat for Shree to sleep in. She had his sleeping bag and pillow, and he strapped the seat belt around her. Dad put on some interesting music that sounded familiar. Despite the bumpy movement and the sound of the tires on the road, despite the occasional bright headlight filling the car with blinding light, despite the slow downs and speedups, the unexpected turns, the sudden noisy gravel, the stop at a gas station amongst giant trucks, the uncomfortable bump in the middle of the seat, the seatbelt making it hard to turn over, despite all of this, Shree felt the night was perfect. She was going on an exciting adventure with her Daddy, moving to Oregon or Alaska, and maybe they would even have a cat.

29. Bosch's Ceiling

August 25th

A vibrating pain in her chest woke Rebecca at 3:27 am. It felt like a medical procedure was being performed without her consent. It occurred to her that the term 'broken heart' had originated from this very pain. Shree's letter had arrived that afternoon. At first Rebecca had been overjoyed. Six days had passed since Shree had been taken. Six days of helplessness. Cycles of frustration, anger, worry, fear, and helplessness. Repeating like the needle lapping at the end of a record. Then the letter! Rebecca had torn it open in a rush of blind hope. Her daughter was writing to her, calling for her mommy, ready to come home. But before she knew it, the whole letter was gone. Every word from her daughter consumed. No call for help. No need for her mommy at all. Rebecca, for the first time in those awful six days, broke down and cried.

After the fifth reading, Rebecca fixated on her daughter's maturity. She was impressed with Shree's ability to defend her dad, to justify their leaving, to decide and say what she thought was important. But Rebecca's admiration was overwhelmed by the obvious truth Shree had conveyed. Anthony hadn't taken her. She had chosen to go with her father. In Shree's eyes, her mother was guilty. In her efforts to protect her precious little girl, she had lost her growing daughter. Rebecca had woken up to her wrenching heart.

She staggered into the bathroom looking for something she could take. A bottle of cough syrup shattered on the floor as she fumbled for Excedrin. Hours before sunrise, hours before she could hope to do anything. Then what. What could she do? On her back, Rebecca stared at the ceiling. Filtered moonlight exposed a single strand of spider web dangling, collecting dust, slowly lilting in the nearly imperceptible air flow of the room. Random patterns in the textured ceiling coalesced into the face of an old man, laughing. Her pain was turning her ceiling into a Bosch painting. She tried to unsee it, but the old man kept laughing.

Her brain returned to the same patterns that it had been tracing for the past six days. The first twenty-four hours after Shree disappeared were numb. She kept thinking it was just a mistake. Shree would show up that night. She would see her in the morning. Surely Anthony would come to his senses. When Shree got tired of his game, she would make her daddy bring her home. Shree would miss home.

But the longer she waited, helpless, the angrier she got. *He has no right. He knows that taking her from her home, from her mother, will be bad for his baby girl. He understands enough child psychology to know this will be traumatizing. He says he loves Shree, but he is injuring her just to hurt me. How long till his wild ideas scare our baby? How long till he does something psychotic that directly endangers her? He thinks he could never hurt her, but I know the truth!*

She turned on her side and tried to drive the poisonous thoughts out of her head. She knew if she let them, they would extinguish all hope. Rebecca forced herself to picture better times. *How proud he was when Shree was first in his arms. So tender, he introduced her to the world, told her how enchanting her life would be, how she had two parents who would love and cherish her with all their lives. That time on the lake, when she was three, she jumped from the boat into his waiting arms and clung to his neck. Their enormous grins shining as white as two moons on the choppy water. Letting a little green caterpillar crawl from his hand onto hers. She was so captivated, hanging on every word he spoke. Even when telling her the cat was reading his mind.*

Rebecca turned to look out the window. Blackness still. The police were less than helpful. Underlying every question, every useless form, perfunctory interview, rambling explanation, patronizing advice…. Underneath it all was the same presumption. *It is only her father. What did you do to make him leave with his child?* Behind all their help was a hunch that Anthony was just a good guy trying to spend time with his daughter. *He is just like them, while I'm just like their ex-wives. Angry, vindictive, not to be trusted.* The only comforting thing in the whole ordeal with the police was what Officer Donnilon had said. "Your husband will make a mistake. They always do. And with that mistake, we will find him and bring your daughter home." *Well there was nothing good about Anthony's condition. But one thing is certain: he's incapable of hiding it forever; his psychosis will be seen. That bastard is gonna be found!*

The pain that Shree's letter had triggered dragged her brain further down. *Why did she leave me? I should have talked to her more, should have told her more about her father.* It was clear to Rebecca that this was not just about a girl wanting her father. This was Shree calling her a 'bitch'. This was their tension that had been growing for months. *Why didn't I fix things? I could have told her how much she means to me. Why didn't I make it clear that I would do anything for her? And now I've lost her. I can't protect her. Can't hold her and stroke her hair and let her know that everything will be alright. Now nothing is right. I've been a vacant mother. Don't know how to talk to her. Never been good at that sort of thing. Why isn't it in me? Words fumble. Choke on expressing tenderness. Punish too easily. I've been a lousy mom, and I don't think I can do any better. She's left because of it. My child left me.*

Rebecca sank into this darkness, sobbing.

Eventually, she tried to pull herself out. For the thousandth time, she asked herself what she could do. She couldn't drive off and look for them, didn't know which direction. She had called Lydia, talked to Shree's friend, no one had any clue where he'd take her. *Maybe call hotels? Would they stay in a hotel? There would be thousands of possible hotels within driving distance of Houston. There must be some way to figure out where he'd go.* It never occurred to her that the letter from Shree, with no return address, did have a postmark.

Instead, another thought brightened her mood. The best person to figure out where Tony would go would certainly be her. *He would probably want someplace familiar, but not where he'd be recognized. Jimmy was confident he'd go home to Boston. If only that were true. Lydia felt sure he would stay in Houston, keeping Shree near her mom. Oh please let it be that. But it wasn't likely he would go to Boston or stay in Houston. One was a direct path back to the hospital, while the other would send him to jail.*

So where would he go? Where would he want to take Shree? If he were thinking clearly, he would take her someplace 'natural', as he used to say. He grew up in a city, but he was always dreaming of living away from so much concrete. And thinking clearly, he would want his girl, his 'Roly Poly', to be surrounded by nature.

But he wasn't thinking clearly. Now Rebecca wished she had read his letters instead of throwing them all away. But she remembered some of his psychotic mythology from when they were still married. *The main element was 'the Universe', some all-encompassing force driving him, driving everyone, but mostly driving him, to grander action than the rest of us could comprehend. The power of the universe was 'natural', was 'wild', was a life and death struggle for creation. Suffering, pain, and joy were mere spices. No, they were also the two sides that drove progress. What did he call it? Pain and joy were* the 'dialectic engine of realization' or some crap like that. But by 'realization' he meant the universe becoming real. 'The universe is wild,' he said as if it were the answer to life's riddle. Rebecca groaned in frustration. Like all those times before, trying to understand him led nowhere.

Anyway, if he is being driven by his delusions, he will certainly want to be submerged in nature. The hardship and the beauty would serve to validate him, prove that the universe had a plan for him. But where does that lead him? He's not much of a camper. Rebecca couldn't imagine him trying to live off the land. *He can't fish or hunt. No, he'll need a job or help of some kind.*

The first traces of color were seeping into the sky. Rebecca noticed the sounds of birds starting to greet the day. She thought of getting up and making coffee, but it was only 5:43 am. At least some time had passed, she consoled herself. She was so tired of the waiting. Sick of having nothing she could do.

By 7:30, she had a plan. She would start tracking down everyone he had known in high school or college. She hoped he would turn to one of his old friends for help. And she had decided that he would head, not to Boston, but to somewhere one of his friends had scattered to. It wouldn't be easy, finding them. She could hardly remember any names. But there was a high school yearbook in one of her boxes somewhere. That would be a start.

At 8:46 am, Officer Donnilon called. Anthony's car had been found in Farmington, New Mexico. It had been in an accident. Two people had been badly injured. A male and a young female.

30. Headless Robots

As the sun was just beginning to rise behind them, Shree woke when the car went from pavement to gravel doing eighty. Tony had seen no one on the road for at least half an hour. There were no houses, or trees, or cows, or anything. The road had been perfectly straight for so long that he imagined tying his belt to hold the steering wheel and taking a nap. But the sudden drop to gravel jolted Tony out of a sort of fog of mindless driving. Slowing way down, he felt prickly needles wash over his fists, which tightly clenched the steering wheel. Had he fallen asleep? Were they still on the road? No and Yes, the answers came into focus. There was road work, complete with signs of warning, but no workers anywhere to be seen. Perhaps this stretch of road has been unfinished since Johnson was president. In about a mile, the pavement returned, so he again increased speed up to seventy-five.

Shree was the first to notice a jackrabbit. It had darted away as the car sped past. The sun, still on the horizon, drew long shadows across the empty landscape, punctuating every rock and bush. So the tall rabbits became easy to spot. One darted across the road and caused Tony to swerve, almost losing control at the speed they were traveling. He slowed again, but the next jackrabbit that darted into their path was not as lucky as the previous. Tony was struck with shame that he had run over a rabbit in front of his little girl. He sought words to comfort her, but Shree said nothing, so he let it pass. Hopefully she didn't notice. Luckily, the zone of rabbits soon ended.

"Dad, look at those towers. Don't they look like headless robots?" And in their sleepy inspiration, they tinkered together a song. "Driving through the desert of the headless ro-bots, headless robots is a-what they are! Driving through the desert of head-less ro-bots, I hope they don't step on our car!" And so on, for multiple verses, some less charmed than others, they filled the radiant morning with their new charmed life. "Driving through the desert of headless ro-bots, see them all toeing the line. In the future we will all-have-our ro-bots, but I tell ya I-don't-wanna meet mine!" Texas disappeared behind them, mountains grew up from the distance, and the headless robots eventually led them to a town with a coffee shop and pancakes.

~ ~ ~

He felt electric after three cups of coffee. A warm magic that was the sun, danced across the desert through living clouds. He felt his mastery over the mechanical beast flying down the road. He was totally unlike the faltering, wisp of a being that had piloted the car under timeless stars. Mere hours before, the car had driven him, and he had doubted he would see the dawn. Now he knew. Now he surfed this wave of certainty, felt the power that had revealed itself in his decisions, in his actions. He had done it. He was making it happen, despite all the doubts. The fears. His catatonic indecision. Despite Rebecca's refusal to see the path. Shree had understood. Now, his smiling daughter beside him, he felt they could accomplish anything. Rather, he knew he would accomplish whatever was important to preserve their happy family. It was destined to be.

Yet coffee's invincibility doesn't last forever. After a sleepless night, he knew he had to find a place to stop. He started making shorter and shorter goals. Drive all day to get out of New Mexico, was followed by drive to Albuquerque, which then was shortened to drive to the next mountain pass. Focusing on the road was becoming hard, but eventually the car arrived in a high mountain meadow, with shade trees and a gravel road up which he steered the tired car.

"Shree, I have to sleep. If you can sleep too, maybe you should. But if you can't, stay nearby. If anyone comes to ask questions, just wake me up." Shree wasn't tired at all, so Tony took the back seat, leaving Shree with nothing to do. She took her backpack, filled with her swimsuit, towel, her notebook, and a few other items she had brought to spend the day with Uncle Jim. Was it only yesterday that she was playing 'hearts' with Uncle Jim and Sirrus? She wondered how her mom was taking it. She imagined Mom being so furious at her and Dad. But it also dawned on her that her mom was probably sad too. She remembered when she and Mom had moved to Houston. It had been awfully strange, the new house, the new neighborhood, knowing no one. Except Uncle Jim, of course, but he lived at his university. It had just been her and her mom. The first night, sleeping in that creaky house that smelled weird. She had her own room, but Mom had come in and lay down with her. Shree remembered how her mommy smelled like home. And Mom said the same thing about her. "We have to take care of each other, now," Mommy had said. In that strange house, they were still home.

She decided that she would have to write her mother a letter. But she had spent so much time resenting her mom's rules, had been disgusted by her lies, and how she was mean to Dad. Now she sat looking at an empty page in her spiral notebook.

Dear Mom,

I know you are probably mad at me and Daddy. Please don't be. Don't worry about me. Daddy and I are taking care of each other. Don't be sad. I do love you and know you love me too. But I also love Daddy. You are wrong to be mean to him. I hope you can understand why I had to go with him. Perhaps one day we will all be a family again. But right now, he is my family. Don't worry about us. Take care of yourself.

Love, Shree

She read it over. It didn't quite say what she felt, but she didn't know how to say what she felt. She was angry with her mom, but felt sorry for her too. She knew she would miss her, but she would never want to go back. Saying 'I love you' felt like a lie, but not saying it felt worse. She decided the letter was good enough.

There hadn't been a single car or person that came by since they got there. She took the time to have a good look around. The trees overhead were some kind of evergreen. There were only a dozen or so, along a tiny creek bed. Beyond, there was a meadow of dry yellow grass, except for one patch of lush green about forty yards away. It appeared there was a little dam creating a pool from the trickle that ran through the trees. Just then she noticed there was something moving at the edge of the green. At first she thought it was a horse, but then realized it was a deer. This was the first time she had ever seen a deer in the wild. She just had to go closer. She crept very slowly, hiding behind trees and then ducking low in the grass. But it didn't matter. The deer looked up, froze, flicked its tail. Then three deer bounced away. Disappointed, she nevertheless laughed at the sight of them bouncing on four legs. She wished she could tell Wendy.

Despite his exhaustion, Tony kept turning over in the back seat, never losing consciousness for long. What did he think he was doing? The police would keep looking for them, whether they were in Texas or not. Rebecca would make sure of that. He couldn't get a real job without using his Social Security number. They couldn't drive the car for long; the license plate would give them away. They couldn't stay in a motel or rent an apartment. The more he tried to sleep, the more he imagined being caught in a net of numbers and names. He couldn't call his mom; the number would be traced. He couldn't write a letter, or visit a friend, or go to the doctor without the chance of discovery. How long till they could live a normal life again? And with that thought came another fear. Would he be able to keep it together to take care of his daughter? For a brief moment, he considered turning back before his wave of worry found even more fuel for his sleeplessness. If they returned, he might never see his daughter again. No, there was no turning around. Shree was relying on him, and he couldn't give her up. He would rise to this task. No irrational thinking, he would take care of Shree.

The day wore on, and Shree was more than bored by now. She had read the only book she had. A boy detective who caught the bank robbers by recognizing their Morse code signals from the gang's hideout. Shree was disgusted with how stupid it was. How can they sell such stupid stories? Two pages in, and she just knew it would end with the ace detective being congratulated by the chief of police. With the book finished though, she had nothing else to do. She thought once more about those early days in Houston, when she had no one to talk to and nothing to do. All alone while her mom was at work. She used to read, she would sometimes draw.

"Shree! Shree! Help, I can't breathe! Hey Shree, get me out of here!" Shree smiled at the recurrence of an old pastime. She had outgrown her imaginary friend. At least that is what she told herself when she was too embarrassed to tell her real friend, Wendy. But now here he was. Growing up can wait.

"Mr. Trains, where are you?" How many times she had wondered that.

"Right here, in dee side pocket of your backen-packen!" Shree unzipped it. "Jeesh! That hola der stinken," he said in a funny voice, brushing crumbs and lint off himself. "Don't you never clean dat ting? I tink you stuff-ed in a half-eaten cheese azandwich, many mont ago, no? Whatever it ees, it ees green und hairy!" Mr. Trains eyed the trickle of water running through the trees. "Well what do we haven a-here? Where dot it come frum? I could sure usa der shower after dat ride. You too, kiddo! Let us go for der swimming swum?" Before she knew what had happened, she had followed the watery path up the hillside till it buried itself under a fortress of rocks. But despite there being no waterfall, Mr. Trains was not wanting. He was busy trying to walk across the water like the numerous skater bugs were doing. Instead, he splashed one, who was none too happy at the insult. Soon splashing and squealing prompted Shree to rescue Mr Trains by the scruff of the neck. Just then, her Dad called.

"Shree, it's time to get moving again."

31. Manny

In Farmington, Tony left Shree in a shopping mall bookstore with her backpack and twenty dollars. Shree bought envelopes and stamps, and had enough money left for a book or two. A woman saw her picking her way through the young adult fiction shelves and handed her The Hobbit and To Kill a Mockingbird. "Trust me," was all the woman said. Shree had heard of them both. Her mom had To Kill a Mockingbird, but Shree had never opened it, put off by the title. The Hobbit however, was read to her as a child. She was excited to read it herself.

When Tony left, he drove straight to a junkyard. He had no trouble selling the car without its title. Of course, he only got a fraction of what it was worth. His plan was for them to take a bus into Colorado and buy a used car there. Hopefully, if someone traced the car to New Mexico, their trail would end here. And the two of them would be able to disappear into Alaska. That was his plan.

The junkyard owner called to one of his employees. "Manny, give this gentleman a ride." Manny was no more than nineteen and was strikingly short for his age. His muscular arms, all the way up to his shoulders, pants, shirt, and a good deal of his face were covered in grease. He didn't say a word while he led his charge with all of his belongings to a beat-up station wagon. Inside, Tony couldn't help but be impressed at how well it was decorated. There were tassels trimming the ceiling, toy dinosaurs glued to the dashboard, a polished wooden steering wheel, and an air freshening cardboard tree dangling from the cigarette lighter. As soon as the car pulled out of the lot, Manny smiled broadly.

"So are you a car thief or what?" The mischievous smile that leaked from Manny's eyes as he spoke these words put Tony at ease. Right away, he couldn't help but like this kid, in whose care he had been placed.

"No, nothing like that. It was my ex-wife's car." Tony had prepared a story, an explanation for selling the car without a title. But the junkyard owner couldn't care less about why there was no title, or even Tony's made-up name. He hadn't asked a single question, though he examined the car carefully. So now, with this friendly teenaged chauffeur, Tony was pleased to tell his tale. "She died last year. I drove out from Boston to scatter her ashes. Now I don't want the car."

"So you gonna walk back to Boston? That will be quite a hike."

"I'll take a bus." This prompted a few stories about long bus rides.

"Another time, on a bus to Mexico, some creepy old dude, hair coming out of his nose, missing teeth, he fell asleep on me. But I was happy to let the guy sleep, since he'd been talking nonstop all day. Couldn't understand anything he said. And the smell of his breath, frijoles, onions, and death!"

They carried on, swapping stories about mutant bus passengers, until finally Manny arrived at his objective. "So I can get you a car if you want. My father sells cars in Durango. He'll give you a bueno deal." He paused for a brief moment, looked out the side window, and said, "No questions asked," with smiling eyes.

By the time Manny had made the proposal, Tony had already guessed it was coming. But he didn't resent Manny for trying to sell him a car. They did need one. But Tony didn't like the idea of this kid becoming a tie between the old car and a new one.

Nevertheless, something about Manny made him relax. It was as if he had known Manny all his life. Think rationally, he told himself. We need another car. "Okay, maybe I'll look him up when I go through Durango. Where does he work?"

"I forget the name, it's right on the highway. Homie, I'll give you a ride. I been meaning to go see my old man." While Tony had anticipated the sales pitch, he didn't understand that Manny's true motivation was to create an excuse to see his father. His dad had barely taken part in raising his kids, and though Manny's sister resented him for it, Manny always believed the best. And now he imagined showing up with a plump sales commission for his father. Then they would go celebrate as true amigos.

"Well I don't know," Tony stretched his words while he thought. If Manny kept their secret, then this was exactly what they needed: an untraceable ride to another state and a friendly, beneath-the-table car deal. "There are two of us."

Manny drove Tony and Shree, or Eddy and Lesley McAdams, as Tony introduced them, to a cheap hotel just north of town. His mother worked there as a maid, and even though she couldn't get them a discount as Manny had promised, she did sign them in herself and gave them extra towels. Tony found it endearing to see Manny's affection for his mom and her worry over him.

Shree, on the other hand, kept her distance around the strikingly dirty Manny and his mother, old and weathered, who scolded her son in Spanish. Shree also hated the name her father had chosen for her. 'Lesley'? She didn't want to be a Lesley! When they were alone in their room, Shree found herself scolding her dad about selling the car. "Now we have to ride with that guy, and he's so dirty!" But her dad explained that he was dirty from working on cars, which is very useful work. And he was just a helpful kid, a teenager. He reminded her that they would meet many strangers on this journey to find a new home. People from different cultures, speaking different languages, and who have different jobs. Slowly, Shree began to realize that what her dad was trying to say was that she was being prejudiced. Shree was embarrassed. She didn't dislike Manny because he was Mexican or Indian or whatever he was. She just didn't like the dirt. But she promised herself to give him another chance. And her dad promised her that she could choose her own name if she didn't like being called "Lesley".

The next morning at half past ten, Manny returned cleaned up and well dressed, topped with a tan cowboy hat. Shree wanted to laugh, but thought better of it. Maybe he was a real cowboy. She had seen plenty of cowboy hats in Houston, and she always thought they were funny. In the car, as he drove, he told them of his friends who ride horses, but that he preferred riding a goat. His friends would all race past him on their sleek horses, teasing him and Bebita, his goat, but he didn't care. See, those friends had to spend money feeding and pampering their stupid horses. But smart Bebita fed him and took care of him. It was only towards the end of the journey that Shree realized that Manny had made the whole thing up. The name Bebita came from his baby niece.

As they approached Durango, Shree felt the tension in the car. Tony was second-guessing his decision to trust Manny's father, and nervous about what kind of car he could afford. He knew next to nothing about cars, so he worried he would be suckered into a bad deal. Manny, on the other hand, worried his father would be too busy to see them. He hadn't seen his dad since winter, and then Dad had been right in the middle of a big sale. So they hadn't talked, and the manager had sent him away after an hour of waiting. Dad had promised to call, but must have forgotten. These were the unspoken thoughts as they pulled into Ace Motors, just off the highway. Shree saw a gleaming red roadster on the roof above the office and immediately declared with a point, "Let's get that one!" Tony and Manny erupted in laughter.

"Sorry, but your dad doesn't work here anymore." That was the greeting Manny received in the manager's office. He wouldn't give much more in the way of details. He hadn't worked there for the last two months. The manager didn't want to say any more, but suggested that he still lived in the area.

After some quiet conversation with the manager, Manny suggested that Tony look around the lot for a car. Tony quickly zeroed in on a Volkswagen van with a bed and storage already built in. Manny checked the engine carefully. While doing so, Manny revealed to Tony that the manager agreed to give him a hundred bucks if he could sell Tony a car. "So I'm not entirely unbiased, but this van seems okay to me. You should offer $400 less, though. And I will throw in my hundred because I told you I could get you a good deal." Tony assured him that wasn't going to happen.

While waiting to close the deal, with Manny in the bathroom, another sales rep told Tony that Manny's dad was a "worthless drunk and a real piece of work! I feel sorry for the kid."

Edward McAdams bought a van without any identification. Tony nervously expected to pay extra, or at least tell his prepared story, but the all-cash deal was all the dealer cared about. Manny was ready to say goodbye, but Tony suggested that they could join him to look for his father, then have a nice meal together. "No amigos, you know you have to be riding your new goat into the sunset. I hope she takes care of you as well as my Bebita cares for me," he said with a wink to Shree.

"I will never forget all your help, Manny Hernandez!" It hurt Tony to have to leave this kid he barely knew.

"And I will forget you two before you get out of the parking lot," Manny said with a wink. "Don't go stealing any more cars!"

32. Little Blue Sailboats

August 24th

"You're gonna have to tell them all you know." Juan Alvarez didn't look so intimidating in a hospital bed, Manny thought. His gown had little blue sailboats on it for some unknowable reason. Perhaps the director of supplies grew up near a lake where they would go sailing on a summer afternoon. Or maybe a box of gowns was sent to the hospital by a practical joker of a shipping clerk, who thought that sailboats in a desert would be funny. Maybe an institutional psychologist thought sailboats were a cheerful image for a building filled with tragedy. Manny decided his habitually angry boss looked tragically funny in a hospital bed with his face badly bruised, an arm in a cast, and little blue boats sailing across his broken ribcage.

"What's to tell, boss, I wasn't in the car with you." Manny knew the wreck was a much bigger deal to his boss than the broken bones. Uncle Juan and his mistress were both drunk when he plowed into a parked car on the edge of town. Angelena broke her neck and currently had her head bolted into a cage to prevent movement. When Juan's wife, Maria, found out, she charged into Angelena's room, but was overpowered by Angelena's brother. Maria then turned her wrath on Juan and very nearly cracked another rib. Now Maria was divorcing her dirtbag husband, and the junkyard would be sold. Manny felt sorry for his uncle, who was losing his wife, his business, and no doubt his mistress as well. But

Manny also felt angry and worried that he would be out of a job. Manny needn't have worried, since Maria intended to keep the business going and needed help doing so. Manny would soon be promoted to assistant manager. But for the moment, Manny felt closer to the unemployment line, and this made him angry with Uncle Juan and his "little thing on the side".

"Not about the accident, Manny. This is about the guy who sold us the car. He's some sort of criminal. You gave him a ride, remember?"

"I can't believe it! He seemed okay." Manny remembered Eddie all too well. He had jokingly accused the guy of selling them a stolen car. Eddie had been kind, though a little nervous. A real homie. And he was such a sweet father to his girl.

"Yeah, they say he kidnapped a kid. Did you see a kid?"

Manny made a split-second decision. "No, I didn't see anybody. I just dropped him off downtown." Manny felt tingling down his neck. He suddenly noticed the room was very warm. He wanted to get out immediately. He needed air; his throat was parched. Was he doing the right thing, lying? It was one thing to lie to his boss; he did that all the time. But he knew he would soon have to talk to cops. Should he lie to them? For Eddie?

"You need to go down to the police station and tell them that. If you don't, they will come to you. I know your mamma will be real worried if they roll up to your house. Do your mamma a favor. Go to the station and tell them what you know."

Five minutes later, Manny was sitting in his car, staring at the dust that had accumulated on his little plastic triceratops, glued to the dashboard. He recalled the day he drove Eddie and the girl to Durango. He was tall and pale as a ghost, but he had honest eyes and a smile he seemed almost embarrassed to reveal. And they looked like family. Same eyebrows, same almost black hair, both wearing glasses. They were so relaxed around each other, too.

Could it have been kidnapping? No, he remembered distinctly that she called him 'Dad' and 'Daddy'. Near the end of the ride, when she finally figured out that the racing goat story was a fib, she said, "Daddy, it's his baby niece! He's been pulling our legs." And how she ran around the lot saying, "Daddy, let's get this one!" and, "Not that one, Dad, it smells weird." It's clear that she was his daughter and that they were good to each other. No, it can't be that he kidnapped his own daughter.

Manny also remembered the end of the day. In the blue light of the Crazy Horse Saloon, his father already drunk at four, insulted his sister and called his mother 'puta'. Still, when Dad asked, Manny gave him everything in his wallet. Soon after, the old man disappeared without paying the tab. Luckily, the barkeep was sympathetic. On the drive home, Manny had thought about Eddie and his daughter. If only he could have gone with them.

And with this, he decided, he would tell the police nothing. He only drove Eddie downtown. Dropped him off at Orchard and Main. Manny wiped the dust off his triceratops, put on his gas station sunglasses, and drove to the police station.

33. Snapping

September 3rd

On Thursday of the first week of school, Wendy was in a bad mood. It seemed like all the other kids belonged with their group, but she didn't belong with any of them. The first few days, she hid her loneliness by burying herself in a book. But today, Francie had stood next to her in the lunch line and confronted her.

"I heard your brother went to jail. Is it true that he stabbed someone?"

"Shut up, Francie," Wendy had snapped, but immediately regretted it. The words had come out too loud and too mean. Now everyone was looking at her, and she felt tears beginning to fill her eyes. She left the line and skipped lunch altogether. She hid in the school library until the lunch period ended.

Nobody said anything about her brother for the rest of the day. And Annabelle even went out of her way to compliment her shoes, light blue high-tops that her mom had bought for her. The fact that the exchange with Francie was not a big deal made Wendy feel even worse. She missed the sound of Shree's voice.

When she got home, she brought in the mail, as usual. One envelope stood out. It was made for a store-bought birthday card, with a light orange color and almost square shape. It was too thick to contain just a card. In careful, large handwriting, it was addressed to her. There was no return address. Wendy had never received a real letter before. She made herself a peanut butter and jam sandwich and took her letter outside to read.

Dear Wendy,

This is your pen pal, Renee. You may not remember but you signed up for a penpal in May. And you wrote me about the reservoir. You wrote about someone named Les Bean. Do you remember now?

It was obvious to Wendy that Renee was none other than Shree herself. She had no idea why Shree was playing this game of being someone else, but she hungrily read on.

I want to tell you of my adventures. I have been driving across the country with Leo who is a Padre, but we will just call him Leo, okay? We have not yet reached home yet, but Leo says there is no hurry. The first night of this vacation I slept in the car and woke up in a desert. Leo said it was a desert, but it didn't look like I expected. There were no sand dunes or cactus that I saw. Instead it looked like hard, mostly flat land with a lot of ugly gray bushes. But we also saw giant headless robots! They weren't really robots. Can you guess what they really are? After the desert, we were in the mountains and I saw three deer bouncing like bunnies. It was hilarious to see the big deer, taller than me, bounce away looking exactly like cartoons.

Leo left me at a bookstore while he sold our car. That's where I bought the stamps. Who is Louis Armstrong anyway? The Padre says he is 'God on Trumpet'. The next day we bought another car, which is a van. This one is better for sleeping, according to Leo, but I liked the old one better.

Anyway, then we drove all day through a desert and we didn't see any cars for what must have been a hundred miles! Can you imagine being in a valley so big that it takes an hour to drive from one side to the other? And in all that time there is no one, absolutely no one in the entire place?! We stopped the car and yelled as loud as we could. But no one heard us! Leo said I should shout whatever I want to whoever I want. I yelled that I missed you! Did you hear me? I'm pretty sure you didn't hear it, though my voice is sore from yelling so loud.

At sunset we made it to one humongous sand dune. I wish I had a camera, because it was an actual mountain made of sand! And the sunlight made one side glow bright orange, while the other side was shaded blue. Leo said it was the "golden hour". He was really really happy that we saw it at sunset. But I had to pee behind a bush and it was scary in the dark. There are rattlesnakes in deserts after all.

Leo doesn't want me to send letters. But I will when I get a chance like now. I need to write to *you. When we get to Alaska, or wherever, you can write back. Will you write back?*

Your best friend and pen pal, Renee

P.S. I look like a boy now! Leo cut my hair.
P.S.S.T. They are the towers that hold power lines.

Wendy loved this letter. Long ago, her anger at Shree had dissipated. What had seeped into that void was a kind of fog of her own isolation. She missed being able to share her days with Shree. The less she thought of her absent friend, the less she seemed to think for herself. Anyone close to her would have told her to "snap out of it". But no one was close.

And now she had the letter. It was to her. It was obviously from Shree. And it was a secret of the highest order! Why else did she call herself Renee? This letter snapped Wendy out of it. She knew she had a role to play. She was Renee's pen pal, and Renee needed her.

34. Germination

The long trip across the arid lands of the Great Basin had taken its toll on Tony and Shree. While much more comfortable to sleep in, their van was burning oil. The heat and long hours of driving seemed relentless, and each agonizingly slow climb up a desert mountain had Tony worrying that the van would give up for good. He had thrown his trust into the teenaged Manny and now imagined that Manny had played him into buying this stupid van. Tony turned against himself, angry that he had trusted a stranger, just because the kid seemed familiar. He wouldn't make that mistake again, he promised himself. Nevertheless, the van topped each mountain pass and then sailed down into the next valley a little too fast for comfort. After a few of these cycles, Tony began to trust the van and renewed his trust in Manny and himself.

The final long rise out of the desert would bring them into the alpine forest of the Sierra Nevadas. Shree was delighted at being surrounded by green trees and cooler air. Tony suggested they imagine what it had been like when early pioneers finally reached the Pacific side of the Sierra Nevada mountains. Catching sight of the deep blue waters of Lake Tahoe, they both felt like everything would be okay now. Modern settlers in their covered wagon. After rushing to get as far away from Houston as quickly as possible, Tony decided they could slow down and enjoy the journey. They stayed at the lake for a whole day, drove down through Yosemite, then set off in search of an even bigger deep blue body of water.

Tony had heard that the Big Sur coastline was special, but nothing prepared them for what they found. Rather than the crowded ocean coasts he had seen before, here was eighty miles of coastline with hardly a house on it. And it was easy to understand why. The mountain sides plunged directly into the raw coast. Jagged rocks, sharp as shards of glass, the size of houses, had tumbled from great heights into the unforgiving abyss. Huge waves marched across an infinite shimmering surface, swept by the wind as if blown by unseen lips, looking like nearly frozen ripples from far above. As they approached land at last, the waves arced and curved, then collapsed in joy, finally crashing in celebration over those giant broken boulders, like great white firework celebrations. The waters then drained down through tide pools and dangling red algae, receding to their embracing home. Shree and Tony crept to the edge of the staggering hillsides. Watched prehistoric pelicans flying in formation just above the waves. They clung like the trees, barely believing they could survive the wind, twisted into dramatic shapes, clutching granite boulders and awkwardly craning neck and branch, determined to spend their mortal moments as part of the timeless scene.

Tony had wanted to visit California on their trip north. But he had imagined it as crowded, touristy, overhyped, and commercial. Surprisingly, this is not at all what they found. No doubt, the downsides of the most populous state, the home of Hollywood and Ronald Reagan, were all too real. But he had purposely taken the less populated paths, had avoided the endless suburbs of southern California, stayed away from the ostentatious and subdued mansions that reminded passersby that the good life was unreachable for most. Perhaps it was the difference between his expectations and the raw, unspoiled coast they discovered that shook his resolve. Alaska was so far away, but the Universe had brought him here. Just a seed, not a decision.

They traveled north and found themselves in Santa Cruz. Many places in California are famous beyond their size. Names of places that wafted out of California, carried on the breeze to suburbs in New Jersey, farms in Arkansas, high-rises in Chicago. Marin, Sausalito, Santa Monica, Palos Verdes, Encinitas. Such names were mythical places to people far away. The name of Santa Cruz was vaguely familiar to Tony, yet it was more familiar to him than any place so far. Santa Cruz is a university town, which certainly set a tone. Yet for some years, it had become a mecca for hippies, surfers, naturalists. It was as if the sixties youth culture had come home. While the rest of the country had moved on to disco, Reaganomics, and condo fees, the residents of Santa Cruz kept growing their hair, starting organic farms, pottery collectives, and guitar stores. Their kids, some with names like Peace and Rainbow, went barefoot to Montessori school or learned to surf before they could ride a bike. Volkswagen vans, many held together with coat hangers, carried nomads from all over the country to one of a handful of shining beacons of alternative living. Santa Cruz was known in certain circles. And here Tony felt at home. The seed was growing.

After seeing sea lions and great waves near the lighthouse, Tony and Shree walked the downtown pedestrian mall. Here, a guitar player with a beat-up acoustic played Hendrix's Castles Made of Sand, and further on, a gray-bearded bandleader, himself on Marimba, filled the sidewalk with admirers and had the lunch crowd swinging. A sculpture of a hypercube, a four-dimensional cube, near a great local bookstore, made Tony realize that Santa Cruz wasn't simply a hippy town. So they drove up to the university and at first thought they were lost, since the campus was sprinkled through a redwood forest, which gave way to golden meadows and expansive views of the ocean below. The sprout, growing strong by now, was watered by the University Library, sounds of gamelan, notices of classical concerts, and Shakespeare plays.

The plan was to grab supplies and look for a place to park the van and sleep, north of the city. The next day, they would see San Francisco. They went into a small store with local produce, advertising ten avocados for a dollar.

"Amherst, is that you?!" Shree looked up at a tall, chubby man with stringy black hair, trim beard, and an enormous smile. Her father stood silent for a moment, as if unable to speak. Did he know him?

Tony was stunned to see Rich standing before him. They were three thousand miles and four years distant from their last contact. How was this possible? "Hey Tufts! I see you broke out!" Having recovered from the shock, Tony was now uncertain if he should grab Shree and run. It had never occurred to him that he would be recognized. Maybe Rich knew, maybe he would turn them in.

"What are you doing in California? Boy, are you a sight for sore eyes." Tufts seemed sincerely happy to see Tony.

"We're just traveling through. On vacation." Tony didn't want to say too much.

"Really! Vacation? Are you enjoying it? Hey, where you staying? You definitely should come to my place. Really, where are you staying?"

"We're camping. Going to San Francisco tomorrow." Tony felt his ambivalence rising. Best to get away quickly, but he remembered how much he liked Rich.

"Great! I love the City. Hey, come to my house tonight, and I'll give you a tour of San Francisco tomorrow. Seriously, Tony. I'm not taking no for an answer. You are a real sight for sore eyes."

Tony weakened. He had bonded with Rich when they were in lockup together. Rich had been the one voice of sanity, it seemed, in the whole place. That included the doctors. They had helped each other survive inside. And see the humor in their lives. Now,

Rich seemed genuinely happy to see him. And realistically, there was no way he could know that they were on the run. Maybe this was another sign. The universe wanted them to stay in Santa Cruz for a while. "Sure Rich, that would be great! Let me introduce you to my daughter.

35. Hydrogen Bonds

"Hydrogen Bonds! That is the subject for today." Shree listened to her dad's attempt to homeschool her. Sometimes it was alright, other times she couldn't follow what he was trying to say, and the lesson would be painful for both of them. They had come to a mutual decision not to enroll her in school for one year, since that could get them caught. But Shree had promised to take lessons from her dad during the whole year. Of course Tony didn't know what was taught in sixth grade. Instead, he taught her whatever he thought was interesting. Two days ago was all about the mitochondria. Yesterday it was the Reformation. A very big problem was that Shree didn't understand enough of the story leading up to the Reformation to make any sense of what her dad was telling her. She had no idea what ATP was, or even that a hydrogen ion was just a free proton, which has a plus one charge. Nevertheless, her father's enthusiasm encouraged her to think of the subjects as interesting, and years later, his seeds bore some fruit. Yet for now, the lectures were their own sort of blight to survive.

~ ~ ~

The most difficult problems for Tony: where to settle, where to sleep, how to make money, all had solved themselves. Running into Rich seemed to be just another part of a natural progression that resolved with 'Leo' and 'Renee' living in a beautiful redwood forest near a creek in a small cement and wooden cabin with a corrugated metal roof. Rich's grandmother owned a property with nine cabins, mostly vacant. She had let the vacation rental business go after she let her husband go. Rich had been asked to help out by his father. But Rich had higher ambitions. He was trying to start a software company with two other people he knew from college. Running into Tony was serendipitous for Rich, too, as Tony could program and might get them past a few roadblocks.

It didn't take long for Rich to convince Tony to stay. And it didn't take long for Rich to figure out that Shree's name wasn't Renee and that her mother wasn't a comfortable subject. Late one night, when Shree was asleep, Rich pressed his friend carefully.

"Her mother is having issues. Renee felt she wasn't safe. I felt she wasn't safe. So we left. But the thing is, Rebecca has legal custody, so she could take Renee back and have me arrested. Then I couldn't protect my daughter anymore. As long as Renee wants this, I'm going to keep her with me, and we're going to hide from her mother and the law." Tony knew he was taking a huge risk by confessing to Rich. But they had shared some things in lockdown. If anyone was going to be an ally, it was Rich. And if not, it is better to find out now.

"That's intense, Tony. She really fired a gun at you? Well don't worry about any of that now. You're among friends here. Is Renee okay? It's got to be hard on her. Anyway, I'll try to call you Leo from now on, or Amherst." His smile was visible even in the darkened room. "You and Renee are safe here. And it's a great place to live!"

~ ~ ~

"Today we are having class outside. Hydrogen bonds. They make this creek beautiful." Tony knew his lectures had been hard on Shree, but he was pretty sure this one would get through. "See this curve, as the water rushes down into the hollow between the two rocks. Is it a thing of beauty? Think how hard it would be to sculpt that exact shape. How smooth it is. How the ridges in the water made by that twig are softened and then blended back into the smooth surface of the slower water. All this can be described with mathematics. All the forces here are the beauty of physics. And one essential part of the physics making this beautiful scene is very simple chemistry. Hold out your hand." Shree did so, and her dad let fall a single drop of water onto her palm. "See it bead up? Now look when I put a drop on this piece of paper." Shree saw it soak in right away. "What do you think will happen when I put a drop on this leaf?" Shree guessed it would soak in, but it bulged up even more than on her hand. The water was like a little ball on the green, supple leaf, and it rolled off the side. "All of this, the shape of the water in the creek, the water soaking into the paper, the bead of water rolling off the leaf, all of this is because the water molecule is slightly polar!" Tony was excited to have Shree learn this. To him, it was a glorious secret to the beauty of the universe. But Shree didn't know what polar meant. Not yet.

But she soon learned. Her dad drew her a picture of some water molecules, explained to her the partial charge because the big oxygen atom pulled the negative electrons towards it, leaving the hydrogen atoms more positive. He then had Shree guess how the water molecules would interact with each other. Finally, they discussed how the molecules would act in 3D versus 2D. "And you can see that in the shape of the water. It is as if the water has a skin holding it together in a bead. The outside water molecules are slightly more bound to each other because they have fewer places to bond." This struck Shree. She had seen water drops all her life, but never thought about why they made that shape. Water has a kind of stretchy skin.

Then her dad pointed to the beautiful swirls and curves in the water of the creek. The reflections of the trees and sky were being bent and stretched around small boulders and old branches. Shree thought about the exquisite detail, how hard it would be to draw or paint or sculpt anything nearly as beautiful. Her dad picked up a fistful of rocks, leaves, and dirt and threw it right into the most beautiful part. Shree was shocked he would destroy what was there. But within moments, the cloudy water flowed away, and the beautiful scene, slightly altered with a few new pebbles, had returned. "The water molecules that make this gorgeous scene are being swapped out constantly. All this beauty that they had momentarily made is instantaneously remade with new water flowing in. The shape of water this creek reveals is because of hydrogen bonds and gravity. And air pressure. Physics. And we are like the water molecules, doing our part momentarily in the stream of the universe, then letting others carry it on. Water molecules do not know the beauty that they make. Perhaps we don't know either. But the fun part is that we can try to learn, to see beyond ourselves. We get to try to see the beauty we are a tiny part of. And that is a very special thing. There are people who say that learning how things work destroys the magic. But what do you think? Does knowing about hydrogen bonds destroy the magic of this creek?" Years later, Shree would recall this question voiced by her father and smile.

36. Arrest

September 24th

Shree had thought carefully about how to correspond with Wendy. Her dad had been very clear. No letters out, and especially no letters in. They could not risk getting caught. But in the isolation of their forest home, Shree missed Wendy even more than she guessed. She had managed to send letters already without her dad knowing. And Shree had no doubt that Wendy would keep their secret. The danger was if Wendy's parents found Shree's letters or if Dad found Wendy's. But Wendy's parents worked, so Wendy could get to the mail first. Besides, would Wendy's parents ever guess who 'Renee' was? Shree's dad, on the other hand, might easily get to the mailbox before she did, and he wouldn't need to guess. Then the perfect solution revealed itself in the form of an unused mailbox. She would have Wendy mail her letters to the vacant cabin behind theirs.

Dear Renee,

Do you remeber Annabell? Do you remember her creepy dad? You'll never guess what hapened. He was arested! It's all over the news! Do you get nuws where you are? He was on TV getting lead away from their front door in hancufs! I feel sorry for Annabell. She hasn't been in school since. And

Jeenie and Shareon B. are already saying mean things. I can't believe it!

The news said thosands of dollers, or mayby like a million, were missing from the church where he preeches. My mom was crying, because she gives money to that church and she thinks the Revrend, Annabell's dad, is so holey. Dad thinks its funny that he got arested. They were also whispring and said it was ashame about Annabells older sister. I don't think Annabell has an older sister, do you?

2 days later: Annabell came to school today. As 1 thoaght, Jeenie and Sharron B. acted like they didn't even know her. So 1 felt sorry for her, so 1 sat with her at lunch. We sat next to your favorate tree. At first we didn't say much. Then 1 told her about my brother. (He's now in a "joovie" which dad says is like milartary school. He hates it!) I wanted to ask her about everything with her Dad, but 1 didn't. She didn't look like she wanted to talk about it, and 1 didn't want to be like Francie. She asked me about you and 1 really wanted to tell her. But 1 didn't! Our seecret is safe! But we did talk about friendship and what it is like when people you care about go away. And 1 told her about the day we first talked at the resevroar. I only told her about my "less bean" idea about Ms. Warner and Ms. Halloway, and how you made fun of me. Annabell ~~laffed~~ laughed and said she was sure our old teacher was a lesbeean. You know I think 1'm going to be friends with Annabell. We will still be

best friends ##### Renee, so don't worry. But I think Annabell needs a friend right now, to. I think all three of us should be friends. If you were here I think you would agree. But our secrett is still our secret so don't worry about it at all!

The next day: No more news about Annabell as today it's Saterday. I got up before everone today and road my bike all over, like you used to do. There were hardly any cars or anybody. It was cool, like it just rained. Mayby it did, because the grass was all wet. Anyway, it was so nice. I wish you were here and were riding with me. I have been riding no hands a lot! I can practacly ride from my house to the resevoar without hands. Some people were getting into their car and a little kid saw me and started yelling and pointing at me. He was so amazed I was riding no hands and I turned the corner! I don't think his mom was empressed, tho. But I'm not doing it for the stares. It just feels so nice to glyde along in just the right balence. Anyway, I sure hope you come back soon and we can ride togather. I got to go now, because my Mom is yelling at me to wash the dishes. You know how that is.

Your best friend and pen pal,
Windy Wendy

P.S. I am embarased about my spelling. But I want to write to anyway.

~ ~ ~

Dear Windy,

Don't worry about your spelling! I'm so happy you wrote me!!! I so wish I was riding bikes with you! I remember how good you were at no hands. I will get there sometime, but not now. I don't even have a bike here in the forest. But I do get to practice my balance.

Our creek has a number of log bridges. These aren't real bridges, just old fallen trees. When we first went for a hike, Leo helped me cross a big log. It was scary because it was a long way down. But now I'm crossing on my own all the time. There is one that is my favorite. It is only a couple of feet up, so if you fall it's no big deal. But the log is thin. It is maybe four inches wide. And while it is still firmly in the ground on one side, the other side isn't attached to anything. It just bounces and sways. It took me five tries to get across the first time. Twice I fell in the water, but it's really shallow. Now I go right to the end and just stand there while it bounces and sways back and forth. I feel like I'm Luke Skywalker, I use the force! Sometimes I challenge myself to wait till I see a bird fly by. And sometimes I just fall off. I don't know if it will help me ride with no hands, though.

I like the forest here, but there isn't much to do all day. Dad is working and, like I said, I'm not going to school yet. I have been hunting animals. Well, not hunting, I don't want to hurt anything. I just want to see all the animals. I have seen raccoons. They come to our cabin at night and Leo has me give them bread. I see a lot of blue birds, and squirrels, and lizards that Rich calls noots. Dad and I saw a snake once, but it wasn't poisonous. I also see deer about every other day. There is a big orange cat that wanders all over the property. He is always very friendly. We don't know his name, but Leo calls him Gunther. He must have two names just like us. Leo says there are skunks and bobcats and maybe even mountain lions (cougars). He told me to act very big and yell at it if I ever see a mountain lion. The most amazing thing I ever saw was a coyote. It was a long ways away, though. It must have been huge but it wasn't scary. I was so happy to see him!

I am glad you are friends with Annabelle. I know we used to make fun of those popular girls, but I always thought Anna was nice. Not like that Sharron B. Anyway, I am jealous that you have a friend in Houston. I only have your letters. But truly I hope you have fun and make friends. And I hope Anna is not too upset about her dad. Tell her hello for me. Wait, scratch that. Don't say anything about this secret. But I do wish her well.

You ended your last letter because your mom made you wash the dishes. I remember all the chores I was made to do by you know who. My Leo never tells me to do any chores. And he never cleans anything either. I have started cleaning dishes because they smelled! And I am cleaning and sweeping too. I guess you know who brainwashed me to want everything tidy. Leo doesn't even notice. Sometimes I wish Mom were here to take me for ice cream after chores. But I will never tell her that! I hope your mom appreciates your work.

I will leave you now that my hand is tired from writing. I hope your eyes don't get tired from reading! I really really miss you and I love love love your letters, so write when you can. Good luck with Annabelle.

Your best friend always and pen pal for now,
Rainy Renee

P.S. I hope you never learn to juggle while riding a bike. If you do, I will never catch up to you.

37. On the Edge

"The future is about to be born, gentleman!" Rich was fond of saying this. Clearly he imagined himself a midwife to the birth. Ever since high school, when he had dialed into a mainframe and written programs on punch tape, he talked about the coming computer age. His father had trivialized that vision.

"Computers in homes?! What on earth would people do with them?" his father would smirk. "Accounting for toilet paper?" Rich just smiled. His father was too old to understand. Not so many years later, his dad bought him an Atari. And now he had two Apple IIs and an idea for a text formatting program. He had joined forces with Larry, from college, who had thoughts about how to correct spelling mistakes. Then Larry's roommate, Kevin, found a customer willing to pay actual money. By the time Tony appeared, the crew was racing to get their first version of their product, 'Scriptmate', ready for release. And with Tony's help, the Gordian knot they had built was finally laced. They met the deadline and got their first real payment.

"You guys dug deep and created a thing of beauty," Rich announced at their regular morning meeting. "As you know, there is a tremendous amount of digging yet to be done to flesh out this product." Mixed metaphors are his talent, Kevin thought. "And when we do that, there will be more products to follow. Right now though, we will take the day to celebrate. We're hiking down to the ocean and we're doing it on shrooms!" Rich had a triumphant smile, knowing a nice trip was the perfect corporate bonding exercise.

Larry cheered, and Kevin looked delighted. "The creative juices will flow. Some thinking outside the little computer box for a change," Kevin said with an air of confidence. No one noticed Leo's irritated stare.

"Well it sounds nice for you guys, but I have my daughter here and I'm not hiking to the beach without her, and we're not taking shrooms in front of her!"

"She'll be okay, Leo, we won't be too wild. I'm sure she will have fun," Larry said. Tony thought for a moment that Larry was suggesting Shree should be taking mushrooms as well. In any case, he announced that he and his daughter would skip the outing and leave them to their fun.

"Look, I understand Amherst. I didn't think about Renee when I planned this. I can understand if you aren't going to take anything in front of your daughter. But still come with us. We will keep it together." Rich, as always, wanted everyone to be happy together. Eventually, the three convinced their reluctant coworker that it would be alright.

It was a gorgeous sunny day, though the marine layer of low clouds still hid the ocean under puffy white cotton candy as viewed from the golden hills above. Tony and Shree were squeezed into the back seat of Kevin's car, swinging back and forth as he raced down winding roads towards the start of their hike. Shree was disappointed that the car stopped long before the beach. Her dad's promise of a beach day had arrived at last, yet there were many miles to walk to get there. Rich made sure everyone was dressed for a long walk into the chill of the evening, meaning Shree had to carry her stuffed backpack the whole way.

The hike started along a dry creek bed deep in the forest. In a little while, the sandy dry creek turned into a rocky canyon with stones smoothed by uncounted years of rushing water. Then the water itself made an appearance. A pool like a big bathtub with sparkles of gold at the bottom. Tony saw that the others were starting to get a bit giggly. He felt irritated with their recklessness. Kevin walked out on a slender fallen tree extending fifteen feet above the rocky creek bed. He scolded Kevin, but the others just laughed. Even Shree was smiling at their buffoonery.

Further along, Rich led them up the side of the steep hill on a barely perceptible path. Tony again felt it necessary to remind them about his daughter. Shree for a moment, felt embarrassed. She could handle her own. She tried to show her dad by standing on a rock on one foot. Larry called out to her in admiration, which put Tony in an even more foul mood.

They arrived at a group of rocks with crudely painted graffiti all over them. Rich pointed with triumph at what to Tony looked like the painted outline of a giant penis. What Rich was actually pointing to was an opening in the rocks. "'Hell Hole'! I brought you guys to the opening of this cave called 'Hell Hole'. It goes in like three hundred yards!" At this, he pulled a flashlight out of his backpack.

Larry and Kevin were quite excited to go in, but Tony felt it was one more stupid thing his friends were doing. Shree was curious, but dubious. What she saw was a dirty hole between the rocks. She wanted to see inside a cave, but the thought of going into that hole filled with spiders and who knows what else, was just hard to imagine. However, Rich talked calmly to everyone. "We will only go in about fifteen feet to the first chamber. It looks bad here, but I assure you that once you're inside, it will be fine. It will be chilly, and it smells a little, but it is perfectly safe. Beyond the first chamber, it is possible to get lost, and there are some steep drops, so we aren't doing that today, okay." Leo said that he and Renee would stay outside. After the three others went in, Shree asked her dad if he had ever been in a cave before. It was clear to him that she wanted to see what it was like. So he called down the hole, and in a few minutes, Rich appeared to guide them in.

Shree practically threw up going through the opening, but once inside, she was encouraged by Rich and the others, told how to squirm around one obstacle in the passageway, and told to back down feet first to drop into the first chamber. It was like a small room. There were places to sit and actual stalactites above. There were flashes of sparkling reflection suggesting they were inside a giant, muddy geode. It smelled like wet dirt. But Shree loved it. She couldn't wait to write to Wendy about being in a cave. It was hard to see since there was only one flashlight, which Rich was using to guide her dad into the chamber. Once they were all there, Larry and Kevin giggled while Rich spoke in a formal voice.

"We have gathered under the earth in this darkness," he began, then remembered to switch off the flashlight. In the complete darkness, Shree couldn't even see her hands. Rich continued with the sermon. "To remember where we came from. Our ancestors lived in caves. They sought shelter from the dangers outside and gathered here to dream. How many times in the history of humankind have dreamers come into the darkest depths and conjured great visions? We are their direct descendants, we are cave dwellers, and we, too, can conjure visions of what is not yet here! We can take the light that exists only in our mind and bring that light out into the world." When his booming voice was done, the cave was completely silent as they each followed the light in their minds.

Shree imagined an amusement park where people could crawl through caves like giant three-dimensional mazes. Larry imagined music that was taking the shapes of the passageways, bending around curves, bouncing off formations, and harmonizing with his cell membranes until he himself was music. Kevin imagined the Earth was one massive organism, and they were as tiny as skin mites, crawling into an ear. Rich imagined the four of them, no, the five of them, were experiencing an awakening to flows of electrons, quantum possibilities of things existing outside the confines of probability curves. Communication of thought through alignment, not language.

But Tony felt disgust. *Imagine Rich thinking himself a spiritual leader in this very moment. His vision was so small. He brings us to a cave and talks of humans some few thousand years ago. But this cave has been here for eons. This planet, four billion years. Humans are mere tarnish on the wild beauty that has been polishing itself for fifteen billion years. How about the trillion trillion stars with countless planets and countless caves? The dazzling crystalline order, and the incalculable, seeming random, but anything but randomness of scattered wildness beyond anything we can guess. Rich wants us to conjure lights. Can't he see that the lights are conjuring us?*

After a while, the crew naturally found their way out of the depths of their thought and sought the daylight again. Their journey continued down the creek, all together, but slightly apart. Tony believed himself in a certain separate grace. The three shroomers took all things in stride, never faltered, always laughed, willed harmony, and believed they had achieved it. Shree too, completely unaware of the drugs that feathered the day, felt a certain harmony with her dad's friends. They praised her sure-footedness, laughed with her at normal things that seemed so silly nonetheless. A banana slug in a race. Squirrels making fun of birds. Two trees in love. Moss that believed itself a forest. Every little observation was another chance for silly joy. But her dad was aloof, in another world.

They came to a clearing to rest, with a log across the now flowing creek. While the three buffoons chortled and Shree giggled along, Tony crossed the log and stopped in the middle, on one foot, fifteen feet above the flow of water. It was exactly what he had scolded Kevin for earlier, but now he was in his world. The blue sky was filtering down as giant trees climbed upward. The log had loose bark and patches of velvety green moss. Below him, the trees and sky were reflected in shallows, algae dancing in the quiet current. Tony wasn't in the sky or the water. In his mind, he was the bridge between them. He felt the pull of gravity while he remained aloft. The tenderest of muscle movements, the curve of his back, the slight movement of one hand, the quiet ease of possibility into an arc and fall, yet there he stood. A bridge upon a bridge, a balance upon a balance. He was a juggler with his own flesh and with the forces of the universe. His weight, his mindful weight, held him in a constantly moving stasis. This was the definition of beauty, he thought. Those three couldn't possibly understand what he felt, how he was art in that moment, while they were mere cartoons. The universe flowed through him, held him there in that one moment, timeless. And they, with their mushroom crutches, their orange sneakers and affected slang, can't even see the wild abyss that stares into us.

The day proceeded, and they emerged from the forest at last to find rolling meadows, golden gray before the first rain of the season. It was a magical moment to emerge to this view. And as they walked, they laughed about the claustrophobic spaces they had left and the stately living room meadows that welcomed them. A grand oak, its massive trunk clothed in gray wrinkled skin, stood as a uniquely ancient witness to all who passed. Light filtered through its leaves, illuminating moss-gilded branches from within. Larry named her Mabel, and they each paid their respects.

And as they crested one more hill, the ocean in all its splendid glory was unveiled. The marine layer had retreated far out to sea, and now the sunlight reflecting off the ocean stretched to the horizons, a spread of shimmering texture that was almost touchable. A few high clouds raced across the sky, and their shadows traipsed across the ocean like massive ghosts swimming just beneath her surface. If the open meadows had welcomed them home, the ocean below was visual music, dazzling them, calling them like a siren's song. Not a mere voice, but an iridescent symphony hypnotizing them with promises unspoken.

Though the ocean was two miles away yet, they traveled undeterred. Even when they saw deer and a red-tailed hawk, they kept their pace. The group traveled on, three, plus one, minus one. Shree enjoyed each new moment, the views, the animals, a weed that smelled like sweet cereal, the silly adults running around like puppies through perfect meadows. Having spent so many days practically alone, she couldn't help but enjoy the camaraderie of these happy, kind adults. She barely noticed that her dad was not as kind. He alone, felt alone. The prattle of their voices barely filtered in as he reaffirmed his connection to truth in all its beauty. He didn't let the children throw off his awareness of the inner vibration of each blade of grass, each tree, each cell of his body. *I sing the body electric*, he thought. *Some roads can only be traveled by those called.*

In time, they crossed Highway One, a moment of sober awareness of the dangers of civilization, then they descended into the vegetation again. The trail they were following had lost them, so they bushwhacked their way towards the roar of crashing waves. Larry found a deer trail through poison oak. Kevin forded a muddy bog before Rich discovered that someone had dragged logs into place to make a trail. When they finally reached sand, Tony broke with the group and practically ran to the waves. Shree followed her father, while the three others plopped onto a low dune and just marveled at the beauty in silence.

Shree was exhausted from the long hike, but overwhelmed by the grand, empty beach they had discovered. It wasn't like the warm flat beaches of Galveston or what she remembered of the beaches back east. It was broad but bound on both sides by rocky, crumbling cliffs. There were massive waves, so big that she couldn't imagine anyone going into them to swim. The waves broke very close to the shore, and white foamy pancakes raced up the steep sand before retreating with a hissing rush. Explosions crashed upon jagged rocks along the far side of the beach. Nearer, huge geysers of white water, engulfing giant boulders, draining back down off black and slippery ledges as the remnants of one wave receded and a new one rolled forward to smash the rocky shore again.

Shree had imagined a beach day of swimming and body surfing, but this beach was no playground for children. It was terrifying, like standing on the rim of a volcano. Each wave could crush her, swallow her up, and never spit her out. She had walked to the edge to feel the freezing water, and the steep, soft sand almost tripped her as the bare edge of a wave tried to drag her into the grinding jaws of a monstrous wall of water above her. She staggered back, frightened but awed. Her dreams of body surfing were obliterated, but she was too overwhelmed by what was in front of her to be disappointed. Then she saw a head pop up at the crest of a wave. Was that a person in the wave? How were they not drowning? The head disappeared as mysteriously as it had appeared. Then another wave revealed a seal, about her size, calmly swimming along the crest, just before the wave rolled over and collapsed into its white frenzy.

Her father called to her through the roar, leading her to the rocks along the right edge of the sand. Shree could see now that the polished rock extended many feet into the ocean, and though waves crashed onto the fractured edges, there was quite a bit of dry rock under the cliff on which to walk. Her dad looked wild, unlike anything she had seen before. He was talking fast and pointing in many directions, in what seemed to Shree as if all at the same time.

She didn't understand what he was saying, perhaps because of the wind and the crashing waves, but she understood that he was thrilled to be there at that moment. She too was thrilled. How could she not be? It isn't every day that you stand on the edge of a volcano!

There was a seagull gliding a mere four feet above them. She could see the wind ruffle feathers on its head, as it slowly drifted, almost not moving forward at all. Then suddenly it turned around and swooped low to the waves before rising above distant cliffs. Shree realized then that there were hundreds of seagulls as well as other birds. Tall black ones sitting on a large wet rock just beyond the range of the crushing waves. Black and white birds bobbed in the water beyond the breaks. There were large pelicans, looking just like pterodactyls, swooping single file above crumbling walls of stone, then gliding down mere feet above the waves. One lone pelican, standing on the same rocky shelf where they stood, was almost as tall as she. Then it stretched out its bill and flapped its wings. And she realized one of the many things her father seemed to be pointing to, were living lumps of rock. The same familiar shape of head that she had seen in the wave was peaking up at her from the cluster of gray, spotted lumps. She looked directly into the eyes of a harbor seal, looking right back at her. "I see you!" the harbor seal seemed to say.

"These seagulls understand, Shree! The seals know it. This is the knife's edge of this planet. The knife's edge of evolution. Of meaning! This is what the universe has created us for. Shree, we are here to be a witness to this focus of beauty, this fulcrum of creative destruction. If you learn anything from me, Shree, please understand this. The wild universe needs us to witness its incredible, timeless indifference clothed in momentary yearning. We are here to experience. If we don't recognize that, then why are we?" These words spilled from her father's mouth, and she tried hard to understand them. But by the end of a sentence, she couldn't connect it to the beginning. Her father was so brilliant, but she was just a kid. She wanted to understand him, but all she could recognize was that he was telling her this was a very special place. She understood that on her own, but his enthusiasm multiplied hers. This was the most amazing place she had ever been to.

Then her father grabbed her arm and pulled her towards the wet rocks and the breaking waves. For a moment, she felt terror as she imagined one of those monstrous waves breaking on top of them. Then she looked into her father's eyes and saw he was calm, so she willingly followed him out onto slippery rocks polished smooth in places, covered in bright green algae in others.

Her father led her to a small caldera of seawater, where a thin sheet of foamy white flowed across a ledge and poured into the pool like a little waterfall. When the pouring ebbed and the surface calmed enough to see through the water, she saw that the pool was filled with life. Large green blobs, radiating tentacles. Flat round shells stuck to the sides. Countless holes seemed to be bored into the stone. A group of hundreds of black clam-like shells tightly bunched together. Dripping down part of the ledge and gracefully folding over into the pool was a large sculpted clump of what might have been mistaken for sand. Closer inspection revealed the tiny honeycombed holes of a colony of creatures. Homes by the thousands, all collaborating in the most graceful shapes, pouring over the rock and dripping down like honey. A sculptured apartment block built by individuals who cannot even see the result.

Shree saw purple and golden ringed shells that looked like jewels, pink plants, green grass, reddish brown algae, a shell covered in what looked like black velvet. Hermit crabs had taken over some of the shells. There was a yellow and blue starfish, itself looking bedazzled in jewels. Tony, kneeling next to the pool, put his finger on the green tentacles of what Shree would soon learn was an anemone. He jerked his hand in seeming pain, and Shree shrieked. Then she saw his smile. He took her hand and guided it to the tentacles, which grabbed her softly, with no sting at all. She touched the starfish, which was hard like a rock, as were the black 'clams', which were edible mussels. The golden, curving sand colony of tube worms was surprisingly delicate. Shree felt terrible to have caved in several worm homes. Her dad picked up a hermit crab and plopped it onto her palm. It quickly skittered and plopped back into its pool. Then a large wave spilled over the ledge once again, and both of them got wet before they retreated to safety.

Rich joined them on the ledge and told them they needed to be more careful and that it was time to go. The sun was setting, and everyone was tired and very hungry. Rich's car was parked nearby. They all ate his store of bread, cheeses, fruits, nuts, and chocolate while sitting on the cliffs. The sun turned everything golden, then orange marmalade with pastel pink gauze and scarlet wisps above a deepening port wine sea. Everyone, even Tony, was happy with the day. On the drive home, Shree shared her impressions of the waves, the seals, and the tide pool. Everyone else was too spent to speak, and too content to want to do anything else but listen. Tony, receding from his isolation, was proud of his little Shree Riley Roly Poly. She was one more marvel of the day.

38. Given

November

Weeks passed, then months. Concern and sympathy evaporated into silence. Rebecca sometimes felt it was only her in a world of ghosts. Only her, who remembered what life had been, while everyone else carried on in their cardboard lives. But it was she who led the empty, hollow existence. Halloween had come and gone. Rebecca turned to loud music to drown out doorbells of excited pirates and candy-craving space aliens. As Thanksgiving approached, Jim talked to their mother almost every day, discussing how to steer his sister through the holidays without Shree. In the end, their mother flew in to try to distract her. And Rebecca agreed to be distracted.

Jim too, was depressed and sought distraction. He worried about his niece, but not as much as he worried about his sister. He was convinced that Tony would never harm Shree and that she must have gone with him willingly. As Jim saw it, his sister had tried to keep father and daughter apart and failed to consider the consequences. He didn't quite blame his sister. He did sympathize with her reasoning. Could she have acted any differently? Nevertheless, Rebecca's pain was hard to watch, and he didn't know how to help. On top of this, he had lost his best friend.

Just after Halloween, Jim and Sirrus had a big fight. He couldn't remember how it started, but somehow she had accused him of not sticking up for her. He didn't even know what that meant. He became angry and told her that he had always tried to be there for her, but now he needed to be there for his family. She insisted it had nothing to do with his family. "If you think Conner is so bad, why won't you stand up for me?"

"What do you mean, stand up for you? Stand up to him? That's not my place. Besides, I have nothing against Conner. I think he's a nice guy." Did he? "Maybe YOU need to stand up to him," he said with an almost mocking voice. "But you never do, do you. You just come in here and cry to me about it." To that, she practically growled that she loved Conner and that he, James, was milquetoast. Then she turned and left without looking back. Within ten minutes, Jim wanted to apologize. But she had offended him. And it still burned. She acted like he hadn't been her best friend all this time. Acted like he hadn't cared enough. She knows that isn't true, and she should apologize. That night, he couldn't sleep. He wanted the fight to be over. He tossed and rolled and was still wide awake at 2 am. Should he just give in to her and let them get over this fight? No, his point was that she needs to stand up for herself, and likewise, he has to stand up for himself. *Milquetoast that!*

The next day, he had a morning class, then lab, then he went to see his sister. He didn't see Sirrus that day, or the next, or the next. They passed each other in the hall on Friday, but she was with Conner and didn't even look at him. After a few more days, it seemed awkward to even broach the subject of their fight. Then two weeks passed before he saw her again. What with Shree's disappearance and trying to get his first paper published, he had forgotten to be mad at her. One day, with a happy smile, he called to her across the lawn outside the library. She saw him, smiled briefly, then turned away and walked briskly in the other direction. Oh yeah, she was still mad. Some perfect world, he thought.

~ ~ ~

Ruth, their mother, arrived on Wednesday before Thanksgiving. Surprisingly, Rebecca had insisted that her mother stay at her house. The three of them would make the feast together the next day. Everything went smoothly between mother and daughter while putting together a shopping list and getting groceries that afternoon. Ruth, not generally aware of her daughter's feelings, was now determined to tread lightly. Rebecca too, kept the conversation pleasant. All through cooking and feasting, the next day, the conversation stayed guardedly pleasant. There were stories from when they were kids. Cousin Evie peed in the corner because she was too scared to knock on the closed bathroom door. Jimmy at six, with a crush on the girl across the street. He brought her their cat as a gift, which promptly killed her hamster. They reminisced about their father taking them for donuts when they were supposed to be going to music lessons. He would imitate their piano teacher as if she was a Nazi until Rebecca was crying from laughter.

Ruth described meeting their father in 1949 outside a dance club. "He was so handsome with his slicked-back hair and his double-breasted blue suit. I couldn't believe he wanted to talk to me." She had her first sip of alcohol with him that night at seventeen. A story she would never have told her children a few short years ago. She also described first meeting his parents, *Bubbie* and *Zadie*, to Rebecca and Jimmy. "Their apartment in Brighton smelled of fish and latkes. They were not pleased that Nathan had chosen me, because I wasn't raised in the Jewish tradition and didn't know anything. But your daddy was so sweet. He would whisper in my ear, tell me things to say that made them smile. I think by the end of that night, we both knew we would get married. A week later, he proposed."

Shree was often mentioned during the day, though no direct talk of why she was missing. Her father was never once mentioned.

Rebecca had set a place for her daughter at the table, and they each, in turn, mentioned her in their list of things to be thankful for. "I'm thankful that I have such a smart and happy granddaughter and know we will all see her soon." After what Jim had imagined, Thanksgiving was miraculously easy.

It wasn't till Friday that the train ran off the track. Jim was at his lab, leaving Rebecca and her mom to themselves. It was Rebecca who was determined to tread new ground. Her aim was to learn to talk sincerely with her mom, so that she might figure out how to do the same with Shree.

"How come we never talked about our feelings when I was growing up?" Rebecca had meant that as a sincere question, but when she thought back on it later, she realized that it did sound like an accusation.

Ruth intended to answer honestly, but somehow the words she came up with were saturated in blame. "We talked about feelings, or at least I tried. But you would close up a lot. You wouldn't talk to me. You always had time for your father, but wouldn't tell me anything."

"You know, I talked with you more than with Dad. He was gone a lot. Also, he always talked to me like I was his little girl, even when I was a teenager." Rebecca hoped to rise above her mother's defensiveness, but her words somehow would not follow her intention. "At least you didn't treat me like a child. Instead, you expected me to figure out everything for myself. You didn't even talk to me about menstruation. You just gave me a book and told me to ask my science teacher."

"Well I'm not any good at those things. At least your teacher could explain it."

"My teacher was a man, Mother. I had to ask Cathy's big sister. And there were other things we should have talked about." Rebecca had blown right past her good intentions and had returned to her familiar resentments. "I told you that Uncle Jacob exposed himself to me, and you accused me of making it up!" Uncle Jacob was Ruth's much older brother. When her daughter brought up his name, a darkness rose in her brain. Certain memories had been shoved down out of sight for many decades, and she certainly wasn't ready for them to surface. She tried to sidestep.

"At the time, I felt that the best thing to do was to let it go. I didn't know if you were telling the truth, but even if you were, I couldn't undo what you'd seen. I thought it would be better for you if you just forgot about it."

"Well, the worst way to help me forget it was to accuse me of lying about it." Rebecca felt righteously energized in pointing out her mother's failings. But even as she said it, she recognized that her real target was her own shortcomings as a mom. "You know, when I was thirteen, I let a boy feel me up, and then I felt horrible. I needed someone to talk to about it. I couldn't talk with my friends, because they were the ones who dared me to do it. It would have been nice if I could have talked about it with my own mother." Rebecca had meant this as another count in the indictment against her mother. Her mother didn't hear it that way.

"Oh you poor girl. Thirteen. Why didn't you come to me?" Ruth responded sympathetically.

"Because you would have accused me of making it up!" Rebecca snapped back.

"Well I'm sorry that I wasn't a perfect mom. At least I provided you with a stable home life." These words slipped out before Ruth could catch them. She immediately wished she could take them back, but it was too late.

"What are you saying?!" Rebecca wanted to strangle her mother at that moment. All the years of putting up with her mother's poison, all that hurt and anger came welling up like a geyser.

"Nothing, Rebecca, nothing," Ruth pleaded.

"What are you saying, mother? What are you saying?" In Rebecca's mind, her mother was accusing her once again of getting pregnant too young, of choosing a terrible husband, of divorcing him when a good wife stays with her man, and of raising her daughter alone in a broken home. Most poisonous of all, she heard her mother blame her for losing Shree to her psychotic father. That is what Rebecca heard, though Ruth had intended no such thing.

"Please, Rebecca, I didn't mean anything by it," Ruth tried meekly to rewind.

"Then why did you say it?" Rebecca said this quietly, then went into her room and closed the door. Two hours later, she realized she was once again staring at the image of the *old man in her ceiling*. He was still laughing in her Bosch nightmare.

Rebecca came out of her room and found her mom packed and waiting for Jimmy to take her to the airport. As if she were once again eight years old, she stood before her mother and apologized for her deeds. But unlike the deep imprint from the past, her mother interrupted and apologized to her. They hugged awkwardly, and her mother said, "Shree will be home soon, Rebecca, don't you worry."

39. Taken

The edge of the ocean exposes many moods. The brilliant, invigorating warmth of an October afternoon can rapidly be replaced with a depleting gray chill as the fog takes possession. Shree was blessed with a father who reveled in the windy and unwelcoming coast even more than the idyllic one. At the end of their long hike down to the sea, Tony had found his religion. What had been so clear to him in previous years, what he had been so unable to explain to Rebecca or his friends or the doctors, what he had felt alone in seeing, that was all being rewritten before his eyes. Now, living on the edge of the world, he no longer needed to explain it. The universe was right there, every day, displaying it all. If people didn't see the casual cruelty, the perfect indifference, where absolutely everything matters, well it was because they weren't looking.

Shree might have been hostage to this reawakening of her father, but his enthusiasm fueled her own awakening. She learned that if she stared into the tide pools, little marvels appeared everywhere. The crashing waves no longer frightened her. She learned the art of careful timing. She also learned about aggregating and giant green anemone; chitons, gumboots and spineys; giant keyhole limpets and their tiny limpet cousins; turban snails, kelp snails, periwinkles, and the precious jewel top snails; mussels; urchins; ocher stars, bat stars, and brittle stars; yellow, orange, and cobalt blue sponges; sand castle tube worms; shore crabs, rock crabs, hermits, and decorator crabs; and even the rare nudibranch. These and more clung to crevassed stone while incessant waves dragged their impatient fingers through the sea grasses, kelp, rock weed, and coralline algae. All of these she knew by sight, yet didn't know names other than the ones she'd made up. Fascinated, she studied the tide pools. She couldn't believe they were right there, treasures so easy to find. Tide pools were like little wildlife sanctuaries, tiny oases where creatures found peace, surrounded by storming waves. While her father was running on the beach, dancing at the foot of the waves, or climbing crumbling cliffs to discover new, unexplored coves, Shree imagined shrinking down to the size of a hermit crab and exploring her Eden with Mr. Trains.

Yet sometimes when they arrived at the shore, the tide was too high, the pools unreachable. So she'd dig into sand, watch for seals, and get to know the birds. Her father always sought the most isolated beaches, but occasionally other people appeared. They brought surfboards and dogs and even kites, yet they were tiny intrusions of civilization upon the untamed wilds.

One day, a large, excited dog knocked Shree over in a friendly greeting. The dog's owner came running, yelling at her dog, and apologizing. After putting a leash on the wet and dirty yellow lab, she asked if Shree was okay. But Shree was fine. Without thinking, she started pouring out what filled her up.

"Have you seen the creatures in the tide pools out there? They're amazing, and there are so many that they're growing on top of each other!" Talking to this stranger felt natural for Shree, though she didn't understand why.

"Oh yes! I just love the tide pools! I especially like watching the hermit crabs. Don't you? Too bad it's high tide now. Not a good time to be on the rocks." The woman responded in a friendly way, smiling at the girl alone on the beach. "Burek seems calm now. Do you mind if I let him off the leash?" Shree nodded, and Burek nuzzled her for a brief moment, then took off running down the beach. "My name is Sandy, do you mind if I join you for a few minutes before I have to chase down Burek again?"

"I don't mind. I'm Shree, I mean Renee." Her true name slipped out before she could stop it. Something about this woman reminded her of her old self. "Do you come to the beach a lot? Dad and I go to different beaches, but this one's my favorite." Her words flew effortlessly on the wind. They were soon talking of the sanderlings running up to and away from the surf wash, looking like marbles rolling across the floor. Just then, Shree saw her father marching up with a tight look on his face.

"Time to go!" He didn't say hello to the stranger or even acknowledge her presence. "It's time to go. Now!"

"Okay, Dad, I was just talking to, uh…," Shree had forgotten her name.

"It's Sandy. You have a bright and lovely daughter. We were just…"

"Okay, but it's time for us to leave." He grabbed Shree's backpack and turned to go up the sandbank and to the trail, struggling to walk swiftly while sliding back down. Shree said goodbye to Sandy and ran after her dad. They didn't say another word until they were in the van. Shree couldn't imagine why her dad was in such a hurry.

"That's not okay, Renee! You shouldn't be talking to strangers. When I saw you, I thought it was your mother coming to take you." That's it, thought Shree. That woman did look a little like her mom. Her hair. She even had a jacket that looked like Mom's. "I thought she had found us and it was all over," her father continued, his eyes looking wild.

It scared Shree to see her father so upset. "But it wasn't her, it was just some nice woman walking her dog," Shree responded.

"You don't know that. Did you tell her anything? Did you tell her our names? Where we're staying?"

Shree remembered her slip. She didn't want to lie, but she didn't want to concern her dad when there was obviously nothing to be concerned about. "I don't think so," came out before she could come up with better words.

"You don't think so?!" Her dad's voice was thundering. "What do you mean, you don't think so?!"

"I mean, no. No, I didn't say anything about us. We talked about her dog and the birds. She called them her 'namesake birds', the 'sanderlings'. That's why she told me her name: Sandy."

Her father seemed to cool down a bit. "Sanderlings? Which birds are they?"

"They're the little ones that run in and out of the waves. They look like rolling marbles."

"Oh yeah, I know the ones," her father said with a relaxing posture. "I've been calling them BB birds in my head. They do look funny running in front of the waves." With that, he turned and started up the van.

This relaxed posture didn't last, however. On the way home, he made Shree swear that she wouldn't talk to anyone anymore. "When we go to the store, or run into people, or anything. Don't look at them. If they ask questions, you can answer, but don't make eye contact. You never know who those people are or who they're working for." When she and her father started on their adventure, he'd told her that they would have to hide for a while, but that it would get easier soon. Instead of getting easier, Shree felt like it was getting harder. She just wanted to have a nice conversation, but now she wasn't allowed to look at anyone?

"Daddy, when can I go to school?" At first, she had been happy that she didn't have to go to school, but as time went on, she missed it. She liked certain subjects, though English grammar was a bore. Mostly, she missed having kids around.

"We talked about this, Renee. No school. That will be the easiest way to get caught. Besides, they aren't teaching you the important things. Don't you like our lessons?"

Oh god, the lessons. Shree had tried to follow, but her father's lessons were getting more and more tangled. He was making her read William Blake. She had no doubt the guy was a genius; her father told her that again and again. But she couldn't make any sense of most of it. 'Standing waters breed reptiles of the mind.' *What was that?! What is a reptile of the mind?* "It isn't that I don't like your lessons, it's just that I wish I had some friends here."

"I know you do, Roly Poly, but we are going to have to rely on each other for a while." His daughter's words had an ominous tinge to them, though he tried his best to hide his reaction. *She wanted friends. Of course she does. But like school, friends will come with parents, who will ask questions, and may figure things out. It didn't take Rich long to figure things out. Maybe later, Shree can have a friend. But for now, it was better they stayed hidden.*

"What about a cat? Remember you said we would talk about getting a cat?"

This set Tony back. "Did I?" He liked cats. *It would be great for Renee to have a pet. But if they had a cat, then they would have to make a home. Was it safe to think of settling down? And if someone came asking questions, wouldn't it be necessary to get out?* "Sorry, but we really can't get a cat yet. We need to be sure we'll stay here for a while. We can't take a cat on the road."

"We aren't staying here?! Where are we going?"

"I'm not saying we're going. It's great here. But if we aren't safe, we may have to leave." Tony said this, even believed this. But the thought of leaving seemed much more frightening than the thought of staying. Tensions in him were rising, but they were intangible worries beyond his recognition.

"So I can't even have a cat?!" Shree said this with obvious

exasperation, which didn't go unnoticed.

"Well there is that orange cat in the neighborhood, Gunther," Tony offered lamely. "I'm sorry Renee, but it won't always be this way. Maybe in a year or so we can get a cat." Hearing this, Shree slid into herself. A year or so! She felt angry. She hadn't felt angry at her father in, in, well, perhaps never.

~ ~ ~

Two days later, Rich knocked on the door. The team, as they referred to themselves, usually had a meeting for a few minutes each day, but Tony preferred working alone in his cabin the rest of the time. He would often even chase his daughter out so that he could concentrate. When Rich appeared, Shree was gone. Tony suspected Rich was going to push him to work faster. *The nerve of Rich, he writes such sloppy code, and he's going to tell me to work harder!* But Rich was actually quite happy with his friend's work.

"Leo, I thought I'd come by to ask you what you're doing for Thanksgiving."

Tony immediately felt evasive. He wants me to work on Thanksgiving? "Renee and I will probably go somewhere," he answered nonspecifically.

"Well Larry and Kev are both going back east for the week, so things will be slow. I thought you and Renee might like to come have dinner at my parents' house on the day. My parents would love to have you over."

Tony was unready for this. Did he want to go? *Renee would probably like it.* Then Tony imagined the prying questions Rich's folks might ask. "I don't know…."

"It will be nice, Leo. My brother's family is coming down. His son is ten. I bet he and Renee can find some trouble to get into.

Besides the turkey, my mom will make her famous coconut pumpkin pie."

"Uh…." Did *Rich's mom see me in McLean?* He couldn't quite remember. *Maybe she'll remember me, though. Maybe Rich was inviting us as a means to expose our secret. What was Rich up to?* "I think Renee has her heart set on going somewhere on Thanksgiving. Big Sur. She wants to go to Big Sur."

"You can go to Big Sur on Friday, Leo. It would be so nice if you two would come over. See where I grew up. I'd really like you to come." Rich's voice was unmistakably sincere. For whatever reason, Rich looked up to his friend. And he wanted his parents to meet him and Renee. But the most he could get out of his friend was an 'I'll let you know.' Yet Tony never did.

Instead, Leo and Renee went to the only restaurant they found open. The two of them ate turkey with soggy stuffing at a hotel diner. Tony used the occasion to tell his daughter about how colonizers had treated Native Americans. Shree kept thinking about school, how she had learned that the Pilgrims and Indians shared the first Thanksgiving meal. She remembered in first grade, coloring the outlined feathers on the friendly Indian bringing corn to the feast. Her dad called it "nation building propaganda," but she wanted to believe everyone could be friends. They finished their afternoon dinner and returned home without even a slice of pumpkin pie.

Her dad went back to his computer. He was always doing something on the computer, though Shree had no idea what. She had asked him once, but he started talking about registers and garbage bins or something, so she never asked again. To her, the computer was boring. So on Thanksgiving evening, she wandered alone in the forest like every other day.

She felt especially lonely in the cool drizzle. She looked, but Gunther, the orange cat, was nowhere to be found. The rain had turned her once dry forest into a lush, magical garden, with mushrooms emerging through rain-dappled sorrel, and deep redwood trunks clothed with velvety moss. Yet Shree was not captured by the transforming beauty; rather, she was held prisoner by her enduring isolation. From a wet and spongy moss-covered log above the now chortling creek, she thought about the previous Thanksgiving with her mom.

Shree and Uncle Jimmy were given tasks, and Mom ran the kitchen. While the turkey baked all day, Shree got to mash the potatoes and heat creamed corn. But it was the making of the pie that seemed like a special time with Mom. Together they carefully measured flour and butter for the crust, then laughed at the sticky mess they made, squeezing the dough. Mom somehow got flour in her hair, and when Shree pointed it out, she was rewarded with a bit of dough plopped onto her nose. Then there was the thick orange pumpkin glopped from a can. Shree got to run the mixer while her mom added eggs, sugar, and spices, all while describing her chain-smoking aunt making spaghetti sauce with a 'secret' ingredient, which Mom suggested was probably cigarette ash. Together, she and her mom would lick the beaters, getting orange faces and hands.

"Is Mom missing me today?" Shree asked a green beetle, the only other creature Shree saw. Then she recalled how she demonized her mom before running away. While wisps of guilt had passed through her like ghosts before, now Shree leaned into the haunting. Her mom must have felt awful when she ran away. And it was Shree's fault. *Maybe Mom wasn't fair to Dad, but I wasn't fair to her. It's one thing to argue and call her ugly names, it was another to leave her.* Shree felt shame soak into her like the misty rain. Her mother and the whole forest were crying because of what she did. *And there is no going back now. Even if I wanted to, I'd only betray Dad the same way.* The ghost of guilt had made its home in her chest: she had hurt her mom.

Eventually, chasing away dark feelings, she conjured thoughts of Wendy. *I wonder if she's having a good turkey day with her family. Maybe her jerk brother is home and is nice now. If only I could spend a day with Wendy. I wonder if she knows how to make pumpkin pie. If I were there, Wendy and I would break the wishbone. I wonder what she would wish for?* Shree broke a twig off a nearby tree and sculpted it further till it approximated a wishbone. She sat back down on her log, the wet having long since soaked through to her skin. Of all the things she might wish for at that moment, she decided to wish that the pilgrims and Native Americans actually were friends. That, and that she could help her mom make pumpkin pie again.

40. Tonic

"Is she asleep?" Rich stood at the door and whispered to Leo.

"She's down. What's up?" Leo said this softly only after stepping out onto the landing and closing the door behind him.

"We missed you at Thanksgiving, and I just wanted to catch up and see if everything's alright." The night had settled into a damp chill, though the rains had already passed. Tony was glad he had a sweater on. In the far distance, a dog was yapping. Was it a coyote, Leo wondered.

"Everything is fine," Leo replied flatly. He felt nervous at the unexpected visit of his boss. "The case-insensitive hashing is now working, but I'm gonna need more time for…".

"Let me stop you there, Amherst. We can deal with work during work hours. This is just a friendly visit. I'm a little disappointed we never just hang out." As he said this, Rich very obviously drew out a joint from his front pocket. "I was thinking about Jeffrey the other day, for some reason. That geezer in McLean, talking to himself, repeating the same thing all day? 'Don't touch the water. It's ionic. But I told him that's not why…'. Remember? All day long he repeated it, and no one knew what the hell he was talking about." With that, he lit the joint and took a deep toke. Tony heard an owl surprisingly close to the cabin. After smoke poured from his lungs, Rich continued. "Ms. Halliday tried to get him to say something, anything different in group, but he never did." Rich casually pressed the joint towards Leo. Leo waved it off nervously. "But *you* got him to stumble once, remember?"

Tony warmed a bit at the shared memory. He and Rich would have little games to try to pass the time in 'Summerville'. "Yeah, it took me forever to do it!" Tony began.

Rich laughed excitedly, but quickly quieted down when his friend motioned to the window, reminding him that Renee might wake up. "You tried everything before getting him to crack. You stole his food, you poured water down his back, what else?"

"I pretended I was his mother talking to him from under his bed." Tony again demurred when Rich absentmindedly offered the glowing marijuana.

"You talked in Pig Latin, you tried Spanish, you tried French. Anything to get him to deviate." Rich enjoyed drawing out the shared memory.

"I know, I couldn't even speak French. I also made up a language." That stupid game kept him occupied for the better part of a week, distracting him from the soullessness of McLean. And now again, the memory was distracting him from his desire to shut Rich out.

"What was it you did that finally made him crack?" Rich asked, knowing full well how it went down.

"Well I stopped him outside the bathroom, and I kept him as long as I could. I had left the water running in the sink. You could see it was getting to him, and then I started chanting his lines. 'Don't touch the water, he says. It's ionic. But I told him that's not why it scalds.' Several times through with him, just like he said it. But then I started varying the order like jazz. 'Don't touch the water, it scalds. He says it's water. That's ionic. Don't touch, he says. It's that he's ionic. Don't scald the water. It's he.' He kept up his lines perfectly for four or more rounds. But then he slipped and said, 'It's tonic!' The look on his face! He stopped a couple of words into the next line. Smiled at me and then pushed past into the bathroom. In that one moment, we connected!" With that, a very satisfied Tony took the joint, which was almost out. He took a long, hard drag, the red glow of the ember lighting his heroic face. A long-ago familiar feeling seeped into his brain almost immediately. The rasping pain along his upper throat. His lungs suddenly full, and yet empty of air. He suppressed a cough, worried he would wake Shree. Smoke poured from his nostrils and teared up his eyes. It had been more than a decade since he'd smoked pot.

"He went back to his normal lines by the next day. But for a moment, you woke him up, man!" Rich was proud of his friend and also pleased with himself that he was bringing the embers of their friendship back to life.

The pungent smoke was rapidly taking over Tony's head, but the momentum of the conversation carried him along for a while. "When I sat next to him in group after that, I would whisper 'tonic' when he got to the 'ionic' and he would shake his head, and sometimes he would smile." Then, after a short pause, "Remember how you got that old man to write a poem for Ms. Halliday?" Tony heard himself say this almost before he thought it. *Did I say it out loud? Did Rich say it?*

Rich felt a little guilty for having played that game, but decided to just enjoy the memory for the moment. "He seemed so sad when his wife didn't visit, so I convinced him that Ms. Halliday had told her not to come because she was jealous. Then I couldn't help myself, telling him how the old lady would look tenderly at him whenever he was looking the other way."

"You even said she wore a special perfume just for him. He was eating it up." Again, Tony's contribution came without him realizing it. Had he had this conversation before, he wondered. *Who is feeding me the lines?*

"Well I probably took it too far. I feel sorry for old man Ritter," Rich quietly confessed. With that, the conversation collapsed into silence.

It was then that Tony realized he was far more stoned than he wished to be. He marveled at how he had just been laughing with Rich. *Had I really? Did I just imagine it? Why is Rich here?*

For his part, Rich thought about the other side of being in Summerville. In particular, why he had been there. He couldn't blame Helen for his depression. When she broke up with him, he felt the darkness take hold and he was crippled by it. At first, he had been obsessed with trying to get her back, but the more he had tried, the more he demeaned himself, and begged, and cried, the more pathetically broken he felt. Then that wild night, after he saw her with someone else. He smashed his moped into a hedge, badly damaging it and dislocating his shoulder. Then, back at the dorms, he tore up his room. He destroyed not only his own, but all of his roommate's stuff too. His notes, the paper he'd been working on, the stereo. When he realized what he had done, how pathetic he was, he had taken a shard of glass from the window he had smashed and tried to slit his wrists. Luckily the proctor unlocked the door and stopped him before he cut himself too badly. And he was in lockup that night. Now he recalled how he toyed with Ritter's emotions. He wasn't proud of himself.

Was he cold? Tony couldn't tell. He was in a cloud of incomplete thoughts, not knowing if any were real. *So Rich had gotten me stoned and is talking about the days in Summerville. Like it was some kind of joke. Is he implying something?* He thought maybe Rich wanted to go back. *Maybe he liked it there? Maybe he wants to drag me back too. Is that what this is about? Is Rich in love with me? He's sitting so close on this bench.* The warmth of Rich's leg against his. *Do I actually feel Rich's leg? Is that in my head? I should get up. But if I do, will he know what I'm thinking? Did he just put his hand on my thigh? Has he?! No, no that's just my imagination. Nothing is on my thigh. Why did I think he did? Do I want him to?*

Tony had his head hanging down now. A stranger passing

might think he was praying. His overgrown mane now hid his face from view, and that was a refuge. He was glad it was dark. He knew he was incapable of interacting with people at that moment, catatonically silenced by a cacophony of thoughts, uprooted from reality. He began wondering if he was smelling a foul bathroom stench, but he wasn't sure if it was just in his head. Maybe he had flatulated? The thought that he couldn't control his own gases horrified him with shame. He was by nature priggishly uptight. His corporeal existence was a circumstance he'd rather ignore. *Maybe Rich farted. I hope to god it was Rich. Let him be the disgusting animal.* Then the thoughts of why Rich even liked him returned. *Is his stench some kind of power move? If there even IS a smell.* Tony just couldn't tell if any of it were true. There was no objective truth, he postulated. *I'm drowning in subjective conjectures.* And now the shape of the words 'subjective conjectures' turned over in his mind again and again, and he wasn't sure if he was saying them aloud. *Like tumbling stones.*

"We've grown up a lot since then, haven't we, Leo?" Tony uncomfortably nodded to the voice from a distant mountain. "Not that I'm perfect, I still screw up plenty. But I'm much happier with myself now. And I am amazed by you, Leo. You are raising your girl, and she's great. I know that has everything to do with what a caring dad you are."

What's he talking about? He's proud of himself? He's happy with himself? Is that code? And what's he talking about Shree for? What is his interest in my daughter? Is he a pedophile? First he's touching me, but then he's going after Shree? Is that what this is about? Is that why he invited us here? Gave me the job? Because he saw Shree in the store that day? That's why he suddenly took an interest. You know, I've never heard of him having a girlfriend. All these years, and he never had a girlfriend? Because he is a disgusting little perverted weasel. I should knock some sense into him right now. I can grab a log from the firewood bin. I could crack it over his head this instant!

NO! I can't DO that. Even if I knew he was a pedophile, I'm not sure I could do that. But do I know? Is he a pedophile pervert, or am I just stoned? I've got to figure it out. And I can't risk having my daughter here. I can't wait till it's too late. But no, this can't be real. He's just Rich. He's my friend. Nothing is weird about him. But…. No, it's Rich. Is he touching me again? No, his legs are clearly not touching mine. Rich is alright. Rich is tonic. Is he crying? "I gotta go in now." Tony got up quickly and almost didn't wait for an answer.

"Okay Amherst. By the way, I've got leftovers from the big dinner. If you and Renee want to come over for turkey and pumpkin pie tomorrow, you are certainly welcome." To that, Tony mumbled something noncommittal and went inside.

The first thing he did was check that Shree was still asleep. She seemed to be, so he took off his boots and climbed into the loft bed, trying to contain the creaking of the wooden supports. Finally, he settled into silence. He was above her alcove and beyond her sight, even if she woke up. In almost complete darkness, he still felt eyes were on him. He felt sure there was something in the dark watching him. *Mice? There certainly are spiders.* Were they looking at him? Judging him? And it was their house; he was the uninvited guest. As he lay there, he felt sure that someone was watching him. He knew it wasn't his daughter. Then he became viscerally aware that it was Rebecca. Rebecca could see him! Rebecca's anger was palpable. In the cabin, he could feel it. She may have been two thousand miles away, but she was there. Hating him. Plotting to get him. And he felt his mother, too. Rebecca had enlisted his mother, and they were plotting. His mom wasn't crying this time. She too was angry. *Her little boy had gone too far in taking Shree. And there is only one way back. There is no way to atone and only one way back. And Rich. Rich too, is looking at him. Lusting. And Rich's mom. She's there watching. Somehow, Rebecca had reached her too, and the network of seething moms is drawing its net.*

Shree suddenly snorted in her sleep, then rolled over. And Tony knew that the seething web of women was going to reach her, too. Their hatred for him had found Shree in her sleep and tapped her on the shoulder. *My sweet, innocent Roly Poly is going to hate me one day!*

41. One Night

December 9th

Jim stopped short before opening the door to Sirrus's building. Over the break, he had a lot of time to think about how much he missed her and what their friendship meant to him. Feeling the weight of regret, he concluded that he had all but lost her as a friend. But from within the aimlessness of his mourning, an idea flickered into his head. If he had lost her, he might as well tell her how he really felt. Thus hope, from out of nowhere, soon dominated his waking hours. He should tell her, maybe this is what she was waiting for. Maybe she felt the same way after all these weeks. Maybe this wasn't the end of their friendship, but the start of something much more. He had turned the conversation over in his head, what he would say, how she might respond… a smile, a hug, a first kiss? It all had seemed so possible in his head, but now he was standing outside her building, and nothing seemed possible but humiliation. Nevertheless, he had to try. So, nervously, he pushed open the outer door.

Her roommate, Claire, answered his shaky knock. "Sue's not here right now." Jim forgot that Susan was Sirrus's given name. She hated it. Claire held the door open for Jim to come in. "She ought to be back any minute."

"Like in the next ten minutes? I have to get back." Jim nervously made excuses as he crossed the threshold. He didn't know much about Claire, but he always felt like she was laughing at him. She was very different from Sirrus, with big blond hair and traditional makeup. Like a cheerleader living with a geek. Anyway, he was pretty sure she didn't like him, so he was surprised she was inviting him in.

"You know you're blowing it with her. She could have really used you the last few weeks, but you were nowhere to be found. She broke up with Conner." Claire said this, hoping that she was telling him something he didn't know. It had been pretty obvious to Claire that her roommate's "best friend" was in love with her. When Sirrus had broken it off with Conner, Claire had expected this puppy dog standing before her would come running. But he had stayed away.

"Broke up? Really? Is she okay?" Jim consciously had to suppress his smile. "Seems like they were heading in that direction for a while now. Seriously, is she okay?"

"She's fine. Conner came over one night after she told him, and there was a lot of yelling." Claire, too, felt her smile was out of place. But after the heat had settled, she found it all hilarious. He had accused her of a lot of ugly things, including sleeping with James, but the only one that struck Claire was that he called her fake and not very bright. While Claire made fun of her Sirrus name, she thought Sue was a whole lot smarter than Conner. "But when the arguing was done and Conner finally left, Sue was kind of, uh, relieved." Claire remembered her wiping away tears and laughing. "She had said, 'It's good to get that over with.' I'm totally impressed with how well she's taken it. Still, I think she could have used your shoulder."

"Well we haven't been getting along lately."

"Yeah, I heard. Not what it's about. But I asked where you were, and she said you had a big fight. Whatever it is, get over it. She needs a friend." Claire, who had an active social life and boyfriend, and was never very close to Sue, still felt responsible for her. Sirrus, on the other hand, felt perfectly fine, not even being aware of Claire's world.

After waiting a few more minutes, Jim felt the awkward pauses in the conversation. "Well can you let her know I came by? Tell her that I need to speak with her. See you." And with that, he slipped out the door.

Buoyed by the news that Conner was no longer an obstacle, he tried to guess where she might be. He was carried by the winds of his hope and the December evening to walk through the library, do a loop of the student union, around a couple of the quads, and even walked through his lab building, irrationally imagining that she might be looking for him. When no sign of her turned up, he thought about returning to her building, though he didn't want to talk to Claire again. It was on the doorstep to her building that he found her, sitting.

"Claire told me you came by." Sirrus said this as an accusation. Her voice wasn't friendly, and she seemed braced for something unpleasant.

"Yeah, I wanted to speak to you." As James said this, he felt he couldn't go through with telling her that he wanted to be more than friends. At that point, just being friends seemed hard to ask for. He sat down beside her without asking. He immediately noticed two things. It was going to be easier to talk with her if he wasn't facing her. And he could feel her warmth beside him, and it never felt more comforting than now. "Well I just wanted to say that I really miss you. I don't want to be fighting, I don't want us to be upset. I just really miss our friendship."

Sirrus let the words sink in for a while. In the cold evening, she too felt the warmth beside her. So much had gone on since they had fought, she struggled to remember why she was mad at him. But one thing she knew still to be true. She had decided to take the reins of her life, to break up with Conner, to be less dependent on other people. Take control of her education and choose her way in life. Her fight with James had been the impetus for change. Now James missed the old her. She knew she missed James, too. She really did. But where once she could imagine falling into a relationship with him, now she knew she mustn't. She felt it was essential to her self-worth that she stay on her own for a while. Besides, she was leaving. Finally, she spoke. "I missed you too, James. But now I need to be alone."

As soon as she said this, she wished she hadn't. She suddenly remembered James's tender, sweet smile. She remembered how much fun they had, laughing at nonsense, talking science, philosophy, the Marx brothers, early Pink Floyd. She remembered how it felt, like coming home, when she entered his dorm room. How she was always safe and happy and herself with him. But with the words she had just uttered, she felt like she had slapped him across the face. Her tears began to well up. But she stopped herself. She would be strong.

Jim was dumbstruck by her phrase. She 'needed to be alone'. He had imagined this conversation many times over, but he certainly never expected this. What was he to say now? "But we can still be friends, can't we? I mean, I don't want to give up our friendship. What do you mean, 'need to be alone'?" As he said this, he had to awkwardly move away from her to let someone walk down the steps between them. The girl moved quickly away from the pain of strangers.

"The thing is, I've made some changes in my life. Claire told you that I broke up with Conner." Jim nodded. "And I have been taking some time to decide a few things." You remember, I told you I was quite introverted in junior high. Well I'm finding a lot of strength again in solitude. Also, I haven't been happy in Hendrick's lab, so I'm transferring to Stanford. Dr. Beal has offered me a place." There, she said it. She had hardly told anyone. Even though she was moving in a week.

Jim was even more dumbstruck. Leaving?! In his chest, he felt a burning sensation. He felt a little dizzy. What had he hoped? It was all ending. She didn't want him as a friend anymore, and she was leaving. "Transferring? Really?"

These words didn't come out in his normal soft timbre, Sirrus noticed. They sounded off-key. She struggled to put her finger on it. Desperation? Anger? Derision? She felt for a moment she had to justify herself, then she recovered her own composure. "Yeah, Dr. Beal is running a great program in leukemia, and I'm hoping to focus on stem cells in bone marrow. Cell differentiation."

Ordinarily, Jim would have loved to fall into a discussion about stem cells, but her words seemed totally beside the point. "But you're leaving! I'm not gonna see you anymore?"

"Yes. You can always come out to visit." She offered this idea as people do, casually. She knew full well what James meant. But she stayed strong, not looking into her own abyss of feeling.

"That's horrible! I've missed you so much, and now I'm going to lose you completely." And now he knew he had to tell her. "You know you mean the world to me. And this just sucks. Of course you'll do what you gotta do. But if you ask me, this is awful. You're my best friend. My best friend ever."

"You're my best friend too, James. But I have to do this. I have to get away from here. I have to take control of my life." Sirrus was strong, but her feelings were bubbling through. She had missed him deeply, and her life in California was going to be difficult without him. She wouldn't miss Conner, but James was another story. She fought her emotions back.

"But you're more than a friend to me, Sirrus. I love you." His voice cracked when he said it.

"I love you too, James, but…".

"You don't understand," Jim pressed on. "I don't just love you as a friend, I LOVE love you. I have for a long time. I have been afraid of ruining our friendship, but you might as well know, since it's ruined anyway. I really love you." Jim was staring down at a flattened coffee cup in the flower bed beside the steps. His words were out, and he felt kinship with the empty, discarded cup.

"Well I... I think I knew," Sirrus answered in almost a whisper. She too, was staring at the cup. "But sometimes the timing isn't right in life. Maybe we could have been good together, but maybe it just would have screwed everything up." She turned to him and spoke more firmly, almost pleading. "I'm sorry, James. But I have to do this. I have to find my way. And it isn't here in Houston anymore."

"When do you leave?" His voice was so steady. Unexpectedly normal.

"Thursday," she answered in a quiet, apologetic voice.

The two of them sat in silence, neither one knowing what to say. Jim tried to put his feelings into a box that he might store on a top shelf somewhere, while Sirrus let her mind dwell on the thought of what might have been. After several minutes of silence, Jim stood up, and Sirrus followed. "Well I'll let you go," Jim faintly said.

As he turned, Sirrus caught him and pulled him into a hug. Before she knew what was happening, James kissed her, and she kissed back. It was sweet. Tender. Then James's passion grew. Sirrus suddenly pulled away, breaking their embrace. "Why did you do that?" She said it, though she knew exactly why. "We can't do this, James. We can't! I can't." And before the moment could get any more awkward. "Just go."

And so they parted in more turmoil than ever. Jim turned back and said, just as her building door was closing, "I'm sorry." But he didn't think she heard.

His dorm room never felt so tiny and empty as when he

returned that evening. Clothes still on, he buried himself under the blanket with his head under his pillow. The normal sounds of dorm life could still be heard through the walls and bedding. He felt like crying, but nothing came out to the muffled sounds of Dire Straits. He could tear up in sympathy with characters in a movie, but he couldn't cry in his own heartbreak. Time passed slowly, but he couldn't coax himself to sleep. He told her that he loved her, but it would never be. It occurred to him that his suffering was nothing compared to what his sister was going through. And Tony had gone through. But it still ached. He knew it would take a long time before he felt whole again. He decided Sirrus was right to have broken off the kiss. She was leaving. It would feel even worse if they continued. She had already let go, which is what he needed to somehow do.

Near 2 am, there was a knock on his door. Then she was standing in front of him. *Is she actually here?* She stood in the doorway, not pushing past him like she'd done so many times before.

"It's like this. We spend this one night together, and then we don't see each other again. This is it. This is goodbye. Promise me. When I get to California, I will write you. But over the next week, we stay away from each other." Jim would have agreed to anything.

42. Higher Still

A forest has its charms at any time. But anyone who walks in a forest after the rain knows it at its best. One needn't ascribe emotions to plants to see that they are at their happiest when wet. With sunlight peeking through and water still dripping from boughs, colors seem more vibrant than physics can explain. This is especially true in the redwood forests of the Pacific coast. For eight months or more, there isn't a drop of rain. Colors recede to drab as nature conserves her resources. Then rain returns, and so does the joy of growing. The moss springs up into a lush, inviting lace, redwood trunks turn a deep red like velvet cake, while sorrel collects raindrops, like pearls. Greens expand to a full, diverse spectrum, across deep, rich warmths, chilly blues, light and vibrant neons, whimsical variegates, and endless gradations in between. And though the greens have expanded their numbers enough to crowd out everyone else, the wet forest still teams with scarlet berries, amber slugs, tangerine fungi, and sapphire and indigo flowers.

Even the dead and the dying seem happier when wet. Vermillion and butterscotch leaves felled by the rain, paint patches of earth. Massive carcasses of trees, toppled decades ago, now soak up the moisture like a sponge and display their bounty of termite tunnels in mustard brown, still sheathed in rusty garnet and coal-blackened bark hosting ferns, moss, and white and golden fungi looking just like fat pancakes. Decomposing branches, charred trunks, and tangled dead roots, recently camouflaged in dust, now glisten and intrigue as ebony silhouettes against the verdant riot. The earth tones themselves have expanded to every shade and pattern of mud, granite, sandy loam, and sculpted rivulet left by spontaneous water flows. The solitary walker in a forest still dripping with rain makes acquaintance with newborn mushrooms peaking up in quiet hope, banana slugs racing along fallen logs at almost visible speeds, birds splashing in momentary puddles, spiders rebuilding, and squirrels passing their gossip. The redwood forest lives for these happiest of days.

Shree didn't notice this transformation right away. She had stayed inside to read when it was rainy out. Then couldn't put down her book when the rain stopped. Sent outside by her father, she still failed to notice, as pictures on the walls of a home are unthought of day to day. But one day, with nothing new to read, while feeling lonelier and chillier than usual, she noticed that the moss on a distant tree branch caught the light in the most extraordinary way. And suddenly, her familiar world was as magical as an alien planet. She couldn't believe she hadn't noticed before, the shafts of sunlight setting the outlines of trees in glistening relief, like a Disney fairy was waving a wand and bringing everything alive. And after a morning of looking at every kind of leaf and sprig, at the tiniest of mushrooms sprouting from the side of a fallen log, at slugs, and newts, and a garter snake. Every happy bird that cuts the airy way. A morning marveling at mysterious paw prints repeating through the runnelled mud. After hours of widened eyes, she found herself lying back on a moss-covered log, in a clearing she dubbed "Fern Glen," looking aloft into the beckoning heights. Some of those trees are really tall, she thought.

"Well let's go see what's up there?" Mr. Trains hung from two arms on a low branch, his feet dragging on the ground, no longer supporting his weight.

"You know I can't climb these trees! I've tried already." Shree braced herself for the trouble her imaginary friend might pull her into.

"Sure you can, Shree. You just haven't had me to give you a boost. Look up there. I bet you can see the ocean from the top."

"I can't even see the top from down here. All I see are branches."

"Yes, and ? Look how easy it is up above. Down here, the branches are few and far between. But the higher you get, the closer they are. The only hard thing about climbing a redwood is the first few branches. And I can help you up those, no problem." Mr. Trains could see the resistance was ebbing. Shree was too curious to hold out for long.

Shree struggled to get a grip on the first branch, which was so thick it could be its own tree. But with Mr. Trains's help, she made it to the fourth branch before things started to seem possible. The bark was soft and easy to grab hold of, with plenty of deep fissures into which she wedged her toes. Of course she had taken off her shoes to help feel her way. Everything was going well till suddenly it wasn't. She slipped from her thirteenth branch, just catching herself. But when she took a moment to assess, it suddenly became clear to her that she was shockingly far up in the tree!

"What are you stopping for, Shree?" Mr. Trains sat on a branch above, just dangling his feet. Shree guessed he wasn't even holding on. 'Guessed', because by now, Shree was too afraid to look around her. She just clung to the trunk, trying not to look. "Come on Shree, we're not even a third of the way up!"

"I don't think I can do it." Shree said this softly, as if too loud a sound might cause the tree to shake. She closed her eyes and tried to convince herself it wasn't as scary as she thought. But all she could think about was what would happen if she fell.

"Sure you can!" *Fall?* she thought. "Look, you made it to here, and the rest gets easier and easier." *It's all too easy if you slip.* "The

branches are getting closer together. It'll soon be like a staircase."
What Mr. Trains was purposefully leaving out is that they would
have to climb down eventually, and that would get harder and
harder.

"I can't move," Shree managed to say through clenched teeth.

"Yes. You. Can." This was said softly but firmly. "You can do
this. Take a deep breath and look into my eyes." Shree's blue eyes
stared into green irises and pupils that returned calm. "Now think
how easy it will be to reach up to this next branch, pull yourself up
and over, then straddle it. I'm right here beside you. You can do
this."

Shree reached up and pulled herself to the next branch.
"Good. Just like that," Mr. Trains encouraged. "Just take it one
branch at a time."

"But I want to go down." Shree was no longer shaking, but
felt certain that she could only relax when this was over.

"But you are going to the top. You've come this far. Down
isn't going anywhere. We will get there eventually. But you haven't
come this far to turn around. Just think of the view you're gonna
get." Mr. Trains, usually playful and often only concerned with
himself, was calm, confident, and assuring.

Shree continued the climb up. It was easier to put the height
out of her mind, especially in the final third of their ascent, when
the branches were so frequent and cluttered that it was hard to
weave through them, much less imagine somehow falling and not
being caught in the net of branches. At one point, they rested to
catch their breath. A stellar jay flew in through the branches and
landed a mere four feet away from Shree. She held her breath,
frozen, hoping not to scare it. The tree itself was slowly swaying. A
second jay flew into the tree. The two trilled rapidly to each other,
then suddenly noticed Shree and took to wing in an instant. Shree
marveled how they flew between the branches so quickly, without

running into even the smallest twig.

After over forty minutes of climbing, they reached the top. Or at least to where the trunk and branches were so spindly that they couldn't hold Shree's weight. Their tree was eerily moving from side to side, though Shree felt secure in her perch. The wind could be heard, but she didn't feel it. They were above most of the surrounding trees, and through the branches, they could see the view.

"Didn't I tell you?! Didn't I?!" There's the ocean."

Shree looked where Mr. Trains was pointing and couldn't see the ocean at all. "That's a large blue roof! It's not even in the direction of the ocean. And we can't see it because there is a whole other mountain in the way." Shree pointed with an outstretched hand toward another forest-covered hill not very far away. Now that she thought about it, she had known all along that they wouldn't see the ocean.

"Look, we can see into that mansion. See that man? He's naked." Mr. Trains said this like a five-year-old boy who giggles when he says the word 'butt'.

Shree looked at the house, a big house, the closest one to them, with large windows and a deck. "That's not a mansion, that's Rich's house. And that is his grandmother, not some man. And she is fully clothed. You need glasses, Mr. Trains."

Her climbing companion was not deterred. "Well we can see what she's doing, nevertheless. We can spy on her and she will never know."

Shree took a moment to consider if they were doing anything wrong. But then realized that she couldn't see much at all at that distance. The only way she knew it was Rich's grandmother was because who else could it be? And as for seeing what she was doing, well. Knitting? Making a jigsaw puzzle? Reading a book? So the evils of spying were undermined by the paucity of tantalizing secrets that could be gleaned.

The way down was fine. At least for the first third. But there came a time when the thought of losing grip and falling through unforgiving branches to a broken neck, grew persistent. And when Shree had to dangle her feet down and find the next branch with her toes, while barely holding her grip, Shree again felt panic. Again, she clung to the trunk, not daring to look further down. Again, she knew she couldn't move.

"Shree, this is nonsense! You are practically standing on the ground, so why not just bounce down the few last branches?" Mr. Trains was no longer the calm, assuring guide. Instead, his impatience with his frightened companion went undisguised.

"We are NOT practically on the ground. We are not even halfway down! We are fifteen stories up! If I fall now, I will bounce off any branches below and and...," Shree shuddered to think what it would look like. She felt needles in her hands and the back of her head. Her chest was filled with a sort of rushing lightness. Lightness in the face of her heavy fall. Shree could not imagine moving again. Yet she knew she had to get down. Mr. Trains wasn't going to help. She had to do it herself. After a long time, she felt a drop of rain. "Oh no."

Silence greeted her. Maybe her climbing partner had abandoned her. She was all alone, far above the ground, with rain about to make everything slippery. So she swung her legs under the branch, lowered her torso, keeping her current branch under her armpits, and felt for the branch below. Nothing. Her toes reached down as far as she could, but there was nothing to catch hold of. She felt her strength ebbing as she released one arm, clinging desperately with the other, stretching another ten inches towards the next branch. Nothing. If she unhooked her second arm and hung by her hands alone, she would never be able to pull herself back up. But she had to reach that branch! She looked down. She could see it, just a little to the side. If she dropped straight down, she would skim it but would fall for another twenty feet before any branch came close. And she would just keep falling. Until…. Again, she was frozen in fear. The tree was swaying, and she felt dizzy. Diz… disoriented. Where was she? Still hanging, that's right. She couldn't hold on with her arms much longer. She doubted she could pull herself up again. So she positioned her loose arm so that she could reach her hands together and make a loop around the branch she was dangling from. And slowly she let loose her armpit and felt her full weight on her hands. Nothing. Still nothing below with her feet. The branch she clung to dipped lower a few feet further out. She shuffled her hands, inch by inch. But this caused the branch to bend and undulate. She again felt the whole tree moving back and forth above the unmoving ground, as she held on only by her now sweating hands. Why couldn't she reach the branch? She had to find that branch. Her whole body stretched to the limit as her left foot pawed the air, trying to find her only hope.

Just then, she heard a crack and felt herself fall. No branch saved her as she rushed by, feeling whips of twigs as she flailed her arms and legs, trying to catch anything. The horror lengthened as time slowed, but nothing saved her from the desperate fall. She felt her ankle hit something, and now she plunged headfirst as all became darkness, and suddenly she felt herself falling up, propelled back up into the maze of branches and then down again. This time, the unexpected woke her from her terror, and she realized that something was around her ankle and slowing her downward journey until she stopped descending again and was gently pulled up a few feet. Then she came to a rest, dangling just off the ground. She reached for a branch that happened to be the lowest one on the tree. Once safely on it, she looked at her ankle and saw a hand and a long, stretched-out arm, like a rope hanging limply from her foot. From above, she heard a cacophony of branches bending and guffaws until the rest of Mr. Trains joined her on the branch.

"Well my fellow spy, what did you think of that?!" Mr. Trains was very proud of himself. Quickly Shree's fear turned to gratitude, then to anger, then back to gratitude.

"Well my stretchy friend, next time let me know what you're up to before I die of fright." And though Shree had thought herself surely dead, but moments ago, she couldn't help but smile broadly and feel proud of herself. After all, the only part of her that had actually left the ground was her imagination.

43. Dancing Mermaids

The morning after Rich had shared a joint with him, Tony stayed in bed. Thoughts that had poured out of him the night before now slowly slinked out of his mind and fell on the floor like so many wet leaves under an autumn tree. As quickly as the familiar feeling of being high had returned, the daylight rejection of those thoughts commenced. His fear of Rich seemed laughable. Lusting after him! A pedophile?! It was Rich, after all. Calm, clever, sometimes arrogant Rich. He is harmless. And Tony had actually thought about cracking him over the head last night. Absurd. Not for the first time, Tony concluded marijuana was not for him.

Had he really imagined that Rebecca was staring at him last night? From thousands of miles away?! Communicating telepathically with his mom? And there was a mom network, all hating him, all searching for him. How could he believe such nonsense? No, the marijuana really did a number on him last night. Long ago, he loved getting high, no matter how paranoid he would get. He had been convinced that there was truth to be found in that fearful symmetry. So he kept riding the tiger. But he had given it up soon after Shree came into his life. The paranoia seemed so out of place in a world with his daughter.

One thought from the previous night persisted in the light of day, however. One stubborn leaf, refusing to fall to the ground, no matter how he shook. He had fallen asleep thinking that Shree would hate him one day. Perhaps she would, he conceded. Was he doing the right thing, taking her from her mom? Keeping her isolated in this redwood forest without her friends? Keeping her out of school. Their lonely Thanksgiving… he had failed her. He would have to do better. Of course he had to keep her safe. Hadn't he done so? Since they left Houston, he had stayed rational. He had kept his mind on what was important. Changing cars, changing names, finding a place to live. But perhaps he was missing one very important thing. Shree needed a home, not just somewhere to live. He thought long and hard about what that would entail.

He got up late in the day and cleaned the cabin, then made noodles for dinner. Shree told him about climbing trees, stories she must have made up. They had a pleasant evening listening to a light sprinkle of rain on the roof as they warmed themselves by the fire and played checkers.

It wasn't until a couple of days passed that Tony remembered Rich had invited them for pumpkin pie. So he and his daughter walked up the hill to Rich's place. 'The Big House', they called it. He lived with his grandmother, who never seemed to leave her room upstairs. Rich had made the house his home. While there were a lot of doilies, ceramic figurines, and old photos pushed to the periphery, collecting dust. A torn-apart computer, soldering iron, miscellaneous other tools and wires, an "Asteroids" arcade video game, and a four-foot-tall plastic Tyrannosaurus had taken over the center of the room.

"I'm sorry, man. I totally meant to share the pie with you, but it was so good that I couldn't stop eating. Tell you what, let's go into town and get some food and pie, my treat." With that, Rich called up to his grandma that they were going, and away they went. Tony suppressed the thought that Rich had not really meant to invite them. And Shree, well all she was thinking about was that pumpkin pie had been dangling, just out of reach, for more than a week. She would believe it when she tasted it.

Within twenty minutes, they were parking near the beach in town. It was like they walked out onto the sky, Shree thought, as they strolled out on the wharf. The sun was slipping slowly towards the horizon, and the water had a calm, glassy look. She had gotten used to the big waves carving up the shorelines north of town, yet here, a soft evening swell lazily arrived at the beach and collapsed like a tired puppy. Seagulls effortlessly hovered above their heads, gliding towards unknown destinations. A lone pelican stood on the railing, looking every bit like a local, quietly judging the loud touristing humans. When the waves up north churned, the sky filled with water vapor, draping the cliffs in a soft gauze. But this evening every detail was distinct, in fresh focus, as if seen for the first time through new prescription lenses. The smooth, silvery surface of the water seemed almost warmed by the golden glints of the late afternoon sun. Shree pictured Mr. Trains skating across the water as if it were ice. How exhilarating it felt, flying between sea and sky. The silvery golden glass was interrupted by a lone sailboat at anchor. A teenage girl on board, busy yet in no hurry.

Her dad and Rich were pointing down in the water right by the massive black pilings. At first, Shree was intrigued by a long stretch of kelp curling at the surface, reaching down, and disappearing into the green depths. Suddenly a sea lion swished past, coming to the surface for a brief moment before twisting over itself, then under and out of sight. It finally dawned on her that the loud barking she had been ignoring wasn't from dogs, but from these wild ocean acrobats. Huge, the size of bears, they lounged on the cross supports under the wharf.

Fish and chips were ordered, and clam chowder in a bowl made of bread. While they ate, the sun went down and the sea changed from silver and golden, to crimson and burgundy. Walking back towards land, over the darkened sky, Shree didn't even notice that they still didn't get pie. Lights from land and from slowly undulating boats were waving reflections across the otherwise hidden surface. Rich shared that his granddad had told him the reflections were dancing mermaids. They crossed over to the opposite railing to witness the mermaid queen, painted by the now rising moon.

"Time for pie!" Rich said as they arrived at his car. He knew his Santa Cruz, and they found pumpkin pie in Paul's Diner on the north edge of town. At the table, Rich asked Shree what she wanted Santa to bring her.

Her dad defended her honor. "Renee hasn't believed in Santa since she was six."

"What, you don't believe in Santa?" Rich teased. "Why I believe in him so much that I live in Santa Cruz!"

"Come on, guys, I'm eleven. You're pouring it on a bit thick, don't you think?" Shree just had to say something, between forkfuls of the long-awaited manna. Not the same as what she and her mom had made, but quite delicious nonetheless.

"Alright, alright! I guess you aren't hoping for a dolly from the fat guy," Rich smiled. "What do you want?"

"I dunno. Maybe a pet sea lion. But not a stuffed one," Shree suddenly added, to be sure her joke wasn't mistaken for a request for a sea lion dolly.

"Well they are protected by the Marine Mammal Protection Act, so I think we will have to look on the black market," Rich slyly smiled. Shree felt happy that she wasn't being talked down to anymore, as she wiped whipped cream off her upper lip.

Her father, on the other hand, felt an unwelcome thought clink in his mind. Maybe Rich really was a pedophile. What was he doing, talking to his daughter that way? No, he pushed back on the thought. Rich was just being a friend. Then he noticed a woman in a booth near the door looking at them. She was trying to hide it, but he saw her. The waitress rotated over to her table, and the two started talking. *About us? Was the woman trying to warn the waitress about us?* The waitress went into the kitchen. *There was the look again. That woman detests us. And a man at the bar. He's in on it too. Is the waitress calling the police?* "We have to go now. Finish your pie."

"Amherst, what's the rush? We're almost finished." Rich looked at his friend, a little concerned.

Tony noticed the look. *What's his attitude mean? I'll have to figure it out later. Any moment the police will arrive... I'll lose my daughter again.* "Just, I think we need to leave now. I can't explain it, but we need to leave."

"Alright, alright. Lemme pay the bill."

"Renee and I will wait in the car," Tony said firmly and quietly. Rich handed him the keys.

Once they were out of the restaurant, Shree spoke. "What's wrong, Dad?" But Tony said nothing until they were in the car.

"I think someone might have recognized us, Shree. We have to keep out of sight until we're forgotten."

Shree felt sure her dad was exaggerating. No one could have recognized them. Just then, a police car pulled into the parking lot. How did her dad know? Shree hadn't noticed anything, but her dad knew! They watched Rich walk past the police officers as they entered and he exited the diner. As they drove out of the parking lot, the two cops chatted with the waitress while she poured them their usual coffees and offered them blueberry pie.

No one said a word on the way home. Not until Rich was dropping them at their cabin. "Thank you for dinner and pie, Rich!" Shree remembered her mother emphasizing how important it was to say 'thank you'.

"No worries. It was a nice evening. We should do it again sometime soon." Rich was sincere. He really did want to spend more time with Leo and Renee. Living alone with his grandmother was sad sometimes.

"Yeah, thanks, Rich." Tony said this in a peculiar way, as if many different emotions braided together to produce speech. Part of him still liked Rich and wanted to be friendly and grateful. But part of him wanted never to leave the cabin again. And he still wasn't sure what Rich was up to. Schemer? Pervert? For Shree's sake, he had to be wary.

~ ~ ~

Over the next few weeks, Rich came by the cabin several times, but each time, his friend had someplace he needed to go. Her father insisted that Shree should come on these errands. They went grocery shopping three days ahead of schedule, just to get away from Rich. In the store, he sensed a mother carrying an infant in a sling was following them around. He first noticed her in the bread section, and again in dairy. When she turned up pretending to examine tomatoes across from Tony and Shree, picking out avocados, Tony was ready to run. Instead, he sent Shree to the car while he returned to the dairy section to see who she would follow. When he lost sight of the mom, he left the groceries in the cart next to a dozen kinds of butter and left the store.

Their sudden rush to a bookstore didn't fare much better. Shree fell into exploring books in young adult fiction, while Tony was absorbed in non-fiction. He took advantage of Shree's preoccupation to buy a couple of books for her for Christmas. But when the sales clerk, with a friendly smile, asked for his credit card, it was as if a bell went off. Obviously he didn't have a credit card, not wanting to be traced. But the clerk seemed to sense this and asked for a credit card anyway. With a smile! *Was it a signal?! Be careful, the management is watching? Were there cameras? That box on the ceiling, was it a camera?* He scribbled a note and dropped it at

Shree's feet without saying a word. She followed the instructions and met him at the car. Shree thought it was weird, but she remembered the cops showing up at the diner right after they left. Her dad must know what he's doing. And besides, it was kind of fun to play secret agents again. This was the last time he took her into a store, however. Secret agent meant staying in the car while he did the shopping.

~ ~ ~

Rich invited his three partners to a Christmas Eve party at his house, and Tony swallowed his anxiety for his daughter's sake. Shree deserved a Christmas. Larry brought his girlfriend, and Kevin brought a guy friend. Rich's grandmother even came downstairs to drink eggnog and tell everyone they were beautiful. Tony stood to the side of a large window with views of the valley. The old woman kept looking at him, he thought. Why was she looking at him?

There was a gift exchange. Shree was embarrassed since she never had a chance to shop for gifts. But she made do. She had found an old fish tank in the back of an abandoned cabin, added a beautiful piece of wood with a blanket of moss, some colorful rocks, and a small patch of sorrel. Her dad loved it and said he wanted to live inside of it. She gave a large abalone shell to Rich, and a feather and large pine cone to Larry and Kevin. Though she was embarrassed, each praised her gifts in turn. Tony thought a bit too much. She received cookies, a locket, a warm sweater with a bobcat on it, and some rain boots. Rich gave her a beautiful book about marine mammals, which she loved.

What is Rich doing? Trying to upstage his own gifts, Tony thought. He presented his daughter with a book about the flora and fauna of the redwood forests, and though she seemed happy,

Tony felt like he missed the mark. When she opened the final gift from her father, a field guide for tide pools, he thought he had failed again. Tony had written in the inside cover a long treatise, much of which Shree couldn't follow. He noticed Rich, smiling smugly in his victory. And the old lady kept staring at him. *Is she in touch with Rebecca? Are the moms plotting to take his girl? No, she can't know anything. But why is she looking at me this way? Is she attempting to read my mind?* Tony forced himself to think about something else. It was then that he noticed how Kevin's friend looked deeply depressed.

What Tony didn't notice was that Shree loved his presents, especially the field guide for tide pools. She immediately showed everyone a nudibranch that she, herself, had seen. 'Her-mis-senda', she sounded out the unfamiliar word. Rich, Larry, and Missy, his girlfriend, were all struck by how happy she was to have the book. It was true that she didn't follow most of what Tony had written inside the cover, but it closed with, "Under the barrage of nature's passions, we build our tranquil home. Love you forever, Dad." This book remains a sentimental treasure to this day.

When it was time to go, Rich gave everyone a hug at the door. When he leaned over and gave a big hug to "the young Marine Biologist," Tony couldn't believe he was doing it. Rich hugged her for extra long, more so than the other guests. *He's so obvious about it. There is no doubt, any longer. Rich is a pedophile!* Tony refused to give Rich a hug, and glared at him as he ushered his daughter out the door. Rich offered his hand to shake instead and beamed his conspiratorial smile. "Don't touch the water. It's ionic!"

That night, Tony tried to predict where the deviant was headed. Would Rich try to take Shree from him? *Not without getting rid of me. Is his grandmother in on it? Is he plotting to get me arrested? No, that wouldn't fulfill his plans. My arrest will only bring Rebecca to take Shree back to Texas. To actually get Shree, Rich will need to kill me. So that's where this is headed?! But I can kill him first.* At this evil thought, he caught his breath. He wasn't sure enough about Rich's plans. *What I need before acting is certainty. The universe has all the answers. Just need to listen. Everything is connected. Everything is known already. Time, an illusion. No doubt this exact dilemma has played itself out countless times before. The wild universe has all its secrets hidden away like a stage magician. But if I pay close enough attention, I will see the mermaid under the waves, before it starts to dance. I just need to understand, before it's too late.*

44. The Call

December 28th, 1981

"Have you heard anything about your brother?" Wendy was surprised to see her dad standing in front of her. She and Annabelle were hanging out at the Dairy Queen next door to the movie theater. If he'd come ten minutes earlier, he would have caught them smoking cigarettes outside. Anna smoked cigarettes because it made her feel older. Wendy was just going along with her friend, never inhaling and trying not to cough. How did her dad even find her, she wondered.

"What's up with Max? Did he get out of Juvie?" Wendy hoped her dad didn't smell the cigarettes.

"Just, if you hear anything, or if you see him, call your mom. She's at home waiting."

"But isn't he still in jail? How'm I gonna see him?"

"Will you excuse us, young lady?" Dad said this to Annabelle, who nodded and went outside. Now it was just the two of them in the Dairy Queen. The guy who worked there was busy cleaning the back counter.

"What's this about?"

"Remember when we got home last night, we saw someone had broken in?" Wendy hadn't forgotten this. When they got home from a weekend at the lake, Dad noticed the front door was unlocked. The thieves had ignored the stereo console and TV, but had taken her little record player and Mom's ring. "It wasn't just your turntable that was taken. Some of your brother's clothes are missing too. And the police told us this morning that three boys left the Boys' Camp without permission Saturday night. One of them was your brother. The police believe he came to our house yesterday."

Wendy was speechless. *Max had broken out? What was he thinking? What's going to happen when the police catch him? He's gonna be thrown in jail for life!* Outside, she saw Annabelle making a face at her. She pretended not to notice and looked at her dad. "Is he gonna be alright? He must be in a lot more trouble."

"Well it won't be too bad if he turns himself in. That's why we need to find him. So I want you to ask around and see if anyone has seen him. If we find him, we can take him to the police and get this all straightened out." Wendy's dad looked calm, like it was just another Monday. The last Monday of 1981.

"I can ask around. Maybe I'll see one of his friends." Wendy felt grown-up. A few months ago, she would have been sent home so her mom would know where she was. Now she was twelve and Dad wasn't treating her like a kid! But growing up suddenly felt scary. Her brother was in serious trouble, and maybe the police were looking for him right now.

"Well just see if anyone has heard from him and call us as soon as you find out anything. Then come home."

"What if I see him?"

"Just tell him that it's very important that we talk with him. Tell him to call us. Tell him that we can help. Will you do that?"

"Sure, Dad. If I see him, I'll tell him to call you." With that, her dad stood up and dropped a dollar on the table.

"Buy your pretty friend a coke." And out the door he went.

Annabelle returned, and Wendy started to tell her everything. But the guy behind the counter came up to their table before she could.

"Hey, was your dad talking about the breakout from Boys Camp? Was it your brother?" Spencer, not more than sixteen, with at least a dozen pimples, seemed uncomfortably nosy.

"Maybe," Wendy responded, "what's it to you?"

"I heard a kid died. Three of them broke out late at night and swam across Mud Lake to get away. Only one of them drowned!"

This sent Wendy's head spinning. Thoughts exploded on top of each other. *Some kid died?! Will Max be charged with murder? Is Spencer making it up? That poor kid. So horrible. Can he really be dead? Cops could shoot on sight! How could a kid, his whole life in front of him?*

Spencer's pimpled face hovered over them, kind of smiling, expectantly. "Well that's horrible! Come on, Anna, let's go."

They started walking towards the rec center, and on the way, Wendy told Annabelle the whole story. "How could he be so stupid?! He can never get away from this. He broke out of jail and got some kid killed? And the first thing he does is go to our house? What an idiot. I'm surprised the police weren't waiting for him there."

Near the rec center, Wendy saw Tristan, whom she remembered from her brother's party. He was smoking weed in the open with two other teens on the otherwise deserted playground across the street. Normally Wendy would never dare go up to kids her brother's age. And certainly not when they were obviously breaking the law. But her dad told her to ask around.

"Hey, Tristan, have you seen my brother?"

"Ooh Tristan! Picking up girls from the playground, now!" Tristan looked embarrassed. His friends were laughing. Never mind that they were kids themselves, literally hanging on a swing set.

Wendy was undeterred. "You know my brother, Max. You were at our house a bunch of times."

"Yeah yeah. You're Max's little sister, Wanda, right?"

"Wendy. This is Annabelle, by the way."

"She's hot!" snickered one of the hyenas on a swing.

"She's what, eight years old?" laughed the other.

"Tristan, have you seen him? It's important."

Finally Tristan caught on. "Yeah. I've seen him. But don't tell…." He stood up and turned to his friends. "Thanks for the reefer, dudes, but I gotta truck." With that, he looked at Wendy and Annabelle. "Y'all coming?"

Tristan led them back towards the rec center. "Max is at Blob's right now. Don't tell him I told you! He's with some douchebag he brought with him from the farm. They're gonna get caught! I'm worried they're gonna get Blob popped too. You heard what happened, didn't you? Man, don't ever tell anyone I told you!"

"You'll take us to Blob's, won't you?" Anna said, looking intently into his eyes.

"I'm not gonna go anywhere near there," Tristan replied, looking away. "I don't wanna get arrested. And I sure don't want Max on me."

"Can you at least tell me where Blob's house is?" Wendy said with annoyance.

"They say the guy who died was trying to stop them. My sister said the warden called him a hero. On the news. But Max says it's all wrong. He said the guy was just too fat to swim across." Wendy's head was spinning again. This is what Max had said about her after he'd held her underwater. *Maybe Max did kill him. Maybe he's an actual murderer. Is this really happening?* All her fear and hatred of her brother seemed confirmed. She knew her brother was evil. *But actually?! Even he wouldn't go that far. What have you frickin' done, Max?!*

After Tristan explained how to get to Blob's, he took off with an "I didn't tell you! Okay?!" Wendy and Annabelle stood in silence for a moment.

"I'll go with you. It'll be okay." Annabelle looked worried. "Maybe you can just call your parents and tell them where he is."

Wendy wondered whether she should be chasing down her brother. Tristan was too afraid to. Maybe calling her dad was the safest thing. She thought about what the right thing to do was. She remembered the party her brother threw just before he got arrested. Tristan and especially Blob had been nice to her. She hadn't wanted to get them in trouble then. "No, I think I better do this myself."

"No you won't. I'm going with you." Anna seemed determined this time. "You aren't going there alone. We'll be safer together."

Wendy relented, relieved that Annabelle would be with her. Max wasn't as mean in front of her friends, she reminded herself. It was a fifteen-minute walk, which gave them time to relax and forget about what was coming. Anna called Tristan 'cute', but Wendy thought he looked like a chipmunk. By the last two blocks, the heaviness returned. Wendy didn't know what Annabelle was thinking, but all she herself could think about was whether her brother could murder someone.

A cigarette dangling from a wrinkled crevasse with one tooth, answered the door. Wendy suddenly realized that this old woman had probably never heard her grandson's nickname. And Wendy didn't know him by any name other than 'Blob'.

"Is, uh, your grandson, er, son at home?"

"Johnny. There are a couple of girls to see you!" the tooth yelled, aspirating with indifference. Then it disappeared back into the depths of the house, leaving Wendy and Annabelle standing awkwardly at the wide-open door. Waiting for several minutes, they heard The Hollywood Squares turned up very loud, two yappy dogs barking at who knows what, a toilet flush, and finally, Blob appeared at the door.

"Oh hello Wendy. Did Tristan send you?"

"Umm, no. Is uh, Max here?"

"Come in," Blob said with a whisper, stepping out of the door to see if anyone else was on the empty street. He led Wendy and Anna into the house, through the smoke-filled living room where the old woman, consumed by her show, was sunken into a blanket-covered couch, through the kitchen, which smelled weird and had a somnolent dog sprawled across a flattened cardboard box, and into the cold and musty garage, half of which appeared to be Blob's bedroom. Max and a stranger were there.

"What did YOU come here for?!" Max was not friendly.

"You need to call Dad!" Wendy had thought she would tell him to turn himself in, but this was all that came out.

"Little goodie two-shoes, come to drag me home. Now why the fuck would I do that? I'll shit on your head before I'm going back there," he said, standing up and walking towards her. "What's wrong with your little friend? She never heard cussin' before?" Wendy turned to Annabelle, half expecting she would be in tears.

Annabelle looked straight at Max, challenging him like an attack dog. "You should *fucking* call your dad before the police fucking shoot you!" Everyone in the room was floored by this pretty little princess of a girl, ready to do battle.

"You're a little firecracker," Blob said with admiration.

"Don't mess with these two," said the stranger.

Max was stunned into silence. Not only was he surprised by Anna's fierce stance. She had also hit her target when she said the police would shoot him. He knew what happened, but the cops didn't. They might believe he did kill Hector. And the thought of them shooting and asking questions later had crossed his mind more than once.

Wendy knew her brother enough to recognize he was worried. "Dad says to call him. He told me that everything will be okay if you turn yourself in." Max was about to speak when Blob interrupted.

"Max, I think you should. The guy dying was an accident. They're much more likely to listen to you if you turn yourself in. Just call your dad and hear him out. At least tell him what you told me."

Max was silent again. But the stranger spoke up. "Hector was an idiot. We should never have let him come with us. Why'd he tell me he could swim long distance? I loved the guy, but he was such a lying idiot. He told me he could swim ten miles. Said he won a trophy. And the water was freezing. I didn't wanna go in when I felt the water. But no, Hector insisted."

"Yeah, he called me a 'pussy' because I didn't wanna swim across in the cold." Max joined in the story. "By the time we were halfway across, I was so cold I couldn't feel my arms and legs. But I kept swimming. I just wanted to get to the other side."

"Yeah, and Hector started slowing down. I wasn't about to stop; we were so close." The stranger was practically crying. Wendy felt very uncomfortable. "When I passed him, I told him he better hurry up."

"Yeah, Ray, shut the fuck up. I'm sick of talking about it." Max stood up and went out the door to the side yard. As he went, he looked at Wendy and said, "I bet you're loving this."

After he left, Ray continued. "Max was behind, so he saw Hector go down. He kept screaming Hector's name. I was on the bank by the time I realized anything was wrong. Max didn't come to shore for a long time." And after a pause, "Hector was an idiot! Why the fuck did we let him come with us?"

After a minute, Wendy whispered to Annabelle, "I better go outside and talk to Max."

"I'm coming with you."

Max was in the backyard, smoking a cigarette. He glared at

Wendy. "I threw your record player in the dumpster. You'll have to dig in the trash to get it back." Between Max and Wendy, this was a peace offering. At least he told her where to find it.

"Dad says it'll be okay if you turn yourself in. Can you just call him?"

"You know you're gonna screw up your life too, Miss Susie Homemaker. I bet you'll get in so much trouble by the time you're my age." Wendy resisted the urge to tell him she was nothing like him. She just kept quiet. Then Anna got out a cigarette and lit it. Max broke into a grin. "See, even your friend knows. I dare you to take a drag off this cigarette, right now, Miss Perfect." Wendy refused. "Come on, chicken shit. Smoke a cigarette like your friend."

"If I have a puff, will you call Mom and Dad?"

"Sure."

So Wendy took a puff from Annabelle's cigarette, but didn't inhale.

"No, that doesn't count. If you want me to make the call, you have to take a big drag and inhale, like this." He demonstrated, and the ember of his cigarette glowed brightly.

Wendy took Annabelle's cigarette once again and sucked a great suffocating cloud of smoke into her lungs. Then she coughed out loud billows of smoke and parts of her throat and lungs. Max and Anna both burst out laughing. Wendy joined the laughter, but this only brought more coughing. It took some time before she could breathe comfortably again. Max loved every humiliating moment of it.

But he upheld his end of the bargain. And Wendy never smoked a cigarette again.

45. The Pour and Rich

Soon after the new year, the rains became serious. A gentle mist of rain had invaded the woods occasionally for the past month. But that kind of precipitation and the rains that attacked the forest now were as similar as a birthday candle and a rocket. Shree sheltered in their cramped cabin all day and at night wrapped a pillow around her ears to block out the sheets of drumming on the tin roof. The power went out, leaving the embers glowing beyond the hatch of their wood-burning stove as the only light in the forest. She couldn't help feeling worried. Just then a sound, like a tree cracking open, broke through the wind and rain.

"It's not anything to be frightened of. This is nature in all its glory!" Tony was beaming, but in the low light, Shree thought he looked different, like a stranger. "You love the ocean, the waves, don't you? This is just like that. The beauty and the power of the universe are pouring down on our tiny oasis." There was a pause as Tony soaked in his own words. "We are like the creatures of the tide pools! We make a home underneath forces so much bigger than we can ever know."

"But Dad, a tree could fall on the cabin?" This was true. Cabins have been destroyed in lesser storms.

"Well that is unlikely. Think of all these trees, hundreds of years old. Some of these trees live two thousand years or more." This was also true. "They can't get that old if they are so easily falling in any winter storm." But was this any winter storm? Water was pouring from the sky as if nature was busy erasing the difference between land and sea.

After an interlude of twenty minutes when no one spoke a word, Tony stood up with determination. "We're going out!"

"What are you talking about? It's pouring!" Shree was not about to go out.

"Yes it is, and that is exactly why we're going out. It's time to meet this universe of ours, rather than to shrink from it."

"But it's dark! We won't be able to see a thing. I'm not going out!"

"Yes, Renee Shree Riley, yes, we are. Consider it our lesson for the day. We haven't had one in a while. But I think you need this lesson tonight."

When her dad called it a lesson, Shree knew she wasn't gonna be able to avoid it. Best to get it over with, she decided. She put on her still-wet raincoat and muddy boots in the kitchen, which was also their entryway. Her dad didn't bother with his rain gear and didn't even put on shoes. Instead, he led them out onto the front porch, through the waterfall of rain running off the roof, and down the slippery steps to the muddy ground. Shree was surprised to realize she could see through the darkness. And the ground wasn't as muddy as she expected. Instead, it was covered with needles and large, fractured branches that had rained down with the water. She looked back at the little cabin and realized that it was now covered in a dark blanket of this same forest litter, even though she could still hear the pounding on the metal and see the water splashing off of it.

Tony was drenched through, and any normal person would be shivering. But he didn't shiver, at least not from cold. Instead, he swayed and sort of danced in place. "Feel the raindrops! Try to predict exactly when each one will hit you. Feel the space between the drops. The space between the notes!" Here Tony was referencing a lyric he liked. "The space between the drops relays the color to the scene." Shree had no idea what he was talking about. "Don't you feel the rhythm? It's nature's rhythm. It's the physics of water and air. We evolved… we were made by the universe to feel this pattern."

Shree was cold and felt the rain soaking through her raincoat. She realized cold water was finding ways in, along her arms, down her back. *We've evolved to protect ourselves from the rain*, she thought. But she tried to follow her father's words. She pulled her useless hood off and felt the rain pelting her head. She turned up, towards the source of the rain, and felt that she could withstand the ocean wave. The water was sweet. She opened her mouth and welcomed the drops. It got into her eyes and stung, but not too much. Perhaps she did understand her father. The rain wasn't to be feared.

But then the hard rain became so much harder still, a barrage of pellets shooting down on them. She turned her face away and cowered with her back to the force of the water. Without even thinking about it, she began making her way to the door again. Her dad remained in the deluge and didn't object to her going. When she was on the porch, under the roof again, she called to her dad, "I'm going inside, okay?" But either her dad couldn't hear her or didn't care. So she went in and got out of her wet clothes, toweling down as if she had just gotten out of an icy shower. It felt a bit smoky inside, but so much warmer and safer.

Tony stayed out in the rain for more than an hour. He was looking for something in that maelstrom. Looking for wisdom in the patterns. Looking for guidance. A path. He felt it was all familiar. Hadn't he been on this path before? How had he lost it? The universe knew what it was doing. It was calling him. The universe had plans for him. The path was there because he alone could find it. Like Morse code, the rain was telling him what to do. He must protect his daughter at all costs, because she was the key. But his role wasn't just to protect her. The universe had chosen him for something more. To counter the conspiracy of mothers? It isn't about Rich or Rebecca or petty things of the flesh. It is about the realization of time through the dialectic. And just as the waves are there to sculpt the coast, he was here as a tool of the universe. And his path is not to follow but to forge.

When he found his way back inside, Shree had lit a candle and was trying to read. The warmth of her innocent face brought tears to Tony's eyes. How lucky he was that the universe had given her to him. He stood in the kitchen, the muddy floor covered in water dripping from him. He sensibly thought of a warm shower, but realized there would be no hot water with the power out. He then thought of warm soup for the both of them and was again defeated. It never occurred to him that the wood stove was designed for cooking. Instead, he poured a can of cold soup into two bowls and brought them over to Shree. He neglected to change out of his sopping clothes, and now the shivering began.

It was Shree who took over. She made him change and get into his sleeping bag. She then put the soup into a pot and placed it on the hot stove. Her father, towering in the doorway minutes before, now seemed like a helpless child, she thought. *It's up to me to take care of him now.* Her father didn't speak another word all night. After dinner, she washed the dishes in cold water, extinguished the candle, and got into bed. By morning, the storm will be over, she reassured herself. The storm did pass, only to be followed by another.

After another day of rain, in which Tony never left his bed, a pounding on the door woke Shree late in the night. She could see the distress of a flashlight, as it jumped erratically in someone's hand. "Leo! Leo, wake up! I need your help, Leo!" Shree recognized Rich's voice, but the agitation in it was not something she'd heard before. As he kept pounding and calling for her dad, she called up into the loft to get him out of bed. He grumbled and told her that Rich needed to go away. She got out of her warm bed and went to the door.

"Where's your dad? I need him to help me? It's important." Shree was just about to tell Rich that her dad wasn't getting up, when Tony arrived at the door.

"Go away Rich! Let us sleep." Shree noticed that her dad sounded scared. His eyes kept darting in odd directions, and there was a quiver in his voice. Shree wondered if he was getting sick.

"Leo, I need your help. This is important, or I wouldn't be asking. The barn is collapsing, and I need help moving the animals." Rich's grandma had two horses and a goat in a barn down by the road. Nothing ever happened with them as far as Shree knew. Rich had said they were too old and lazy to ride anymore.

"I can't help you," replied her dad, looking at the muddy boots by the door.

"*Please Leo*, I really need help. The creek is shifting its banks, and if we don't get them out soon, they're gonna be trapped. They could drown. Please!"

"I know what you're up to. I'm not going." Shree couldn't understand why her dad wasn't going to help.

Rich was floored. The animals could die if he didn't do something quickly, and his friend was acting so alien. Rich got angry. He wanted to scream at Leo. He let them live in the cabin for free; he gave him a job. And Leo couldn't be bothered to help when he actually needed it?! The thought suddenly came to him that Leo's behavior had been increasingly disturbing lately. But there wasn't time to confront him, so he just yelled in exasperation, "FINE! I'LL DO IT MYSELF!" He saw Shree's concerned face and, turning to her, said, "I'm sorry. It'll be alright." Then a flash of fear hinted that Rene wasn't entirely safe with her father. But he turned definitively to the task at hand and quickly left. The last Shree saw of Rich was his car slipping in the mud as it swerved around the turn.

~ ~ ~

Rich's anger tempered when he almost slid off the muddy road and into the steep ravine. It was not worth getting into an accident because of Leo. Nor was it so important to rescue the horses that he was willing to hasten his own funeral. He slowed and carefully drove to the barn. A neighbor had seen that the barn was collapsing and had stopped by the house on the way to saving his own livestock.

When Rich finally arrived, it didn't look so bad. But when he got out of the car and walked around to the door, he stopped abruptly. The raging creek had torn through twenty feet of pasture and was already inside the barn. Three corners of the building were barely holding the collapsing roof, while the fourth corner was now a shamble of splintered wood on the other side of the rush of water. The animals were trapped as the only door was now a low triangle of roof above the disgorging torrent. The sound of the terrified horses could be heard over the rush of water below and the din of rain above.

Rich saw there was barely three feet of ground closest to the wall holding one side of the former roof. But as he shined his light directly at it, he could see another few inches collapse into the hungry creek six feet below. Without further assessment, Rich darted inside the building. He reached the goat first and quickly unlatched its stall. The goat ran out bleating and bucking and was not seen again. Now for the horses. Without halters, it would be hard to guide the frantic animals. And merely releasing them from their stalls didn't convince them that safety awaited outside. Of the two, the older, gray mare was less frightening to Rich, so he entered her stall and tried to calm her.

"It's okay Bess, we're gonna get you out of here. You know me, Bess. It's going to be okay." He eased his hand onto her neck. The whites of her eyes could be seen even in the dark barn. Nevertheless, she let him hold her neck and took steps in the right direction at his urging. All went well until her head was ducking under the roof and into the pouring rain. She pulled back, and Rich worried the ground would give under her weight. So he slapped her rear as hard as he could, and she shot out of the barn, taking some of the roof and earth with her. Who knows where she would run to in the dark, and who cared, Rich thought. She would be found the next day at one of the neighbors', no doubt. She had lived on this property for twenty-five years. She knew all the neighbors and their horses a lot better than he did.

Now Rich turned his attention to Beau, the gelding. This horse scared Rich. Years ago, he had tried to ride Beau, and it did not go well. Ever since then, he felt sure that Beau hated him. His mom had told him he was paranoid, that "Beauregard would never hold a grudge." Whether his mother was correct or not, Beau was a lot harder to handle than Old Bess. Rich decided to take the time to halter the horse, which, in his wild state, proved hopeless after several attempts. As an alternative, Rich managed to get a rope around Beau's head. This didn't exactly calm the beast down, so Rich took a while longer to get close and put his hand on Beau's neck and try to ease him forward.

"That's it Beau. We'll get you out of this in no time. Bess is waiting for you, Beau. Easy does it." Rich had never been a fan of horses and never played cowboys as a kid. But for a moment, he pictured himself in a different life, roaming the west on his trusty steed. As they approached the exit, the remaining ground not yet carved into by the rushing water was less than two feet wide. Beau reared back a bit and made it clear that he didn't trust the path enough to take it. Rich looked around desperately for an alternative, but there was no other way out. So he took hold of the rope and tried to drag Beau through the exit. But Beau had no intention of following. So Rich decided he would have to push the horse out somehow. And that end of the horse did not appeal to him. He noticed the manure shovel and decided to use it as a paddle. At least this way, he hoped to stay far enough away that Beau couldn't kick him.

"This is for your own good, Beau!" And he smacked him hard on the rear. Beau jumped forward and threw his head up, hitting the slanting roof. This caused Beau to jerk back and to the side, towards the creek edge and towards the reluctant cowboy. Rich stumbled back off the edge and down the collapsing bank. As he fell, he saw Beau sliding down on top of him. *Uh oh*, he thought.

46. Guardrail

January 12th

He couldn't believe it was this cold in Houston. In Boston sure, but he didn't even have a decent coat down here. The sting of the wind jolted him awake as he trotted down the steps of his building at 6:43 am. Naked branches laced in ice were catching the early sun. The grass crunched under his shoes, and plumes of steam announced each breath as he picked up the pace. He regretted leaving his car in the cheapest lot, and leaned against the stinging bluster to cross the campus. It took three attempts before the engine kicked over, and only then could Jim begin to hope for warmth. He had volunteered to pick up Dr. Riccaboni at the airport before he knew how early the flight arrived. And now he was late.

Driving block after block of still empty streets, he glanced over at the freeway, where traffic was painfully slow. After another five blocks, he decided he couldn't avoid the freeway any longer. From the top of an icy overpass, he winced at the stop-and-go traffic below. At least he could listen to music, he thought as he reached over to get another cassette from the glovebox. The light on the far side of the overpass turned yellow, and Jim tapped the brakes to slow down. Unexpectedly his car had a mind of its own, sliding to the left, then quickly to the right. It kept turning on the ice until Jim witnessed the overpass guardrail disappear beneath his hood. Then suddenly a jolt caused him to hit his head and lose grip of the steering wheel. But the car was not done spinning, and after bouncing off the railing, it slid through the deserted intersection backwards and came to rest perpendicular to the road, thirty feet beyond.

"Fuck!" Jim didn't need this right now. "Fuck!" He tried to start his car and heard only clicks. "Fuck! Fuck! Fuck!" he banged on the steering wheel. Jim had always been proud of his vocabulary, but his erudite and evocative lexicon had dissipated in trepidation at the expletive now exploding from his gut.

As if on cue, a patrol car rolled up, lights flashing. Jim watched nervously as one of the officers got out and walked to the back of his car, which was facing towards a vacuum repair shop that no one had entered in years. Through the foggy rear windshield and marijuana leaf window decal, he watched the officer radio in his license plate. When the officer finally approached his window, Jim, expecting the worst, rolled it down and was greeted by an icy gust of wind.

"Do you have any questions for me?" the officer said with a friendly smile.

"I'm sorry, what?" Jimmy's voice quivered a bit, and not from the cold.

"Your bumper sticker. You want to 'Question Authority'? This is your chance."

Contrary to Jim's assumptions, the two officers were nothing but helpful, pushing his car off the road, trying with him to get it started, then calling a tow truck when hope was abandoned. They even helped him bend his hood enough to close it. In the warm tow truck, though, the driver's silence allowed Jim to dwell on how much it was all going to cost. In the garage office, he phoned the lab and let them know Dr. Riccaboni was not being greeted. Since the garage was only a mile from his sister's work, he decided to walk. The bitter cold he accepted as further punishment.

"Rebecca, some long-haired guy is in the lobby, says he's your brother." Rebecca knew something bad must have happened, but was relieved when Jimmy told her about the accident.

"I feel so stupid, like I didn't learn to drive in Boston winters," Jim clutched the styrofoam cup of coffee, hoping its heat would reach his fingers.

"It could be worse, Jimmy. You're not hurt, are you?" Rebecca needed to get back to work, but Jimmy didn't seem to notice and inventoried the busted headlights, cracked windshield, and myriad other details. Eventually, she pawned him off on Mr. Spruill, who sat him in a chair and told him it was a quiet office. Her company was short on programming staff, and though she was a 'computer operator', she had taken to fixing bugs on overnight jobs so that they could be completed before her shift was done.

As the weeks and months had stretched out since her daughter was taken, Rebecca found it harder and harder to talk to people. It seems life had to go on, even though a nightmare was gripping her helpless, sleepless mind. Either people knew about her situation and tiptoed around her feelings, or they were entirely ignorant and stepped right into them. Surprisingly, it was her brother Jimmy that she found most annoying to talk to. Pollyanna Jimmy was sure to let it be known that Tony could never harm his daughter. Jimmy had no idea what Tony was capable of. Talking invariably reminded Rebecca that she had exhausted all she could do. The only thing left was to wait. At least when she was working, the clock seemed to run a little faster. She found herself dreading the empty weekends.

As Jim waited in the break room, Charlie, the head of IT, struck up a conversation and slowly steered it to familiar ground.

"So, have you learned any programming up there at your university?" Charlie queried.

"I've done some Lisp and C here and there. Mostly trying to

determine statistical significance for ...".

"Well, if you're half as sharp as your sister, you could do well here." Charlie stared intently into Jim's eyes, hoping to see a spark of interest. But the comment seemingly went unnoticed as Jim carried on explaining why statistical significance had proved annoyingly beyond reach. Charlie ended the conversation soon after.

"What were you chatting with Charlie about?" Rebecca asked as they got into her car. Charlie had never once held a conversation with her, though she told him when she had fixed his bugs.

"I think he was offering me a programming job," Jimmy answered like he had received a gold star on his fourth-grade book report.

"You've got to be kidding me! I'm fixing their bugs, and they won't even consider me? Then you walk in off the street, long hair and all, and they offer you the job!" Even her little brother was welcomed into the good ol' boys club.

"He didn't actually offer me a job. But are you serious? They won't consider you for a programmer job?"

"Yeah. They told me that they can't afford to lose an operator, so I'm stuck."

"Why don't you quit? Get a programming job elsewhere?"

"Life isn't that easy, Jimmy. Things don't fall from the sky for most people."

"Well I do feel particularly unlucky and incompetent at the moment, having just smashed up my car. Seriously, Rebecca, I wonder if I will ever be a capable adult, like you and Tony are." Little did he realize, but he had just hit a guardrail for the second time that day.

"Tony? You consider Tony capable?" Patience ran out, and the geyser began to boil. "Do you even know Tony?!"

Jimmy noticed the change in Rebecca's voice, her posture, the look of certainty in her eyes. Certainty? Maybe just fury. "Well I…".

"There isn't a moment that goes by that I'm not thinking about what he's capable of. Shall I tell you about…" She leaned her head towards her brother and pushed her bangs out of the way. "…the time I woke up…" There, just above her left temple, "…to my loving husband…" for her brother to finally appreciate, "…slicing into my head with a paring knife?" was a three-quarter-inch V-shaped scar. "He said he was cutting out a receiver that was poisoning my thoughts. THAT, Jimmy, is who kidnapped my daughter!"

47. Fission

It wouldn't stop. The pounding on the roof would not let up. Wrapped up in his sleeping bag, Tony twisted and twisted, trying to block out the icy wind, icy fingers down his back. Stomach foul like burning tacks, churning, twisting, reconstituting into putrid chicken bones, then disintegrating into toxic ashes inside his gut. The weight of the heat, oppressive, hard to breathe. And then the fingertips, icy cold, swiping across his forehead, clutching his neck, and the hammering on the roof, inside his head.

"Are you okay, Dad? Can I get something for you? Soup?" Shree didn't know the sound of the word 'soup' made him gag. "Are you warm enough?" She laid his winter coat over his sleeping bag. "Just let me know if I can do something."

"You should go. Go outside. No use getting sick, too." Tony's throat felt dry. Words scraped across his larynx. Sick. That's what it was. Tony was sure the universe was punishing him for not figuring out what it wanted from him. Maybe he's sick because he can't figure it out. But maybe the cruel universe knows he can't figure it out because he's sick. The laughing rain on the tin roof jeered at him.

Shree put on her rain jacket and muddy boots and went outside again. Was it a lull in the string of storms? The wind had died down. Shree searched the breaks in the trees for any sign of blue sky. There was a hint, but as she watched, a gray mass rolled in and let her know that the clouds were not done with her forest yet. She looked around, surveying the little oasis she knew so well. The ground was flowing with water and mud. The creek, it was frightening. It was so high that whole trees were submerged, bent over in the relentless gush. Large branches had fallen across the gravel road. The road itself looked precarious above the raging creek. Some of it had fallen away and been consumed by the river. A massive tree had fallen over from its perch above the road and now hung down across the road and spanned the creek as well. How were they going to get out? There wasn't enough room to drive under it to get to town. Their cabin looked secure, but one near theirs had a strange slant to it.

~ ~ ~

Inside the cabin, Tony fell into a stuttering sleep. He awoke to a hand around his throat. Rich stood over him with black holes where his eyes should be. "You know what they'll ask of you!" said the apparition. "Have you any choice here?" As Rich said this, the arm that clutched his throat dropped off at the shoulder. Tony recoiled as the weight of the disintegrating flesh turned into maggots on his chest. He frantically brushed them off, and the maggots split open under his fingers, and flies erupted from so many pimples popping on his skin. One of the flies flew into his mouth and down his throat, and before he could block them, they all flew into his mouth and buried themselves in his stomach. There they fizzed like carbonation, and soon the fissioning seeped out of his stomach and into the rest of his body. He could feel it in his bones and muscles, his heart and lungs. *When it gets to my brain, I'll die*, he thought. Every cell in his body wanted to vomit up its maggoty poison.

Then Barry, from elementary school, Barry, who had been hit by a car right in front of him, Barry walked in from a door in the wall that Tony had never seen before. "Why do you think we've chosen you? Did you think you could just wait this out? All you have been given, every breath, every thought, has a cost. And now you need to pay up." Barry stood opposite Rich, but then stepped closer, bent down, and stared uncomfortably close into Tony's eyes. *The terrible nearness of his eyes.* And inside the eyes, he saw an attic, and in the attic, he saw his… *Daddy?* Not Barry's dad, Tony's own father!

"Did you expect someone else? You need to wake up now, so they sent me."

"But Dad?! Are you… are you Barry's father, too?"

"Barry is my father, son. We all live in the eyes of God! Go ask your sister."

Then Barry stepped back, but it wasn't Barry. It was a well-dressed stranger with a violin case and enormous hands. *How can he play the violin with hands so big,* Tony wondered. "Soon we will ask of you a favor." The voice was deep and heavy with command, yet somehow ended up sounding exactly like his late sister, Tina. " That's what this is all for. The rains were sent for you. You already knew it." And with that, his sister put her arm around Rich and walked to the phantom door. But just before they stepped through it, she turned around, but it was Rebecca's father.

"She pulled a gun on you, Anthony. You know what you have to do. Before all the mothers join in. Solids have started to flow. What will be left when the paint can't dry?"

Then just like that, there was nothing. Tony felt exhausted and still felt like flies were fissioning into more flies inside his stomach. But his lungs were fine, his heart was whole again. There it was. The universe was sending him a sign, and one that was hard to miss. Soon his time would come. The rain was his sign. It was calling for him! He knew it; his own sister had told him. *This rain is mine.*

~ ~ ~

The next day, the sun was out and so was Shree. Since her dad kept mumbling to himself in his sleep, never even getting out of bed, she took the hint that she was on her own for the day. She would explore, take stock of the damage. And damage there was. Much of the wild areas seemed fine. More trees and branches had fallen, but plenty of trees full of branches remained. Moss was still mossy, and most of the plants never looked happier. But not all of her favorite trees were happy. At the top of the hill, near Rich's house, there was an old wild oak tree that looked to be a thousand years old. Shree had imagined it growing in The Hobbit's Shire. The tree was still standing, but one of its massive lower boughs had fallen to the ground. Where it had broken from the tree was a frightening raw wound as the skin of tree bark was ripped and the tendons of wood were torn into giant splinters. Shree had sat on that branch many times. She had read five whole chapters one day, right there on its moss-covered perfect spot, where the branch curved up and supported her back. Shree tried to sit on it again, but the angle was off, and it wasn't comfortable anymore. So she stood on it and pulled herself up to a higher perch. It wasn't quite the same, but at that moment, the sunlight poured through the myriad filigree of twigs and warmed her face. "We can work with this," came the voice of Mr. Trains, a few branches away, turning to face the sun.

Shree also investigated the road down to civilization. While a car would have difficulty getting under that one fallen tree, she had no trouble getting through. "It's more fun climbing over," her imaginary friend chimed in. Then he got himself hooked in the branches and pulled his sweater off over his head to get free.

The fallen tree wasn't the only obstacle. Another fifty yards beyond, more than half the road had slid down into the creek. She could see black roots sticking out of the orange-red clay, the new cliffside. Once holding up and feeding trees, now sticking out into oblivion, the roots had no purpose left. What was left of the road, with a drop down on one side and a steep wall of soggy black dirt on the other, was too narrow for cars. Their van was now as pointless as those airborne roots. Shree walked carefully along what remained of the road, worried that the rest might give out at any moment. "It's just like at the beach," said Mr. Trains, standing on the very edge, watching a crack in the sand open up around his feet. "Here we go!" as the cleaved section of road slid rapidly down into the current below. Shree made it safely past, while her imaginary friend used a bent tree in the creek to sling himself up to the road again.

Further down the gravel road, she saw that the hillside above had given way. Here was a perfect example of a mudslide. This term would be used on national news that night, but she had no way of guessing this. Yet here it was. In her description, the hillside had simply moved over, so that the road seemed to angle into the hill itself. A road to nowhere. The new hillside had plenty of broken branches and displaced rock, but it also had several plants and a young tree, still growing peacefully, if a little slanted, in the displaced earth. As she started to climb over this new obstacle, she realized that the hill was not firm. It was a massive ooze of mud. Where was the safe foot trail? Stepping onto this new steep hillside, she felt the mud below slide away and the mud above move in to take its place. Shree began to realize this situation was dangerous. Not only could she slide into the creek below, but she could be buried under an avalanche of mud from above. She decided she would have to back out, and imagined the mud would suck her boots right off of her feet. No sooner had she imagined it than that exact thing happened. She lost her right boot to the mud and, losing her balance, lost her right sock too. Mr. Trains thought it was hilarious, till she shook the mud off her arm and splattered his face.

With some effort, she extracted the boot and sock. Then she slip-walked back up the road with one squishy, cold booted foot. "You walk so elegantly!" Mr. Trains then grandly marched as if one leg were so special that each step was a gift to the ground. "Feel the lovely mud hugging and kissing your toes? They are your subjects, oh queen!"

Above their cabin was a bridge over rushing water. She remembered thinking the bridge was too big and sturdy for the little creek. Today, she understood why. As it was, there was a pile-up of logs on one side of the cement bridge, and at the far end, water was spilling over the top and pouring back into the creek on the other side. As Shree stood over the most powerful part of the flow, she dropped a stick, just as she had done many times before. Usually she would watch her 'boat' float down the lazy little creek, and she would predict how far it would make it before being stopped by the various obstacles populating the creek. The trick was to get the stick to land in the perfect spot to start its cruise. This time, there were no obstacles in sight, and she could drop the stick into any exact spot she wanted, since the distance to the water was barely a foot. But her aspiring boat immediately vanished into white water, never to be seen again.

On the far side of the flow was a walking path. At one place, where the creek fanned out, she found a place to wash her boots, socks, feet, and hands safely. Mr. Trains dove in, but then got too close to the current and was swept away. At first, he was whooping as he raced along the surface, as if on a ride at Astroworld. But then he smashed into a tree, half-submerged. The full force of the torrent pushed him underwater and out of sight. Shree ran to the spot but could see nothing. Sometimes her imagination was a little too real, she decided. Mr. Trains popped up twenty-five yards downstream and dragged himself out of the creek, looking every bit the exhausted puppy.

She followed the path along the creek, down to the paved road. Before reaching the road, the valley spread out, and she saw the remnants of the old barn. The whole building had collapsed, and there was no sign of the animals. The creek had been some distance from the barn, but now it ran right through the remains of the building. There was yellow tape around the pile of broken lumber and still-shingled roof shards. Shree saw three men standing in the small parking lot next to the mess. There was also a small tractor, Rich's car, and a police car. She looked for Rich but didn't see him anywhere. Good thing he got his car out before being trapped by the fallen tree, she thought. Shree wanted to ask about the animals. But knowing her dad would be upset if she talked to strangers, especially the police, she just walked by quietly.

It was another couple of miles till the paved road met the main, four-lane road. Since it was sunny, Shree decided to walk down to it. After so much rain, it was kind of comforting to see the world hadn't ended. Along the way, she passed another huge fallen tree that had already been sawn through to let cars pass. Shree wondered how big the saw must have been to get through that trunk, almost as wide as she was tall. The cut-out section was rolled to the side of the road, and Mr. Trains decided to roll it into the creek to see if it would float. Shree helped him, gave it all she had, but the section of tree trunk didn't budge the tiniest bit. How did they manage to move it to the side of the road, she wondered.

A little further on, Shree almost leaped out of her skin when a dog aggressively charged at her. The dog stopped short behind a chain-link fence. But even though it couldn't get to her, Shree worried that it would rip her apart if only it could. "It's okay Bowser, no one wants to hurt you. Relax, little doggie," she tried in a gentle, calm voice. But there was no calming this beast. So she got up her courage, looked fiercely into its malicious eyes, and yelled, "Go Home!" To her surprise, the barking stopped. Nervously, the dog looked at her, then turned and walked away.

"What a chicken! You are such a scaredy cat," Mr. Trains yelled after the mutt. But where was his bravado when the dog's teeth were visible?

When she got to the main road, she realized that the storm damage was a big event. The road was closed, except for one lane of traffic. There was a bulldozer scraping mud off the other lanes. The mud was at least four feet deep in cross-section! She could see this along the edge of the lane, scraped clear. All four lanes had been overwhelmed by a river of mud, and at least one car was all but submerged. The white car top stuck out of the ground like a giant mushroom. There was no one inside, and the window was open where the driver must have climbed out. Shree imagined the mud pouring inside the car as soon as the window was rolled down. *The driver must have been very scared. Maybe it was a whole family who had to swim through the mud river to safety.* Shree worried for them when she remembered losing her boot and sock.

As she stood there watching the cleanup, a man walked by. "This is something, isn't it? Talk about a natural disaster!" The man had a strangely delighted look on his face. Shree didn't know what to reply, but the man didn't wait for an answer. She noticed several other people, in twos and threes, were also watching the clean-up. Mostly they seemed somber, but as the guy passed one couple, they all broke out in laughter, like it was a big, funny joke. *A natural disaster*, she thought to herself. *I've lived through a natural disaster. Wow.* And Shree too, felt a certain joy in it all. *Nature is wild!* Shree didn't learn the extent of the disaster till years later. She didn't know it was an international news story. She didn't understand that thousands of mudslides resculpted the Santa Cruz Mountains in three days. While many locals felt joy or relief, having witnessed the beautiful power of nature, more than twenty people had not survived.

~ ~ ~

Several days passed, in the same pattern, with Shree exploring and Tony staying inside. While her father was getting out of bed and no longer seemed feverish, Shree couldn't convince him to eat anything. The power was still off, and the inside of the refrigerator smelled disgusting. The few things in there started changing color. White when it should be brown, green when it should be pink. Shree vowed not to open it again until there was power. The food was running out anyway, and they clearly weren't driving to the store anytime soon.

One morning, there was a knock at the door. When Shree answered, she saw a stranger, a tall man with a gray beard, looking very tired. "Hello, you must be Renee. Is your father at home?"

"I'll get him," Shree offered, but then her dad came cautiously up behind her.

"What's this about?"

"You must be Leo, right? I'm Glenn, Rich's father. Can you come outside for a moment?"

Immediately Tony's mind flew to thinking this was some sort of trap. Rich was getting him to come out, and the two of them would trap him. He cautiously went out onto the porch anyway, darting his eyes back and forth, looking for where Rich might spring at him. But all he saw was an older woman, forty feet down the dirt driveway. She looked somehow familiar.

"Thank you for coming out here," Glenn said, after the door was closed. "I'm not sure you want your daughter to hear this right now."

"Hear what, what's this about?" Tony was ready to dart back

inside. He already eyed a log from the woodpile that he could use to defend himself. Still, it was only this old man, Rich's 'father', and the woman, who was staying far away. Then the father put his hand on Tony's shoulder and walked him down the steps, further away from the door and also the woodpile. Tony suddenly knew this man was a priest of some kind. *I will not be part of your flock*, Tony said to himself.

"I'm afraid Rich passed away." The old man's face looked so tired. And sad. "It happened in the storms. He was rescuing the horses from the rising creek, but there was an accident."

Tony heard the words, but maybe they were lies. *Rich couldn't be dead. He was just here. Didn't he just help Rich with the horses? Did he? Oh but this is some sort of trick. This priest is trying to collect souls.*

"I know you were his friend. And his business partner. We thought you should know." *The eyes are blank. Shouldn't he be crying if it is his own son? But of course, he knew about the perversion. And why did he specifically want me to know? Maybe he thinks I did it? Maybe he knows I did it. Maybe he's trying to get my confession for his collection?*

"There are a lot of things to take care of, we're just trying to get through it," Rich's father continued. *Trying to get what?* "I see your van there." *What is he implying?* "With the road damage, you can't drive out." *So he has me trapped!* "We will get the road open as soon as we can." *But the joke is on him, because I took out the road. The rain is me!* "In the meantime, maybe you can use Rich's car if you need to." *Oh he knows! He is just trying to get on my good side. A favor for a favor.* "It's at the bottom of the hill." *The valley? He's sending me to the valley of death?* "You can find the key hanging inside by the door in the main house." *The key! Shree is the key! I must never let Shree go up to the main house again!* "And don't worry about rent." *Favor for a favor, says the priest of perversion.* "We can work that out when we get the road open." *Again with the road. What is the significance? Is he referencing when Shree and I took to the road? Maybe he knows, maybe he is telling me that he approves.*

"Well that's all." Rich's father had said all of this with a flat voice, as if the words had nothing to do with him. Just words that had to be said. As he talked, Tony became increasingly agitated. But despite the defiant thoughts, he was frozen with fear.

"Leo, are you and your daughter doing okay?" This was the woman who had walked up now. Suddenly Tony recognized her. She visited her son in lockdown. She must recognize him as well. *This is the mother! Don't let mothers connect! Rebecca is already communicating with her. Rebecca is going to find us through her! She must be stopped. What's that in the priest's face? He knows too! But he looked just like my dad in that twitch! He's on my side! He is going to help me against her. The road will be reopened!*

"Rich loved you, Leo," she continued, emotions uncomfortably spilling out. "He talked about you all the time." *What did he say? What did Rich tell her?!* "He told us what a great father you are." *That's it. She knows it all. But maybe she isn't in contact yet?* "And your girl is smart as a whip, I hear. Like her dad." *Is that a threat? A warning? Don't be too smart?* "Rich told us that you saved his little company when you showed up." *The company? Did I not understand what the job was?* "You were such a great friend to our little Richie." With this, she broke into a short sob and silence, turning away. *Wait, did she just reveal that Rich is working for the CIA?! Again, Rich's father's face twitched.* Again, like a bolt, a message from Dad. *He's on our side. Rich and his mom are CIA, and the priest is working with Dad.*

Throughout these words from Rich's grieving mother and father, Tony stood in silence, looking lost, suspicious, with wild and frightened eyes. But this didn't seem strange to Rich's parents. They understood his shock, his inability to process their news. They were touched to see how much their son had meant to Leo. "We are having a service on Saturday at two. It will be right here, at the main house. We do hope you and your daughter will be there. It would mean so much." And with this, they took their leave, slowly walking up the path towards the other cabins.

Shree never found out what was discussed outside that day. The only thing her father said was that she wasn't to go anywhere near the main house. Shree wondered if she had done something wrong. And when people streamed up the path in suits that Saturday, she stayed far away.

48. Why People Don't Talk

November 14th

"I'm really sorry." Annabelle softly broke a long silence that had followed the two girls as they walked through the drizzling rain.

"Why, what d'you do?" Wendy asked, sure Annabelle had done nothing to apologize for.

"You know… *that* day." Annabelle said this as if it should be obvious. Wendy stopped and looked at her, puzzled. "The day we stole balloons. I'm so ashamed." Tears welled up in her eyes and escaped down her cheeks to mix with the rain. Despite the salty and sweet droplets making Anna look even more adorable, like a lost kitten, Wendy turned decisively and walked away. Annabelle had to hurry to keep up with her. "You only did it 'cause I asked you. I stole too, but I've been too ashamed to admit it. Sharron and Jeanie told everyone you did it, but I stayed quiet the whole time. I should've stopped them! I should've told Sharron it was me. How can you ever forgive me? I'm so sorry. I'm ashamed, how I treated you."

Wendy slowed down again. The memory of her own humiliation seeping into her mind, like the cold trickling down her back. Even now, she couldn't bring herself to speak. She just looked blankly into those wet blue eyes. Then Wendy turned and stared down at the water rushing along by the curb.

"Sharron's family knows my family. She goes to our church! If she knew I stole, the whole church would hear about it. My dad is the, uh, was the Pastor. I know it's no excuse, but I couldn't let it come out. I couldn't let Sharron know." Anna reached out and pulled Wendy towards her. Wendy tried to look away, but again Anna's sparkling eyes caught her up in a spell. "Don't hate me. I'm so so sorry!"

Still, Wendy couldn't talk. She didn't know how. It was too confusing. Did Anna owe her an apology? If she did something so terrible, why had Wendy been her friend these past few months? Why, in that very moment, did she want to hug Annabelle and assure her that everything would be okay? All she knew was that she needed Anna to stop. Stop crying. Stop apologizing. Stop talking about that horrible day. Stop looking at her with pleading eyes. "Forget it Anna! Just forget it! I have!" And once more, she broke away and all but ran.

"Don't hate me, Wendy. I'll tell everyone it was me. Just don't hate me."

"I can't hate you, Anna," replied Wendy, still walking away. " But don't ever talk about it again."

And with those words, Wendy locked the vault for another seven years. She just couldn't imagine the day when Benny and Liam would snort Dr. Pepper out of their noses when she told them the story of her great balloon caper.

December 22nd

The lamp glared down on vacant paper. Five abandoned attempts lay wadded on the floor like crumpled cars at a wrecking yard. Sirrus gave up. The promised letter to James was sounding more forced than sincere. Celebrating their closeness with inside jokes and soulful gratitude was her intention, as she launched that ship off into their past. "A friendship and a time in my life that I will always cherish, even as we sail off to our separate lives." Trite. The problem was, she knew what he was waiting for. Only it required her verdict on *that*… their final night together.

It had been… awkward… sleeping with James. She still didn't understand what went wrong. In their friendship, no one had seen her as well as James had. She knew him and felt safe sharing anything. Yet in his bed, he felt like a stranger. Clumsy, impatient, while she felt… alone. Afterwards, James, sleeping in the moonlight, was oblivious. She, staring at the glowing red digits of his alarm clock, wasn't. Had she ruined everything? Let her curiosity forever stain their friendship? Was it unnatural? Immoral? James too naive? Or was it because she lit the match, knowing she was running away from the flames? She did love James, but she couldn't face him after that. The long, empty hall silently judged her as she slipped out before he woke. Called her dad to help her move out that morning. The last time she saw James, he was blissfully asleep. Couldn't she just leave him that way?

Looking down at the wrecking yard of words discarded, mistake upon mistake, she pledged herself to another attempt in the morning.

January 23rd

"D'you guys hear about that Reverend Riddley?" Spencer, working the counter at Dairy Queen, was bored and wanted to start a conversation with the only customers for the last forty minutes. Annabelle gave Wendy a sharp look, making it clear that she didn't want Spencer to know she was the Reverend's daughter.

"Don't you have some work to do in the back?" Wendy never really liked Spencer. Though he was five years older, he acted like he was their friend or something. But he had given them free ice cream occasionally, and that was one of the reasons they would hang out at the Dairy Queen.

"He was banging a sixteen-year-old! That's what they're saying anyway." Wendy was shocked beyond words and knew she had to get Annabelle away from there immediately. "She killed herself! And her parents got her diary." Wendy was too terrified to look at Annabelle and couldn't think of how to shut this kid up fast enough.

"You don't know what you're talking about. Come on Annabelle, let's get out of here." Wendy stood up, but Anna stayed put.

"What did the diary say?" Anna said this in a perfectly calm voice.

"She wrote all about how she and Riddley were in love and doing it for a whole year. They're saying he might have done it to other girls, too. And he's a Reverend!"

"Such a damn hypocrite!" Anna said this with a calm certainty. "Were there more details in the diary? How did it start?"

"They're saying it started when she was going for her teen 'step up' or whatever. The police have the diary, and they're not releasing anything more."

"And she killed herself?" Wendy watched Annabelle talking with Spencer, as if the gossip had no bearing on her life. How could she listen to *that* being said about her dad?

"Yeah. Took some pills or something. I can't believe that perv lives right here! Well not anymore. He's gonna be living in Huntsville, in the slammer for a long time."

"One can only hope." With that, Anna got up to leave, and Wendy followed in horror and amazement.

When they were outside, they started walking to the rec center out of habit. Wendy wanted to say something, but didn't know what.

"I bet it isn't true. Spencer makes stuff up all the time."

"I know it's true, Wendy. You have no idea." Anna said this with a mean, condescending edge. If Wendy didn't know what to say before, she felt entirely rebuffed by Annabelle's fortress. They walked on in a silence that weighed more than the moon. Just before they got to the rec center, Anna spoke.

"You know I think he expects me to do the same as her. I've thought about it. But that's more Mother's style than mine." Wendy was so confused. What was Annabelle talking about? She wanted to help, but she didn't understand at all. She really did 'have no idea'.

"So your dad is really bad like that? I'm so sorry, Annabelle. I'm so sorry."

"I don't need your sympathy. I'm not gonna do it."

"Do what?"

"Take a bunch of pills. God knows Mother might, but I'm not going to give him the satisfaction."

Wendy was again overwhelmed. "Oh Anna, don't say that. Don't even think about it. Or your mom neither." She was flustered and helpless. What could she possibly do for her friend?

"Look, I'm sorry I said it. I ain't gonna do nothin' so don't worry. And don't tell anyone. You hear me?! *Don't tell anyone* about this conversation!" And with this said, Annabelle turned on her radiant smile. But for once, Wendy recognized something in it she had never noticed before. It wasn't filled with joy as she had always thought. The smile hid a hard edge to Annabelle. Wendy, not knowing what else she could say, stepped in and hugged her friend. But Anna pulled back. "Not now," was all she said. Then she ran off to the basketball courts because she thought she saw Tristan.

49. Famine

January 28th

A thick envelope was in her mailbox when she got home from school. Wendy wanted to read it right away, but the phone rang. It was Lloyd. She and Lloyd had been paired to give a report on the Battle of San Jacinto. Unfortunately for Wendy, one of Lloyd's great-great-granduncles or somebody had fought in the battle, and Lloyd needed to educate her about his multiple heroic acts carried out in the course of the eighteen-minute battle. Those acts took Lloyd twice as long to retell as it did for his ancestor to perform. Evidently, many enemy soldiers had surrendered personally to Uncle Lloyd, and Wendy was fairly certain she understood why. Eventually, the anecdotes ended, and the two of them agreed on how to divide up the work.

By the time the call ended, Wendy had forgotten the letter and turned on the TV to watch Gilligan's Island. After that, her mom came home, so Wendy had to clean her room and then do her homework. It wasn't until after dinner, when her mom and dad were preoccupied with The Love Boat and Magnum P.I., that she returned her attention to the letter.

Dear Wednesday,
    I have to admit life is hard right now! Remember my dad was sick. Even though he's better, he still just stays in bed all the time. And

it's so dark! The power still hasn't come on since the storms. And Dad keeps the windows covered up. I think he's working on something. Maybe it's for the computer, but there is no power for that. He keeps talking about something as if he's talking on the phone, though we don't have a phone. Is that weird? I don't bother him during the day, because I'm usually outside. One time I woke up at night and heard him crying! It sounded horrible. Did I do something wrong? Sometimes I hear him arguing. But no one else is here. I thought he was mad at me, but when I asked him, he suddenly got quiet and told me everything was okay. I don't think he's telling the truth. I wish I could help him, but he doesn't let me. I do make all the food and I keep the fire going. But whatever is bothering him, he won't let me help.

Speaking of the fire, I have to tell you about the big orange cat we call "Gunther". Sometimes days go by and we don't see him, but after the storms he came to our house one evening. He was very friendly and I let him in. He was purring on my lap. But then he started crying and went to the door. I let him out and thought that was the end of it. But then I heard him crying real loud on the porch and scratching at the door. So I opened the door and he ran in and kept crying. He was running around in circles in our little cabin and crying like crazy. Dad told me to put the G__ D___ cat out, so I opened the door and he ran out. But he kept crying. I was about to cuss at him too, when I noticed a strange cloud going out from our door. And it was smoke! Our cabin was filled with smoke and Gunther was trying to tell us that. I went back in and saw that the box of paper and kindling was pushed against the wood stove and had caught fire! Luckily it was easy to put out. Gunther had saved us! Can you believe it! Saved by a cat! I wished I had a fish or something to reward him. Our hero Gunther! Unfortunately, I haven't seen him since that night.

The road isn't fixed yet, so this place is really deserted. All the other cabins around here are empty now. I guess people don't want to hike in and out each day, so they don't bother coming home. It's kind of spooky. Remember I told you about the cabin that fell off its posts. Well all the people's stuff is still inside but some raccoons have moved in and made a mess. You never saw a kitchen so messy!

I had to go in once and I was scared the raccoons were going to jump on me. Why did I have to go in, you ask? Well I'll tell you. Since we can't drive to the store, we can't get food. What we had already was already gone. But Dad wouldn't get out of bed to hike to the store. So we're getting hungry. After a full day and night without food, I was REALLY HUNGRY. I tried eating some plants that looked like they would be okay and didn't smell bad, but I threw up and my stomach hurt. So I went into that cabin and searched for food there. I didn't find much, the racoons had gotten most of it, but there were some cans of soup and tomato paste. The whole time I was in there I felt like there were eyes staring at me. It was creepy.

Anyway that food didn't last us long. So I yelled at Dad to get up, but he wouldn't. He told me to go to the store myself. Man, I would have gone that instant. I was THAT hungry, but it was dark already. So next morning, yesterday, I got up as soon as there was light, and went to the store. I took my dad's big backpack. It is almost as large as I am. I know where Dad keeps his money and so I took a handful. Later I counted it and it was $87!

Anyway, it is a long walk to town. First I had to walk along the path opposite the mud road. Remember I told you about losing my shoe and sock in the mud. Well the path is ok, but it was real early in the morning. Suddenly I was face to face with a coyote! He wasn't as big as I thought they were. There are dogs that are much bigger. But he looked so wild and beautiful. It was like being in "The Wild Kingdom" on TV. He was looking directly at me and I was looking at him! We were frozen. Then I realized there were three of them. One was to the left, in the bushes. He looked a little scruffy. And mean. And one was behind me, but when I looked at him he looked scared and took a few steps back. But the one in front of me, he was only about six feet away. And he wasn't mean or anything. He was just quietly looking at me like "what do we do now?"

Were these guys going to attack me? Should I have been scared? I wondered for about an instant. I mean no one else was around. It was just me and three coyotes. But it seemed ridiculous that I should be scared. I decided to be friendly. Maybe they could be my pets! "Hello little doggies!" I said. But as soon as I spoke, the one in front of me turned and walked to his buddy to the left of me. Then all three trotted off into the forest away from the path. They looked so cool with their fluffy tails behind them.

Anyway, after hiking down the trail past the collapsed barn, I got to the paved road. The creek isn't so flooded as in my last letter. And the downed trees and branches have been cleaned up by somebody. But it is still nobody around on this road. There are a lot of animals, though. There are horses and cows and chickens and even a peacock. I saw where the horses from the wrecked barn are now. The older one came straight to me. I think she knows me! The goat came up also, but didn't let me pet him. Also there are a couple of cats that are very friendly. I think they know me too. But there is a dog that I hate. Everytime, no matter how prepared I am, he scares the ba-JEES-us out of me! I mean it! He runs up out of nowhere. And even though there is a fence, I always jump like he's going to leap right through and bite me. The coyotes are sweeties compared to him.

Anyway, it is a long walk down the paved road and then the big four lane road. They cleared the mud away and everything looks normal, only you can still see the dried mud where the mess was. I still wonder what it must have been like to be in that car when the mud almost buried it.

It takes about 2 hours to get to town, but when I got there, the store wasn't even open yet! Imagine how I felt, I hadn't eaten in a day and a half! I was soooo hungry and the store was closed. Well I sat by that door for the longest time before I noticed some people going into a place down the street. And you will never guess what that place was! It was donuts! I practically ran there. And I got the biggest donut thing they had. They called it a "bear claw" and it was filled with apple jelly. It was great! I ate the whole thing and then felt stuffed for the first time in weeks!

Shopping was fun. I was thinking about all the meals I could eat. But when I packed up the backpack, I realized I had bought too much! I had difficulty stuffing everything in and then it was so heavy. And if going to the store is 2 hours downhill, going back is four hours uphill! I sat down a lot. I ate snacks of course. Marshmallows! The only thing that got me back up was my plan to make Dad macaroni and cheese that night.

On the path, the very last part, I tripped over a root and smashed the milk carton! I was so mad. I carried it the whole way, and at the very end I spilled most of it. No use crying over spilt milk, but I did cry a little. And my ankle now hurts! Slowly I managed to make it the rest of the way to the cabin. Boy I was tired! I hope the swollen ankle is better before I have to go back to the store.

Only thing, when I finally got home, my dad wasn't here! He wouldn't get up for days to go to the store, but now he left?!! I waited all day for him, but he never came home. I made dinner, but he still didn't come home. Now it is the next day. And he hasn't come home still!

Well I will end this now and get it down to the mailboxes at the paved road before it gets dark. Please write to me soon. You don't have to write all these pages. I'm glad you like my long letters, but if you even only write one sentence I'll be happy.

Anyway, I hope you are having a great time doing homework. :0) Seriously, I miss school a little and I miss you more than you can imagine.

Your coyote training secret penpal,
Ren-A S. Sure-E

It was past Wendy's bedtime when she finished reading. Lying on her bed in the dark room, she wrestled with her thoughts. This letter pulled Wendy in two directions. Like all of Shree's letters, it made Wendy feel special to share the big secret with her best friend. But unlike the others, this letter bothered her. A lot! Shree was hungry?! Her dad was being so weird. Now he went away, and she was all alone in the forest with wild animals? What if the coyotes came back for her? What if there was a fire in her cabin and the cat wasn't there to save her? What if she couldn't walk to the store and get more food? What if her dad never came back? Or what if he did come back and he's crazy?

Wendy went to the bathroom as an excuse to turn on a light and reread the passages about Shree's dad. He was crying? Arguing with someone who wasn't there? Refusing to get out of bed for days? Then he disappears? Didn't Shree's mom tell her he was brain sick? Wendy had heard of "mentally ill" people who talk to themselves. And she heard her mother mention a friend's brother who disappeared. And it was because he was "mentally ill". If Shree's dad is mentally ill and he disappears, what will happen to Shree? Wendy felt sick to her stomach.

50. Undertaken

Shree's ankle was still painful to walk on, but her enthusiasm to mail her letter carried her down the path to the mailbox. On the way back up, she stopped many times, wincing in pain. Before she started, she had imagined meeting her coyote friends on the path again. But now, as light was fading and she had a long way still to go, she started thinking such a meeting might not go too well. She remembered the raccoons she had seen many times now. How cute and innocent they were, when alone, hoping for a handout. But their sweet friendliness would change in a flash if they felt threatened or thought it would give them advantage. One had darted up and grabbed a bag of bread from her hands, snarling like the dog she hated. Once her dad threw a single slice of bread into the middle of five of them, and they exploded in teeth and claws, viciously growling as they fought for the scrap. What if she met the coyotes now and they suddenly turned on her like that? She had seen nature shows, how the lions would pick off the lame wildebeest. With her ankle, she was ripe for picking. She looked for a big stick or some rocks just in case. It was a good thing she did, because the stick she found helped her hobble the rest of the way home.

The cabin was empty. Still no sign of her father. This would be the second night he was gone. Why wasn't he coming home? She had begun conserving candles, so the only light was from the wood-burning stove. She ate cornflakes in water and listened intently for any sign of her dad. At one point, she was certain that she heard several animals on the front porch. Probably raccoons, she thought. Nevertheless, she quietly crept to the door and made sure it was locked. It crossed her mind that she hadn't been frightened the night before. Just worried about her dad. Now she couldn't stop imagining dangers to herself.

She remembered Rich had told them a story on Halloween about a mountain lion that had developed a taste for people. Her dad told her it wasn't true, that mountain lion attacks on humans were extremely rare. But Rich's story came back to her now.

The big cat had been attacking people and livestock for years, and no one could catch her. A professional hunter had been called in. He eventually tracked her down with dogs, trapped the cat in a tree. "Right here on this property!" Rich had said. He didn't want his dogs attacking her beautiful fur. So the hunter turned to tie them up before he shot her out of the tree. "That's when the mountain lion leapt on him. Her weight knocked him to the ground, and her lion claws shredded his skin. He fought with all his strength to keep the vicious cat from biting his throat, because if she did, he knew the mountain lion would kill him! Instead, she bit his skull and almost crushed it. His dogs were doing all they could to help him, and the cat finally let go of his head to sink her fangs into Maggie's throat.

"Maggie was his favorite dog," Rich paused. "Maggie had been rejected by her mother, and the hunter rescued her. Raised her by hand. And Maggie was devoted to him like nothing you've seen. Now Maggie was giving her life to save him. The man freed himself from the preoccupied cat and got to his gun. The predator turned towards him and challenged him again, Maggie dangling from her jaws. The gun was slippery in the hunter's bloody hands. As he took aim, the mountain lion lunged forward, knocked him over in passing, and disappeared into the steep overgrown ravine. That was the last he saw of the magnificent cat and the dog he loved. Three days later, a horse was killed a quarter of a mile away. That mountain lion is still hunting to this day!"

Rich had been beaming when he told his tale. According to him, the hunter lost one eye, was horribly maimed. He never hunted again. According to her dad, the story was made up to scare kids.

Now Shree heard something on the roof and imagined it was that very mountain lion. It knew she was inside, alone, wounded. The mountain lion was hungry, and Shree was on the menu. She held her breath, waiting to hear the big cat's footsteps again. Hoping that if she stayed quiet and still enough, the hungry cat wouldn't know she was there. Wouldn't wait for her when she went out in the morning. She heard another step on the roof, then another. Then she realized it had started to rain again. Probably, there was no mountain lion. But Shree felt especially alone that night.

~ ~ ~

In the morning, she discovered her dad. Asleep. On the front porch. He was covered in dry mud, including in his hair. And his clothes had multiple rips she hadn't seen before. She was so relieved to see him, and she started crying as she beat him with her fists. "Where were you, Daddy?! Why did you leave me alone?!" But her father didn't answer her and didn't hug her warmly as she expected. Instead, he put his fingers to his lips and hushed her, looking around as if someone else was there. But there was no one else. Only the two of them. They went inside, staying as quiet as possible. Once inside, her dad locked the door, made certain all the windows were completely covered, and then began whispering.

Shree had great difficulty understanding what he was saying. Something about the CIA watching them. He whispered that a war was coming, and he had been drafted. Only both sides wanted him to kill people. The story was so twisted that she couldn't tell who the two sides were. The CIA? Maybe the Mafia? Dad also whispered about circus clowns. And a network of women on teleplaffys or something? He was clearly very frightened, and what he was saying was really scaring Shree. She was afraid for him. Her dad had been right about so many things, but she couldn't believe what he was saying. He said things that were obviously not true. The CIA was not watching them in this forest! There are no people! No clowns had visited them. How could he possibly be serious? Maybe he had seen someone by the road, carrying a violin. But why is that anything to worry about? And her dad kept talking about Rich as if he were dead, which surely wasn't true. And when he told her that Rich's dead body had been in the cabin too! Talking to him?! Her dad was talking nonsense, yet he was very insistent. His eyes kept darting back and forth, looking behind her. Telling her she was 'the key', pleading with her not to join with them. Telling her one moment that her mom was behind it all, the next that 'they' had brainwashed her mom and were planning to brainwash her too. "Don't listen to them, Shree! Promise me you won't listen to them!"

"Dad, stop this! You're scaring me! Please stop it!" This plea quieted her father for a few minutes, but soon he started up again. Shree thought maybe he just needed to eat, but her dad refused to eat anything. He said it was poison and insisted she didn't eat anything either. Eventually she got him to drink some tea that she made on the wood stove. He always liked tea. But after three sips, he accused her of trying to poison him. Shree begged him to stop again. She cried for him to believe her and stop talking nonsense. This finally had an effect. Her dad became very quiet. He also started drinking his tea again. So she made him a peanut butter sandwich and quietly put the plate next to him. Over the next hour, he ate it bite by bite, while whispering about the universe ringing a bell, needing him to make it right.

After a long while, he stopped whispering and stayed silent. Shree was too frightened by his rant to prod him to talk again. She was dying to know where he'd been. She wanted to know if there was anything she could do to help him. She also wanted to tell about her adventures going to the store and meeting coyotes. But most of all, she wanted to know if he would ever sound normal again. Instead, the sound of rain on the metal roof painted the cabin with a staccato dirge. It took a while before she realized her father had fallen asleep.

Now her mother's words came back to her. "Your father is ill. He doesn't always say the right thing, and he doesn't always understand. Sometimes he doesn't realize he's doing dangerous things." Maybe her mom had been right about Dad all along. A deeper rush of shame washed over her. Her mother had tried to warn her, but Shree hadn't listened, called her a liar, a monster, a b____. How could she ever face her mom again? Not that she would ever get the chance. The shame at the thought of her mom, mixed in with her fear for her dad, multiplied her isolation. Mom had said he was getting better. Shree was pretty certain that wasn't true. He was getting a lot worse. What was she supposed to do now? Shree knew it was impossible to erase the shameful way she had treated Mom. But she would have to do better with Dad. She decided she must take care of him somehow. But how could she get him to be better again?

~ ~ ~

For four days, the cabin settled into an awkward dual rhythm. During the day, Shree was awake, taking care of chores, rationing food, reading, entertaining herself. All while Tony slept or pretended to. At night, Tony was up, quiet and fearful, watching over his precious child and making sure nothing bad happened to her. This dual existence shielded Shree from her father's worst moments. But she knew her father was struggling and she had few ideas of what to do. Her mother used to tell her, when she was sick, that sleep was the best thing for her. So as long as he was sleeping, Shree had hope.

Of course she went to the main house to try to get help from the only other adults she knew. But Rich wasn't there, no one answered the door. The second day, when Rich didn't answer, she opened the unlocked front door and called up to ask his grandmother. But she didn't answer either. By the third day, she went inside to see if anything was wrong. The house was deserted.

The remains of a gathering were evident. Food dishes and glasses scattered about. No one had cleaned up, and ants were mining multiple treasures. The living room was filled with wilted flowers. There was a large photo of Rich prominently displayed with big candles and flowers on either side. He looked happy, like when he told the mountain lion story.

Shree remembered people in suits who had quietly streamed up the path a while back. Could it be? Had it been a funeral? For Rich? Shree was stunned. Was her father right? Rich had died? She didn't want to believe it. No, she had seen Rich after that. She tried to remember when she had seen him last. That night, was it still storming? When he came to ask Dad for help? NO! She was sure she had seen him since then. At the wrecked barn? Not sure of herself, she looked around for evidence. She found photo albums filled with pictures of Rich. In high school, he looked so young, with a smooth, round face, long before the beard Shree had known. With his older brother when he was Shree's age. Rich as a toddler, she could recognize him in that goofy kid's face. Slowly, it began to sink in. Rich was gone. She vaguely remembered her grandpa's death. But Rich had just been here. How could he be here one day and not the next? As if it were haunted, Shree suddenly felt she couldn't stay in that living room another second. She went outside and sat on the front step.

Maybe if he had helped Rich that night, her father would be dead too. It was too awful to think about. Maybe that's why her dad was sick. Maybe he's just mourning his friend? Maybe, but maybe Shree didn't want to think about any of it anymore. She didn't actually know what had gone on in the house. Maybe Rich was perfectly healthy. Maybe he and his grandma moved to his parents' house until the road can be fixed. Maybe everything is fine. But as much as she wanted to believe it, Shree was pretty certain it wasn't true. It occurred to her that she should be crying for Rich. But tears didn't come. Instead, her mind was a fog. She felt like she was watching herself sit on the step. If this was growing up, she wasn't ready. Life was moving by, and she could do nothing about it.

~ ~ ~

A wave of warmth spread over him. There was a tingling to his being, he hadn't noticed in a long time. Every molecule of him vibrated in harmony with existence. How could he not have noticed? Like his jaws were finally opened wide enough to engulf the breath. Yes, the breath! So many breaths in a lifetime, but each one is a gift. He opened his mouth and yawned inward, pulled air into his vibrating shell, his tinker toy construction of a vessel. But the vibrating vessel that is Tony is not separate from the harmonizing bed, the pulsating cabin, the singing forest, the endless cacophony of the universe. A symphony so complex that no individual player can comprehend the whole, as all possible melodies are played simultaneously. Yet he heard!

~ ~ ~

A chill shadow passed through his being. Isolated, bound by gravity, habit, fear, incomprehension. Long fingers poked through the bars, accused him of unspeakable acts, shamed, taunted, toyed with his helplessness, and licked his bones. What they knew! Snapping their fingers. Smug smiles and furtive looks. Laughter, dismissive yet accusatory. Ice cold under blankets. How could he ever show himself? Stillness calling. The harmony dissipating until all is cold and still.

~ ~ ~

Come on, Tony, this can be worked through. I was sick, had a fever, that's all. But somehow I can't… get… out… of bed. Shree will need my help. I have to be stronger than this. Come on Tony, hold it together like you did. You got us here. You can rise to this.

~ ~ ~

The door in the wall opened, and Glenn stepped towards the bed. With him, the smell of warm, wet hay rolled through. "The priesthood has directed me to prepare you." *For what? Am I to be ordained?* "The old boys say you can figure it out for yourself, but some of us feel you need a little help." *Liturgy? I'm certainly not figuring out doctrine on my own.* "You killed Rich according to plan, but you did it too soon." *Rich is dead? I killed him? Of course he's dead!* "He wasn't ready to kidnap Shree, and the kidnapping was our path to learn their organization. Shree was the key!" *Yes, Shree is the key!* "But you jumped ahead and tripped over the plan. It's on you when the Mafia kidnaps more children. More monsters will be trained." *The mafia again? Who is in this mafia?*

~ ~ ~

Tony felt the icy air clutching him. He couldn't move a muscle, and the grip of the cold air tightened around his chest. Squeezed, he felt the cold morph into knives. Knives pricking his skin, pressing at a thousand points.

Suddenly he realized there was someone else. Right next to him. Whispering into his ear. Albert? "We know some names already. Rich's mom, your mom, Rebecca, of course." *Oh yes, telepathy links Rebecca and the Moms.* "Until we take the whole group down, the mafia will still grab kids. You've seen them. Priests, of course." *Glenn? Glenn is a priest. Wasn't I to be anointed?* "School teachers. And clowns. Perfect disguise. Kids love clowns. They roll into town, all the parents bring their kids, the Ringling Brothers and Barnum & Bailey Circus. Innocents go missing, and then the circus moves on. But they can be stopped. You can stop them! Just be ready. We'll call. Think it through. A new sign, then you'll assassinate the leaders. We'll wipe up the rest."

"But why me? Why do you need me to kill?"

"You can figure out that one, Amherst." Tony was shocked to see Rich standing over him. Was he there the whole time? His eyes were still two black holes, but now a fly was eating the decomposing flesh around the eye sockets. Rich's teeth were mostly gone now, and his gray skin was hanging off his forearm. Tony could see the muscles giving way to bone. He suddenly realized he had known Rich was dead before the priest ever told him! Only one way he could know! Because he himself had assassinated Rich! He saw it vividly now. Smelled his fear. Pleading eyes. Yet somehow, here Rich was! "Just because you did me in, don't think you're done with me. It wasn't enough to shatter my skull. To be rid of me, you will need to take us all down. We are bigger than you think. We exist in music. Fleetwood Mac! They worship at the same dark altar. And I'll rise like Christ." *Musical devil worship? Truth ringing through a cliche?*

"I hate you, Leo Anthony Amherst Vomit. I despise you." Rich's decomposing corpse spat on Tony. "I anoint you!" The spittle burned like a tattoo. Only it was no longer Rich, but Tina? His face was etched with his guilt. The little brat that he'd ignored as she descended into addiction. "Why you? You have the gall to ask?" And rising as the very wind, "You let me die!" And the wind carried away his sister's voice.

Rebecca's father materialized from the facade of Tony's little sister. A quiet truth now spoken. "Because you started it with Rebecca. You persisted, and that led directly to here. Shree is the key, but either you or Rebecca must turn her to unlock us all."

~ ~ ~

It kept getting louder. Like a tea kettle, but it kept getting closer and louder and more insistent. Then another note, off a half step. The two notes demanding, yelling, ear-splitting. The dissonance between the notes began wobbling back and forth, accelerating, sharper, louder, painful as he felt his eardrums about to rupture. Then all of a sudden, silence.

Oh so grateful for the silence. But is it truly silence? Embers of smoke, tiny rattling sounds, hisses, churnings, textures. A golden tissue of longing. Cyan lilt. Soft lavender lament of sound. The voices rising out of nowhere. A choir of weaving voices like wisps of cloud, so fragile. Female voices. Muses. Inviting. Seductive and yet poisonous. "Give her back," whispered in amber-green. "She belongs to us," hissed in lilac. "She is life." "She is light." "She is night." "She is wild." "She…" "Shee…" "Shree is…" A hundred voices, all different, hypnotic, threatening, chanting. Disembodied voices. Female ghosts calling from around the world. His mother's voice. His third-grade teacher's. Rebecca's voice stirred into a stew of swirling flavors. "She doesn't need you." "She is not you."

"Shree will kill you." "She controls you." "She can hear you." "Shree hates you." "She defies you." "Shree will fight you." "She is frightened of you." So many voices, like an ocean, carving away at his crumbling shell.

~ ~ ~

'Kill the girl. It's the only way. Kill her." Tony knew this new voice was evil. But it persisted. A man's voice, just behind his left ear. "It's the only way." Tony fought back.

"GET OUT!" he screamed. He woke Shree.

"Dad? Are you okay?"

"Nothing. Um, don't worry, Shree." *Kill the girl, it's the only way.* Tony struggled with this new sinister command. *I WON'T LISTEN*, he yelled inside himself. *I won't listen to you!* And still a familiar whisper. *Kill her.* Tony wrapped his head in his pillow, trying to block out the sound, while wondering who was producing it. *It's the only way out.* His father's voice? *Kill her.* Robert MacNeil's? "KILL HER!" Tony screamed again.

"Dad, what's wrong? Is it a bad dream? Dad? Can I get you something?" Shree thought about what she could give her dad right now. They had no medicine. There was almost no food left. Though it was pitch black, Shree thought about going to the main house and seeing if there was any medicine that could help. She vowed to go back in the morning, see if she could find anything. At least find tea or coffee. He would drink those.

Kill her and be done with it. Please stop. Otherwise they will get to her. Stop it! *You must protect her from the ugliness of the world. Prevent them from TURNING her. SHE is the key.* "Stop!" Tony pleaded, but the voice hissed on. *It's the only way. If she lives, it will be torture.* Another voice! *She'll be the torturer!* Don't say such things. *The change that's coming. You must save her.* I will save her. *She*

HATES you. They are turning her already! My voice? *Release her from the fundamental contradiction that is life.* Yes, the contradiction. It's the ONLY answer. *Kill her. Save her from all of this.* No you're lying! *KILL HER. Not murder, it's mercy.*

Tony desperately fought. If only he had something to stab into his eardrums, he wouldn't have to hear these lies. He will NOT listen to these incessant lies. Even if they were true. Even if she was doomed. *Yes, kill the girl.* Tony snarled back: "I'm NOT listening!" Get out of my head. Devils! *End this!* Get out. *But kill her!* NO. *Just do it quick.* "GET OUT!" his voice erupted. GET OUT OF MY HEAD! Then he flung himself out the door and into the drizzling night.

Shree stood in the doorway, calling to her dad. He hadn't even put on his shoes. She could hear him in the distance, yelling, "Get out!" Somewhere in the dark of night, he was crashing through trees, fighting with vines and poison oak. Shree wanted to go after him, but she was afraid of her father, too. She had no idea how to get him to come home. She went back inside, put on her raincoat and boots, lit a candle, and walked out into the mists of rain. The candle went out before she made it down the steps. She listened for where he was. She heard nothing but some creaking trees and the muffled sound of rain. She went back inside and cried. It was a long time worrying. A long time stewing in dread and shame and tears. A long time till sleep finally ended her helpless thoughts.

51. Voices

Shree spent the day looking for her father. There were signs that someone had ripped through the brush up the hill. She found footprints, clearly her father's bare feet, in the mud. But about a hundred feet from the cabin, she lost all sign of where he went. Shree realized that she couldn't search the whole forest without a plan. If she found him, how was she going to help him? If she looked in the main house, maybe she could find medicine and bandages. Then she could walk beyond the main house till she reached the next property. If anyone was there, she would ask if they had seen her dad. After that, she could loop around, keeping the cabin at the center of the circle. If she found her father and brought him home, she wasn't sure what would come next.

~ ~ ~

After scrambling blindly, Tony had fallen down a hillside in the dark. Luckily, he was caught by a ring of trees before he rolled over a ledge into a deep ravine. Believing this cozy ring of redwoods had been put in his path by the universe, just for him, he crawled into its embrace and stayed there through the night. Voices swirled while he shivered. Sleep may or may not have touched his fevered mind.

Chaotic fragments of images toyed with him. Waves sculpting clay. Screams of wind ripped through creaking tree masts. The darkness was penetrated by flashes of shifting light and clawing shadows. These disembodied shapes were coming, reaching branches like arms clawing for... *for her.* The furies wouldn't stop. Voices chanting they must be fed. Shree's cadence among them now, crying from a crumbling height, giving voice to the agony just starting to envelop her. It was unbearable to hear. His little girl was beginning to be eaten alive by an awakening dragon. Virtual particles of birth and death, the divorce of heaven and hell, fissioning in and out of existence in the vast emptiness that is the fabric of the universe. The empty fabric of flesh and the immeasurable void between minds. This particulate symphony rising to paint the dawning day. Creative destruction will not be stifled. Roly Poly girl standing in the hurricane's path. The chanting choir marched towards the inevitable, her pleading wail barely audible above the din. He had to save her! The only thing he could quite comprehend was that he had to save his daughter. She was the key to him.

Shivering in the mud, surrounded by fairies holding back ghosts, listening to celestial music cascading through chemistry and genomes, saxophones and civilizations, galactic tides.... Then, in a blink, a phase transition. Ringing, true as a bell. He saw it all now! *The universe must take her, but I can save her too!* A warmth now flooded him and held him close. Yes he knew. *Consciousness is all there is! Flowing like a river. Without it, there is no pain. She will drift off to a final sleep and never have to know... life's excruciating entanglement.*

Tony was ecstatic now. He found himself swaddling his baby sister as she gave herself over to bliss. And in promises whispered by the tints of dawn, Tina welcomed Shree to follow. *Yes, the furies will do their worst, but precious Shree shall receive serenity. Even a wretched father like me can give my daughter that!*

~ ~ ~

In the icy stillness of the morning, through the mist that clung to branches and veiled the earth with rising ghosts, he heard his daughter calling. He remembered his fevered decision. And he remembered why he had run from the cabin. Whatever the tides of the universe were up to, he knew he was a danger to his own daughter. He almost burst out sobbing at this realization. But he had to stay hidden from her. And for hours, he could hear her plaintive voice calling him. Occasionally, he heard other voices. They told him that they knew. They told him he had killed his friend and would kill his daughter. They told him to hide. He would be called. His fairy ring of trees held him. But his refuge was growing on the ghosts of past trees. Ghosts were everywhere in the forest. How long till the trees would be choking him?

Midday, or was it, he couldn't tell, when Shree was so far away that Tony couldn't hear her anymore, he snuck back to the cabin and got his shoes and coat. Voices also told him to take the money. "And get the matches." He was about to start the van when someone whispered not to. The road was washed out, remember? He was stepping back onto the muddy ground when he saw something moving. He ducked and crawled beneath the van as quietly as he could. From there, he watched as a bobcat trotted by. When it was no more than ten feet past him, it abruptly stopped and turned. It stared right into Tony's wild eyes. The regal face of the cat, its striped mane and tufted ears framing rich yellow eyes. Tony felt certain this was the face of God. God hissed at him, then trotted away.

The voices, however, stayed. They told him to get the keys to Rich's car. "They're dangling in the darkness at the pedophile's house." The priest named Glenn told him so. And Glenn's voice told him to find the gun. Tony gave in to the priest. He found the keys hanging by the unlocked door. But where was the gun? He searched and searched, yet found no gun.

A new voice told him to leave. "The ocean!" he heard his mother say. And that seemed right. His loving mother knew what was best. Tony pictured the glorious waves sculpting the land. This forest feeds on ghosts, but the coast is giving birth.

As he moved along the path above the creek, he realized he was limping. His torn pants leg was stiff with dried blood. When had that happened? Suddenly he heard someone coming up from the road. As stealthily as he could, he left the path and hid in dense growth. As he knelt, holding his breath, two uniformed police officers passed by. "They are looking for you, Tony. Shoot them before they shoot you." Frightened by voices, Tony felt safe in one thing. He hadn't found a gun.

~ ~ ~

Shree had spent the whole day searching for her dad and had found nothing. Her plan to ask at other houses if they'd seen her father didn't quite work out. A scary-looking man with a tattoo on his face caused her to hide. An old woman with dogs warned her that she shoots trespassers. Now it was starting to get dark, and she was cold, wet, and hungry. Also, she was lost. She had spent the last hour following a creek that she thought would lead back to the cabin, but instead it came to a gravel road she didn't recognize. She had followed the wrong creek! She knew it was a bad idea to try to find her way back up to her creek in the dark forest. Instead, she decided to follow the road. But which direction? Since downhill was easier than up, it won out.

In half an hour, the gravel road joined a paved road that she was pretty sure was the one she knew. It was quite dark by this time, but she spotted the broken remains of the barn, clothed in a settling fog set aglow by headlights. A police car was leaving the little parking lot. Immediately Shree hid, though the headlights never turned her way. After months of avoiding cops with her dad, it didn't occur to her to do anything else.

It didn't take long to negotiate the dark but familiar path back to the cabin. No father. Inside, it was pitch black. It reminded her of that muddy cave. She needed to see to start a fire in the wood stove. She decided to light the candle first. But the matches weren't in their place! No matches, no light! No fire, no warmth! She spent uncounted minutes very carefully feeling around every place she could think of, but she couldn't find the matches. Next, she felt for food. She knew there was almost nothing left. Tomorrow, she would hike to the store again. Tonight, she found the last box of macaroni and cheese. Oh yeah. Without fire, no cooking. Instead, she ate the last of the Fruit Loops and scraped the peanut butter jar clean. Then she crawled into her sleeping bag and tried not to think about her dad.

Eyes closed, she pictured a birthday party from long ago. There was so much pizza! She had never seen so many boxes of pizza. She tried to remember each of the kids and what they were doing. Annabelle, with her followers: Sharron B. and Jeanie. Elizabeth, mad at Albert. Lloyd's bubble rings. Sharon G. imitating Annabelle's mom. She remembered talking about religion with Wendy. What she would give to see Wendy again. Would she ever see her again? Or her mom? Special moments entered her thoughts, one by one. How her mom had held her close in the windy cold. Had read to her all day when she was sick. Had kissed away tears when she got soap in her eyes. Mom had taught her to roller skate. And ride a bike. She had bandaged Shree's knees so many times that Mom joked about earning a medical degree. Shree remembered the smell of her mom's chocolate chip pancakes waking her on Saturday mornings. She even made blueberry cheesecake, her favorite, for her last birthday. It occurred to her that she would be twelve in a couple of weeks. Shree wondered what her mom would be up to then. A bubble of guilt rose to the surface as she thought of Mom alone.

A small cry and scratching at the door slowly caught her attention. Gunther had come back! She felt her way in the dark to let him in. His thick, wet fur felt so warm as she rubbed his back and was rewarded with loud purring. She was sorry she had no food to offer him, but he didn't seem to mind. He lay across the bed, and his purring kept her warm inside and out.

~ ~ ~

Shree woke up hungry, and there was still no sign of her dad. Gunther cried at the door, then ran out as soon as she opened it. There was nothing but a box of mac and cheese and a can of Cream of Mushroom soup that she had bought because her dad liked it. Since she still couldn't find the matches, and the wood stove was as cold as the creek, she opened the soup and ate straight from the can for breakfast. "Concentrated grossness," she had complained to her dad. Only now she was hungry.

Then she made a list of what she would buy in town, put on her dad's backpack, and went out the door. She was halfway down the path to the road when she realized that she had forgotten to take money. When she returned, she discovered her undoing. There was no money! No money, no groceries. No groceries, she was gonna starve. Through tears, she searched high and low. No money.

She also discovered her dad's coat and shoes were gone. Her dad had been at the cabin when she was out looking for him! And he left again! If she had stayed home, she would have seen him. Could have stopped him from going! She threw herself on the bed and cried like she hadn't in months. Not since she called her mother the bad word. Would she ever see Mom again? All alone, she was frightened and hungry and angry with herself. Why had she let her father down? Not taken care of him? Kept him healthy? Why didn't she believe Mom? Unless Dad returned, what was she going to do? And if he did return, still talking craziness, what was she going to do? She felt sick herself. Was it the cold, disgusting soup? Or dread of what would happen to her now? She fell asleep in her shoes and her tears, face down on the bed.

Much later, she got up. Starving. She decided to go to the main house, under the shadow of Rich's death, and search for food, matches, money. Soon after she stepped out of the cabin door, she heard voices. Was it her dad? Of course not. She heard at least two people, and though her first thought was to hide, something familiar made her stop. It sounded like… like… but that couldn't be. And yet the laugh was just like his. Was she imagining things? *Am I going crazy now?*

52. Burning a Friendship

January 29th

No one answered the door, so she sat on the cold cement porch and waited. The wait spilled over with worries. She had made a decision, but it wasn't too late to leave. Thoughts of how angry Shree's mother would be returned. Like food she couldn't keep down. Jump on her bike now, and no one would ever know. *But Shree's letter!* The storm, the hunger, the coyotes, her scary father. Shree sounded upbeat, but she must be afraid. *How can she not be worried?* If anything happened to Shree, it would be Wendy's fault for not saying something.

Still, Shree was her best friend. And this will be the worst level of betrayal. Shree had trusted only her with the secret. And now Wendy was about to reveal it to Shree's worst enemy. Shree called her mom 'the monster'! But Wendy would call her own mom even worse, and her mom probably cared about her. *And what will happen when I tell? Her mom will be furious that I kept the secret for months. Shree will be in so much trouble, and then her mom will call my mom, and I'll get it too. And Shree's dad will probably go to jail.* This too, made Wendy pause. Shree loved her dad. *She may come home, but that doesn't mean I'll get my friend back. Shree will never ever forgive me for this.*

Wendy stood up and got on her bike to go. But she didn't leave. Shree needed help. *I need to be her friend, even if she'll never see it that way.*

Rebecca was surprised to see Wendy on the porch as she pulled into the driveway. *She still misses Shree after all these months,* Rebecca thought. *She's hurting too. It will feel good to talk to her for a while. Feel that youthful energy in the house for a moment.* "Nice of you to visit, Wendy. Would you like to come in?"

"I'm sorry, Mrs. Kreisler." Wendy couldn't hold back her tears.

"Oh Wendy, it's okay. We both miss her." With this, she wrapped her arms around Wendy, and Wendy went limp.

"I'm so sorry, Mrs. Kreisler, I'm so sorry I didn't tell you."

Rebecca pulled back, holding Wendy up by the shoulders. *What hadn't she said?* "What is it, dear? It's okay. Tell me what?"

Wendy held out Shree's letter, tears still streaking her dusty face. "I think she needs help."

Rebecca frowned and swiftly took the letter, diving into its words. After reading but a few lines, she looked at the envelope and saw the return address. Now tears flooded her eyes. She grabbed Wendy again in a hug. "Oh thank God, you brought this to me. Then she rushed inside, leaving the door open for Wendy. In an instant she was on the phone.

"Jeff, I have her address! She's in California." Rebecca excitedly talked through tears, reciting the exact address. "No, I'm not waiting. I'll fly there tonight if I can. Why should I wait?" Rebecca listened intently, her eyes still wet with tears. "Okay, but if we haven't heard anything by tomorrow, I'm flying out anyway. See you soon."

Rebecca wanted to do everything at once, but she mostly wanted to read the letter still in her hand. Wendy knew she was in the way. But Shree's mom's excitement was infectious. She wanted to stay there and watch, half expecting Shree to be home that night.

"Wendy, I can't thank you enough. I just called the detective on her case. They will get someone out to check on her tonight. If all goes well, I may be bringing her back this weekend. I know she'll be happy to see you. I'll let you know as soon as she's home. Right now, I have a lot of things to take care of, but do you mind if I read this letter before you go?"

"Of course, Mrs. Kreisler." Wendy was surprised that she asked permission.

"You can call me Rebecca! We're friends here." Then Rebecca buried herself in the letter, tearing up again. At a couple of points, she laughed, and sometimes she seemed very serious. "You did the right thing, bringing this to me. I think you're right that she needs help. I see you've been corresponding with her for a while." Wendy nodded guiltily. "While obviously, I wish you'd let me know sooner, I think I understand." Rebecca was too buoyantly hopeful not to be generous. "I'm so grateful she's had a friend like you this whole time. Now, do you need a ride home?"

No Mrs. Kreisler, I…" Wendy saw the look on Shree's mom's face as she mouthed her name. "I mean, um, Rebecca. I have my bike."

"May I hold onto this letter for a couple of days? It might help."

"Sure. Please let me know how Shree is." And with this, she turned to the door. Rebecca caught up to her on the porch and gave her another hug.

"Thank you for giving me my daughter back."

~ ~ ~

The police in California had reported no trace of Shree or her father at the given address. Only an abandoned cabin with heavy water damage. Rebecca knew better. Even Jeff, Officer Donnilon, who had been her best ally for months, agreed she had to go herself. Not that anyone could have stopped her.

Ruth, Rebecca's mom, insisted Jimmy accompany her and offered to pay expenses. "Jim will take care of the details, while you take care of what's important," she said over the phone. Lydia, Shree's other grandmother, would meet them in California. Her son would need her help, Lydia felt certain. Now, sister and brother were nervously quiet amid the disjointed chatter at the airline gate. Both tried to contain their hope, just in case. Yet hope kept levitating.

However, one thought kept popping up in Rebecca's mind, uninvited. What if Shree didn't want to return home? What if she wanted to stay with her dad? Rebecca knew that if they found Shree, her daughter would be flying home with her. But if it was against her will, well…. Rebecca was determined to be a better mother than she had been. That would not be a good first step.

53. The Big Turn

January 30th

Emerging from the cabin, Shree heard voices and wondered if she too, was going crazy. How could Uncle Jim's laugh find her from so far away? Then suddenly, she saw them. Uncle Jim and Mom! Time sped up, and before she knew it, they were running, and she was running, and Mom was holding her and crying and laughing and hugging her tight.

Rebecca and Jim were shocked by the girl before them. She was as skinny as a refugee and was strikingly taller than they expected. Her hair was short and dirty, her clothes muddy. This girl had changed so much in six months. Yet she was every bit the Shree they remembered. Her eyes glistened with the same life. They all had so many questions and apologies and explanations and words tripping over each other.

"I'm so sorry, Shree darling, I'm so sorry!" Shree didn't understand why her mom was apologizing, since she was the one who ran away.

"But I'm sorry, Mom! I didn't mean to hurt you. I missed you so much." Shree's words tumbled out, while her head was buried in her mother's hair, her smell so familiar and warm. Long ago, she had called her mother a liar, a monster, and worse. Believed she had hurt her mother so badly that she could never face her again. All of that seemed insignificant now. Her mom had come for her. She had missed her mom so much more than she had realized.

"Oh Shree, I can't tell you how wonderful it feels to have you back in my arms!" Tears and laughter, smiles and hugs.

Jim had stood back to let mother and daughter enjoy their moment, but when a pause came, he jumped in. "We're so relieved that you're safe and healthy, Shree. I can't tell you how happy I am to see you two smiling!"

"I missed you too, Uncle Jim! I even played Dad's Yes tapes in your honor." Shree said this with a sly look at her mom. Jim was happy to hear his niece thought of him and his taste in great music. Her mom, though, recognized the joke was meant for her. "Let me get a picture of you and your mom to send to your grandma." Jim had his orders.

Slowly, Rebecca weaved in some important questions, and learned her daughter was healthy, if hungry. She also learned that her ex-husband wasn't there and had left the day before. He was clearly having delusions. But when her daughter told her that she wanted to come home, renewed tears of gratitude flowed through Rebecca.

Shree got in a few questions, too. Wendy had given Shree's letter to her mom. "She was worried about you, darling. Wendy is a *real* friend." Shree couldn't imagine what she had written in that letter that would worry Wendy enough to tell. Until recently, such a betrayal would have been unforgivable. Considering how she felt this morning, though, she thought maybe Wendy had saved her life.

Since Shree was hungry, they decided to pack up her things quickly and go get food. Shree wanted to leave a letter for her dad, but then couldn't figure out what to say. Rebecca promised they would come by the cabin before flying back home. "But what if he shows up and I'm not here?"

"Just leave him a note that you're with me."

"Can he visit us in Houston? Can I invite him to visit us?" Shree was so hopeful that Rebecca had to say yes. All the anger she felt towards her ex-husband had to be managed if she was going to be a better mom. After all, Shree knew all about her father's condition now and just how bad it could get.

> *Dear Dad,*
> *Mom came to get me. I need to go back home now. I'll miss you every day. But you can come visit me. Mom says it's okay. Just remember, "Under the barrage of nature's passions, we build our tranquil home."*
> *I Love You Forever!,*
> *Shree and also Renee*

She quoted him from his note in the back of her tide pools book. Half an hour later, while waiting for pizza, Shree was showing off the anemones and nudibranchs in that book, especially the ones she had seen herself. Her mom loved them. Shree told them story after story, about Gunther, Rich, the cave, the ocean, coyotes. Jim sat back and watched his older sister beam as his niece chattered away nonstop. Rebecca's happiness was a long time coming. And it gave him hope for his own plans.

~ ~ ~

Back at the hotel, they met up with Lydia, who hugged her granddaughter for a solid two minutes. She hadn't seen Shree in close to two years and was amazed at how grown-up she was. After a while of catching up, Lydia asked Shree about her son. Shree described how he would talk to himself. And she tried to explain what he was saying. Lydia and Rebecca stopped her there.

"There's no use trying to make sense of it. It's his illness. His brain is just not working right," Rebecca assured her daughter.

Lydia held Shree's hands. "Both your mother and I have seen him at his worst. It can be quite frightening. You should know that, no matter what he may have said or done, your father still loves you and would never mean to hurt you." As Lydia said this, Shree's mom stroked her hair and nodded in agreement. "He just gets lost, and the world doesn't make sense to him for a while. It's a genetic disease. This runs in his father's family. He has a great aunt who also suffered from schizophrenia." Shree saw her mom give Grandma Lydia a quick, stern glance. "Their brains just don't work like they should. But there is medication. We will get him on his meds again, and he should calm down, and the world will make sense to him again. Don't you worry."

"You will be able to cure him, right?" Shree tried to find hope, but thinking about her dad with a broken brain was very sad and scary to her. Like night had fallen, and there would never be a dawn.

Rebecca took over. "I'm sorry, honey, there's no cure for this. His medication helps. And when he stays on them and gets treatment, he is mostly okay. You said yourself that he wasn't acting this way until recently. You said he had a job, had friends. These are all signs that he was in what is called 'remission'. When he's in remission, it can be hard to see any sign of his illness, even though there are some. But I have to be honest with you. His illness can come back again at any time. And it can be very difficult for him and everyone around him. I'm so sorry you had to deal with him on your own."

"But he's my dad! Of course I should be there to help him."

"Oh sweetie, no." Lydia was quick to jump in. "You may want to, but there isn't much you can do to help him. There isn't much I can do, and I'm his mother! We can steer him back to taking medication and getting therapy. But when his brain isn't working, he may not listen to our reason or even our love. We have had to call the police to restrain him and take him to the hospital. I know you want to help him, but sometimes that is simply not possible." To Shree, Lydia's voice sounded flat. But Rebecca and Jim both heard her pain as she was saying this. Tony was her son. Soon after, she left for the police station to start the search.

January 31st

The next afternoon, Rebecca and Shree would fly home. Despite Shree wanting to help look for her father, Rebecca suggested a tour of Santa Cruz led by her daughter. There were only two places on the agenda. The ocean and the forest. Shree wanted to take them on the 'forest to the sea' hike, complete with going into the cave. But she knew she couldn't find the right place, and they didn't have that much time. Uncle Jim suggested that they could go to the famous Boardwalk and ride the wooden roller coaster. He had a pamphlet from the hotel lobby.

"Locals don't go to the Boardwalk," Shree said with an insider's smile. Jim checked out of the hotel, and they climbed into the rental car heading towards the north coast. She hadn't been down to the ocean since before the big storms and was struck by how different it all was. The golden bluffs had been replaced by vivid green hills rising into the fog, and lush meadows that her mom said looked like Scotland.

"Here, here it is!" Shree excitedly directed them to her and her dad's favorite beach. But as they were trying to park, a police officer waved them away.

"He says the beach is closed." Jim waited for cars to pass so he could pull back onto the highway. Why would they close a beach, Shree wondered. As they pulled away, Shree thought she saw Rich's car. But maybe she was mistaken.

Soon she was again insisting, "Here, here! This is a great place too." And moments later, they were hiking down a trail under a gray overcast sky towards the beach populated by washed-up kelp and driftwood, three other people, and a lone pelican. There was a prominent hole in the cliff that they walked through, revealing an even more secluded beach. High, crumbling cliffs stood above piles of splintered shale, which advanced towards the waves that would churn them into sand. Twenty or more seagulls nervously eyed the newcomers intruding into their sanctum. Rebecca and Uncle Jim, wind twisting their hair, were not dressed for the penetrating chill. To Shree, however, it was just as glorious as her first visit. The waves were huge, the tops whisked away in the wind, with white caps far out on the ocean. They walked right to the edge of the continent. A wave curved up, up and over, then broke just before the sand, sending a sheet of racing white foam straight towards them. Uncle Jim immediately got soaked well above his knees because he wasn't fast enough. Rebecca stayed high on the dry sand watching the young ones cavort. Shree felt completely at home, darting down as a wave receded and then racing up just in time to avoid her uncle's fate. Unfortunately, the tide was too high to see much of the tide pools, though Shree did show them a giant green anemone, reachable during lulls in the surf. She even played the same trick her father had. She let the anemone grab her finger and then pretended to be in terrible pain. Her mom screamed and scolded Shree for scaring her. Then a big wave raced up and over the rocks, and the three of them skittered like crabs to higher ground.

As they left, her mom and uncle praised the postcard beauty of the scene. Shree was so proud to have led them there. But she was a little disappointed in their reaction. She remembered how her father was captivated by everything about the coast. He told her it was a work of art made by the universe. Shree had been swept up in his enthusiasm and felt how amazingly raw and naturally magical this place in the universe was. She wished she could show *that* to her mom and Uncle Jim. If her dad hadn't shown her, she wondered, would she see it like her mom did? Just a beautiful postcard? She decided to be glad that she herself could feel how gloriously special it was, even if others didn't. She knew her father would be proud of her.

Showing them the forest went a bit better. Her mom really liked the velvety green moss. She said it reminded her of visiting the mountains back east and how she loved the forests and creeks whenever she was there. And Uncle Jim knew about the bonds her dad talked about. "Hydrogen bonds," he reminded her. When, after pointing out soft curves reflecting all the colors, Shree took a fistful of gravel and dirt and threw it into an idyllic spot in the creek. Her mom loved the demonstration of how the beauty naturally returns. Shree felt like her dad for a moment. She was giving them a homeschool lesson.

Then it was time to go to the airport. Shree was excited to be going home, but in the car along the winding highway to San Jose, she was quiet, absorbed in her thoughts as trees raced by her window. She didn't get to see her father before leaving. The last time she saw him, he was running out of the cabin yelling, "Get Out!" Was he okay? Would he take his medicine and get into 'ramisun' or whatever it was? She hoped Grandma Lydia would find him soon so he could start getting better. And she wished he would visit them by her birthday. But as the car pulled around a remarkably big turn, she considered that it would probably be a long time before she saw her dad again. She knew it was the right thing to do, to go back to Houston, to school, to her friends, Wendy, and of course her mom and Uncle Jim. But it didn't feel right not seeing her dad before she left. All they had shared in these months…. Like it wasn't supposed to be over yet.

54. Chosen

January 31st

The sun had broken through the clouds and cast its warm smile on a little house on a tree-lined street in Palo Alto. James knew the address from her letter, but little else. When no one came to the door, his optimism leaked out of the plan of surprising her. What if she were out of town? What if she'd moved? He couldn't remember the name of the lab she had joined. He went back to sit in the rental car and watched as the clouds cast shadows across the little house once again. Maybe she was with someone else already. Time slowed while he watched an elderly man walk his dog. He noticed a couple at least three blocks away. Their step-by-step progression built like Bolero till they inevitably arrived at, then passed his car, continued down the block, and anticlimactically, they turned a corner.

Her letter had been ambiguous. It included her new address, but no phone number. She told him she loved him and always would. But she wrote as if their time together had permanently come to an end. She wished him all the happiness in this life that he deserved. Yet she denied him the thing that would make him the most happy: her in his life. He had thought about surprising her during spring break. Then Shree popped up in California, so now he was at her house, a couple months early. As he waited, he realized more and more that this was it. Either she would be delighted to see him, or irritated that he had come. Any moment, his fate would be sealed. And the longer he sat, the more he feared her imminent arrival.

Then her eminence appeared. It was already dark when a car pulled up to the curb, and she hopped out. He watched as she said goodbye to an older man, her face lit by the open car door. Her blue hair was now a subdued dark brown. Then the door was shut, the car slowly pulled away, leaving her in a red glow as she approached her front door. Jim quickly jumped out of the car, causing her to turn in his direction, yet she didn't recognize him in the dark. She returned to unlocking the door. As Jim got close to her, he called up the steps, "Surprise!"

She spun around, and her smile was radiant. "You Jerk, why did you scare me like that?" Then she threw herself down the steps and into his arms. "What are you doing here?"

~ ~ ~

Together they cooked pasta, while he talked about finding Shree, and she described the quirky people in her lab. It felt like old times again, like their friendship had never been in doubt. After dinner, her housemates started watching a movie, so they retreated to her bedroom. James reenacted his perilous guardrail calamity for Sirrus, complete with his failure to question authority when he was given the chance. With her laughter billowing his courage, he decided to make his pitch.

"I'm going to look for a position out here. Maybe as a lab tech at the medical school. I'm sure something will turn up."

"James, your PhD! You're not done with that."

"I'm ready to leave it," he said with blind confidence.

"I've seen how excited you are with your research. You can't walk away from that!" Sirrus was agitated.

"I can leave it for now." Jim didn't expect that she would raise his PhD. Now he was stumbling with what to say. The truth was that he wasn't comfortable leaving his thesis research. But there was at least another year and a half before he would be done. And that was an eternity. "Maybe I'll continue with one of the professors here."

"Yeah? Which one, James? Do you have a professor in mind?" Sirrus snapped. She wasn't sure how she felt about James moving to Palo Alto, but she knew he had to finish his PhD.

"Sirrus, I love you. I want you in my life."

"I love you too, James, that's why I know you can't move here." Her words hurt. She didn't mean for them to, but didn't regret them.

"You decided to move here, and I'm happy for you," Jim responded. "And I can decide to move here too." The little speech he had imagined had turned to mush. "I may believe in determinism, but if I can choose some things, well, I mean… You showed me that I can, so…. What I mean is, I choose you! School is secondary for me. It can be figured out. I have decided to move here."

Sirrus gave a long sigh, while she searched for words that would express her feelings clearly. "James, you have to complete your PhD. I would never forgive myself if you gave it up for me. I have given this subject a lot of thought over the last, what, three months. Five months, really. Way back before we weren't talking, I thought a lot about what's important to me. Obviously you're important. Even when we weren't talking, I knew that. But I had to make a decision that would be best for me, for the long term. If you quit your PhD now, there will come a day when you recognize it was a mistake."

"But I love you. I choose you!"

"You can decide for yourself, but you can't decide for me. Look, now is not the time. Not for me and not for you. If we're meant to be together, a couple of years apart won't change things. But if you walk away from your PhD now, it'll be very hard to return to it." Even as she said it, she knew that a 'couple of years' would likely change everything.

Sirrus sat before him with as lovable a smile as he had ever seen. And this sweet, adorable Sirrus was ripping the floor out from under him. He knew she was right. He did have to return to Houston. He would finish his PhD. Not because he wanted to, but because she didn't want him to stay. It would not be the Hollywood ending that he and Sirrus used to make fun of. Instead, it felt achingly unfinished.

In awkward conversation, after he spent the night on the living room couch, they agreed that they would visit each other when they could. She had family in Texas, and he would visit California again. She also insisted there would be no surprise visits. She agreed to be open to the idea of a future together in some hypothetical couple of years. And he accepted that they were friends only, not a couple. If other people came into their lives, so be it.

~ ~ ~

Driving to the airport that afternoon, he wondered if he just wasn't worthy of love. This depressing thought gripped him during his wait at the gate. As strangers walked passed in twos and threes, it surprised him to notice that everyone carried themselves with a quiet dignity. Each was beautiful in their own way. A bald man in his forties, with a drooping mustache and brown leather shoes. A middle-aged woman in lavender slacks and matching eyeshadow, reading a paperback mystery. A curly-headed three-year-old throwing a tantrum. His exhausted mother trying to calm him with a stuffed giraffe. A businesswoman in a teal blazer with padded shoulders. A husband and wife, seething over an unfinished argument. Each one somehow had a style, a rhythm, a beauty unique to themselves and universal to all living things. They each were deserving of love. He alone felt pathetic. His eyes filled with tears that he wiped away in embarrassment.

Later, as his flight rose into, then broke through the clouds, he noticed a wisp of relief breaking through his self-pity. Maybe he deserved someone who wanted him. He even smiled to himself for a moment. When he finally agreed with her that he had the free will to choose his fate, she proved to him that it was out of his hands.

55. God's Joke

February 1st

Lydia was driven to the morgue by Officer Morales on Monday. An unidentified deceased male, estimated to be thirty years of age, was discovered at a beach approximately seven miles north of Santa Cruz on Sunday. A local surfer had located the body amongst the near-shore rocks, shortly after dawn. An automobile parked in the vicinity was registered to a 'Richard Campbell'. Mr. Campbell, also deceased, had a last known address corresponding to the property identified by Mrs. Andersen as her son's most recent domicile.

"This won't be easy. The body and face were badly damaged in the fall and then tumbled by heavy surf. There is no hurry. You can take a moment to prepare yourself." Unlike the police officers, who all seemed to speak in the same desiccated cadence, the medical examiner spoke softly and with empathy.

The thought of looking at a dead body was extremely uncomfortable to Lydia, who could faint at the first sign of blood. Yet as soon as the police had told her a body was found, deja vu, something inside her knew it was Tony. While praying she was wrong, she now prepared herself to see her son one last time. The examiner, mid-thirties, pudgy, with a new wave hair style and noticeable tattoo on his left wrist, pulled back the starched sheet.

And there her boy lay. His color was all wrong, and there were holes, like punctures, on his hollowed face. But she could clearly make out her little Anthony. His regal eyebrows. His soft, perfect ears. His lips downturned as if he were pouting. She reached to stroke his cheek. But as she did, she understood that he was no longer there.

She turned away and suddenly felt too weak to stand. The examiner led her to his office and an armchair. Her son had died, and she found comfort in an armchair. It's not meant to work that way. Her precious baby was gone. What was she supposed to do now? God had tortured both of her children till they could take no more. And in a cruel joke, God left her behind.

Epilogue: Tides

July 22nd, 1991

The address was three blocks from Golden Gate Park. The summer fog had yet to burn off, though occasional peaks of blue promised a beautiful afternoon. Wendy gave her partner a quick kiss before ringing the bell. "She's cool, she's gonna love you! Here goes." Wendy pushed the button, but heard no bell. Inside, however, she could tell the button had triggered a commotion.

Jim answered the door in bare feet and a blue sweatshirt spattered with paint. Clinging to his left leg, a shy toddler with wavy blond hair tried to hide behind him. "Wendy, is it actually you?" Wendy was practically as tall as he was and had grown into a strong and confident young woman. Her youthful beauty lit up with her smile. "I haven't seen you in, what, six years? Come in, come in."

"You haven't changed a bit, Uncle Jim. Sorry, um, James. I always called you what Shree called you."

"Of course you can call me Uncle Jim. As Rebecca says, you're part of the family!" He was proud to hear her call him 'uncle'. As for not having changed, he knew he looked older. His long hair had shortened considerably, though it was still over his ears and collar. And no one had called him James in years.

"Welcome to San Francisco and our little home," Jim said while leading them into the comfortable, though cluttered, living room. "Shree went with Shelley to the store, but they'll be back any minute. This is my little monkey pie, Allie. Allie, can you say hello?" Allie wasn't ready to say hello. She clung to his pants and kept her dad between herself and the strangers.

"Nice to meet you, Allie!" The toddler buried her face into

her dad's leg. "She's a cutie, alright. This is Trish. She's my roommate." Trish cringed a little at the white lie. This was San Francisco, after all! "We just drove up from LA."

"Welcome Trish, so nice to meet you." Jim held out his hand, and they shook with a humorous awkwardness. Then Trish, who was already the second shortest in the room, knelt down and offered her hand to Allie. Allie shook hands with the friendly lady with purple hair, a studded dog collar, and a tattooed fish on her arm, then immediately showed her a little plastic tiger she was holding.

"Is that a tiger? What's your tiger's name?" Trish felt in the way with the old acquaintances catching up, but perfectly at home talking to Allie.

"Shree told me all about your trip. She's really looking forward to driving to British Columbia with you." Jim also knew that Wendy and Trish were more than roommates, but didn't want to embarrass anyone. "So you're in Eugene, right? Are you at the university?"

"Yeah, I'm a bit behind. Just completed my first year. I had to establish residency and save some money so I could afford it." Wendy was worried that Uncle Jim would judge her for falling behind. After all, he was a professor.

"I hear you. Yeah, it can be hard to put yourself through school. It takes commitment. On the other hand, most of the students I see who are paying their own way are getting a lot more out of their education. I hope you're studying things you enjoy."

"Well so far it's just prerequisites, but most of it was really interesting." Just then the front door opened, and they could hear two people laughing.

"Shell, we have guests," Jim announced.

Shree appeared, dropped several shopping bags on the table, and fell into Wendy's waiting arms. They hugged, laughing for more than a minute. When they emerged, Wendy immediately pulled her friend up. "Shree, this is Trish! I wrote you about her. You're going to love her."

"Well, if you're good enough for Wendy, then I won't hold it against you," Shree said with a wink and a smile. Unfortunately, the comment fell flat with Trish. "I'm so glad to meet you at last!' Shree was surprised that Trish was so tiny. She had imagined her with Wendy's strong build, but this girl was almost a foot shorter and thin as a feather, with fading purple-blond hair and strikingly blue eyes. She wore thick black eyeshadow and lipstick, while neither Wendy nor Shree wore makeup. Shree admired the tattooed fish. Meanwhile, Trish sized up Wendy's best friend since fifth grade. Medium height, kinda slim, straight dark hair, just reaching her shoulders, pale, plain face, wire-frame glasses. The only thing that stood out about her was her great affection for Wendy. Trish slipped her arm around Wendy's waist, consciously declaring her rightful place.

"You two look great together. Don't you think so, Uncle Jim? Shelley?" Shree said a bit nervously.

"Shelley, this is Shree's best friend, Wendy. And Wendy's, uh, roommate, Trish," Jim introduced their guests.

Without missing a beat, "And I'm Jim's, uh, roommate, Shelley!" Smiling warmly, she slipped her arm around her husband, mirroring Trish and Wendy.

Wendy looked at Shelley and tried to figure out if this was the same person she had met so long ago on the day they all went to the beach. She remembered Shree saying that Uncle Jim was in love with her. It could be the same person, though the hair was no longer blue. Wendy decided it would be better not to bring it up. Soon they got down to business, packing Shree's things into the car and saying goodbyes.

~ ~ ~

Though they would be heading north, the first destination was south to Santa Cruz. Shree had not been back since her mom had taken her home. As soon as Wendy suggested the road trip, Shree thought of Santa Cruz. Finally, she would get to show Wendy where she had lived with her dad.

"So did your uncle's wife go with us to the beach that time?" Wendy was driving, but kept looking in the rearview mirror at Shree.

"Um, what time?" Shree's mind was wandering and hadn't quite heard the question.

"In Galveston, remember? She had blue hair!" Trish heard this and became interested. She just couldn't picture Shelley with blue hair.

"Oh, you mean Sirrus. Yeah, no Shelley isn't Sirrus," Shree said with a laugh.

"Who's Sirrus?" asked Trish.

"Shree's uncle was in love with this hippy chick a long time ago. I remember thinking she was so weird. Blue hair in Texas! In the 80s! I was such a judgmental little hick. So what happened to her, Shree? D'you know?"

"Not really. Maybe Uncle Jim moved out here because of her. Mom was sure they would get married. But they didn't. I was there when Mom asked him about it once. He said they were better off as friends. It never worked because they were 'in different phases', but that was all he said. I remember his words 'cause I remember thinking they didn't explain anything. And now, years later, that's exactly what I felt when I broke up with Jason. Now it makes perfect sense. Whatever we tried, Jason and I were just a little bit off."

"Don't miss the turn to Highway One," Trish interrupted. She had been interested for a bit, but then Wendy's friend just started talking about herself.

Wendy, on the other hand, was not done with her questions. "So what happened to her, though? Are they still friends?"

"I don't know. He never mentions her."

"Good thing I didn't ask Shelley if she remembered that day in Galveston!" Wendy winked into the rearview mirror.

"Yeah, that would have been awkward." Shree laughed. "But Shelley's great for him. And she's hilarious! You should have heard her last night, making fun of how he sounds talking to grandma."

"So how's your mom? Did she divorce Jeff yet?"

"No, they're working it out. I think I might have been the problem. I never gave him a chance," Shree reflected. "And you and I were getting into so much trouble together before I left Houston. The poor guy was just trying to be a parent."

"He grounded you for like a month when he found your pipe. And took your door off its hinges!" Wendy resented him for interfering with their high school years.

"Sounds like a real jerk," Trish contributed.

"Well he *is* a cop!" Shree laughed. "I snuck out anyway, you'll recall. I think he didn't know what to do with me. And Mom felt guilty and took my side. They argued about it a lot." Shree had thought seriously about it since going off to college. She came to realize she had made things difficult for her mom. She had even called up and tearfully apologized. "Anyway, now that I'm out of the picture, Mom says she and Jeff are doing okay. After all, Ben and Alex deserve to have their dad at home."

"Bosco and Ax! How are those two rugrats?" Wendy enjoyed teasing Shree's little brothers, especially since they worshiped her.

"They're good. Ben wanted me to tell you he rode the whole block with no hands."

"No! Did he go around the block?! Is he turning?" Wendy was

proud of her little protege.

"Not that I saw. And Alex is trying hard, but he can't get more than two feet. Mom says Alex is gonna knock out his teeth trying to impress you."

"Is he still on that tiny bike?" Shree nodded. "Well, tell Alex that I couldn't ride without hands til I was nine. He's got years yet."

"Tell him yourself. One of these days, I'll call and put you on the line. Of course they'll fight over the phone. Oh speaking of rugrats, you'll never guess who I ran into. Sharron and her boy! Zack is four already. Looking goofier than ever."

"What! Four! Seems like yesterday when she suddenly dropped out, then showed up months later with that wrinkly pink sausage," Wendy recalled. "Trish, you remember I told you about that girl I used to hate? That's Sharron!"

"The girl who took you to your first gay bar?" Having only heard stories, Trish felt a certain affection for Sharron.

"Yeah, that's her," Wendy confirmed. "So glad we grew up," she continued, then turned back to Shree. "Are they doing okay? Is Wayne in the picture at all?"

"She didn't mention him. I only saw them for a moment 'cause she was late for work. And Zack ran into the pet store in the two minutes we were trying to talk. As she dragged him out to the car, she was smiling, though. Last thing she said over his screaming was, 'call me if you wanna babysit!' I think she was joking, but I didn't call her just in case." Slightly embarrassed that no one acknowledged her joke, Shree redirected the conversation. "So how are your parents?"

"I don't know. I haven't called them in six months. They're still in the La Hacienda. Last time we connected, Mom was talking about becoming a foster mom. What a joke! Like she did so well with her own children."

"You turned out alright." Shree knew Wendy had a long-running game of pretending not to care about her parents. "How's your brother, though? Any word?"

"No one's heard anything in four years. I still think he ran off to South America with his friend, Luis."

"Didn't you say they were wanted for armed robbery?" Trish joined the conversation.

"That was just Anna's joke. But I wouldn't put it past him. Oh, speaking of Anna, we saw her in LA!"

"Really? I've been wondering what she's up to." Shree had become close with Annabelle. But they lost touch when they each left for college.

"Yeah, she's still at USC and she's in a band."

"What?!" Shree never would have guessed.

"Really! They're called 'Asperger's Cafe'. We went to one of their shows."

"Very Tom Tom Club crossed with Annie Lennox," Trish added her assessment. "I thought they were pretty good, if five years too late."

"Yes, our Annabelle is the lead singer. And she's great. She had the whole crowd eating out of her hands," Wendy said with pride.

"She's always had charisma. Guess it makes sense she would be on a stage." Now that Shree thought about it, it seemed obvious.

"She has a really interesting song called 'Preacher in Hell'. I bet you can guess what that's about. And there is a hilarious one, 'Smoking on the Swing-set'. Our teen drug use has been immortalized!" Wendy beamed. "She told me they're hoping to do some shows in Seattle. We may be able to catch them on the way back down."

"I would love that! I've missed her a lot these past three years. At least with you, we've been writing the whole time." Shree slid back into silence in the backseat, while Wendy asked Trish if they were still on Highway One. They had gotten a few glimpses of the ocean already, but now they descended towards a beautiful beach with a rocky coastline in the hazy distance.

"Looks like this is still One. I think we're going to get to Devil's Slide soon." Trish seemed more informed than Shree expected. "Shall we stop at Taco Bell first?" It would be difficult to keep to her budget, Shree suspected, with Trish on the trip.

When they started driving again, Trish was behind the wheel. It didn't take long for Shree to realize that their new driver was dangerous. She sped out of the parking lot, almost hitting a car pulling in. Then she tailgated, like seriously tailgated. They were only two feet behind the car ahead. Soon the road narrowed, with crumbling granite walls on either side. She chose this time to swerve past the car in front, even though there was a blind curve ahead. They only avoided getting hit because the car she was passing slammed on the brakes and let her in.

Then suddenly they were on the side of steep stone cliffs that plunged hundreds of feet into the glorious Pacific Ocean. All eyes were transfixed by the glittering sun on the expanse of water and jutting rocks far below. Transfixed, for a moment in time, before Trish suddenly jerked the car back onto the road, barely missing the cement barrier, which was the only thing between them and the breath of eternity transfixing them a lifetime ago.

As the road itself swerved and descended, Shree tried hard to silently communicate to Wendy that Trish should not drive anymore. What neither Shree nor Wendy had noticed was that Trish was now shaking with fear. The first turnout she could, she pulled the car over and killed the engine.

"That was intense! For a moment I thought we were going over. Don't make me drive anymore." Trish felt her job was done. In the prehistoric era of ten minutes ago, she had intended to show off a little. Scare Wendy's friend a bit. But maybe that wasn't such a good idea on Devil's Slide. She heard David Byrne's voice in her head, "I don't wanna die-ie!"

"I can drive," Shree offered. *As long as Trish doesn't touch the wheel again,* she thought.

After reliving the excitement of their shared near-death experience, the car grew quiet again. Shree drove calmly through Half Moon Bay traffic. "So what's the deal with your dad and Santa Cruz?" Trish wanted to make peace with Shree and thought a conversation would be a start.

"Well I don't know what Wendy has told you, but my dad and I ran away from my mom and hid out in Santa Cruz for half a year." From there, Shree happily told the story, with Wendy adding in here and there and Trish asking lots of questions. Trish had started just trying to make peace, but soon warmed to Shree's story. As casually stunning ocean views shimmered on the right and lovely golden brown hills fringed with redwoods rolled by on the left, Shree began to feel the excitement of that time all over again. She was so happy to be driving towards her own lost world.

"So what happened to your dad?" Trish knew some of it already, but she wanted to hear what Shree would say.

"You know he was mentally ill, right? Schizophrenia."

"Yeah, Wendy told me. My mom's bipolar." Trish said this in a quiet, matter-of-fact way.

"What, really? I didn't know that," Wendy said in surprise.

"Yeah. I don't like to talk about it. So what happened with your father?" she asked, turning back to Shree.

The car got quiet as Shree recalled the final weeks of her time with her dad. Trish would add encouraging comments here and there. "That sounds familiar." "My mom would disappear too." "It's hard to make any sense of it."

Then Trish took over the conversation for a while. "My mom is labeled bipolar, but a lot of people who were labeled schizophrenic in the old days are being labeled bipolar now. What you describe is pretty similar to my mom. She was once convinced our neighbors worked for the CIA and were trying to reprogram us. I'm a Psych major, and I talked to one of my teachers about her. Professor Holtz said something that surprised me. These major mental illnesses: schizophrenia, bipolar, depression, are all genetic, and are found in similar numbers all over the world. When it's so clear that these conditions are debilitating, why hasn't evolution weeded them out? It can't be good for fitness. She suggested that in full strength, the genetic traits are harmful. But in milder forms, the same traits might be advantageous. The visionaries, the prophets, those who see the dangers and prepare. Those who see what isn't there and ask, 'Why not?' Unfortunately, your dad and my mom got a full-strength dose. And we are left to wonder how big a dose we get."

Seemingly out of nowhere, her childhood imaginary friend popped into Shree's head. She hadn't thought about Mr. Trains in ages. After seeing her father's illness, there had been a time when she wasn't just ashamed of Mr. Trains; she had thought he was a symptom of her own schizophrenic tendencies. Would she travel the same path as her father? No, she had concluded. Mr. Trains was just an invention of a bored and lonely child. And she knew she would follow her own path.

"In the end, my dad stood on a cliff above our favorite beach and asked, 'Why not?'" In the awkward silence after Shree said this, she recalled that when her mom finally told her what happened, it had made her so angry. Why did he leave her? Why did he give up? Then later, why did he do that horrible thing at their special place? The magical edge of the planet, where he showed her the universe's soul. Forever stained by the image of his suicide.

~ ~ ~

And just like that, they arrived at the very beach. Shree pulled over, unsure if it was the right place. The unpaved parking area was more worn and full of ruts. The start of the path was much more overgrown. But everything else said it was the right place.

"Hey, we don't have to go to this beach. We don't have to go to any of these beaches." Wendy worried that visiting Santa Cruz would be hard for Shree. Seeing where her dad died would be too much.

"No, I have to see it. This place is magical. I want you to see it." Shree said this, but she felt a weight on her that was hard to ignore. And as they crossed the railroad tracks and the path widened into an old dirt road, Wendy took Shree's left hand, and Trish took her right. Shree let them hold her, though she felt like it was comforting them more than her. The path rose, and soon they could see the ocean and august cliffs on the far side of the beach.

Shree suddenly broke off from them and ran down a side path to an overview of a tidal marsh. It was glorious, with perfectly still water reflecting the reddish rushes, feathery green grasses, and perfect sky. A snowy egret stalked hidden prey. The creek wandered its way out of the marsh and through the windswept sands to the ocean beyond. Shree could see through the pale aqua water of the creek to its rippled, sandy bottom. This marsh was more beautiful than she remembered. The whole scene as perfect as a tide pool. And the ocean still called.

As Wendy and Trish caught up, all Shree could say was "Can you feel it? Can you feel it?" like a chant in a song. Wendy recognized that look and knew her friend was fine.

Though a fog bank covered the ocean a mile out, where they stood, the sun warmed their shoulders and the wind teased their hair. Shree urged them on, and soon they were stumbling through the dunes, their shoes in their hands. Leaving the first human footprints of the day, Shree ran across the sand to the edge of the earth. The waves were not as big as the very first time, when she was overwhelmed by them. But they still rose up and crashed in explosions of white water. A pancake of foam rushed up to greet Shree, and she let the shock of cold soak her to the knees and bury her feet in rushing shards of shells and pebbly sand.

Wendy was worried that the waves would sweep her friend away. But Trish dropped her shoes and ran into the next rush of foam and shrieked at its icy welcome. A seagull, not twenty feet away, watched the awkward land-bound animals stumble and splash in the surf. Soon all three of them were wet to their thighs.

In the sensory overload of her return to the beach, Shree had completely forgotten the funeral weight she carried as she left the car. Now, as Wendy and Trish held hands next to her on the warm sand, her thoughts turned to her father again. Of course it was horrible, how he ended his life. But all of Shree's anger and sadness had drained away like a wave rushing back to the sea. Her dad was cursed, but gifted also. And he passed on some of those gifts to her. Like the water molecules, he had played his part in shaping the beauty of the stream. If he felt he had to end his life, why not here? As he might say, where the universe, with all its wild power and elegance, was in the very act of destroying and creating itself? And as if the universe wanted to ring a bell, a harbor seal popped its head out of the surf and looked at the three terrestrial mammals hauled out on the sand. "I see you!"

~ ~ ~

Appreciation

I would like to thank my daughter, Natalya Dreszer, my sister, Cindy Davis, and my close friend, Bill Fellows. They each gave generously of their time and patience reading the first draft. Their insights were extremely helpful, both large and small. I apologize for my inability to correct my most egregious failings. Instead, I'll pretend they were as intended. Additionally, Natalya's creativity enhanced the cover design. I would also like to thank my wife, Lena Dreszer, for patiently listening as I stuttered and misread the entire manuscript aloud. As always, her questions and suggestions inspired me to look deeper. Finally, I would like to acknowledge the motivation imparted by my mother, Norma Y. Parkinson. She announced many years ago that she expected me to write a book. Her words have haunted me long enough.

Independently published novels quickly evaporate unless readers share their thirsts. Please consider pouring an honest review into your preferred pond of books.

About the Author

Timothy grew up in Houston, within NASA's pious penumbra. At seven, he endured mundane family trauma when his parents divorced and he was forced to live with his mother against his will. By his twenties, when his brother was diagnosed with schizophrenia, Tim learned to appreciate the poetic humor in his own 'tortured' life. Escaping family and suffocating humidity, he found refuge in the redwoods on the edge of the Pacific and distraction in nature, science, and engineering. This led from psychology to biology to bioinformatics via degrees and a career along the way. While his head was occupied with writing code and scientific papers, his heart was beating stories colored by complicating human emotion. Though he anticipated living alone with a cat, his wife and two adult children have rescued him from that ascetic fate. Presently, he's most likely riding his bike with no hands near the ocean.